THEY MAKE MOVIES

George Thomas Clark

Published by GeorgeThomasClark.com

ISBN: 978-1-7332981-4-8 – Trade Paperback

GeorgeThomasClark.com
Bakersfield, California
webmaster@GeorgeThomasClark.com

Books by
George Thomas Clark

Down Goes Trump
King Donald
Paint it Blue
Hitler Here
The Bold Investor
Basketball and Football
Death in the Ring
Echoes from Saddam Hussein
Obama on Edge
Tales of Romance
In Other Hands: Revised Edition
After the Movie

Introduction

This fast-moving collection blends fiction with history to illuminate the lives and careers of noted actors, actresses, and directors. Talented but tormented Louise Brooks and Anna May Wong open the show, and major stars Marlene Dietrich, Vivien Leigh, and Bette Davis follow, revealing their experiences or yielding to characters who offer creative comments about them.

The parade continues with Joan Crawford, a gifted actress who's difficult on and off the set. Olivia de Havilland becomes a star and then challenges a rigid studio system that locks her into inferior parts and bans her from movies while she fights the moguls in court. Marilyn Monroe is glamorous and gifted but seldom escapes emotional agony. Lupe Velez, *The Mexican Spitfire*, is similarly doomed.

Contemporary actresses Meryl Streep, Cate Blanchette, Halle Berry, and Kate Winslet usually have better creative choices and earn more money than their cinematic predecessors but must also deal with challenging screen roles and, on occasion, outrageous co-stars.

Leading men next step before the cameras. Humphrey Bogart battles his violent third wife while finally moving toward screen immortality. Errol Flynn, a compelling but unstable young man not long removed from sailing the seas around Tasmania and New Guinea, rapidly becomes a star and almost as quickly undermines himself with alcohol, narcotics, and bad decisions. Clark Gable marries two much older women, one teaching him to act and the other showing him how to behave in high society, before he combines polish and charisma to start getting what he wants.

Laurence Olivier and John Wayne differ stylistically but both dominate the screen and delight moviegoers. Kirk Douglas also proves he's a star and so does his son Michael, and some creative scenes enliven their stories. Ernest Hemingway arrives, trying to help Burt Lancaster survive his debut in *The Killers.* In other roles the actor swims through backyard pools on estates in suburban Connecticut and studies birds not at Alcatraz but less scenic Leavenworth. Marlon Brando again fascinates in *On the Waterfront*, this time making alternative efforts to avoid becoming a bum. The youngest star is Chadwick Boseman, portrayer of Jackie Robinson. Character actors appear next and include Robert DeNiro, Dustin Hoffman, Claude Rains, Edward G. Robinson, Ernest Borgnine and, more recently, Jesse Eisenberg.

The performers above are guided by directors such as John Huston, Alfred Hitchcock, Billy Wilder, Clint Eastwood, Woody Allen, and Spike Lee. And where do they get their raw material? It emerges from numerous too-little-appreciated screenwriters like Ben Hecht, Budd Schulberg, and Aaron Sorkin as well as directors who write well. Huston, Allen, and Lee are among the finest.

And these talents coalesce to form fantasy teams about which we confidently state: *They Make Movies.*

Contents

Lovely Ladies

Smooth Operators

Characters

Behind the Camera

LOVELY LADIES

ANNA MAY WONG

Delicate Flower

The judge evidently thinks I'm a movie mogul rather than a UCLA English professor and awards my hard-shopping wife more than half my estate and my entire Santa Monica home. I rent a couple of places that prove dreary before I diligently study classified ads and drive by what may be a suitable residence. It was once a fine Hollywood house that's been quartered. The landlord lives in one of the residences and on that door I knock. A middle-aged oriental lady responds.

"Hello," I say, examining her.

She exhales cigarette smoke and says, "Are you going to gawk at me all afternoon."

"No, ma'am. I just feel I've seen you somewhere."

"Is that the most clever line you've got?"

"I'm here in response to your advertisement for a place to rent."

"Just a minute," she says, and shortly returns with a large key chain. "This way."

Walking a couple of steps ahead she leads me to a furnished ground-floor apartment of medium size and consisting of a living room, kitchen, bathroom, and one bedroom. I agree to rent the place, sign the contract, and ask to whom I should make out the check.

"Anna May Wong," she says.

"I should've known right away.

"Evidently, I've aged to the point I'm unrecognizable."

"It's more likely a matter of my incipient senility," I say.

"I doubt it. How old are you?"

"Fifty-two last month."

"You're only two years older than I."

Feeling enthused, I say, "You were great in *The Toll of the Sea.* First movie I saw in color."

"First movie ever made in color, 1922, when I was only seventeen. Maybe the audience didn't appreciate I gave my child to my white bigamist husband who'd returned to China with his gawky wife. I thought it odd the script dictated my child would somehow be better off with two strange adults in the United States. My decision to enter the sea was also troubling, but poignant. Perhaps these tragedies added to the beauty of the film.

"I expected my career to blossom but two years later I had to play a decidedly minor part, as a Mongol slave in *The Thief of Baghdad.* Movie people told me I should be delighted that Douglas Fairbanks had requested me."

Looking through layers of time I still sense young Anna May Wong dancing on screen. She was lovely, graceful, exotic.

"I confess I fell for you in *Picadilly.* In the way one sometimes fantasizes about movie stars."

"Many men did. I hope they weren't too smitten since I died again. This time my oriental boyfriend shot me because I was in love with another man, a white one. That was expedient since people of different races weren't allowed to kiss on screen, a rule rather limiting my opportunities to play romantic leads."

"I'd like to see more films from that period."

"So would I," she says, "but careless people at the studios have lost about fifteen of my silent movies."

Noting her neat but plain dress, I say, "I remember newspaper photos of you always attired in chic outfits."

"Someone or other voted me the world's best-dressed woman one year. Another group judged me the world's most beautiful Chinese girl, an unusual honor for one born and raised in downtown Los Angeles, albeit in Chinatown."

"In the late twenties you went to Europe, made some silent pictures, and acted on stage with Laurence Olivier."

"Most people there treated me as a star."

"Lots of men must've wanted to marry you."

Lips curling down, she says, "I've always been married to my career. In the play with Olivier, critics excoriated me for having a voice that lacked professional timbre and dignity. I got lots of training to improve and also learned and performed in French and German."

"That brings us to your career in motion pictures with sound."

"We'll have to talk about that promising but ultimately tormenting era on another occasion, Mr. James. It's time for my afternoon libation."

"It's eleven a.m.," I say.

"In my lifetime of waiting, that's late enough."

A few days later I move in. At UCLA I frequently mention my new landlord Anna May Wong and, without contrivance, link her to American and European literature. Films, after all, begin as scripts adapted to the screen.

Entering and leaving my apartment and taking frequent afternoon walks, I hope to see Anna May but don't and instead notice her drapes are always closed. This frustrates me until I decide to pay my rent a week early. I knock on her door. I knock again. Her car, bearing ten years and losing paint, sits in the driveway. It's only four p.m. I step to her picture window, tap a bit harder than intended, and say, "Anna May. Are you all right? This is Bob James."

In seconds drapes are jerked open, Anna squeezing material in each hand as she frowns. "What the hell do you want?"

I hold up my check.

"Come back at the start of the month," she says.

Initially, I think I've interrupted an afternoon assignation. I then conclude I more likely aggravated her hangover.

A few days later, a weekday evening, there's a knock on my door and I'm delighted to see Anna May smiling.

"May I come in?"

"Of course. I'll get your check."

"Okay, but that's not why I'm here. Let's talk about movies."

Motioning to the sofa, I say, "We were moving into the era of sound."

"I was ready and in 1931 I starred in *Daughter of the Dragon*."

"I remember. You had the presence of a star."

"I also had a Caucasian father painted yellow: Warner Oland from all those Charlie Chan movies. Never has a white man fathered so many pure Chinese. My Chinese boyfriend in this movie was Sessue Hayakawa, a fine actor from Japan. He moved to the United States as a young man and starred in silent films but in talkies he spoke English with such a thick accent it marred all his scenes. At least he proved a good shot, killing me and then dying on my body as our rivals, a white couple, embraced.

"May I smoke?"

Ordinarily I'd ask a visitor to do so outside but say, "Certainly. I don't have an ashtray but I'll get you an old cup."

She inhales deeply and blows dense funnels of smoke illuminated by lamps on each end of the sofa.

Relaxed in my reading chair, I say, "I wish you had a much larger part in *Shanghai Express* in 1932 when your beauty and dynamism were at their peak."

"Are you suggesting they've plummeted?

"Not at all, Anna May. I'm simply saying that you and Marlene Dietrich, two high class courtesans, were superb in that railroad car encounter with the puritanical old lady. I love how she tells you, "'I'm sure you're very respectable, Madam.'"

Anna looks perturbed. "And I say, 'I must confess, I don't quite know the standard of respectability that you demand in your boarding house.' One of the best lines in my career."

"Marlene was gorgeous in that scene, teasing as she asks the lady, 'Don't you find respectable people terribly dull?' I've read you and Marlene were good friends."

She takes a big puff and exhales. "That's correct. I prefer not to elaborate."

"I understand."

"Do you have anything to drink, Bob?"

"Plenty of white wine."

"Bring us some, please, because I know what you next want to talk about."

"What's that?"

"*The Good Earth.*"

I pour Anna May a wine glass almost full and she drains it in a few minutes and pushes it forward for a refill.

"As a scholarly fellow, Bob, you know how much I wanted to play O-Lan, the Chinese slave in northern China before World War I. They started casting in 1935. But they told me I looked too Chinese. So they chose an Austrian, Luise Rainer."

"And she won the Oscar for best actress."

"I haven't watched the movie and never will. Have you seen it?"

"Yes," I say. "I'd have chosen you."

"I've been told, perhaps by people who know what I yearn to hear, that Rainer spends much of the movie grimacing and cowering. I'm certain I could've played the role with more dignity."

I sip my wine.

"Anna May, I've heard two versions about why you didn't play Lotus, the prostitute."

"Did I turn down this secondary part because all the principal roles would be played by whites and I'd be the only Asian and playing a disreputable woman? Or did some chubby producer say I didn't seem beautiful enough to play the prostitute? It suffices to note they hired another Austrian."

"At least that gave you time to visit China," I say.

"Sadly, the Chinese government, for whom I had great sympathy in their war with Japan, published many scathing newspaper reviews of my work, accusing me of disgracing China by playing loose and violent women. That was as primitive as Hollywood's miscegenation laws. I still needed to see my ancestral homeland, especially since my father moved back after my mother was hit and killed by a car in Los Angeles.

"The people were wonderful. No matter what their station, they treated me as a distinguished actress of whom they were very proud. Meeting them was the most gratifying experience I've had. I'm so pleased we filmed a lot of documentary footage."

She extends her glass.

"Are you sure?" I ask.

"Yes."

"After your return from China you starred in a good film, *Daughter of Shanghai*."

"It was a B movie but my best role since they let me lead and have a boyfriend, oriental actor Philip Ayn, and whites were the bad guys."

"You must've been encouraged," I say.

"I was, but a few more B movies followed that weren't as good. Every actor needs a good script and budget for a first-rate production. You either move up to A pictures or slide into oblivion. By 1942 I was thirty-seven, not young for the screen, and starring in *Lady from Chungking*. I battled the Japanese whose two top officers were played by Jewish guys from New York. The Japanese executed me at the end and, as imaginary bullets entered me, I knew my chances of being a major star were dead. I didn't appear in another movie for seven years. *Impact.* Did you see it?"

"No," I say diplomatically about a decent film in which Anna May Wong, aging fast, had a minor role she performed without distinction.

She finishes another glass and points to it.

"Please consider what I'm about to suggest. There's a new organization called Alcoholics Anonymous. Have you heard about it?"

"No."

"They get together and talk about their problems and provide support. A couple of my colleagues at UCLA go to meetings and they've quit drinking."

Anna May drops her cigarette into the cup and says, "I don't want to quit drinking. Why would I?"

"Because you have a problem."

She stands and says, "From now on just pay your rent and quit analyzing my life," and walks out and three months later sells the place and moves into her brother's home in Santa Monica. Even those on the edges of Hollywood can ask a few questions and learn what's going on. Anna May Wong's been depressed for years, maybe all her life, and she sometimes bleeds internally, and a few years later has a stroke but continues smoking and drinking, and at age fifty-six, when she doesn't wake up, newspapers report she dies of cirrhosis of the liver. Hell of a sad story.

MARLENE DIETRICH

Marlene Rides Again

I first smile then laugh as I discuss *The Blue Angel* script about a cabaret singer who seduces a stuffy schoolmaster, sending him into a life of degradation and destruction.

"This isn't supposed to be quite so funny," says director Josef von Sternberg.

"I hope you won't be jealous, Josef, but this so reminds me of my schoolmaster in Berlin."

"You seduced him?"

"I'm not sure who kissed first but I remember crying when he lost his job."

Our film is a hit soon after Josef leaves Germany for Hollywood. In a few months I follow and he gives me a Rolls Royce and Paramount hires Gary Cooper to star with me in *Morocco.*

"Gary's a lovely man but much too tall," I tell Josef.

"I'll fix it so he has to look up to you."

Gary protests to studio heads who side with the lanky American.

"I hope we're still friends," I tell him.

"I barely know you, Miss Dietrich."

"Let's meet for a drink after work."

We don't spend much time in the hotel lounge. We get a room.

"Goodness, Gary, I confess I'd heard about you."

We meet a couple of times a week, more when I can convince Josef to stop asking why I'm getting home late. I also have to beware Gary's crazy girlfriend Lupe Velez. I know Lupe's got spies and one tells her where Gary and I will be this evening. She pounds and kicks the hotel door, screaming, "You filthy beetch, I'm gonna tear your eyes out."

"Please take care of this, Gary."

"I'm staying right here," he says.

Fans love exotic *Morocco* filmed in Los Angeles. I highlight the movie by kissing a surprised lady's lips in a nightclub. After another picture together, Josef and I collaborate for the fourth time, in *Shanghai Express.* There's something sexy about being on a train. Also mysterious and funny. I love working with Anna May Wong. We met a few years earlier at a party in Berlin where I summoned her into a private place.

I'm delighted she has a good role as a strong and intelligent courtesan like me. After a Chinese warlord, white Warner Oland, rapes Anna she stabs him and survives. I also get my man and have another critical and box office success.

I'm proud of all my films with Josef von Sternberg, including the final three, but our professional association loses creative energy as personal relations rupture, and new Paramount production manager Ernst Lubitsch declines to renew his contract. Meanwhile, I've got a 1936 date with Gary Cooper in *Desire.*

I assure you I never steal jewelry from men but in this picture I tell a psychiatrist and a jeweler that I'm married to the other and ask the jeweler to deliver my pearl necklace to the good doctor who thinks my husband's a patient and asks him personal questions such as how do you sleep and all my jeweler husband wants is his check for two million francs and while they're bumbling I take the necklace and drive fast out of Paris toward the Spanish border and don't mean to splash muddy water on Gary Cooper and only of necessity do I secretly hide my jewels in Gary's coat pocket at customs and later steal his car. This movie's much fun to make especially since Gary's rid of Lupe Velez and we do some shooting in France and Spain far from Gary's wonderful but rather suspicious wife Rocky. I've been married for years to Rudolf Sieber. He understands I enjoy many men and women and approve of, and financially support, his separate life with our daughter and whomever else he chooses.

I'm honored to become Hollywood's highest paid actress in 1936, receiving two hundred thousand dollars for *Garden of Allah*. Cost overruns unrelated to me result in a large loss. Nevertheless, for *Knight Without Armour* I agree to a quarter million and ten percent of profits that, regrettably, never materialize. *Angel* also fails to inspire the public and film distributors crudely place me on their Box Office Poison list that also includes Greta Garbo and Katherine Hepburn, and Paramount pays me to let it shred my contract.

"At least the Germans want you," says a dim acquaintance.

"That's right. Do they want you? Does anyone? I don't want to be the preeminent star in Nazi Germany. Hitler's a curse who craves war. I'm ready to fight for the United States. Meanwhile, I'm taking a rest."

Visitors flock wherever I'm staying in Hollywood or Europe. I entertain young John F. Kennedy and others. Maybe I'll sing and dance and be a star without the countless complications of moviemaking. Two years later, in 1939, I'm offered an excellent role for a modest salary.

"You should take it," says Josef von Sternberg, still tutoring me on occasion. "You'll soon be forty. That's old for male stars and ancient for women."

Jimmy Stewart, seven years my junior, thinks I'm nice on set and off in *Destry Rides Again.* I'm having a great time as queen of the saloon owned by my boyfriend and tough town boss Brian Donlevy. In my place I throw a drink in the face of one smartass and push another down and bump into a man playing high stakes poker and can't help it he loses his ranch in that hand. The weak old sheriff asks me how card games are turning into land grabs. He should keep his mouth shut and will now that he's shot dead. The new sheriff's a drunk and won't make trouble. We townsfolk don't know what to think about Jimmy Stewart, playing Tom Destry, the new deputy who refuses to wear a gun.

I'm always ready for trouble, and scratch, wrestle, and roll with jealous bitch Una Merkel surrounded by excited men in the saloon. If Jimmy doesn't pour water on us we'd still be fighting. I guess the movie code prudes are too shocked to object. Like people all over, they love my song *See What the Boys in the Back Room Will Have.* Jimmy whispers he likes the song, too. On screen he borrows a gun and shows how to use it, shooting six knobs off the sign over a store. More serious now, he visits and tells me he knows what kind of stuff I'm involved in and that he needs to find the corpse of the previous sheriff so he can convict the killer. Jimmy's very smart how he tricks the bad guys into revealing where the dead sheriff lies. I won't spoil the ending but concede after production ends Jimmy Stewart drops me. I assume he thinks I'm too old. He doesn't know I'm pregnant and planning an abortion.

I have a refined eye for handsome men and tell a studio executive, as we talk in the commissary, that I want that big fellow over there for Christmas. He's John Wayne and, enabled by my success in *Destry Rides Again*, I get him gift wrapped for three films we make the next two years. My pay is good and our cinematic results decent but everyone sees my still-striking face has entered its forties. I don't need movies now, anyway. I'm a United States citizen entertaining our troops all over the country in 1942 and 1943. Hundreds of thousands cheer my songs, jokes, and personal style. I'm beating every actress at this game, and really heat up on USO tours as we close in on Hitler in Algeria, Italy, England, France, and, ultimately, Germany where many are calling me a traitor. I think Germans who followed Hitler are the traitors. This nightmare will soon be over. Our troops liberating Europe are led by great generals like George Patton and James Gavin. Both men privately tell me about their adventures.

After the war I make some movies. *A Foreign Affair* directed by Billy Wilder and *Stage Fright* by Alfred Hitchcock are rather good but I feel more heroic on stage. A hotel in Las Vegas pays me thirty thousand a week and I love the applause. Audiences await me in Europe and Australia. Guided by young musical maestro Burt Bacharach, we expand my repertoire and ensure dresses, tuxedos, wigs, makeup, and lighting hide some of the truth.

Occasionally, I get a wonderful screen role. I hope you have seen *Witness for the Prosecution.* If so, don't give away the climax or Billy Wilder and Charles Laughton will rebuke you. Perhaps worse. I think I can tell you this. My much younger husband, Tyrone Power, is accused of murdering a quite old widow who ne'er do well Tyrone is trying to fleece. She changes her will, leaving everything to him, and shortly thereafter is murdered in her home. I'm my husband's only alibi. But am I legally married to him? I imagine Tyrone on the gallows, and even Laughton's courtroom skills won't save him unless I do something decisive. Can I, as a native German, fool people with my Cockney accent? And why would I need to try? You'll be surprised more than once.

My best opportunities are on stage but it's difficult to carry a show in my sixties and overwhelming in my seventies when I fracture a leg and break another and sedate myself with increasing quantities of pills and alcohol. That recalls the line from *Just a Gigolo*, when I'm seventy-seven and making my final screen appearance: "Dancing, music, champagne, the best way to forget until you find something you want to remember." I can't dance the final decade bedridden in my Paris apartment but I read and drink and call people all over the world. I'm still Marlene on the phone. When you want to see the whole woman, watch my movies. You haven't seen anyone like me.

LOUISE BROOKS

Dating Louise

People have been telling me. That's her. Louise Brooks is selling clothes at Saks Fifth Avenue. I probably would've recognized her, though she no longer wears the luminous black helmet hairdo she had when I loved her in the late twenties. I would've married her on the first date, if I could've gotten one, when she starred in silent classics *Pandora's Box* and *Diary of a Lost Girl.* What a stunning lady. And even around age forty, with long hair, she's a special presence in our store just after the war.

"Hello, Miss Brooks, I'm Mr. Dexter, the assistant manager, but please call me Bob."

"I would have, Bob. You can call me Louise."

"I was shocked when I heard you worked here."

"Why? People need to work."

"Yes, but since you're a movie star..."

"I haven't made a movie in almost ten years and that was a rotten B western with John Wayne, who got all the good scenes. One producer told me I better get out of Hollywood or I'd end up a hooker."

"I'm surprised things didn't work out."

"When talkies came, they claimed my voice wasn't right."

"I like your voice," I say, and begin figuring how to assign myself sales and inventory tasks in women's clothes.

In less than a month, more excited every day, I think Louise may be interested in me, too.

"Would you like to have dinner tonight?"

"I'm busy," she says.

"What about tomorrow night?"

"Still busy."

"Would you ever have time for me?"

"Saturday night."

"Wonderful."

"You married?" she asks.

"Yes, but it's over. We sleep in separate bedrooms."

"Naturally."

I meet Louise at a fine steakhouse in Manhattan, and in our booth

I ask, "Do you drink?"

"I suppose you don't know much about me."

We order martinis and she downs three before I finish my first.

"Aren't you drinking a little fast, Louise?"

"Don't be a dimwit. I bore easily, even with men far more distinguished than you."

"Where are those fellows now that you're a sales clerk?"

"Screw you."

I motion for the waiter and say, "Please hurry up."

We talk little before dinner arrives. I pick at mine while she eats fast. The moment she finishes, I ask, "You full?"

"Let's go."

We take a taxi to the address she gives and climb three stories to a studio apartment smaller than my kitchen in suburban Connecticut.

I don't want a drink but reflexively ask for one.

"No time for that," she says, tossing cushions from the sofa she pulls into a bed where she swarms me.

Afterward, she says, "You're a soft guy."

"I try to be."

"They don't excite me."

I'm willing to get a little tougher but she always ignores me when I come to her department. That hurts but soon some of the other sales clerks tell me Louise has started entertaining rich old men. Then she leaves Saks Fifth Avenue and, I assume, becomes a different kind of star.

BETTE DAVIS

Bette in Bondage

Bette Davis blows by the cautioning hand of an executive secretary and opens the big door, marching straight to the desk of Jack Warner who glances up and says, "Bette, we don't have an appointment today."

"I just learned you don't want me to play the lead in *Of Human Bondage.*"

Warner places his pen on the desk and says, "I've already made the decision to protect your career. RKO knows I won't loan you for the role of Mildred Rogers."

"That's an outstanding part and will enable me to rise above the creative rut you've put me in."

Warner stands, motions to a chair, and says, "Please sit down, Bette."

"I really must have better roles."

"You're under contract."

"I'll find a way to break it," she says.

"Bette, I'm not going to let you destroy your career. Several stars have already refused to play Mildred Rogers because she'd turn the public against them. Will you sit down?"

She places her purse on his desk before sitting.

"J.L., I wish those ladies had more ambition."

"Actually, Bette, they've considered the consequences of playing such a disreputable woman."

Poised on the edge of her chair, she says, "They're competent actresses but lack imagination. This is a great dramatic part."

Warner picks up his pen and squeezes before tossing it back onto the desk.

"She's a cheap little cockney waitress, Bette. Remember, Philip Carey will be played by Leslie Howard, a man most women adore. They'll be rooting for him to overcome his clubfoot and rejection as a painter and go on to become a doctor. Let's look at the script."

"I've got everyone's part right here," Bette says, tapping her forehead.

J. L. opens a drawer and puts his script on the desk.

"I can't stand the broad," he says. "Philip offers her champagne, hoping it'll make her 'more friendly.' And when he tells her he'll never see her again if she doesn't change, she says, 'Good riddance to bad rubbish.'

"You're only twenty-five and starting to be considered glamorous, in your own way, but if you act like that you'll frighten men and alienate women."

Pointing to Warner's script, Bette says, "Philip's 'so in love with her' he can't study and fails his medical test. It's my task to at once be adorable and hateful."

"No one will like it when she rejects his proposal so she can marry Emil, a guy who has 'very good money.'"

"Remember, J.L., Philip doesn't treat his new girlfriend Norah well despite her being sincere and loving. The moment Mildred Rogers shows up unannounced, after getting impregnated and dumped by Emil, Philip's delighted to be with her. And when Norah asks why he hasn't been to see her, he tells her he doesn't care for her."

"Leslie Howard, a major star playing an admirable character, can get away with behavior that a young actress playing a wretch cannot," says Warner.

"There's wonderful tension when people offer unrequited love."

Warner says, "Mildred's not a star. When she has the baby she turns it over to a nurse for care and runs off with Philip's friend Harry and tells Philip she doesn't want him."

"That's how things often develop, J.L. Philip's no saint. He ignores another lovely girlfriend so he can help Mildred with her 'hard times.' That saddens me as does his decision to go to her apartment and bring her and the baby back to his place 'just to help.' At least, when Mildred asks what happened to his love for her, he tells her she disgusts him. I can't wait to deliver Mildred's response: I hated being kissed by you."

"Frankly," Warner says, pushing the script away, "lots of guys would've killed her if she'd torn up their apartment, cut up their paintings, and burned their stocks and bonds before walking out. Maybe that's what Philip should do. I'll discuss it with the screenwriters."

Bette interlocks hands in her lap. "That's reasonable, J.L., but if we let Philip murder Mildred, he can't undergo successful foot surgery or get evicted from his apartment for failure to pay rent."

"I think it's unlikely Philip's most recent girlfriend would still want him and even less likely her father would invite Philip to live with them and give him a job in a clothes store."

"The audience will be happy Philip has help," says Bette. "And I'm confident they'll care when Philip learns Mildred is coughing and quite ill and her baby has died."

"I confess, I'm happy Mildred's found dead in her apartment and Philip, having moved forward, plans to marry his very nice girlfriend. That's the role I'd like you to play."

"That's a supporting role, J.L. I guarantee Mildred Rogers will make me a star, or, rather, I'll make her one."

"If you're wrong, Bette, you'll either end up in B movies or acting in obscure plays around the country. Incidentally, Leslie says you need a lot of work on your cockney accent."

Notes: Bette Davis received her first best actress Oscar nomination in this movie and many observers were surprised she didn't win. The following year she received the academy award in *Dangerous* and another in 1938 in *Jezebel.* During her career she earned eleven Oscar nominations.

Our Integrated Life

I finish serving lunch to some actors in the Warner Brothers commissary when from another table I hear, "Oh, excuse me."

I turn toward a voice that thrills millions, and say, "I'll get your waiter right away, Miss Davis."

"I've already eaten. This is business. Please sit down."

"I'd love to, but they'd fire me."

"Nonsense," she says, waving at my boss and nodding. He nods back, looking impressed. "What is your name, young man?"

"Ernest Anderson."

"Do you have any acting experience, Ernest?"

"Yes, Miss Davis, I graduated from Northwestern University's School of Drama and Speech."

"That's impressive. You're also very handsome and friendly and would be perfect for a part in the movie we're making: *In This Our Life.* I've already pointed you out to director John Huston, and he's agreed to give you a screen test."

"That's wonderful, Miss Davis. Thank you so much."

I get the part and am thrilled to be on the set with Bette Davis and Olivia de Havilland and other big stars, watching and learning.

Just before shooting begins one morning, Davis tells John Huston, "John, I'm not wearing this frumpy dress. And you need to change the lighting. I'm not letting them make me up like this."

"We all age, Bette," he says. "You're still only thirty-three. I'll do everything I can to shoot you softly."

"I'm too damn old to play bad sister Stanley. I should be playing good sister Roy."

"You're the screen's most accomplished bad lady, Bette. Olivia's generally the sweetheart."

I can see why Bette Davis is worried. The night before marrying her lawyer boyfriend, George Brent, she runs off with her sister's husband, Dennis Morgan, a surgeon who soon starts drinking too much while Bette wastes money and tells him she hates him. Morgan kills himself and Davis comes running home for help then has to travel far away because her real husband's quite ill but studio chief Jack Warner wires her to get back to work. She ignores him and when she does return John Huston's gone because the Japanese attacked Pearl Harbor and he has public relations duties in the army. Davis hates the new director, Raoul Walsh, and they often yell at each other, and Olivia de Havilland's probably not happy about Walsh, either, since everyone says she and Huston fell in love before he left. I keep smiling and behaving deferentially but I'm thinking these white folks are as crazy in life as in the movies.

The final part of the movie is written to unfold this way: Bette Davis wants to get back George Brent, the husband she dumped, and invites him to a bar he wisely avoids. She gets drunk and rushes to her car and speeds away, swerving all over, and hits two people, killing a little girl and injuring her mother. I've been working in Brent's office to pay for law school and am content until Davis tells police she loaned me her car before the accident. I'm arrested right away and you know how that could turn out. Thankfully, de Havilland talks to my mother, Hattie McDaniel, a maid in many movies including *Gone with the*

Wind, and she swears I was home all evening those people were run over. The investigation points to Davis who, sober but agitated, runs to her car and tries to get away from the police but crashes and dies.

"Damn it, they've got to rewrite the end of this," Davis tells Raoul Walsh. "I'm not going to be the only demon in a movie of angels and suffer a predictable fate."

"I'm tired of your damn complaining," he says.

"Listen, you one-eyed buzzard," she says, referring to the patch covering an eye taken out by a jackrabbit that flew through Walsh's windshield as he drove near Palm Springs years earlier, "either this script changes or I'm going to develop a few weeks of laryngitis."

Walsh calls Jack Warner who marches down to the set. In front of everyone he looks at Bette and says, "When I want you to be the good girl you want to be bad. Now it's the opposite. We've already had too many wars, illnesses, and cost overruns. That's the script."

"We haven't shot the final part yet, J.L."

"By tomorrow morning you have one paragraph on my desk telling me what happens and how we can shoot it in the same amount of time currently allotted."

At the end of the day Bette Davis walks to me and says, "Ernest, I called one of your professors at Northwestern. He says you're a fine writer. Will you come over and help me tonight?"

"Of course, Miss Davis."

She greets me alone in her home. Her husband is improving but still hospitalized in another state.

"Have you eaten, Ernest?"

"Yes, thank you."

"I hope you type faster than my twenty words a minute."

"A little," I say.

Discussing our ideas as I type, we finish the first draft of the paragraph in about an hour and then revise a little before I retype our ending: "Adventurous Bette Davis invites Ernest Anderson, an employee of her former husband, to her home for dinner. They relax and laugh and that evening begin a romance. They usually meet at her house on Friday and Saturday evenings as Ernest is busy studying other nights. Bette lobbies for marriage or at least living together.

Ernest fears this would weaken his opportunity to become a lawyer. His concerns grow when she gets pregnant. Bette's family disowns her. Ernest's mother is also distraught. After he's fired from the law office, Ernest suggests Bette get an abortion. She counters they should move to California where they may have better opportunities to raise a family. After several days consideration, Ernest agrees, and they get married in a private civil ceremony. The movie ends as Ernest drives Bette's car into a beautiful sunset."

In the morning she rushes to Jack Warner's office and hands him our paper. "I think we've done a marvelous job, J.L."

While reading, he several times glances up at Bette.

"You know I can't accept this, and neither would those bluenoses who enforce the movie codes."

"Too bad," she says. "It would be a helluva movie."

"Maybe in fifty years."

Investigating Now, Voyager

I drive right up to an old Boston mansion and tell the maid, "I'm Detective Sullivan and must speak to the daughter of Gladys Cooper, Bette Davis."

No doubt alarmed, she comes to the door and says, "What is it, Detective Sullivan?"

"I'm quite sorry about the untimely passing of your mother. May I please come in and confirm some of the details?"

"There really aren't any details. My mother was quite old and frail and she died of a heart attack."

"We're going to need a copy of the autopsy report."

"There was no autopsy."

I examine her face a few seconds before saying, "If you'd be more comfortable discussing this at the station, I'd be happy to drive you."

"Shall I call my attorney?" she asks.

"I don't know, Miss Davis. Do you need one?"

"Very well, Detective Sullivan, come right in."

We walk down a long hall and turn into a large living room where I sit on a sofa and she in a chair.

"Would you like something to drink?"

"Never drink on duty, Miss Davis."

"I was offering coffee or tea."

"No thank you."

"This won't take long, will it, Detective Sullivan? I'm expecting guests for dinner tonight."

"Just a few details."

I open my notepad, glance at several underlined items, and say, "You don't look at all like the person in photos from a couple of years ago."

"Is that a question?"

"No, Miss Davis, it's a compliment."

"I've lost more than twenty pounds."

"You also look more becoming without those glasses."

"I agree."

"And you're dressing more stylishly."

"Are you going to ask me any questions, Detective Sullivan, or provide commentary for a women's magazine?"

"How did you get along with your mother?"

Miss Davis silently examines me before saying, "I don't like your insinuation."

"Then answer the question."

"I gather you already know. She bore three much older brothers whom she adored. I was an accident. She had no love for me, only ridicule. I felt shy and awkward around a mother who treated me like her servant."

I start taking notes.

"Why didn't you leave home?"

"I was hardly in demand. But even before I got heavy, my mother insulted me in front of men and drove them away."

"Did you hate her?"

"You're really quite impudent, Detective Sullivan, but I've found talking about painful experiences can be therapeutic."

"Have you ever had professional treatment?"

"You damn well know I have. Claude Rains is a brilliant and compassionate psychiatrist. Spending several weeks in his sanitarium changed my life. I was also delighted to be away from my mother. I blossomed when I went on a cruise and met Paul Henreid. We knew we were in love, but he was married, and we parted not knowing what to do."

I flip to another page and say, "Two weeks ago Mr. Henreid's wife drowned in the river near their home. That confused authorities since she couldn't swim and never entered natural bodies of water."

"That's not in the script," she says.

"Neither is this conversation."

Bette Davis stands.

"You'll be leaving now, Detective Sullivan."

I stand and say, "We've talked to various people who confirm that your mother resented your growing independence. Since she controlled the purse strings, she tried to force you to resume being dowdy and weak. You resisted, demanding 'complete freedom.' Shortly thereafter, your mother almost died rolling down the long staircase from the second floor to the first. Where were you when she fell, Miss Davis?"

"I've told you to leave."

"Did your mother threaten to write you out of her will? Did she say you'd be a spinster with no means of support?"

"Detective Sullivan, if I had a gun, I'd shoot you."

"Did you want to shoot your mother? We're going to exhume her body to determine if toxic substances caused her death."

Making fists at her sides, Miss Davis says, "I'm calling the police to have you arrested for trespassing and harassment."

"By now, Miss Davis, we have two squad cars outside. You'll be going downtown in one of them."

"This is insane. You can't possibly have any evidence."

"We have a special witness, and we don't need to wait for the trial to introduce Olive Higgins Prouty, author of *Now, Voyager.*"

Miss Davis dashes to Mrs. Prouty and says, "Olive, thank goodness you're here. Tell him I didn't do it."

"You didn't do it in my book, Bette, but I like the detective's movie ending better. You poison your mother and Paul Henreid wrestles his wife into the river and holds her down."

"You can't let this crazed detective destroy your finest work, Olive."

"Don't worry, Bette, the book won't change. Just the screenplay."

All About Bette

I'm already forty-two and you know what Hollywood and most fans think of aging women especially if they make only three movies in four years and all flounder at the box office. A lot of people in this gossipy town would like to send me away, perhaps in a box. I think it's strange my Oscars aren't helping me get the role of Margo Channing in *All About Eve*, the upcoming production everyone's enthused about.

I adore director and screenwriter Joseph Mankiewicz and producer Darryl Zanuck but, in better times, would rebuke them for even considering others. As a professional courtesy, I won't reveal names but two beautiful ladies are entirely too young for the part of an aging actress, two are much less appropriate than I, and of the two others they prefer one is unavailable and the other injured. I say not a disparaging word when Joe, quite belatedly, offers me what I cherish most.

The day production starts I'm as ever prepared and externally confident but concede my heart seizes when unknown Marilyn Monroe shyly says hello. I'm relieved this gorgeous girl, a generation my junior, has a small part and, so far as I can discern, a correspondingly small talent. In a simple scene she bumbles her lines a dozen times before I say, "You better study the script at night instead of whatever you're doing that makes you late every day." She dashes away in tears.

Anne Baxter worries me. Though less luminous than Marilyn, she's much prettier than I, fifteen years fresher, and a recent Oscar winner, albeit for supporting actress. Anne wants what I've got and, as Eve Harrington, slithers her way into becoming my omnipresent aide and companion quick to praise and serve me while also studying my techniques as the preeminent stage actress on Broadway.

I hope Anne won't try to steal Gary Merrill. Rumor is he plans to have an affair with her off screen. I won't let that happen. I love hairy and handsome men like Gary, especially when they're several years younger, and overwhelm him with passion while deciding to replace my third husband. Before the cameras Gary is also my boyfriend and rejects the flirtations of scheming Anne. I'm further distraught when theater critic George Sanders tells me Anne's wonderful when she secretly reads my part and becomes my understudy. I'll stay sharp and keep her offstage. Renowned playwright Hugh Marlowe and his wife Celeste Holm, the latter of whom I rebuke the first day on set for being too cheery too early, are supposedly my onscreen friends but contrive to make me miss a performance so eager Anne can perform and delight the audience, arousing acerbic George Sanders to praise dynamic Eve and revile me for being an old cow hanging on.

The rest of the original script is irrelevant because I demand a private meeting with Joseph Mankiewicz and Darryl Zanuck and slam soiled and annotated papers on the producer's desk and say, "That's enough. The other players are fine but as usual I'm dominating this movie and insist on the following changes. Anne Baxter as planned lures Hugh Marlowe into leaving his wife, cheery Celeste, but on their way to a seaside wedding they blow a tire and fly off the road into a thicket where their remains won't be discovered for a fortnight. The dry Mr. Sanders, we discover, has a history of ungentlemanly behavior with women and attempts to disrobe terrified Marilyn Monroe who, thankfully, is able to grasp a wine glass on the coffee table next to the sofa on which she's pinned and smash the glass against Sanders' temple prior to thrusting her jagged weapon into his throat. Marilyn thereafter moves to Hollywood to launch a career in pictures. And I marry Gary Merrill and we drink and screw a lot when we aren't berating and beating hell out of each other."

"That's even better than what I wrote," says Joseph Mankiewicz.

"Let's do it as long as it doesn't blow the budget," says Darryl Zanuck.

"Our efforts will still earn us many academy award nominations and with this script I'll surely win the Oscar."

"We better change the title to *All About Margo,*" says Mankiewicz.

"I like it," says Zanuck.

Defending the Dead Ringer

Deep inside a high security prison the meeting room is small and windowless except for an eye-level square of thick glass in the door. A large guard, accompanied by another, lets me in. I wait for the door to close before stepping to a small table where sits a lady in her fifties. I shake her hand and say, “Good morning, Mrs. DeLorca, I’m Joseph Brady.”

“Forgive me, Mr. Brady, but I’m no longer sure I want to appeal my sentence.”

“In that case, you have less than a month to live.”

I put my briefcase on the floor and sit across from her.

“This is quite a unique case, Mrs. DeLorca. What we currently know is that you’ve been convicted of using arsenic to murder your wealthy husband Frank. Your lover Tony Collins also would’ve been convicted but your Great Dane attacked and killed him. Didn’t you try to call off the dog to save a man I assume you cared for?”

She averts her eyes and says, “It was so sudden. I must’ve been in shock.”

“Mrs. DeLorca, given your circumstances, I’m going to be frank. I’ve interviewed two of your employees and learned the dog hated Margaret until the death of her identical twin sister Edith. At that time Margaret, who hadn’t smoked in years, suddenly began chain smoking. Edith was a heavy smoker, wasn’t she?”

“I think so. I hadn’t seen Edith for eighteen years prior to Frank’s funeral. Afterward, I invited her to my mansion in Beverly Hills. And that evening I was delighted she called and asked me to come to her apartment above the cocktail lounge she owned. She offered me a cigarette. I still haven’t been able to quit.”

“Later that night, your sister committed suicide. Did she seem despondent?”

“Not at all. We enjoyed talking about old times.”

“What about the present? How was her business, Mrs. DeLorca?”

“Not very good. She faced eviction.”

“So, after being estranged almost twenty years, she suddenly felt comfortable asking you to come over and give her some money.”

"I think she still loved me and knew I'd help. I promised to cover her business expenses."

"What was the nature of your estrangement?

Looking skeptical, she says, "Surely, Mr. Brady, you've already looked into that."

"Indeed, I have. Frank DeLorca was Edith's boyfriend until Margaret swept in, won his affection, and told him she was pregnant. Were you pregnant, Mrs. DeLorca?"

"I certainly was."

"I'd like to talk to your doctor."

She points to the heavens. "You can't. He's dead."

"But his records are somewhere still alive."

"What's your point, Mr. Brady?"

"I've talked to some of your friends, those of Margaret DeLorca, that is, and most tell me you aren't Margaret."

"That's preposterous."

"Is it? I have three ladies anxious to come here and ask you questions only Margaret could answer."

She says, "I won't agree to see them. Besides, what's the difference?"

"Living and dying…"

She closes her eyes and rubs them. "It's all so frustrating. Maybe if you'd defended me, Mr. Brady, I'd have been found innocent."

"Not guilty is the correct legal term, and I don't think that would've been the finding of the jury."

"I wanted my attorneys to put more blame on my boyfriend Tony Collins."

"Collins only procured the arsenic. He had no way to feed it to Frank DeLorca. Only his wife had the opportunity and motive to do that."

"What do you recommend, Mr. Brady?"

"First, we can easily prove you aren't Margaret DeLorca. Even a *Dead Ringer* isn't exact."

"But then they'll know I shot Margaret, wrote a suicide note, and changed her hair to the style I wore."

"That's correct."

"What would happen?"

"No defense attorney can get you off, but with the new trial for the murder of Margaret, and vigorous appeals, we can keep you alive a few more years."

JEANNE EAGELS

Code of The Letter

I'm Jeanne Eagels proud to report when I star in *The Letter* of 1929, before the Motion Picture Production Code lengthens dresses and stifles hearts to promote moral hypocrisy, we ignore melodramatic compromises and tell the truth about passionate, profane, and imperfect human beings, and I pump several shots into my longtime lover Geoffrey because he no longer wants me. He's fallen for and begun living with a Chinese woman played not by a Caucasian but an oriental, Lady Tsen Mei. She doesn't stab me, or take any other punitive action, for murdering her husband. As in life, criminals sometimes get away with vile acts. In my case, the reprieve is unappealing since vengeful husband Robert vows to force me to live with him forever. Poor Bette Davis also gets to shoot the same Casanova in a 1940 remake, but The Code won't permit the decedent's wife to be Chinese, she must be Eurasian and played by Gale Sondergaard, a decidedly white lady from Minnesota.

Bette and I might be doomed to the gallows if our attorneys don't enable us to purchase our letters from the widow. These emotional messages, for which we secretly spend all of Robert's money, are written in our own hand and urge Geoffrey to come and see us and emphasize our husbands will be away and we're "desperate" to talk. Indeed, we're desperate for his love in hot and horrid Malaya where our husbands are more concerned with rubber than romance. Absent the letter, Bette and I testify in court that Geoffrey attacked us and tried to force himself on us, and we survived only by grace of our husband's revolver in a nearby desk. In my final scene, and Bette's penultimate, we tell weak husbands still eager to cherish us that we cannot promise the same, for "with all my heart, I love the man that I killed."

Bette should not be asked to emote any more, but The Code demands punishment, and this the Eurasian widow delivers with knife strokes to Bette's gut beneath a full and clear moon suddenly darkened by clouds as a policemen walks by, at least alluding to consequences for the avenger.

I have another moving story to offer. A beautiful and talented actress marries and has a child who dies, and she breaks down but recovers enough to continue acting on stage and in silent films and marry again and, despite years of alcoholism and abuse of heroin and other drugs and several stays in sanitariums and periodic hallucinations and another divorce, she is poised when motion pictures appear with sound and she stars in a classic. Shortly thereafter she completes another movie, *Jealousy,* and then spends ten days in a New York hospital following eye surgery, and upon release begins to behave erratically, more so than usual, and goes into convulsions and dies at age thirty-nine. Her last film is lost. *The Letter* remains. Her life story would make a fine picture. The Code wouldn't have permitted Bette Davis to faithfully portray me. But someone could do it now.

VIVIEN LEIGH

Vivien in the Hotel

I work at a great Manhattan hotel whose name I better not mention. I'm just a bellhop and only twenty-two but know I'm going to have a great job someday. Today, I'm rolling a cart with the luggage of a special guest: she's Vivien Leigh, Scarlett O'Hara in the flesh, and as beautiful now as she was several years ago. I'm not nervous, though. I do this for quite a few celebrities. They usually don't say much. Vivien's different.

"You're very handsome," she says.

"Thank you."

"And in marvelous condition."

"I still play baseball with my friends."

"Do you know Babe Ruth?"

"No, he died recently but he'll always be my favorite player. Here's your room, Miss Leigh."

I unlock the door and bow as I motion to enter first, and she walks in and says, "Oh, this is wonderful."

"Let me open the drapes. You'll love the view of the city."

"Incredible. Will you please put my bags in the closet and unpack them."

"You want me to unpack your bags, Miss Leigh?"

"I hope that's not too much trouble. What' your name?"

"Mike."

"Please, Mike."

"It would be a pleasure."

I start pulling out fancy dresses, skirts, and blouses and hanging them in the closet.

"Here, hang this one up, too, will you," she says, handing me the dress she's been wearing as she stands there in panties and bra.

"Sure, Miss Leigh."

I hang up her dress.

"Come here, Mike."

I do what she says and she hugs and kisses me. A couple hours later I wash up in the bathroom and put my uniform back on.

"Thank you, Miss Leigh. I better go now."

She gets out of bed and says, "I want you back here tomorrow."

"Yes, ma'am."

Back downstairs in the lobby my boss marches up and says, "Where the hell have you been?"

"I was helping Miss Leigh."

"Get back outside and take care of our guests."

Waiting by the curb in front is Howard, the cabbie, and I lean through the open passenger window and say, "I visited Vivien Leigh this afternoon."

"Mike, she's like that."

"You're lyin'."

"She's not well."

"Who's says?"

"An actress who rides with me sometimes."

"What's the matter?"

"Manic depression."

Improvised Care

In a dark bedroom at their beautiful estate outside London, Laurence Olivier says, "Where have you been, Vivien?"

"Don't interrogate me."

"A simple question about your whereabouts last night doesn't constitute an interrogation, my dear."

"We needn't discuss details."

"Were you with him again?"

"Who?" asks Vivien.

He grabs slender shoulders and shakes before shoving her onto the bed.

"Please, Larry, violence so diminishes you. Just accept that Peter and I have a passionate bond that you and I lack."

"If I weren't a civilized man, I'd kill Peter Finch."

Olivier turns and storms from the bedroom. That night he sleeps in a guest room. In the morning at breakfast, he says, "You were wonderful in *A Streetcar Named Desire* but more than three hundred performances have stressed and weakened you. I don't want you to play Blanche Dubois in the movie."

"I was born for that part."

"Unfortunately, that's true, and precisely why I must forbid you to leave this estate until you've recovered."

She scoffs. "I'm recovered. My difficulties mustn't have been too awful or I'd remember them."

"Talk to those who do remember, like your husband."

"I've already apologized to everyone, especially you."

Olivier points to the newspaper on the table and says, "Disgusting. Here's Kenneth Tynan, a critic who wishes he could act, calling you a 'mediocre talent' who 'forces' me to undermine my gifts."

"Damn you for throwing that in my face."

"You were certain to find out and I had to be here to care for you."

"Then you better visit me during filming. I suppose you know, the noble director Elia Kazan has called me a 'small talent.'"

"He won't even allude to such nonsense when I'm on the set."

Moviemakers transform a Burbank film studio and several mundane exterior shots into New Orleans. Olivier meets with Marlon Brando, an incandescent young man, and says, "My wife is unwell and…"

"Whatsa matter with her?"

"Frankly, she's much like Blanche Dubois."

"Christ."

"I can't be here all the time to care for her," he says, handing Brando a card. "I ask that you call this local doctor if you see any signs of emotional difficulty. And I can be reached at any of these numbers. Call collect, of course."

Brando pats Olivier's arm and says, "Happy to help. It's an honor to meet you."

"Based on your notices playing Stanley Kowalski in *Streetcar*, the honor is mine."

They warmly shake hands.

"I see that my conscientious husband has been talking to you," says Vivien, approaching Brando after Olivier departs.

"Listen, Vivien, I gotta ask how much that coat cost. And that jewelry. How're you paying for all that stuff? Where are the papers from the sale of your parents' place back in Auriol? My wife's got as much right to the money as you."

"Is this a rehearsal, Marlon?"

"I don't like you telling Kim I'm 'common, like an animal,' just because she and I are in love. Where's your man? What happened to him?"

"You just met my husband," she says.

"You're starting to look pretty old. I don't see any husband. You told him you didn't respect him and that you despised him. He shot himself but you might as well have pulled the trigger."

Vivien suddenly raises both hands to adjust her long blond wig. "I hope Tennessee stops by to discuss the script. He'll be impressed how you're immersing yourself in his work."

"You better stay away from my buddy Karl Malden. He's lonely and might make a mistake."

"I resent your insinuation that I'd be bad for Karl. I think I could love him, at least in this movie."

"This isn't a movie, Vivien. The paperboy told me you kissed him and called him a young prince. You got a thing about kids? I've got people checking this stuff out."

Vivien backs away and says, "I'd prefer to rehearse in a more formal setting when our colleagues are present."

"Fine. I want people to know how you carried on in some hotel called Flamingo. That's a strange place for a teacher to live."

At their factory job Marlon and Karl clash. Tennessee Williams finally arrives and thrusts himself between the agitated friends. With one hand inside the collar behind the playwright's neck, Karl jerks him out of the way, and says, "You started this, Tennessee. Hope you're happy. You too, Marlon. I'm in love with Blanche."

"Go ahead and marry her," he says. "She's gonna need a place to stay cuz she's had five months in my house and that party's over."

At home that night Marlon tells Kim, "She lost her job at school because she screwed a kid seventeen-years old."

Vivien enters escorted by Laurence and Tennessee.

"What has he been saying about me?" she asks.

"I've been telling your sister the truth," says Marlon. "Here's a one-way ticket back to Auriol. You've got a lot of customers waiting at the hotel."

"God, Vivien, you haven't been carrying on there, too," says Laurence.

"Relax, Larry," Tennessee says. "If that's an intolerable problem, I can reduce the tension. After her dalliance with the boy and losing her job, I'll put Vivien in the hotel, but as a maid, nothing more."

Karl Malden hammers the door and marches in and says, "Vivien, I confirmed Marlon's sources at the hotel and am never going to see you again."

"Blanche Dubois had many meetings with strangers," she says. "But I didn't."

She turns to Olivier. Expression firm, he looks away. She walks to Malden and kisses him. "Marry me, Karl."

"You're not clean enough," he says.

Olivier confronts Malden who hits him with a straight right, sending the Englishman down.

"Stop this violence," says Tennessee. "Stop it."

"You're damn right, Tennessee, you're going to put a stop to it before that animal assaults my wife," Laurence says, rising from the floor and pointing at Marlon.

"That's a compelling scene, Larry, the broken mirror serving as metaphor not merely for a violated woman but one who's barreling into madness. I won't change a word of that."

Looking at Karl, Laurence says, "If you want a woman stable enough to be your romantic partner for life, you won't permit this to happen."

"He's right, Tennessee," says Karl. "She's suffered enough."

"Did you not hear my proclamation about the sanctity of the remaining script?"

"It'll have to be revised," says Karl.

Tennessee angrily walks out and Karl locks the door.

"I've got something to say about this," says Marlon.

"You don't know what you've got to say until I tell you the new ending," says Laurence. "It unfolds in this manner. When Marlon assaults Vivien, she's able, from the table behind her, to retrieve a long kitchen knife that Marlon, sloppy while his pregnant wife's in the hospital, has left there. Vivien stabs him one, twice, perhaps even a third time before the brute falls. She thereby not merely avoids being raped but is empowered to receive a real telegram from the cultured gentleman who wants to cruise the Caribbean with her."

"There was no telegram," says Marlon.

"You wish there hadn't been," Karl says.

"Here's the telegram," says Larry, writing it now. "The gentleman has long treasured Vivien's beauty and sensitive nature, having known her before her marriage and, not having seen her in fifteen years, is as usual overwhelmed when he sees her during a visit to his native Auriol. He's not worried about her dalliance with a husky teenage lad, and not in town long enough to learn about hotel activities since he takes Vivien on a romantic vacation to Florida. Throughout her time in New Orleans, in the home of her supportive sister and uncouth brother-in-law, the gentleman writes regularly, urging her to come to him."

"What about my relationship with Vivien?" says Karl, agitated.

"This story's evolution now demands she leave Louisiana and everything it represents, and join her suitor at his estate near Dallas," says Laurence.

Karl clinches both fists. "Maybe I better write the script."

"You'd try to make yourself the star, which you ain't," says Marlon. "I'm the leading man here."

"Despite your successes in recent years, I still outrank you," says Laurence.

"You aren't in this movie," he says.

"Neither are you, Marlon. You're bleeding and dead on the floor."

Clasping hands in front of her chest, Vivien Leigh says, "I'm delighted I'll be honeymooning instead of suffering in a mental institution."

"But you won't get the Oscar that way," says Marlon.

JOAN CRAWFORD

Joan Reveals

Right now I'm quitting these interminable college classes and dedicating myself to dancing and soon get work in chorus lines and at various gentlemen's clubs some call strip joints. A few jealous people say I'm dancing naked for mechanical film clips used in peep shows and have been arrested for prostitution. That's ridiculous. I simply parlay my lovely face and grace afoot into a contract with MGM and at age nineteen head to Hollywood.

I crave to be a star, and know I will be. By 1926 I'm being embraced in onscreen silence by major leading men John Gilbert and Ramon Navarro. And following three years study of diction and elocution, I flow into talking movies with Robert Montgomery in *Untamed.* Clark Gable and I soon become a romantic pair day and night, but priggish studio dictator Louis B. Mayer demands Gable drop me since I'm already married to Douglas Fairbanks, Jr. Mayer can't keep us apart permanently. In 1933 we star in *Dancing Lady.* At first I woo rich Franchot Tone who pays Clark's character, dance producer Patch Gallagher, to let me perform in the chorus, but when I'm about to become the star Franchot feels insecure and withdraws financial backing. I drop him and fall for Patch, committing to his better version of the show. A little later Franchot and I marry off-screen.

By then I've divorced Douglas and become box-office magic adorned with the most creative hairstyles and elegant clothes; a half million dresses like mine in *Letty Lynton* are sold despite the film not being out long because of a plagiarism suit. In public my husbands and boyfriends open doors for me and walk several feet behind my dramatic entrances then place napkins on my lap, light cigarettes, and pour my drinks. This should last forever but MGM gives me weak scripts three straight years and by 1938 I'm called box-office poison. I recover doing three films with George Cukor, who understands and directs women in ways heterosexual men cannot. But MGM is grooming younger actresses Judy Garland, Greer Garson, and Lana Turner, and the studio doesn't think it needs me. I know I don't need them. I clear out my dressing room, pay them a hundred grand to get lost, and move to Warner Brothers.

At age forty I'm both major star and compelling actress as *Mildred Pierce*. My first husband is bitter about his financial incompetence, and divorcing him leaves me with two daughters and no means of support. I humble myself asking doubters for work as a waitress and then learn the business so rapidly I open a restaurant that booms and I quickly start two more. That doesn't forestall tragedy: my youngest daughter dies and my oldest remains a wealth-obsessed demon who deserts me. I respond by marrying a former boyfriend, now the penniless scion of an old Pasadena family. He demands a third of my business interests. I agree, and also buy his old mansion and appoint it lavishly, inducing my daughter to abandon her misguided life as a nightclub dancer. I'm so happy she's back, until I catch her with my husband and she proclaims they're getting married. I drop the gun and leave. Instead of gaining love and luxury, my daughter is told she's disgusting and she picks up the gun. Afterward, police arrest me for murder. I win my first Oscar and know that gnaws Bette Davis, the other queen at Warner's.

The year I divorce Franchot Tone, I adopt my first child, Christina, and after marrying Phillip Terry we acquire a son, Christopher, who's all mine after my 1946 divorce. The following year I become the mother of four, adopting twins Cindy and Cathy. Imagine the pressure of singlehandedly raising a large family and being a movie star. These struggles give me emotional depth. So do my many affairs, hangovers, and cigarettes.

The public doesn't realize how much of myself I offer as Helen Wright in *Humoresque.* I'm a wealthy married woman who smokes and drinks incessantly as younger men encircle me in front of my weak husband. Any man I want is mine. I pray that's true when struggling violinist Paul Boray, played by John Garfield, comes to one of our parties. Later, I send him a beautiful cigarette case, and we meet for drinks. I ask if he goes to concerts and he says not much because if they're good, he's jealous, and if not, he's bored. He needs the break I give him, paying for a recital at Manhattan Hall. His reviews are great but he accuses me of adding a violin player to my collection.

That's not it at all. I'm in love and worried and drinking more. His former girlfriend, much younger than I, is after him and his mother warns about older married women. He then leaves on a tour he wouldn't have had without me but doesn't call. I urge him to keep me in his life. It's all so possible. My husband offers to divorce me. Why does Paul Boray say I'm a "hangman's noose" to him? He surely doesn't mean it. He says he loves me and wants to marry. I go to my beach house before a major concert. Paul calls and I tell him "it's so quiet here, rest and quiet are doing me a world of good." But I'm really quite nervous inhaling smoke and booze as I think about Paul. Now the music's getting louder at his concert and in my head, and I need to walk on the beach. It's dark and cool and the waves are rough yet alluring.

I'm proud that despite my beauty studios cast me in challenging and often unflattering roles. Surely my age isn't a factor. I'm only forty-two when I appear in *Possessed* as a disheveled and incontinent woman wandering streets far from home, asking for David. Doctors place me on my back in a hospital bed and stare into a strange and silent face. A flashback shows me yearning to marry David, Van Heflin's character, who says he can't love me the way I love him and that I know it and accuses me of choking and smothering him and insists we not see each other for a while. I cry and offer to do anything he says. All I can do is marry a man I don't love, Raymond Massey, husband of the crippled woman I cared for until she committed suicide. Now her daughter, Carol, resents me. I try to tolerate this since Carol's lonely father is David's employer and my lifeline to him.

It destroys me when I learn my stepdaughter is having an affair with David. I can't cope because I have schizophrenia. I think I've just pounded Carol's wretched little face and knocked her dead down the stairs. I also believe I'd taken her mother to water's edge and failed to help when she rolled herself into the water. My husband assures me I was off that day and he took her down there and left only briefly. I know I'm not hallucinating at the nightclub with my husband and David and his slutty girlfriend. I'm speaking with evermore joy and intensity.

Later I tell Carol that David doesn't love her. He loves me. The hussy doesn't believe me. I confront David and he says he's going to marry Carol. I can't permit that. I shoot him in the stomach and escape into psychosis. As I lie unconscious in a hospital bed, my loving husband vows to help me. For this performance I receive my second Oscar nomination.

In Hollywood men still love me. My boyfriend is Greg Bautzer, a dashing attorney several years younger who dates many of Hollywood's fairest but always comes back to me. One night he says something dreadful and I lock him out.

"Let me in."

"No, go away," I say.

He climbs to my second floor bedroom and punches the window, reaching his hand through and forcing his way inside.

"You're cut."

He grabs me.

"Stop, you're bleeding, Greg."

He rips my gown off.

"Don't, wait, stop, god, this is incredible..."

Nineteen fifty isn't a stellar year. As menopause envelops me I learn my dear daughter Christina, age eleven, has been screwed for the first time. I punish her in an entirely appropriate way that is my business. I have to decisively resolve family problems to be ready for *The Damned Don't Cry.* I'm not threatened by the title. I'm blessed. My character isn't as fortunate, having a blue collar husband who yells at our son to bring back that bicycle I've bought him, against his father's orders. At that moment a truck runs over the child. I escape by working in a shop where I also model dresses and earn extra entertaining gentlemen and meet a nice certified public accountant. I urge him to be ambitious and he responds and is hired by a mob boss. The CPA proposes but I dump him to become the boss' lady, the now much publicized heiress Lorna Hansen Forbes. The old man thinks he can use me, sending me to get information on a rival gangster, who I fall for. He's killed and the old man is gunning for me.

It's shameful how men try to take advantage of mature women. That's what Jack Palance's character does in *Sudden Fear.* I'm a talented and wealthy playwright who rejects him for a role, despite his dramatic ability, because he isn't romantic enough to be a leading man. Off stage he charms me into marriage and happiness I never expected. He doesn't want me, though. He and a reunited girlfriend want my money and are trying to kill me. I plot to stop them. Moviegoers are riveted, and I earn my third Oscar nomination.

I also exercise exceptional discipline at home. When my battalion of domestic helpers doesn't get things clean enough, I grab the mop and make things civilized. I have to be careful, even at Hollywood parties. One would expect hosts to properly clean their mansions but very often they don't, and I scrub with wet toilet paper before I dare sit down. I expect my four children to be clean and orderly as their mother. If they don't measure up, I swat them.

Christina's frequent misbehavior at school aggrieves me and threatens to become public. Christopher's equally difficult. He runs away from home at age nine after I refuse to let him put chocolate syrup on his ice cream. He's lucky to have ice cream, and I tan his rear with a brush. When he and some other teenagers break windows and injure a girl with air rifles, police bring him home and tell me I should've spanked him harder. They're right. At age sixteen Christopher's arrested for car theft.

Even as a young woman Christina bedevils me, frequently pressuring me to help her enter show business. I feel she should do it like I did, but I arrange a screen test. She gets some work but is unpleasant on the set. You can be that way when you're Joan Crawford but not Christina Crawford. She's jealous and threatening. That's why I slap her face when she kisses Alfred Steele, my fourth husband and the one who makes me happiest. He's president of Pepsi-Cola and spends four hundred thousand in the mid-fifties to connect and remodel two opulent penthouses overlooking Central Park. I know Alfred and I will last forever. I think about him every day but want to stop seeing him heart-attacked on the floor of our apartment.

You can't forget that. I want to lose myself by working but there are no appropriate offers. I'm alone and bored at night, too, since men aren't asking me out nearly as often as they used to. I pour another drink and hope there'll be something for me soon. I need money. Despite his position, Alfred left only six hundred thousand, and after paying former wives and other debts everything's gone.

At fifty-seven I understand I'm no longer a star but at least I look like I used to be one. Director Robert Aldrich agrees, hiring me to play Blanche in *What Ever Happened to Baby Jane.* I don't argue with his decision to cast Bette Davis as my sister, Jane, even though I know there'll be difficulties. Bette's been angry and jealous since she fell in love with Franchot Tone, who cold-shouldered her and married me. She knows who has glamor, and in an interview shortly before filming she fires a shot, calling herself an "actress" and me merely a "star." She's so proud of her extensive stage training, which I lack, and her "little gestures with the cigarette, the clipped speech, the big eyes, the deadpan… I'm just as much an actress as she, though I wasn't trained for the stage, but we're both competing in the same medium, so aren't we both actresses? Film Stars? Former film stars, whatever? She's had almost as many failed marriages and troubled children and financial problems as I."

I respect her as an actress but am depressed she's going to have all the best scenes. "I'm the cripple, physically, and she's demented… and the mental always wins out on the screen." Look at her face plastered white like a clown. Sure, she hams it up and overwhelms almost every scene, hoarding my fan mail, serving me my cooked pet bird and howling at her act, disconnecting the phone, locking me in my upstairs bedroom, telling me I'm never going to sell our house and never going to leave it, serving me a cooked rat from the cellar, forging my signature on checks, kicking me on the floor until I'm unconscious, killing our maid (who liked me) with a hammer, always misbehaving to attract attention. As a result many people say look how Bette Davis trounces Joan Crawford. Nonsense. I play my part with dignity and restraint. Near the end of an otherwise fine script, I reveal that years ago Baby Jane, the former child star, didn't jealously run over her adult star sister, but I paralyzed myself by trying to crush Jane and instead hitting a gate, and Jane hasn't realized this because she's been incontinent and run away.

I can't let Bette win the academy award she's nominated for, and "secretly campaign" against her and tell other nominees I'd be delighted to serve as proxy if they're unable to attend the ceremony. On that night I'm enormously gratified to shoulder past Bette and say, "Excuse me, I have an Oscar to accept." Anne Bancroft certainly deserves it.

Understandably, I'm determined not to work again with Miss Bette Davis and she's doubtless just as determined to avoid me. After we sign to make *Hush…Hush, Sweet Charlotte* in 1964, she harasses me in so many ways I have to be hospitalized for stress and exhaustion, and Olivia de Havilland takes my place in purgatory. I suppose that's where all older women are, especially in show business. My last four movies are *Straight-Jacket, I Saw What You Did, Berserk,* and *Trog.* I'm willing to forsake glamor – it has forsaken me – but unwilling to be the focus of an eternal horror show.

I do a little television work, appearing on *The Lucy Show* and having to answer if it's true, as loudmouth Lucy repeatedly asserts, that I'm frequently drunk on the set and unable to remember my lines. I'll respond simply by saying that Lucy is a bigger bitch than I. So is Christina, who's offering the media material and interviews about my private life. She can't accept that she alone was responsible for losing her job on the TV show *The Secret Storm.* It wasn't my fault. When she was ill and hospitalized the year before, I generously offered to fill in and, at age sixty-three, play the part of my daughter. So what if I'd been tipsy? That isn't why they let Christina go. She's a complainer. And Christopher's just as malignant. At an elegant Miami hotel I agree to receive him and the illegitimate young daughter he's fathered a few years earlier as a teenager. He soon tells people I glanced at the child and said, "It doesn't look like you. It's probably a bastard," and that he walked away forever. I remember making no such statement.

I know I need goals but can't think of any. After years of serving on the board of directors of Pepsi-Cola, which Alfred Steele led to record profits, I'm forced out by an executive I've always privately referred to as Fang. I continue to play backgammon, a passion for decades, with anyone who wants to sit with a distinguished but cantankerous old woman, and die alone from a heart attack aggravated by cancer. All four of my children attend the funeral and afterward are read my will. My delightful young twins, age thirty, receive about seventy-seven thousand each, and several friends and employees get bequests up to thirty-five thousand. For my two eldest children, I simply dictated: "It is my intention to make no provisions herein for my son Christopher or my daughter Christina for reasons which are well known to them." My ashes are then interred next to those of my beloved final husband.

Cowardly Christina doesn't write *Mommie Dearest* while I breathe but within a year tears up my image and throws it to the buzzards, portraying me as a child abuser and alcoholic. I did have a drinking problem but, other than traditional slaps and spankings, never physically abused either Christina or Christopher. I'm sure the financial abuse of being disinherited is her true complaint. Most outrageous is her cry that I once beat her with a wire hanger. The falsity of that is best presented by the impartial website "The Joan Crawford Fan Club." As the chairman of the club points out, in Perry Mason fashion, I "insisted on keeping expensive clothes on padded hangers so they wouldn't ruin the cut of the garment. It is possible that wire hangers were present when garments returned from the dry cleaners but these would have been changed by the housekeeper for padded ones when she returned the garments to the walk-in-wardrobe. Cindy and Cathy Crawford are adamant that Joan never used a wire hanger to beat any of the children."

Rather than refute each of Christina's serious allegations, I will briefly play a cross-examining defense attorney using information from my fan club's website.

"You still claim that I beat you with a wire hanger?"

"I certainly do. The physical wounds have healed but the psychological pain never will."

"Since this was supposedly such a traumatic episode, isn't it bizarre that you would trivialize it by making public appearances with a bad actress waving a wire hanger while you sold autographs for five bucks apiece?"

"I needed the money. I had a stroke and my second husband left me."

"That happened in 1981. Your assassination of me was published in 1978."

"You know how difficult you were."

"Difficult, yes. And you were a distressing child. But your portrayal of me as clinically cruel is dishonest."

"It's honest and helpful to millions of others who were abused in dysfunctional families."

"Our family was sublime compared to the disaster I escaped from. My stepfather molested me. Right now, however, I'm more concerned with your inconsistencies. On Larry King's show he asked what happened to the wire hangers, and you said, 'Well, the basis of that is true.' Something so devastating is either absolutely true or it isn't. You also implied that I was involved in the death of Alfred Steele, spewing that he 'somehow fell down the stairs.' I'll edify you by noting our apartment had no stairs. Furthermore, doctors certified the cause of death as cardiac arrest.

"Whatever you really think I did, I must congratulate you on thoroughly successful revenge. You made a lot of money and ensured that forevermore most people will believe my most famous movie is *Mommie Dearest.*"

OLIVIA DE HAVILLAND

Starring Miss de Havilland

I swoon for Errol Flynn the moment we meet and after our debut in *Captain Blood* I sense the stunning couple on screen must be destined to marry in life. I want to work with Errol again right away and am just as enthused making *The Charge of the Light Brigade* and forgive him, after a strong rebuke, for putting a dead snake in a dress he knows I'll soon be putting on.

"Olivia, we need to see each other away from work," he says.

"I want to more than anything, Errol, but I simply can't as long as you're married."

His wife is beautiful French actress Lili Damita, who no longer acts. She devotes herself to keeping track of Errol. I understand why. All the time he slips into trailers and storage rooms and other convenient spots with women who evidently can't resist. I know this must bother Lili. It certainly disturbs me, and I assume Errol knows I'm aware what he's doing.

In 1937 we're making a wonderful film of romance and adventure, *The Adventures of Robin Hood,* and I sense it's time. I really can't wait and wonder how he can. He climbs a balcony to my bedroom and I kiss him with more than usual cinematic passion and say something to ruin the take. We reshoot and I kiss him just as hard and find another way to prompt another take. I repeat this about ten times and Errol gets very crowded in his tights and I know he's ready until the day Lili comes to Bidwell Park in Chico where we're filming. If this is the woman who smothers Errol and bores him with frivolous talk, I wonder why they hug and kiss like newlyweds. She's got some kind of hold on him.

Errol and I continue making a picture or two together a year and he keeps telling me, "It's over between Lili and me."

"Have you filed for divorce?"

"Not yet."

"Do you still live together?"

"Only for the time being and rather like brother and sister."

"Sorry, Errol."

Finally, I learn that Errol really has separated from Lili and think it's all right to be David Niven's date while Errol doubles with another lady and the two new roommates entertain us for dinner at the home they now rent. When we get ready to drive to a formal dance at the Ambassador Hotel downtown, Errol slyly escorts me to his car while David guides the other lady to his, and we have a wonderful time. Afterward, Errol says, "I can no longer wait."

"Nor can I. Have you filed for divorce?"

"Not yet."

"Errol, I really can't become involved with you until you're free of Lili."

"How can you resist?"

After making humorous *Four's a Crowd,* dusty *Dodge City,* and rather dreary *The Private Lives of Elizabeth and Essex*, we sign to star in *Santa Fe Trail*, based on the life of abolitionist John Brown. By now I've become more active romantically and dated Howard Hughes and am currently involved with Jimmy Stewart. During this film I'm also quite sociable, in a strictly conversational sense, with handsome Ronald Reagan, who loves talking to me about union issues in our Screen Actors Guild.

"If you have a moment away from young Reagan, I'd like to go over our next scene," says Errol.

"You haven't been very friendly to him."

"You're amiable enough for both of us."

"Jealously doesn't become you," I say. "Perhaps we shouldn't work together anymore."

"I agree."

In a year he tells Jack Warner they can't properly make *They Died with Their Boots On*, about General Custer, unless I costar. Warner concurs. I tell both men this is the last time. It has to be. Being with Errol causes pain. During our final scene together, before he leaves for the Little Bighorn, General Custer tells his wife, "Walking through life with you, ma'am, has been a very gracious thing." I can't watch this without crying.

* * *

Studio chief Jack Warner rises, smiles like a devil, points to a chair, and says, "Please sit down, Olivia."

"I've sat in your pupil's chair many times, J.L. This time I'll stand while I tell you again I'm no longer interested in the inferior scripts Warner Brothers sends me."

"We've made you and Flynn the finest romantic couple in the history of movies."

"I'm tired of walking around in frilly dresses and huge hats, flirting with Errol before I disappear so he can lead men, sail ships, swordfight, fistfight, shoot arrows, fire guns, and become a hero until I'm summoned again."

Looking at me like a concerned guardian, he says, "Olivia, in your several short years here you've also been nominated for two academy awards."

"Good point, J.L. *Gone with the Wind* was for MGM and *Hold Back the Dawn* for Paramount. I don't get that kind of material from you."

Face tensing, Warner stands and says, "Listen, you were an immature girl just a year out of high school when I made you a star in 1935."

"We made several excellent adventure films but I'm determined to change my career."

Jack Warner points to a clock on the wall and says, "Your contract isn't ticking, Olivia. Every time you reject a script I keep suspending you and putting the production length of that movie on the end of your contract. Someday, you may be playing grandmothers for me."

"Your contracts are illegal, J.L., and I've already hired lawyers to prove that in court."

He's shaking his head as I turn to walk out.

At my modest home I worry how I'll pay huge legal fees while not working. After three tense months, in late 1943, the superior court rules I'm right but Warner instantly appeals. Finally, the following year, the court of appeals also backs our position. I'm ready to celebrate when I learn bitter Jack Warner and his minions have sent letters to all movie studios in the nation, urging them not to hire me and for two years they don't. I hope you don't consider me unladylike for saying that upon my 1946 return to movies I metaphorically kick Jack Warner in a most delicate place.

In *To Each His Own* for Paramount, I fall for a man but we have only a single night alone before he has to leave to fight in World War I. Doctors tell me I'll die if I don't have an operation that may kill my unborn baby. When I learn the father is killed in action I decide to have our son but lose him because of society's rigid mores and my bad decisions and the motherly greed of another woman whose child has just died. I age a generation in this role, while becoming a successful business owner, and eventually am reunited with my adult son. This creative opportunity enables me to win an Oscar. Also this wonderful year, *In The Dark Mirror,* I play a stable young lady and her evil twin, and evoke kindness and stability on one side of the screen and harshness and cruelty on the other.

Two years later I'm in *The Snake Pit,* running from a boyfriend I love before getting married, not sleeping at night, not knowing what month it is, undergoing many rounds of electric shock treatment, feeling confused, crying often, feeling more confused, being shoved into a straitjacket, and at the end being cured, at least temporarily, and in the arms of my husband. I earn my fourth Oscar nomination and accept another significant challenge. I must portray *The Heiress* as a plain and diffident young lady whose father rebukes her for believing handsome and gallant Montgomery Clift could possibly be interested. I stretch myself to convince audiences that Clift only returns, after leaving me, because of my father's wealth, and voters award me another Oscar for best actress.

Mercurial John Huston for a few years becomes the greatest love I've known, but he frequently wanders and I hear hurtful rumors about his debauchery and one morning I read he's married Evelyn Keyes. Good luck to them. I marry, too, and with Marcus Goodrich have a boy, Benjamin. Some people wonder why I choose a man almost twenty years older. I suppose I like mature men who are fine writers but do wish Marcus Goodrich had told me about his four previous marriages.

I don't need to work all the time and take a three-year break while I divorce quarrelsome Marcus and marry Pierre Galante and move to Paris where he's the editor of the magazine Paris Match. We have a daughter, Gisele, and I take another long stroll away from the screen and act only intermittently until I'm forty-eight and Joan Crawford is fired from *Hush…Hush, Sweet Charlotte.* They try to get Vivien Leigh. They call Barbara Stanwyck and some other actresses. They're desperate enough to fly director Robert Aldrich to find me on vacation in Switzerland. I'm really not anxious to disrupt my peaceful life. I do feel some excitement, though, and would like to make another movie, our sixth, with Bette Davis.

I'd rather play a nicer person than Bette's cousin but, as in *Whatever Happened to Baby Jane?*, opposite her rival Joan Crawford, Bette plays the disturbed and therefore more exciting character while I'm the attractive but evil lady who drugs Bette, kills her maid with a chair strike to the head that sends her tumbling down the stairs, slaps Bette to make her understand I'm in charge and that she's losing her mind and has shot poor Joseph Cotten, who's helping drive my cousin into hell. It's an entertaining movie, I suppose, but rather melodramatic and not up to the standard I established and after this final lead role I only appear on screen a few more times.

I'm a Parisienne and reasonably happy though I've had to learn I can't maintain a marriage and Pierre and I separate and ultimately divorce. More disturbing, my son Benjamin dies at forty-two after a twenty year battle with cancer, and no parent fully recovers from that. My daughter Giséle, thankfully, is healthy and successful in journalism. And I have friends and am active in church and love the home I've lived in more than sixty years making me more than a hundred and amazed people still appreciate my days of drama and romance.

Joan Fontaine Greets Olivia

Joan's waiting at the gate as Olivia enters, sees her sister and quickly looks elsewhere.

"I'm not here because I want to be, Olivia. I feel obligated."

She stops, turns to Joan, and says, "You're in no way obliged, and I frankly view your presence as more of a warning than a welcome."

"That's quite peculiar, Olivia, it was always you who menaced me and initiated hostilities."

"That's absurd. What are you talking about?"

Placing hands on hips, Joan says, "Can you name one nice thing you ever did for me as a child?"

"I protected you as my little sister."

"Really, Olivia, you're experiencing cognitive decline. You should've read my memoir and interviews over the years."

"I'm rather too literate for such drivel."

"Let's review, shall we? You're fifteen months older and used superior strength to wrestle me to the floor any time I displeased you. You pulled my hair. Once, surely you haven't forgotten, you grabbed my arm and jerked me into the swimming pool, breaking my collar bone."

"You know that was an accident," says Olivia.

"Do I? All right, I'll grant it may have been inadvertent. But you always belittled and intimidated me."

"And you were perfect?"

"I can't imagine what I did that made you, as editor of our high school newspaper, write that a girl needs to learn how to win hearts of boys, a skill Joan doesn't have."

Waving a vertical index finger, Olivia says, "No, no, I didn't write that, at least in the way you indicate. Show me the newspaper clipping."

"You know I don't have that at hand. Perhaps what I should really do is thank you for moving to Hollywood and working for Warner Brothers and becoming a star right away. Without particularly wanting to, you provided a Hollywood residence for Mother and me. Otherwise, I might not have had the chance to act.

"You were quite imperious about the whole enterprise, Olivia, telling me, 'Warner Brothers is my studio. You'll have to find another one. And de Havilland is my professional surname. You'll have to find another one of those, too.' I'm surprised our hateful stepfather didn't charge me for the use of Fontaine."

"Don't you have anything pleasant to say, Joan?"

"I think it's entirely pleasant to note that despite your head start I was the first to win an Oscar. I know two years earlier you were quite frustrated not even winning best supporting actress for *Gone with the Wind.* The following year, you must've been acutely uncomfortable, sitting there without a nomination, as I waited to be crowned for my role in *Rebecca.*"

Olivia says, "I'm still stunned you didn't win for *Rebecca.*"

"The year after that I actually thought you might win for *Hold Back the Dawn.* I didn't consider my next Hitchcock role, in *Suspicion,* to be comparable to *Rebecca.* But they called my name. And where were you?"

"I was standing outside the circle of people congratulating you as you ignored me."

"Olivia, if I'd seen you, I surely would've acknowledged your good wishes. Several years later, after you finally won, we have photographic evidence I was thrilled and tried to tell you. Remember that picture of me smiling in profile as you twisted your neck in another direction and grinned like a wolf. When people asked you about this, you said I shouldn't have approached you since I knew how you felt about me."

Looking over and around her sister, examining a lovely landscape rolling green, Olivia says, "I can't imagine we'll be forced to do here what we for decades avoided in life."

"Quite correct," says Joan. "This will be the last time we see each other. I just wanted to remind you that in addition winning the Oscar first, I also married before you, had a child before you, and arrived in this splendid place before you."

"At least I won two Oscars, twice your tally, and kept growing as an actress, and am delighted to have outlived you."

"I'm quite happy with the ninety-six years I had," says Joan. "I'm guessing your additional eight weren't so grand."

"Is there a swimming pool on the premises? Let's take a dip."

MARILYN MONROE

Knocking on Marilyn's Door

I'm okay. I don't really think Clark Gable is my father though that would be nice. Everyone has fantasies. I want to be a fine actress. Some people tell me I already am and to relax but I worry a lot and throw up every day before going on the set of *Don't Bother to Knock*. I really don't want to be there because everything's so real. I feel like my mother who's never been well.

I'll get better. My Uncle Eddie operates the elevator in a hotel and calls me for a job he thinks I'm ready for. Two guests are going downstairs to a ball tonight and need a babysitter for their daughter Bunny. I love children, especially little girls, and read her a bedtime story before saying good night and returning to the front room.

What a beautiful jewelry box and clothes her mother has. I think I'll try on her negligee and bracelet and earrings. They make me feel so good I dance until I notice a man in the room across the way. He's staring at me so I close the blinds. Then I open them to make sure he's still looking. He's smart and figures out which room I'm in and calls to invite me over but of course I can't go. I'm working and have to close the blinds. I can't help thinking about my boyfriend Philip. I'm waiting for him but he may have died in the Pacific during the war.

Uncle Eddie shouldn't just stop by and scold me for wearing the lady's jewelry and tell me I need a new boyfriend to get what I need. When Eddie leaves I put the earrings back on and open, close, open, close the blinds really fast and the man comes over. He's cute because he's Richard Widmark, a strong and confident man I like and try to impress by telling him I'm going to South America but by now he knows my name's Nell and that luggage with other initials couldn't be mine nor a man's shoes and hat.

"It's wonderful you're a pilot," I say. "I knew you'd come home someday, Philip."

"My name's Jed."

I'm not sure who he is but happy he kisses me and angry that bratty little Bunny comes out and says, "Take off my mother's clothes and jewelry."

"Go back to bed," I order.

She's back there crying when Jed or Philip brings her back into the front room and she and I look out the window she leans from and almost falls. I didn't push her like that screaming old woman thinks across the way.

"Go to sleep and you'll live happily ever after," I say.

I haven't been out in a long time and tell Jed, "I want to go dancing with you."

"You're silk on one side and sandpaper on the other."

"We need each other forever."

"That's not in the script, Marilyn," he says.

"I don't like this script. It's too much like my life."

He looks at director Roy Ward Baker who says, "Please stick to your lines, Marilyn."

"You stick to them."

Richard Widmark or Philip or Jed, whoever he is, follows my order to hide in the bathroom when Uncle Eddie comes to the door.

"Everything's fine, Eddie."

"What's that water running in the bathroom?"

"I don't hear anything."

"I thought you were getting better after three years in that institution."

"You're just like my folks, always trying to lock me up."

When Eddie heads for the bathroom I hit him on the head with a tall ashtray and also hit the wonderful man as he tries to help Eddie.

"Hold it, hold it, Marilyn," says Baker. "You're only supposed to hit Eddie, and not for real."

They're both hurt pretty bad on the front room floor. The nosy old couple comes over and discovers Bunny is gagged and her arms and legs bound in bed. I had to keep her quiet. If she hadn't interrupted I could've married the wonderful man. Now Bunny's hysterical mother, alerted by hotel detectives, attacks and throws me on the floor. Thankfully I get away from these crazy people but can't hide from so many chasing me and in the lobby put a razor blade to my throat and would kill myself except Philip is here and loves me but Philip had black hair and this man's blond and must be Richard Widmark. I know he's got a girlfriend but guess it doesn't matter what the script says. They're going to put me away.

Notes: *Don't Bother to Knock* was Marilyn Monroe's first starring role. Daniel Taradash's screenplay offered Marilyn the opportunity to tap into her real mother's disturbed life as well as her own emotional problems.

Marilyn Reverses Niagara

On a scenic trail near powerful Niagara Falls I'm kissing my very handsome young boyfriend and we're planning what to do about my husband Joseph Cotten who's been released from an army psychiatric hospital but is even worse now, a haunted man wandering around early every morning, and later today he scares guests in our motel room by breaking a record and storming out. Pretty Jean Peters goes into the other room to put a band aid on his cut and is shocked when Joseph says I'm always parading around, showing my body, and that I'm a tramp. He warns Jean not to let love for her husband get out of control like the falls.

Joseph keeps right on embarrassing me, telling Jean and her husband about his job failures, and he accuses me of wanting people to think he's crazy. Then he throws something at the wall and breaks open the wound.

"You like to suffer," Jean tells him.

I guess he does but what Joseph really likes is making me suffer and I'm not going to tolerate it anymore. On the phone I tell my boyfriend I'll bring Joseph, who everyone can see is suicidal, near the falls. While he's hiking, I buy two bus tickets and wait for a better life. The next day I'm still holding two bus tickets and haven't heard anything and tell people I'm worried about my husband. At the place where people leave their shoes and rent galoshes I'm told there was one pair of unclaimed shoes yesterday. They're Joseph's, and a body has been found under the falls. I try to look sad but am a relieved widow at the morgue to identify the body. When the sheet is raised, I faint, and they sedate me in a hospital.

When I awake I demand, "Get the director in here."

Henry Hathaway soon arrives.

"I'm getting the man I want," I say.

"Marilyn, that's a major part of the script you agreed to."

"I'm not going to live like that."

"You have to," Henry says.

"Then you live with Joseph Cotten."

"Even if I agreed with your aspirations, I could do nothing. Your boyfriend, as you know, has already been maimed."

"You'll make an even more important change or I won't film anymore."

"Marilyn, either fulfill your professional obligations or you'll be terminated from this film and likely all in the future."

"Get out," I say.

I've got to quit being so weak and vulnerable. I'm the one millions want so shouldn't always be mistreated on and off camera. I know what to do. I get up and dress and slip out of the hospital. I'm going to get out of Canada but there's Joseph, wearing my boyfriend's shoes. He chases me and I run up stairs of the bell tower, and then up more stairs, but he's a big strong man and catches me in a room at the top and with both hands he grabs my neck. The bells toll not for me but Joseph on concrete, my knife in his gut.

"Goddamn it, Marilyn," shouts Henry Hathaway. "You've ruined my great getaway when Joseph knocks out Jean Peters in a boat heading rapidly toward Niagara Falls."

"I'll wait until night and hire a couple of men to carry Joseph's body to the boat and cut it loose," I say.

"That's terrible."

"I think it's a nice dramatic touch."

"I'm speaking morally," says Hathaway.

"From now on I'll be writing my scripts and this one's fine because I'm sparing Joseph Cotten a lifetime of hatred for murdering me in *Niagara.*"

She Likes it Hot

The star of *Some Like It Hot* knows she moves and sounds like no one else.

"Where have you been, Marilyn?" asks the director, Billy Wilder.

"I've been sleeping. How about you?"

"You're two hours late, again."

"I'm sorry, Billy, but I couldn't sleep last night and took some pills that just knocked me out."

Wilder sweeps his hand toward fellow actors and crew members who're watching. "I'm paying them to wait for you."

"I hope the studio's paying, not you."

"I'm responsible."

Tony Curtis approaches. He and Marilyn had a romance several years ago but it didn't work out. It never works long for her. Too many men think she's easy. She's really not but needs a lot of help to feel good.

"Before I started waiting for you, Marilyn, I sat two and a half hours for makeup to become this delightful woman in a too tight dress that's uncomfortable as hell and wonder if you even care," says Tony.

He wants to be pretty as Marilyn but isn't quite.

"Sure, Tony, I care," she says before turning and walking to a female assistant who hands her a glass of orange juice.

"What's in that glass?" Wilder asks.

"What's it look like, Billy?"

"It feels like vodka," he says.

Marilyn takes a gulp and sits at the side of the set while she finishes the drink. Tony Curtis and Billy Wilder are watching with the crew. Billy grimaces and motions Tony to follow.

"Did you study your lines last night?" the director asks.

"I already explained last night," Marilyn says.

"Very unprofessional," says Tony. "You're wearing us out."

"I'm pretty damn tired, too, Tony."

"Okay, Marilyn, today's going to be easy," says Billy. "Your only line is, 'It's me, Sugar.' Got that?"

"Sure."

Billy Wilder announces, "Action."

"Sugar it's me," says Marilyn. "It's Sugar me. Me it's Sugar. Me Sugar it's." More than twenty times she repeats every possible sequence but the right one.

"That's all for today," Wilder shouts.

"Don't raise your voice to me, Billy, or I'll walk off the set."

"I'd love for you to do that but we'd all get fired and some of us like our jobs."

"I'm sorry, Billy. I just don't feel right."

"What's the matter, Marilyn?" Wilder asks. "Maybe I can help."

"I don't think anyone can," she says.

LANA TURNER

Loving Lana

I'm just Judy Turner being followed by boys down the halls of Hollywood High and that's pretty good but not nearly as exciting as when a reporter spots me cutting class in a cafe and sends me to an agent. Right away MGM signs me and says I'm one of the most beautiful women in the world and ready to work with gorgeous and talented actors and become a star.

I think I can do it and know I already love that tall, handsome clarinet player Artie Shaw who's so sexy playing his long black instrument. We're starring in *Dancing Co-Ed*, and I like the way he looks at my legs when I'm tap dancing. I say yes when he invites me to a private place where, after just a few times, I convince him to drop Betty Grable, his famous blond girlfriend. I'm thrilled we marry in 1940 when I'm nineteen and know this will last for life. I love being married and making love and having a special man. My dad was murdered when I was nine but now I've got someone to take care of me. My mom's a little worried since Artie's eleven years older and has already had two short marriages.

"Why don't you cook me dinner more often?" Artie asks after a couple of months.

"Why don't you cook? I work as hard as you and am just as tired."

"I'm sick of the silly things you talk about. Read a book. Read the goddamn newspaper."

"Be a better husband. All you do is blow your horn then come home and read."

"The world's more than Hollywood, Lana."

"I've got plenty right here."

"There's a war going on. Think about something besides your makeup."

"I don't want to think about it."

Shaking his head, he says, "You're so shallow."

I don't know what to do except cry. What happened to the man I loved?

"Lana, I know you're a glamor goddess, but will you make the coffee this morning?"

"I made it last week."

"And I've made it every day since."

He grumbles climbing out of bed and in a few minutes storms from the bathroom. "What did I tell you about the goddamn toilet paper? I want it rolling from the front, not the back."

He's mean like this almost every day and I'm crying at home and work and at my mom's and when I visit my friends, and they say leave him, and that's what I do. I escape but have to see some doctors who give me medications to keep me from going crazy. Cigarettes and alcohol help even more and are always available.

I sure don't need Artie. There are many great looking guys on movie sets and plenty want to be with me, and I plan to go out with them and others. I think I'm falling for Joseph Stephen Crane. He owns a popular restaurant and is a good looking gentleman. I know he's the one. I've matured and am getting better roles all the time, most recently as an alcoholic dancer in *Ziegfeld Girl.* By 1942 I'm ready for the man of my life.

"You told me your divorce was final."

"It is. It was. It was supposed to be," says Joseph.

"You're a liar and this scandal could ruin my career but it isn't because I'm divorcing you."

"Lana, please."

"Go to hell."

He tries to kill himself and I feel guilty and beg him to remarry me when I learn I'm pregnant, and we have a girl, Cheryl, the following year. I'm anxious to return to the screen before people forget me and I just don't have much time for my daughter but always hire people to take good care of her. I really don't have time for Joseph, either. Other men excite me more, so I divorce him. My career keeps going quite well and in 1946 I get my best part as the wicked wife of a boring old man in *The Postman Always Rings Twice.*

In real life I've fallen for the most beautiful man in the world, Tyrone Power. He's such a talented actor and craves me as I do him. I'm free and want to marry him. He's not really married anymore, they're separated. I urge him to divorce. He says he will but has work in Europe. I'm very lonely without him. I don't think it would hurt to have some company while he's gone. Neither does his buddy Frank Sinatra. I know MGM starts publicizing this to drive Ty away from me. Studio executives are always worried by publicity about my private life, and now they suspend me.

"I'll do what I want with my life," I tell them, and they look at my box office receipts and agree.

Besides, I'm getting married. He's a very rich socialite named Bob Topping. I love his mansion in Connecticut where we'll live when not in Hollywood. This is an incredible time. We honeymoon for two years, traveling and going to parties and spending lots of money.

"Bob, please ease up on the booze."

"You're not exactly a teetotaler, my dear."

"I'm not the one becoming bloated."

We go on another vacation and Bob asks me to pay for it. He starts telling me to pay for lots of things.

"I keep reading about 'millionaire Bob Topping.' It's time for you to be the man."

"I just need a little help," he says.

"You evidently need my purse."

"Just until my investments start paying off."

"Haven't they been doing that?"

"Not lately. And the family's cutting back my share of the trust."

If I stay with millionaire socialite Bob Topping I'm going to be broke actress Lana Turner. I just don't want to see him anymore. I've met a divine South American actor, Fernando Lamas, and we travel together. He makes me feel so good. And so does Lex Barker, a big beautiful Tarzan who loves to hold me. We marry in 1953, and I'm happy, but a few years later Cheryl tells me the most horrible story. After wiping away tears and composing myself, I open the dresser drawer, grasp my revolver, and walk into the living room where Lex is sitting.

"Get out of my house."

"What is it, darling?" he asks.

"You're a despicable dog."

"What are you talking about?"

"You feel like a big man, fondling and raping a little girl from age ten on?"

"She's lying."

"I know my daughter."

"How? You rarely say anything to her besides, 'You can't hug mommy now. You'll ruin her hair. You'll smudge her lipstick.'"

"I said get the hell out now."

He hesitates. I point my gun at his head. "I should shoot you now."

He leaves rather rapidly. I know I haven't been a good mother. I've had to travel and make movies and marry four times and love many unreliable men. Perhaps I should shoot myself. MGM recently declined to offer me a new contract. To hell with them. I'm still desirable and prove so at age thirty-six starring in the hit *Peyton Place* for another studio. I'm still box office and a woman who can attract handsome Johnny Stompanato. I've never had a better lover or even one as good. He's also kind to my daughter. I tell people they're wrong when they say Johnny's a gangster. He is a little possessive, though. In fact, he's becoming a pest, asking for money and where I've been and where I'm going.

"I'm going to Europe to make *Another Time, Another Place*," I say.

"I'm coming."

"No, you're not."

"You think you're going to go over there and fuck around on me."

"I'm going to do whatever I want."

God, every woman should meet Sean Connery in 1958. He's a leading man. Johnny Stompanato's an extra who shows up with a gun Sean takes away before punching him in the mouth. I know Sean, nine years my junior, is too young, handsome, and talented to be interested in me for long, and am lonely when I get back to Hollywood where Johnny's waiting to embrace me. Still, I have to tell him, "You can't come with me to the academy awards ceremony tonight."

"You want me in bed but not in public."

"Everything must look right if I win the best actress award."

"See you when you get back, sweetheart."

"Don't be here, Johnny."

I fail to get the Oscar for my role in *Peyton Place* but at parties afterward everyone treats me like a queen. When I get home, Johnny's watching TV.

"So sorry, sweetheart. You'll be thirty-seven next month, an old thirty-seven. All that drinking and smoking. You're lucky to have a guy like me."

"I'm sick of everything about you."

He grabs and kisses me. I jerk away and rush upstairs to my bedroom. Johnny follows. I try to slam the door but he shoves it open and says, "Fuck you," slapping my face and knocking me down.

"Stop it, Johnny."

"I'll cut up your goddamn face."

"Please stop."

He leans down and keeps slapping me and says, "I'll kill you or find someone else to do it."

"Mom, are you okay?" asks Cheryl, age fourteen, standing terrified at the door.

"Close the door, Cheryl," I say. "I'm fine."

Johnny keeps looking down at me.

"Please close the door, Cheryl, and go to bed," I say.

She pulls the door almost closed, and Johnny smacks me again, and grabs my neck and I think he's going to strangle me, and I scream.

Cheryl opens the door a little and says, "Johnny, no."

"Shut the fuck up." He whirls and storms to the door, yanking it open, and lunges into the hall.

"Cheryl..."

I get up and run out to discover Johnny on his back, bleeding fast from his stomach and breathing in a strange way I know can't last.

"He ran right into it, Mom," Cheryl says, holding a ten-inch knife.

What should I do? It's too late to call an ambulance and too early to call the police. I dial Jerry Giesler, the lawyer stars in need depend on. He gets here right away. We tell him what happened and he tells us what to do and say. Truth is our ally. At the inquest I explain what happened, and many call the testimony my finest performance, but I wasn't acting.

I'd love to return to movies but no one will hire me and I'm almost broke from all the bastards in my life. Despite Cheryl driving drunk and romancing other girls and many other concerns, I remain poised, at least externally, and get a great role in the film *Imitation of*

Life. Universal Pictures spends a million dollars on my wardrobe and jewelry, and moviegoers love the glamor as well as my kindness to a single black mother, played by Juanita Moore, who earns an Oscar nomination. I'd farsightedly accepted a smaller salary in return for half the profits that total two million dollars.

I'm comfortable again and in love and marry Fred May, a rich and attractive rancher, and we last a couple of years. In my early forties now I know my time as a star has passed. Fine, I have more time to relax, and husband number six, Robert P. Eaton, is a sexy guy as well as fine tennis player, golfer, and gambler, and for a few years we have fun. In 1969 I rush from divorce to marriage to husband number seven, Ronald Pella or Ronald Dante, I suppose it depends on the scheme of this self-proclaimed greatest nightclub hypnotist in history, and he must be hypnotizing me since I write him a check for about thirty thousand he doesn't use for investments he said he needed, and I don't watch him closely enough because he also steals a hundred grand worth of my jewelry. I still don't give up on men, not entirely, but promise myself I'll never marry again.

I spend a lot of the seventies drinking and smoking and losing weight and squandering most of the few acting opportunities I get, but in the eighties I convert to Roman Catholicism and embrace celibacy and do a little work on TV. I suppose it's ironic that despite being a woman addicted to men I end up loving most my daughter and her girlfriend and especially my maid and companion of more than forty years who gets most of my estate when I die from throat cancer at age seventy-four.

GLORIA SWANSON

Gloria's Honeymoon

A couple of weeks ago I get this great job as a bellhop at one of the finest hotels in Pasadena. I love coming to work in a clean uniform and not having to work outside getting hot and dirty with a bunch of grubby men. In the hotel all the guests look important, and lots of the women are pretty. I'm excited the night Wallace Beery and Gloria Swanson check in. I've recently seen them in *The Broken Pledge*. She's stunning and only about my age, seventeen. Wallace Beery's much older and not very good looking but bossy and I hustle when he tells me to take suitcases up to their suite which is next to the suite of Gloria's mother, who smiles as she says her daughter just married Beery and will someday be a big star like her new husband.

Down in the lobby we all talk about beautiful Gloria. One of the maids says she's crazy to marry a chubby guy like Wallace Beery. I agree. He looks like a bum. She should've married a young guy like me. I'm not an actor or anything but definitely handsomer than Beery. I picture myself punching him. I'd like to but know Gloria wouldn't like it and I'd lose my job. I return to the lobby and stand, talking to other employees about two stars in bed upstairs.

A couple of hours later a lady comes rushing down in her pajamas and says, "Help, the man in 231's killing his wife."

The night manager says he'll look into it but I grab the key and run upstairs to their suite and hear, "Stop it, please…"

I bang the door and say, "Miss Swanson, are you all right?"

"Get the hell outta here," Beery shouts.

"Help me…"

I shove the key in and unlock the door and run in to see Wallace Beery's ass pointed at the ceiling and the rest of him pinning Miss Swanson to the bed.

"Stop this right now," I order.

"Out before I kill you," he shouts.

I dash to the bed and grab his arm with both hands and pull him onto the floor, and stand staring at Miss Swanson until Beery socks me in the jaw. I stagger and almost fall but am still thinking pretty well and put up my hands and move in, throwing a few jabs that miss but make Beery back up, and he looks pretty worried as I step in and throw a roundhouse right that hits him on jaw, and he drops his hands and I throw another right to his head and another and he doubles over and I left hook the back of his neck, sending him down, and I step back and kick him in the ribs.

The night manager and other employees are standing at the door, and the manager says, "Don't worry, Miss Swanson, we'll call the police."

Miss Swanson has the sheets pulled up to her chin when her mother pushes in and says, "Absolutely no publicity must come from this. Wallace and Gloria just had a little honeymoon spat. Gloria, you can sleep with me tonight. Will you all please leave?"

We walk out, looking back at them. They leave real early in the morning and must have used the rear exit because none of us see them. I write Miss Swanson several letters in care of her studio but she never responds. In a few years I get married, anyway, and eventually quit yearning since she keeps getting married and divorced and having more affairs than newspapers can keep track of. That's a different Gloria Swanson than the beautiful girl who stayed in our hotel.

Norma Desmond on Trial

I'm the best defense attorney in Los Angeles and have never lost a murder case despite representing some pretty hopeless guys but in this predicament I tell my client, "Miss Desmond, you're facing overwhelming evidence and better let me plead you were unaware you shot Joe Gillis."

"That's outrageous. I'm neither cruel nor crazy and, anyway, I'm innocent."

Norma Desmond was a silent star when I was a kid but disappeared soon after sound revolutionized the screen. I'd forgotten about her until she made unpleasant headlines.

"In that case, I must advise you not to take the witness stand."

"Nonsense. I'm going to speak eloquently in my defense."

"I can't stop you from testifying, Miss Desmond, but if you do, at least pretend you're disturbed. You can do that, can't you? You're an actress."

"Naturally, I could marvelously portray a woman beset by any problem, but I'm going to maintain my dignity and reclaim my career as a splendid actress."

I offer a reassuring nod while picturing her being led to the gas chamber.

In a few weeks, during which she's examined in a locked psychiatric facility and spends the rest in a solitary jail cell, the prosecution presents its case and I offer the defense. Prosecutor Wilfred Parker and I question several witnesses, during seven days in court, before Norma Desmond, smiling as if for fans en route to the academy awards ceremony, sits on a stand she views as a throne.

"Miss Desmond, the prosecution has portrayed you as an aging and jealous has-been who was obsessed with the late screenwriter, Joe Gillis. Is that accurate?"

"Absolutely not. I'm only fifty and in marvelous shape thanks to good genes and my daily diet and exercise. I certainly wasn't jealous or obsessed with Joe Gillis. He sped onto my estate in his junky car as he tried to escape his creditors. He was a whipped puppy."

Standing with a frown, Parker says, "Objection, Your Honor."

"Sustained," says Judge Samuel Farmer.

"Please restate your assessment of Joe Gillis when you met him," I tell Miss Desmond.

"He was in trouble and I felt sorry for him."

"Do you often invite fleeing strangers into your home, Miss Desmond?" I ask.

"No, but he promptly revealed he was a screenwriter, and I thought he'd enjoy reading a screenplay I've been perfecting for years."

"Did he do so?"

"Indeed he did. He said it was great but needed, let me use his words, a little 'editing, dialogue, organization.'"

"Did you and Joe Gillis make a professional arrangement?"

"Yes, I let him stay in the bedroom above my garage."

I look pleasantly at twelve squares on the jury, seven men and five women, and turn to ask, "Did you have a good working relationship with Joe Gillis, Miss Desmond?"

"Oh, wonderful. He loved to come into my mansion to discuss

the script, and we often watched my legendary silent films. I also showed him the many fan letters I still get from people begging me to come back."

Looking arrogantly at me and then at Miss Desmond, Wilfred Parker says, "Objection, Your Honor. Max von Wayerling, her longtime butler and former movie director and ex-husband, has already testified he wrote the fan letters."

"Of course he's going to say that," she says. "He's always loved me and renounced his career so he could be near me even after I left him for other men."

"Miss Desmond," says the judge, "handwriting experts have already proven that the letters were indeed written by Max von Wayerling."

"That's irrelevant to the issue at hand," I say. "Mr. Wayerling stayed on his own volition. And so did Joe Gillis."

Standing again, Wilfred Parker says, "Objection. Miss Desmond imprisoned Joe Gillis by allowing his car to be repossessed."

"Overruled," says Judge Farmer. "Joe Gillis was an adult and free to leave the estate of Norma Desmond whenever he chose."

"Thank you, Your Honor," says Desmond. "He enjoyed living at my estate. I took care of him and bought him beautiful new clothes so he'd look great when we accepted awards for our new movie. He knew I loved him but he didn't want to admit he also loved me and went to stay somewhere and told me he was moving out and for me to send his belongings. I couldn't bear his throwing away our love and our glorious future."

I dash to the witness stand, shouting, "Hold it, Your Honor. That's enough for today."

"You go back to my hellish cage tonight, young man," she tells me. "I'm going to speak to this court."

"Have a seat, Counselor," orders Judge Farmer. "Please proceed, Miss Desmond."

Nodding at the judge and ignoring me, she says, "I didn't want Max to tell Joe I'd slashed my wrists that night but was elated he rushed home so I could tell him I love him and let him console me and I knew this was the happiest I'd ever been.

"I concede I was distraught when I discovered Joe was seeing some little tart, a script reader, but she left when I called and told her how he'd been making his money. Frankly, I realized that Joe had used me from the start. Good riddance. I've known lots of rotten men. I know Max thought my grief might compel me to try to kill myself again. That's why Max shot him. I was devastated when I saw Joe bleeding and still near the bottom of my Hollywood swimming pool. I'm partly, though not legally, to blame. I unintentionally fed Max's obsessions by letting him be my butler. He should have moved on. I'll move on from Joe."

"Your Honor," I say, "may I please speak to you and the honorable district attorney in private?"

Notes: Gloria Swanson's performance as deranged Norma Desmond in *Sunset Boulevard* earned an Oscar nomination for best actress. Billy Wilder directed and William Holden co-starred.

LUPE VELEZ

Mexican Spitfires

I'm a lover and hate people who in Mexico City say my mother rented my teenage body. That's a lie. I was always a good singer and comedienne and first appeared in Hollywood films before turning twenty. I've loved many leading men and others and still do and for a few years adored Gary Cooper and his beautiful face and the rest but all the time we lived together he was screwing other women so once I stabbed him and another I shot my pistol but wasn't really aiming or he'd be dead. I wanted to marry him but his mother kept telling him to leave me, that I was crazy and causing him to lose weight and ruining everything.

I'm not crying he ran away. I'm in tears because the world always hurts no matter how well I do in films during the thirties. I'm not a major star but bigger than Dolores del Rio, an arrogant bitch who thinks she's queen of Mexican actresses. In truth, she's pretentious and boring, and I only think about her when I'm imitating her in movies or at parties. She says she attends better parties but I don't care. I've got another man, gorgeous Johnny Weismuller, the greatest Tarzan, and when he marries me I give him two pairs of boxing gloves but am only joking. We're a couple people love to see and happy except when he misbehaves and I scream and attack him. I don't care if we're at home or in a hotel room. When I feel bad I punch him scratch him kick him fire things at him. I don't care if the police come. I curse them too. I don't care when he's scratched and bruised next day on the movie set but worry when he gets home and love Johnny even when we divorce.

I know devout Roman Catholics aren't supposed to divorce but in Hollywood I think it's all right especially since I'm so religious I fill my bedroom with lit candles and say many Hail Marys before jumping on men in bed. They love my slender five-foot body and big chichis and passion. I need lots of strong men. Not like ham Orson Welles over there in the restaurant booth with Dolores del Rio who's ten years older than Welles and showing off her prize as if she believes publicity he's a genius for making *Citizen Kane.*

"Good evening, Mrs. Tarzan," says Welles. "Or should I call you Jane?"

"Take your fat ass to hell."

"Where's Tarzan, by the way? I'm hoping he'll cast me in some of his splendid movies."

I run to their table and punch Welles on the nose. He grabs his nose and moans and Dolores del Rio stands and says, "You've always been a slut."

An instant before I claw her, she grabs a steak knife, points it at me, and says, "Let's handle it like ladies."

"Fine." I turn to my new boyfriend, who's looking timid, and say, "Go get my boxing gloves in the car." Johnny left them behind.

"Hurry up," I say. My boyfriend knows he better not refuse if he wants to watch me pray tonight.

"Aren't you going to run?" I say to Dolores del Rio.

"No, but you should."

My boyfriend rushes in and puts my gloves on and goes over to help Dolores. I step up, shadowboxing, calling Dolores bad names in English and Spanish, firing combinations, and only remember colors racing through my head.

Next day in the hospital the nurse says, "Dolores del Rio conked you with a chilled bottle of champagne. You've got a concussion but should be all right in a month."

My head healed pretty well outside but inside I've always hurt and it's getting worse now that I'm thirty-six. The last three years I've made seven films with *Mexican Spitfire* in the title and know my career's sinking and am scared I'm in love with a handsome Austrian actor eight years younger and taking many pills and drinking to feel less nervous especially after he says he won't marry me and doesn't care about the child I'm carrying. I know what to do. I invite two close amigas to my Beverly Hills mansion, which Gary Cooper helped me buy, and we eat a wonderful hot Mexican dinner and drink fine liquor and they don't believe me when I say the shame is too great and would be for my baby too. You'll be fine, they say. They don't really know me. I wish someone did. When they go home I brush my teeth and freshen my makeup and then light every candle in the house and swallow about seventy capsules of Seconal and ease onto my bed. Don't believe liars who say my head's found in the toilet. I'm beautiful in bed, my dark hair dyed glowing blond.

SHIRLEY BOOTH

Lunch with Shirley

As appointed I arrive at a Cape Cod restaurant to interview Shirley Booth two weeks after she won the best actress Oscar for portraying Lola, a sad and submissive homemaker in *Come Back, Little Sheba*. She's waiting at a table and shakes my hand with the force of a longshoreman.

"Congratulations," I say.

"Thank you. Have a seat."

"That was quite a debut. I've wondered, like many others, why you waited until your early fifties to make your first movie."

"Hold it, young man, I'm only forty-five."

"I beg your pardon," I say, glancing at my notes. "The librarian at my newspaper read you were born in 1898."

"Well, he's wrong. I was born in 1907. You trying to age me out of show business?"

"Of course not.

"Not being a Hollywood beauty, I never had many offers to make pictures. Before Sheba, nothing was good enough to tempt me to abandon my career on stage. I'd been getting good roles on Broadway for a long time. I won a Tony for playing Lola, you know."

"Certainly."

She has a sweet smile.

I say, "Lola carried a lot of pain about the loss of her child, and I think that's why she was so anxious to please her husband, Doc, despite his alcoholism. At least he'd built a year of sobriety after drinking away his inheritance and becoming 'sickly.'"

"I'd rather be single than tolerate an unstable guy like Doc. A year ago I lost a wonderful husband. He worked himself to death on our farm. He didn't know he had a bad heart. I know I'll never find anyone else like him. I'm fine, though. I love being alone. On the Cape I can go days without talking to anyone but my dog and cats."

"That's a lot of solitude," I say, concerned. "You're a lot more independent than Lola."

Shirley says, "She spent too much time in her bathrobe and needed to fix her hair and put on some makeup and quit talking all the time about sad times like her parents throwing her out years earlier when she got pregnant, and the way Doc 'used to be,' and grieving over the loss of her dog, Sheba, who she knows is never coming back. But it's understandable she still mourned her daughter, even a generation later."

As we order she gazes at the waiter, young as Lola's movie child would've been.

"I don't have any kids," Shirley says, "but I think everyone knows it's horrible losing one and living with a moody man who gets crazy when he drinks. That's why Lola was so talkative with the mailman and insisted he come in and drink a glass of water."

"Doc was a lonely character, too, and jealous when your pretty renter, Marie, slipped into the bedroom with her boyfriend. Lola wasn't angry about Doc's feelings but said, 'I was pretty then, wasn't I, Doc? Maybe you're sorry you married me. I didn't know I was going to get old and fat… If the baby had lived, she'd be just like Marie.'"

"That's what set Doc off the night he took his sealed liquor bottle out of the cabinet and came home drunk and said Marie and Lola were a 'couple of sluts' and Lola was too lazy to even clean the house and he didn't want to come home and look at her and picked up the butcher knife and attacked. Thank god she got two of his AA friends on the phone and they rushed over and took him to the hospital."

"Lola evokes a lot of empathy," I say. "When she called her mother to see if she could come home for a while, her father said no, and I thought what a bastard. At least there was some Hollywood magic and Doc dried out and came home."

"And he begged me never to leave him."

"Do you think the reconciliation will last?" I ask.

"This ending is forever."

KIM NOVAK

Dealing with Vertigo

I'm not worried Alfred Hitchcock's a legendary director more than thirty years my senior or that Jimmy's Stewart's been a star since I was a child. I'm honored to work with them and looking forward to our story conference this morning. We sit at a small round table.

"Hitch, how the heck am I supposed to pull myself up when I'm hanging from a gutter in the sky?"

Hitchcock smiles at me before turning to Jimmy.

"Our viewers will never consider such a matter. They'll only mourn the brave but unfortunate policeman who extended a helpful hand before slipping off the slick roof into eternity."

Quite handsome for a man of fifty, Jimmy shakes his head and says, "This whole thing is pretty complicated, Hitch. How could my old friend be sure I'd follow his wife?"

Sweeping his hand toward me, he says, "Jimmy, please behold Kim Novak, a beautiful young blonde most men would not merely follow but chase."

I raise my chin, getting Hitchcock's attention, and tell him, "I'm concerned about playing a weak and unstable woman."

"My dear, you read the script before accepting the part, for which you're being paid rather too much. Your job is to perform what's written and that I direct."

"I'm not questioning your authority, Mr. Hitchcock, but is it realistic that after falling in love with Jimmy I'd go with him to the mission at San Juan Bautista and run up the stairs to the tower and jump?"

Perturbed, Hitchcock says, "You didn't commit suicide. The man whose wife you were emulating threw his real already-dead wife out of the tower."

"I know, but I don't think it makes sense."

"What's nonsensical is a callow young actress being so literal and tone deaf."

Extending his hand to the center of the table where he places his palm, Jimmy Stewart says, "Hold it, Hitch. I don't think it's believable, either."

Hitchcock leans back, locks his hands on an enormous stomach, and looks at us for long seconds before saying, "Jimmy, your character is terrified of heights and still traumatized by the death of the unfortunate policeman. Otherwise, you'd have more rapidly dashed up the steps to save her. Everything I've planned makes perfect cinematic sense."

"Mr. Hitchcock, you're very tough on female characters," I say. "My character helped that awful husband but, after getting his wife's inheritance, he disappeared and left me broke in San Francisco and obliged to work a lousy job."

"This sets up some scenes that I believe will someday be classics."

"I wonder if the audience will sympathize with a woman who's not only devious but stupid. Do you think pretty blond women are stupid, Mr. Hitchcock?"

He doesn't reply.

"It's insulting to think I'd dye my hair red and stay in town, giving Jimmy the chance to find me. And I assure you, I'd never permit a man to transform me back to the blonde he loved but now suspects was involved in a murder. Jimmy, you should be ashamed, kissing a criminal like that."

He smiles sheepishly.

"That's why it's called acting, my dear," says Hitchcock. "Of course, if the dramatic demands are too complex, I'll simply wait until Vera Miles has her baby. I preferred her for this role, you know."

"Your budget and the availability of Jimmy and the whole crew dictate that I co-star in this film."

"Maybe I'll bring in Marilyn Monroe," Hitchcock says.

"I don't think she's available, Hitch. Besides, I kinda think Kim's ideal for this role."

"Do you think I exude the characteristics of a murderess?" I ask Jimmy.

"Come on, Kim. That was a compliment."

I stand and say, "Furthermore, Mr. Hitchcock, it's preposterous that I'd let Jimmy drive me back to the murder scene at San Juan Bautista and force me up the stairs into the bell tower. I'm not going to fall to my death to satisfy the censors or movie fans. Jimmy may be the one going down."

"We can't let you do that, my dear. Jimmy's one of the most beloved men in the world."

"Maybe you should take the fall," I say.

Hitchcock laboriously rises and says, "Young lady, if there's any impertinence on the set, I shall suspend you."

Notes: *Vertigo* underwhelmed many moviegoers and critics in 1958 but has since steadily grown in status.

MERYL STREEP

Grand Alliance

A refined young actress faces a wall, her back to the costar, and practices her lines moments before the most challenging scene of her career. The director tells everyone to get ready. Suddenly, in an unscripted act, the star steps up and slaps her face and says, "John Cazale, where the hell's he. Huh?"

She holds her cheek, which bears red finger marks, as her mouth drops open.

"All right, action," says the director.

Confronting her short husband, Joanna says, "I'm leaving you, I don't love you anymore... Here are my keys and my credit cards... I'm not taking Billy with me... I'm not good for him..."

The scene's a success. Most feel bad that Ted Kramer's selfish wife has launched an unholy domestic strike.

"Great job, Meryl," says Dustin.

Without replying she pivots and walks away.

This is a Dustin Hoffman vehicle, and while his wife swings unseen in California, the dedicated New York dad takes Joanna's photos off desks and tables, struggles to cook decent meals for Billy, and gets a promotion at work where he's told not to blow it but begins to arrive late and perform erratically. He can't even supervise his son on the playground and the boy falls from a jungle gym, gashing his cheek near an eye.

Ominously, Joanna Kramer returns to New York and spies on her son from a restaurant across the street before telling her estranged husband she wants the little boy. Ted's crushed, especially when he's fired and his attorney tells him he has "no chance in hell" to win a custody case without a job. The attorney says he needs fifteen thousand dollars and permission to play rough. Ted takes a pay cut to get a job and they go to court.

Just before they film Joanna taking the stand, Dustin walks to her and says, "Where's John Cazale? Seems like he oughta be here."

Meryl Streep puts a hand on her cheek, though it hasn't been slapped, as her mouth drops open.

"Action," says the director.

The attorney asks, "Have you failed at the most important relationships in your life? You've abandoned your son… You've divorced a husband…"

It's a tough day on the stand for Joanna Kramer. Magnanimous Ted Kramer tells his attorney, "Don't do that again."

Dustin Hoffman leaves the set and is walking to his dressing room when a mature and authoritative woman grabs his arm and says, "Sir, let me quote you: 'Don't do that again.'"

"Who the hell're you?"

"I'm Margaret Thatcher."

"You a London stage actress or what?"

"Evidently you're so ensnared in method acting that you don't follow world affairs. I'm the new Prime Minister of Great Britain, and if you again invoke the name of Meryl's tragically departed young fiancé, the fine actor John Cazale, you and I shall clash."

Hoffman looks at her unpleasantly until she shoves her not large but quite hard fist under his prodigious nose and says, "Did you understand me?"

He slaps her fist away and brandishes his own. Streep runs behind him, drops to all fours, and Margaret two-hand shoves him flying onto concrete.

Notes: In *Kramer v. Kramer*, Meryl Streep won an Oscar for best supporting actress and Hoffman claimed the award for best actor. In the ensuing forty years she has garnered a stunning twenty-one nominations, winning three times, including for her role as Margaret Thatcher in *The Iron Lady*. Hoffman has seven nominations and two Oscars.

About thirty years after their contentious collaboration, Streep was asked in an interview to consider three of her distinguished costars – Robert Redford, Jack Nicholson, and Dustin Hoffman – and determine which one, if compelled, she'd kill, which one she'd shag, and which one she'd marry. She said she'd shag Nicholson, marry Redford, and, drawing a hand across her throat, kill Hoffman.

There is one confusing element. Why did Streep, rushing toward stage to accept her first Oscar, pause to kiss Hoffman on the cheek? She must've been intoxicated by the moment.

CATE BLANCHETTE

Carol Meets Jasmine

He's walking fast near the expensive small room he rents in an old San Francisco house when he sees a blond woman crying and talking to herself on a park bench and instinctively glances away but looks back because she's well-dressed and rather attractive.

"Pardon me, ma'am, are you all right?"

She looks up, sniffling and quite disheveled. "No, I'm not."

"Anything I can do to help? I'm Dwight."

"Please sit down and talk to me," she asks. "Call me Jasmine or whatever you want. Evidently my name doesn't matter anymore. My sister just threw me out of her apartment and took back her dumb blue-collar boyfriend and my boyfriend dumped me because my sister's ex-husband told him I'd ruined his life and taken his and my sister's money. I didn't do that, my husband did."

"Where's your husband?"

"He hung himself in prison," she says, dabbing tears with a tissue. "Maybe I shouldn't have called the FBI but after years of shady financial deals and screwing any woman he could he found someone he was 'serious' about and shoved me out the door. Our son was traumatized by having a thief for a father but when he found out I'd betrayed his father he told me to get out of his life."

She reaches into her purse and opens a bottle of pills and pops a few and keeps sniffling and crying as she tells Dwight wild stuff.

"Easy… What is that?"

"Xanax or some other tranquilizer. It doesn't matter as long as it calms me."

"Jasmine, it smells like you've been drinking. You shouldn't combine alcohol and pills."

"What are you, another loser judging me?" She points to a short slender old man about twenty feet in front of them. "And you, Woody Allen, take your truckload of neuroses and eat them."

Allen nods and tells his cameraman, "That'll be all."

"Why are you still filming? The movie's supposed to end with me alone on this bench and my life ruined but you're recording while a buzzard eats my corpse. If all of you don't disappear, I'm calling the police."

Woody and the cameraman stare at Jasmine, and Dwight, too, until Jasmine shoves him and shouts, "I told you to leave.'"

"Did you not understand the lady?" says a striking blond woman wearing a long mink stole and red cap.

Dwight gets up and walks away. Looking at his cameraman, Woody shakes his head and whirls an index finger at his ear.

The elegant lady sits close to Jasmine and says, "I'd like to help."

Jasmine introduces herself and seems to relax a little despite telling her the same sordid story.

"I was married to an abusive man who wouldn't let me see my daughter because he found out I didn't care about him. I loved a beautiful young woman. The movie takes place in the gloomy nineteen fifties. It's called *Carol.* Have you seen it?"

"Not yet. This movie is *Blue Jasmine.*"

"You're going to be a star," she says.

Jasmine manages a little smile. "Some people already say I may win an award."

"That's wonderful."

"Are you and your friend living in San Francisco?" Jasmine asks.

"No, we aren't together anymore," says Carol. "I'm here visiting friends. Would you like to join us for dinner tonight?"

"Thank you so much."

Notes: Cate Blanchett played *Carol* and *Blue Jasmine,* winning a best actress Oscar for the latter.

HALLE BERRY

Queen of the Ball

I never pick up hitchhikers, figuring some are bound to be criminals, and plan to ignore the one standing ahead on the right and waving next to her hood-up car smoking like a bonfire. What kind of woman drives something that old and beat-up? I look over and decide to quit being so damn judgmental. It's daylight and she's alone and not really a hitchhiker but a motorist in distress. I've been stranded a few times, too.

I pull over and get out and say, "Good afternoon, ma'am. I'm sorry your car's having trouble."

"I've got every kind of trouble you can imagine."

"Can I give you a lift into town?"

"Please. And let's hurry so I can get to my job at the diner."

"Are you going to send a tow truck?"

Shaking her head, she says, "No way. That car's dead."

At the diner in this small Georgia town I say, "I haven't eaten lunch. You guys have good food?"

She smiles and says, "Not especially."

"You're just being modest," I say, opening my door and getting out.

She rushes in, puts on her apron, tells her boss what happened, and starts taking orders. I sit in a booth and read the menu, trying not let her catch me glancing at her pretty face. I order a turkey sandwich and fries. When I'm finished, I say, "We don't even know each other's names. I'm Johnny."

"I'm Leticia.

"Ordinarily, I wouldn't ask this so soon, Leticia, but I wonder if you'd like to have dinner tonight."

She looks down.

"I'm sorry. I can't. My husband…"

"Pardon me. I didn't know you were married."

She cries softly.

"Is he okay?"

"No, that man was never okay. That's why they're executing him tonight."

"I'm really sorry."

A couple weeks later, after thinking about her too much, I return to the diner where the boss says, "Leticia isn't here because I fired her. She was late damn near every day."

"She's got some problems."

"Too many problems."

"And you're perfect," I say.

"If you aren't eating, there's the door."

I drive around town, asking people about Leticia. Most don't know who she is but have heard about the execution. After a while I find a woman who knows where Leticia rents a small old home.

"You a friend of hers?" she asks.

"I just met her once. We planned to see each other again at the diner."

"Leticia's in a bad way. Her son was hit by a car and killed. I don't know how much one woman can take."

I buy some flowers and that evening drive to her place. There's a car outside. Dim lights burn inside. I feel uneasy but have got to see her and walk to the door. Holding the flowers in my left hand, I prepare to knock with my right when I hear Leticia passionately say, "I want you to make me feel good… Can you make me feel good?"

I should leave. I know I should but lean my ear next to the door and hear things going on that make me cry inside. I drop the flowers and walk toward my car, stopping to get the license number of the other vehicle. When I drive by early next morning the damn car's still there. That afternoon a friend with contacts gives me the name and address of the owner, and I drive to his place outside town. I try to decide what to do. I hate seeing that car and the house where the man lives who makes Leticia feel so good. I consider knocking on the door but what would I say? I'd just feel worse. I put my hands on the steering wheel, preparing to leave when a slender man walks out and says, "Can I help you?"

"Yeah, is Leticia here?"

"Who are you and what do you want with her?"

"You rotten bastard," I say, and turn and drive away.

Notes: Halle Berry won the best actress Oscar for her portrayal of Leticia in *Monster's Ball*, and Milo Addica and Will Rokos were nominated for best original screenplay. As Hank, Billy Bob Thornton adroitly plays a prison executioner, sadistic father, and racist neighbor as well as a great lover.

KATE WINSLET

Three Kates

"*Heavenly Creatures* is make believe," says Kate.

"That's a rather convenient excuse, isn't it," I say, surveying the rich green forest in Victoria Park above Christchurch. "Wasn't this natural beauty enough to tame you and your bloodthirsty friend, Pauline?"

"I don't have to talk to you."

"Quite right. It's back to jail for you."

"I want to be housed next to Pauline."

"Housed? That's a quaint term. You're incarcerated and awaiting trial. If you weren't only fifteen, you'd hang."

Kate had a bad lung and Pauline a bad leg and both saw things the way they wanted in their wondrous Fourth World of art and beauty where Mario Lanza serenaded them and they pulled babies from their wombs and killed irritating ministers and physicians. Pauline at age fourteen tried a real affair with an awkward young boarder in the family home and got caught by her father and slapped by her mother, Honora. Pauline much preferred the company of Kate. Their four parents were quite concerned, suspecting homosexual desires, and Honora threatened to exile Pauline to a life of menial labor if she didn't study harder in school.

Kate's mother had tired of her brilliant but difficult husband, a scientist and university official being forced out, and begun an affair. The estranged pair planned to divorce and leave their daughter in South Africa before separately returning to England. Honora told Pauline she was only fifteen and not going anywhere with Kate who responded she'd rather die than be separated from her special friend.

For weeks the girls were hysterical about their impending separation and even the splendid vocals of Mario Lanza couldn't prevent Pauline from telling Kate her plan and picking up a pen to reiterate, "Next time I write in this diary, Mother will be dead."

"Kate..." I say.

"I don't want to talk to you."

"Too bad. I'll forever be in your ear."

She turns and flops face down on her cot.

"I can't imagine two girls in their mid-teens committing such an act," I say. "You both lured Honora for a lovely nature walk. Your heart must've been quite heavy as you carried a purse concealing half a brick in a stocking. How deviously nice you and Pauline were to her mother. What were you thinking?"

"None of your business."

"You had to be concentrating on what you were going to do. I imagine you wondered if you could do it. And if so, who would take the first swing? What would that be like? Would Honora scream? Or would the first blow knock her unconscious? How many times would you strike the helpless woman? How much would Honora bleed? If you'd reconsidered, you could've stopped yourselves."

"We didn't want to."

"You don't really think you'll get away with this, do you? You'll be convicted and spend years in prison, and you have no idea how many."

* * *

"Come on, let's go to *Revolutionary Road,"* I say.

"I don't want to," says Kate.

"It's a delightful neighborhood."

"It's dreary and dull and full of people too timid to pursue their dreams."

"Is your dream to be a housewife?" I ask.

Kate looks at me in a way I'd hoped she reserved for Honora on nature walks.

"I aspired to be an actress. I could've been one."

"What happened?" I ask.

"What happens to most women in the nineteen fifties? We get married and have children and give up everything else."

I say, "Your husband's sacrificing, too."

"It hurts to watch a talented man work hours a day at a sales job he hates. Every night I tell Frank we should move to Paris. He's as enthused as I until they offer that promotion, about the time I get pregnant. I tell him we already have two kids. Does he really want another?"

Slowly we walk in the large front yard of her white two story house surrounded by big trees.

"When Frank accepts the promotion I feel our lives disintegrate. He doesn't need that job. I'm ready to work to support us in Paris. He has no faith in me or himself."

"I understand Frank's concern about taking your family to Paris without either of you having anything lined up."

"That's part of the adventure," Kate says.

"Few women are ready for a risk of that sort. Not many men, either."

"I've got the spirit of an artist."

"Artists often starve," I say. "And quite a few decide not to have kids."

Pointing at the pretty house, Kate says, "This place is a burden."

"It's a home for you and your children."

"You sound very bourgeois."

"So be it."

"I feel suffocated living here."

"Kate, you and Frank have already discussed the possibility you may need psychiatric care."

Smoldering, she says, "You're saying I need to be shocked thirty-seven times like that nightmarish son our friends brought over."

"I'm not presuming to know the treatment, but all chronic ailments should be assessed."

"I was fine until Frank sold our spirits."

"Are you still considering an abortion?"

She turns her head and looks into the trees.

"Promise me you won't try to do this alone," I say.

* * *

"I hate Coney Island," says Kate. "All they've got is a roller coaster, a carousel, a boardwalk, smelly hot dogs, dirty beaches, and miles of sweaty people."

I look around and nod. "Why stay?"

"You know I can't get any acting jobs."

"May I be frank?" I ask.

"Go ahead."

"You can't seem to stay out of other men's beds. Screwing around cost you your first husband and who knows what Humpty'll do when he finds out you're carrying on with Mickey."

Pointing at a clam shack, Kate says, "All I've got's that horrible job, a disturbed little boy, a sloppy husband who hates his stepson, and now his daughter Ginny, who's hiding from the mob. You bet I love Mickey whenever I can. I'd like to marry him."

She looks at the *Wonder Wheel* her husband operates, and says, "He's too old for me and so unsophisticated. Mickey's writing plays."

"Has he sold any?"

"Not yet. But that doesn't matter."

I hadn't met Mickey but saw him with Kate a few days later. He's a nice looking young man and I think she's got a few years too many to keep him. Sure enough, the following week I hear he's started seeing lovely young Ginny.

"I'll kill her," says Kate.

"You want to fry in Sing Sing?"

"Ginny's got a lot of enemies. People like that don't last."

I get pretty upset and tell Kate so.

"Then get the hell out of my life and stay out," she says.

"Damn good idea."

I try to contact director and screenwriter Woody Allen who's damn hard to get a hold of. After several days I spot him leaving his apartment building and run up to say, "Mr. Allen, please do something."

"About what?"

"Kate's going to let Ginny be murdered."

"Don't worry about that," Allen says.

"So you're going to take care of Ginny."

"Aptly phrased. But the form of care I selected may not be what you have in mind."

Notes: Juliet Hulme and Pauline Parker were fortunate to serve only five years in separate prisons and leave New Zealand soon thereafter. Juliet changed her name to Anne Perry and has earned thousands of dollars a month writing murder mysteries. Henry Hulme, who had long squabbled with colleagues, was forced to resign his university rector position in Christchurch and returned to England where he became one of the country's preeminent scientists developing thermonuclear weapons. Pauline Parker assumed a new name and managed a school for special needs children before retiring.

In her debut, portraying Juliet, Kate Winslet launched a distinguished career that has earned seven Oscar nominations and one statuette for *The Reader.*

JULIA JENTSCH

Save Sophie Scholl

This mission is going to be difficult and dangerous in the extreme, and only a resourceful person will have even a grim chance to complete the imperative task – save Sophie Scholl in 1943 Nazi Germany. We've rejected applicants interested only in rescuing Julia Jentsch, star of the new movie *Sophie Scholl: The Last Days.* Julia is being praised for her performance in a free and democratic Germany and doubtless receives hundreds of offers from gentlemen smitten by the young actress herself as well as the heroine she portrays. Julia Jentsch doesn't need help. Sophie Scholl does. Since you oppose Nazism, and time is urgent this morning, I select you and pray you're ready.

Sophie and her brother Hans are already walking to the University of Munich, where both are students, to hand out The White Rose's sixth leaflet. They've been reckless three times recently. Rather than secretly writing critical works and buying large numbers of stamps and envelopes from a variety of sources and mailing their leaflets from numerous locations, they – Hans and two male friends, in this case – rushed down wide Ludwigstrasse in nighttime Munich, painting walls with "Hitler Mass Murderer" and "Down With Hitler." The Gestapo, already alarmed by White Rose written matter sent primarily to scholars, medics, and pub and restaurant owners, is determined to crush every opponent. After all, the Fatherland recently lost more than two hundred thousand men in Stalingrad, and deformed but electric Joseph Goebbels has just thrilled and terrified the nation with loud demands for Total War, a commitment Germans embraced with millions of breathless Ja's.

Unless you intervene, Sophie and Hans Scholl will arrive while class is in session and scurry around the elegant atrium, placing stacks of leaflets they've carried in a briefcase and suitcase, and they're going to get away with it, walking out into fresh cold daylight, until they discover they still have some papers to distribute. Foolishly and with youthful impetuosity – yes, with hindsight we proclaim – they'll dash back into the atrium and, as a historian notes, "climb a grand marble staircase to the upper level of the hall (where) Sophie flings the rest of the documents high into the air."

In captivity Sophie, only twenty-one, will for several hours brilliantly confound her veteran interrogator with convincing denials she has any knowledge of or involvement in White Rose activities. She'll attribute her "apolitical" paper launching to "either high spirits or stupidity." This might work except for another tragic error. In Hans' pocket the draft of a seventh leaflet will be found in handwriting that matches friend Christoph Probst's in a letter soon seized at Hans' apartment. Then a defiant Sophie will proclaim she's proud to oppose a regime that's already lost the war and butchered countless civilians.

She and Hans will independently claim they're the only authors and by themselves hand-crank duplicated, mailed, and distributed several thousand leaflets. It's a dramatic tour de force undercut by logic. A few days later she and Hans and Christoph will appear before rabid Roland Freisler, the red-robed judge of the People's Court, and he'll rail at them and order they be taken to the guillotine that afternoon.

You, sir, must stop that. Our window is narrow. There they are. Hurry.

"Excuse me," you say in fluent in German.

"I'm sorry, but we're quite busy," says Hans.

"Listen to me, please."

"Excuse us, sir," Sophie says.

"I'm sorry, but you must listen. I'm on your side."

"Who are you?" Hans asks.

"A friend."

"Let me see your papers," says Hans.

You reach into a rear pocket and hand him your wallet containing a California driver's license.

"You were born in 1980?" he enunciates. "Let's go, Sophie."

"Doesn't that prove something?" you offer.

"We're going to the police," he says.

"Great. Anything's better than going to the University of Munich today."

Their eyes cut me.

"If you're on a special mission, why are you so careless with ridiculous documents?" Hans states.

You shoot a hand into Hans' coat pocket and jerk out Christoph

Probst's draft. "Saving this for the Gestapo?"

"Please, come with us," he says.

Passing soldiers and police, students and civilians, you in a bourgeois business suit walk through Hitler's Munich to the Scholl apartment, a haven where Sophie draws and paints and reads, and she and Hans and their White Rose friends discuss literature and philosophy and theology before going to concerts and plays and lectures. That's how they began, sharing the aesthetics of a good life, until they realized decent living had become impossible.

"You're very brave but just as naïve," you tell Sophie in the living room, after Hans has gone to bed.

"I appreciate your sentiments, and the horrific details, but I still think everything would've been fine this morning at the university."

"In your position, you need to understand your vulnerability."

"I do."

"Then be careful."

"We can't worry about ourselves."

Sophie pulls some papers from a folder.

"What're those?"

"Listen," she says. "This is from our first pamphlet: 'Nothing is so unworthy of a civilized nation as allowing itself to be governed without opposition by an irresponsible clique that has yielded to base instinct. It is certain that today every honest German is ashamed of his government. Who among us has any conception of the dimensions of shame that will befall us and our children when one day the veil has fallen from our eyes and the most horrible of crimes reach the light of day?'"

"You wrote that beautifully."

"Hans and a friend have done almost all the writing. I suppose I did contribute a few phrases."

"May I see some of your poetry?"

"Later, perhaps. Listen. This is from the second leaflet: 'We do not want to discuss here the question of the Jews, nor do we want in this leaflet to compose a defense or apology. No, only by way of example do we want to cite the fact that since the conquest of Poland three hundred thousand Jews have been murdered in this country in the most bestial way. Here we see the most frightful crimes against human dignity, a crime unparalleled in the whole of history.'"

"Amazing how few Germans, and others around the world, really know," you say.

"They know."

"No, most really don't. The Jews haven't passively gotten on trains knowing where they're going. And, Sophie, I must tell you: it's going to get much worse. The six extermination camps in Poland still aren't fully operational. You can't imagine."

"I certainly can," she says. "Hans and three others now with us served on the Eastern Front. My boyfriend's there now, too, and sends word through friends. I have many sources."

"Here, let me read part of that one," you say. "The fifth leaflet: 'Germans! Do you and your children want to suffer the same fate that befell the Jews? Do you want to be judged by the same standards as your traducers? Are we to be forever the nation which is hated and rejected by all mankind? No. Dissociate yourselves from National Socialist gangsterism. Prove by your deeds that you think otherwise. A new war of liberation is about to begin.'"

"Everyone in The White Rose is prepared to die," Sophie says.

"Let's prepare to live. Hand me that draft of the seventh leaflet. I'd like to finish it. I'll reveal disasters before they happen."

"And then?"

"Then, Fraulein, we'll quietly mail the leaflets as you had been. No more public pamphleteering. I insist."

LINDSAY LOHAN

Letter to Lohan

Dear Lindsay,

After grading about four hundred pages of adult ESL tests during the week and feeling increasingly tired, tense and lethargic, I didn't exercise or write Saturday morning, as I usually do. I just wanted to shower and get out and relax at the movies. Frequently, there aren't any good ones in Bakersfield, just car crash and explosion flics craved by the poorly-educated majority and well-educated but hidebound minority in places like this. I found a capsule review of one that looked good, though – *Georgia Rule* about a grandmother, daughter and granddaughter who're battling each other. Jane Fonda is the granny and, as you know, you're the granddaughter.

Fonda rules her home and rebukes her family with energy. Your mother, Felicity Huffman, is an alluring drunkard. Family friend and widower Dermot Mulroney maintains dignity while he resists your advances. Young Garret Hedlund is charming when you introduce him to irresistible pleasure. And Cary Elwes is convincing as your incestuous stepfather. But you turned them into supporting players and dominated the movie. You didn't do so with scene-stealing tricks but your edgy charisma. I was going to email a few people about your performance but an online bulletin delayed me: Lindsay Lohan has again crashed a car and been arrested.

I'd heard you partied and drank a lot and probably didn't limit yourself to alcohol. And just two weeks ago at my school, a fellow employee, smiling, read me a quote, attributed to you, in which you unleashed a Herculean list of male stars you'd bedded in recent months. Lindsay's a wild chick, he said. I guess so. Last Saturday at five-thirty a.m., an ominous hour, you misdirected your Mercedes, bounded off a Hollywood street, over the sidewalk and crashed – as softly as one can crash, evidently – into some trees. The paparazzi tailing you asked if you were all right and another follower – stars have so many – gave you a ride to a hospital where the police found you being treated for minor injuries, arrested you for driving under the influence, impounded your car and therein discovered a white powder believed to be cocaine.

I'm not writing to you about upcoming court dates when you'll be represented by slick, excuse-making attorneys. I don't want to hear that crock. I know more about these matters than either you or your attorneys. And I'm stating, in avuncular tone, that anyone who recently got out of an alcohol rehabilitation facility and had been going to Alcoholics Anonymous meetings and who – depending on which news service your trust – has been in three, four or five car wrecks the last couple of years, is beyond out of control. If you were waitress Susie Smith, you wouldn't have a driver's license and you'd probably be in the slammer.

It's surprising a woman only twenty has experienced so much. You became a child fashion model at age three, overcame numerous rejections at auditions for TV commercials, finally got one and turned that into sixty, one for Jell-O pudding with Bill Cosby, who administers (rather than consumes) drugs. Soon you were speaking more lines "than any other ten-year old in daytime serials." You were ready for the big screen at age eleven when Disney summoned you for the *Parent Trap* and you played twins and, according to critic Kenneth Turan, became "the soul of the film…creating two distinct personalities" who helped generate ninety-two million dollars at the box office.

For several years while the Lindsay locomotive was building speed, your father, wealthy by inheritance, languished in prison for securities fraud. That doubtless damaged you personally, but not professionally. You turned down Disney for another flic, soon made a couple of TV movies, won another audition, your first for a film, to capture the lead teen role in *Freaky Friday,* which brought in a hundred sixty million. Most kids would consider themselves bulletproof if they had powerful adults scurrying around them with money and praise and opportunities for more fame.

By 2003, at age seventeen, you were given the honor, and considerable burden, of carrying a major motion picture – *Confessions of a Teenage Drama Queen.* For the first time, the critics didn't like your work and the film grossed only thirty million. Most people won't gross that in a lifetime. From that "setback" you immediately rebounded with an adroit performance in *Mean Girls,* which generated a hundred thirty million worldwide. Other parts followed, and in *A Prairie Home Companion* you crooned a smooth rendition of "Frankie and Johnny."

I hadn't known you were a singer but discovered you'd already made two good albums your producer said showed an "incredible ability to connect with the audience."

Partying as you progressed, you moved into heavy subjects in *Bobby* as part of an ensemble cast battling each other at the Ambassador Hotel the night Robert Kennedy was shot in 1968. Professionally, that brings us to the above-mentioned *Georgia Rule* and two other soon-to-be-released films that millions will see because you're in them. You've got it, Lindsay, but you may not live to enjoy it if you listen to attorneys, agents, publicists, hairdressers, makeup artists, friends, and hangers on who say what you're doing is okay. In fact, you should fire or otherwise disassociate yourself from anyone who fails to say at least some of the following: part of your problem could be organic since your father is an alcoholic once tossed back into prison for "aggravated unlicensed driving and aggressive assault"; your mother's carousing with you has been a destabilizing influence; you've long been under stress competing in a world that rewards on box office winners but also discards them when they begin to fade; and you must make an ongoing commitment to treatment – psychotherapeutic and medicinal – prescribed by your psychiatrist. If you don't already have one, get one. Your chances of cleaning up, and surviving, will be much better.

That's not preaching. That's the truth.

Sincerely,

GTC

SMOOTH OPERATORS

ERROL FLYNN

Arnella, Too Much Like Errol

For decades the inside cover of Parade magazine has been like it is today, a page glistening with faces of beautiful and famous people. And as I write this, one of those pages stands out more than hundreds of others I've read. It was from an early seventies issue featuring the delightful image of Errol Flynn's daughter, Arnella, sleek and sexy at age nineteen, and – I remember the precise phrase – "like her father, marvelously photogenic." Fashion photographers were shooting her and magazines running her graceful features on their covers and, like her father, she was becoming a star. And that was all I ever heard, until recently.

I'd been studying some Errol Flynn websites and posting news that my short story collection, *The Bold Investor*, offers a tale titled "Fallen Star" about a character named Martin Stevens who looks like the swashbuckling movie star but doesn't have his talent, only his problems. And on a couple of the sites, I noticed that Arnella's life spanned 1953-1998. That stark listing was the only indication she had died. More publicly pertinent to owners of the sites – which include her mother, Patrice Wymore, Flynn's third and final wife – was that Arnella had continued to be photographed and placed on magazine covers and had lived in New York and married a photographer and in 1976 borne a son, Luke, who People magazine last year named one of the fifty hottest men.

That's of interest. But what happened to Arnella? I scoured more Flynn websites. Arnella either wasn't mentioned or was again merely listed as having died in 1998. Meaningful facts were essential, and in this age we know what to do. We plug her name into a search engine. There weren't many responses, and only one offered substantive information. That was an October 1998 piece by Kevin Smith in Splash News. Smith had also been wondering what befell Arnella and to find out he hustled to Jamaica where she had spent a lot of her youth and returned for the final sordid years of her life.

The privileged patch of Jamaica that Arnella came home to in 1995 is known as Errol Flynn Estates, a three thousand acre plantation caressed by several miles of sea. The island's beauty seduced Flynn in the late forties after his yacht was hurled ashore during a storm. He soon purchased the land where cattle are now bred and coconuts grown. Patrice Wymore, evidently, is a fine entrepreneur, and also owns a boutique and a hotel nearby.

We infer from Kevin Smith's article and the websites that Arnella was no longer married and that her modeling career had ended. Her mother provided a place in the family home and plenty of money. Thus, the woman who had never really known her legendary father – he left his wife for fifteen-year-old Beverly Aadland when Arnella was four and died when she was six – could live like Flynn as a celebrity on the island, filling endless idle hours with drink. She didn't just put away a few cold ones. She drank Overproof White Rum straight and, like her father, was an alcoholic who used other drugs, including ganja. From there they diverged in their methods of self-destruction, Errol preferring opiates and barbiturates and Arnella craving the white demon – cocaine.

This is the sad sight that emerged: Arnella daily staggered up and down the beach with her Rastafarian buddies and boyfriends as they drank booze and smoked the region's high-grade marijuana. Kevin Smith talked to a lot of men and all said they liked Arnella, that she'd been very pretty and cool and unpretentious but had a lot of problems, the principle one being perpetual consumption of cocaine. The laid back Rastafarians said they didn't do coke with Arnella and tried to talk her out of using the drug.

Patrice Wymore was not interviewed for Smith's article but one doesn't need to read any quotes to know how she was affected by her daughter's plunge into the abyss. She doubtless had innumerable conversations with Arnella, urging her to quit. She probably invoked the image of Arnella's once heroic father battering himself into an unrecognizable old man dead at age fifty. Such warnings rarely work. I know. I was unfazed by reminders that my father had drunk himself into ill-health by his mid-thirties and later cigarette-smoked himself to death. I might not have been able to stop drinking if I hadn't squandered my modest inheritance and lost the option of too much leisure.

Easy money enables addicts. Patrice Wymore understood that. She first cut off Arnella's allowance – and it's an ominous sign when anyone that age isn't working and needs such assistance – then banished her from the main house but provided a smaller place on the estate. One supposes she also tried to get her daughter into treatment. Nothing worked. Arnella began growing tomatoes and carrots and selling them at roadside stalls. She used proceeds to buy more cocaine. But the white death is infinitely more expensive than edible produce and Arnella frequently ran out of money and started heisting coconuts from the family plantation. Her mother then hired security to guard the cash crop.

It was too late. Arnella Flynn's once flowing golden hair pulled back severely, her face crinkled by exposure to the tropical sun, her body emaciated, she continued to stumble around in a haze, downing straight rum and getting coke any way she could. When someone found her body, the response was similar to what it had been when her father died: people were shocked but not surprised. Both had made a pact with death: take me early, just let me be loaded till I arrive.

Dashing Luke Flynn has not commented publicly about his mother's death, but said this about his grandfather: "He was a cool guy…who had a lot of fun… and I intend to do the same." To young Flynn, I offer this unsolicited warning. Have fun sober. Otherwise, it won't really be fun.

Errol Flynn v. John Huston

I don't know how much I've had to drink but always drink too much at Hollywood parties because I fear the beautiful and talented actresses there are a bit more wonderful than I, and that I'll only be a walk-on as long as I last and that won't be long, and then I'll have to either find a regular job, which I dread, or a wealthy husband, which I prefer, and I'd love to marry either Errol Flynn or John Huston or maybe both at once since everyone understands neither can long commit to one woman.

It's ironic these two men, perhaps more than some of the leading ladies at Warner Brothers, Bette Davis, for example, force me to understand that I lack the essential ingredient of a star – presence. I feel I look better than Bette but can't light up a movie set as she does.

At least I sometimes outshine her at parties, and walk away with men she wants, but I never can hold the floor once either Errol or John start talking. It matters not if they're merely saying hello or, more likely, spinning tales about their adventures at sea and on land the world over. Most of the hundred or so people present this night encircle the thespians in the living room.

"I can knock men out with either hand and often do," says Errol.

"You must be fighting jockeys. I doubt you'd give me a decent workout."

"Easy, John, I represented Australia as a middleweight in the 1928 Olympics."

"Maybe someday I'll film that fantasy."

"Your distrust saddens me. I may have to give you a hiding in front of all these people."

"For your edification, I boxed professionally before I turned to the craft of writing and directing movies."

"One assumes most of your opponents were ladies, like Olivia de Havilland."

"That's a foul comment borne of jealously," John says. "Care to back it up?"

"Indeed I do."

As they walk long and lean toward the side door and into the garden, I guess Errol's about six-two and John a couple inches taller, and I mention this because right after Errol says, "Ready, old boy?" John nails him on the nose with a long left jab drawing blood from one of the swordsman's nostrils. Enraged and grunting, Errol charges, hurling punches with each hand, and John either dodges or blocks most of them but Errol does land a right to the jaw that backs John up and prompts him to open and close his mouth a few times to ensure nothing is broken.

I've never been to a boxing match but right away figure out Errol punches harder while John fights more skillfully, continuing to jab Errol's chiseled but reddened and soon quite bloody nose and following with right crosses that cut his lips and evidently inside his mouth and cause him to spit blood before he counterattacks, not worrying if he misses, knowing he'll surely land some, and he does, and now John has a swollen eye and bloody nose, and all the men shout like they probably do at professional fights, and most of the women are fascinated, or at least alarmed, by two stars pummeling each other.

"Hit him in the solar plexus," urges an older gentleman.

"Where's the solar plexus?" a lady asks her husband, who makes a fist and holds it between her breasts and stomach. I bet that would hurt.

Errol and John rarely aim there. "A couple of headhunters these fellows are," comments a gentleman.

"Had enough, old boy?" Errol asks.

"I'm a decent fellow who's had enough of hurting you."

They quit talking and resume swinging. I don't know how long they beat each other but it must be fifteen minutes that feel like an hour. Both look sweaty and beaten, and since they're huffing hard one of the male mob says, "That'll be enough, won't it, boys?"

Errol and John embrace that idea and each other, and the men cheer and then the ladies do too.

"You better go to the doctor or a seamstress," says John.

"You as well. I'll drive."

"Champions don't drive after title fights," says a portly producer. "My chauffeur will deliver you to separate hospitals so there's no public stink about this."

Wives of a Womanizer

Even at rest on a green hill overlooking Hollywood, I still sometimes think about Lili Damita, my first wife, who I should hate, and really I do for she loathes me and, with hungry attorneys, pursued me the final twenty years, clawing for money, my ranch on Mulholland Drive, and, ultimately, my dignity. I nevertheless concede, and indeed emphasize as a matter of historical revelation, that Lili was the greatest lover of all, queen of a rather large group. During a moment of unmatched passion, we conceived our son Sean, prettier than both of us but like his father he loved danger, and pursued the Vietnam War as a photographer. One afternoon, sharing his motorcycle with a colleague, he disappeared into Cambodia. Lili hired soldiers, mercenaries, attorneys, and others to search while she waited for a miracle. Senility overcame her before she received uncorroborated reports that Sean perished in a filthy prison about a year after his capture. We no longer needed specifics. He was gone.

After parting with Lili I met Nora Eddington, sweet and legal at age nineteen, during my statutory rape trial, a farce staged by district attorneys anxious to publicly flog a celebrity. The process was punishing but they couldn't convict me of seducing two star chasers whose birth certificates I failed to check. Afterward, the judge said he was sure everyone had enjoyed the trial. I wish his ass had been in the dock.

Nora sometimes understood we were happier living apart. She didn't like to see me drink and was appalled by narcotics. I told her they produce heaven and she might enjoy them. Only twice, when she was particularly unpleasant, did I grasp and shake her. She needed to settle down. I hoped our having two daughters would help but sensed she was screwing around, and my private detective reported she often visited the home of Dick Haymes, who I called the Boy Crooner. I could dally but when my women misbehaved I felt quite betrayed. Please, stay with me, Nora, I urged, and several times she returned but decided I couldn't be reformed, and she was correct. I'm sorry she too became an alcoholic but pleased she lived a long time.

I certainly wasn't without companionship. Character actors, stuntmen, and various roisterers regularly visited my Mulholland ranch, and we drank and gambled and rode horses and hosted an array of beautiful young women famous and unknown. Sometimes I stepped into the attic over a special bedroom to watch festivities through a one-way mirror in the ceiling. Most guests never learned. Those who did weren't always pleased.

I didn't care. My career was sliding. I blamed Jack Warner for offering mediocre roles but realized I'd begun to look rather weary on screen. While making a dreary western I met Patrice Wymore, who at twenty-three was not too old. She was lovely and ready to dedicate herself to me as I forsook Hollywood, where I no longer had a house anyway, and we sailed the seas in my yacht the *Zaca,* my home and refuge from Hollywood and former wives.

In Italy, Patrice and I had a daughter, Arnella, and there I resolved to produce my own movies, beginning with *William Tell.* I invested hundreds of thousands to be matched by investors in Italy where sets were being built and we started filming. They disappeared and I couldn't pay anyone and the project collapsed. I'd deal with it. I'd have another drink and all the morphine I could find.

Patrice was wonderful but she soon bored me. I always needed someone new and in my late forties became enchanted by beautiful blond Beverly Aadland.

Fool, friends said, she's only fifteen.

She's a girl no more, I countered.

We traveled and lived together. I didn't care what authorities might say. Beverly amused me and I sensed I wouldn't live long enough to be prosecuted. Now she was seventeen, anyway, and we were flying to Vancouver to sell the *Zaca* to pay Lili and others who believed it's just Flynn, take the bastard for everything. I'd need more time to make a deal. As our hosts drove us back to the airport, my chronic back pain became unbearable, and in other respects I didn't feel at all well, either.

Quit drinking and taking drugs, you might say.

At an ancient age fifty it's rather late for that. I asked to be taken to a doctor who received us at his fine home. After he examined me and administered a shot, I braced myself in a doorway and told stories about John Barrymore and others and noted I could still delight an audience.

Let me lie down on the bedroom floor a little while before we depart.

Fine, said the doctor and his wife.

When Beverly later stepped in to check, I barely breathed. They tried to revive me but couldn't. I wished this could be easier on Beverly, who was hysterical. She needed to understand I'd had all I wanted. And I'm thankful, a half century later, that I wasn't there when diabetes and congestive heart failure consumed her. That's the best part of dying young. You're less exposed when others depart.

Fallen Star

Producers and directors often exhorted Martin Stevens to beat or at least be like Errol Flynn, and that seemed attainable. In terms of facial structure, Martin looked as if Flynn had fathered him. Hell, maybe he did. So the sequence was logical enough. Martin was outfitted in tights in his first starring film role and told to be dashing and athletic. Regrettably, costume dramas had expired even before Flynn and that was a generation before Martin became an adult. Now, at age twenty-six, the same as Flynn in his smashing debut in Captain Blood, Martin Stevens was being hooted by the few who attended his movie.

"He's no Errol Flynn," said the critics.

They were entirely correct. The splendidly handsome Martin Stevens had the physique of a philosophy professor, a young professor, true, but decidedly unheroic.

All right. They simply changed strategy and cast Martin as a brilliant scientist struggling with a larcenous wife. He was supposed to be sympathetic but was merely maudlin, and filmgoers stirred when his smoldering patent attorney bedded Martin's breathless spouse.

"You can't let them cast me in subordinate roles."

"That was an opportunity for some real character acting."

"I'm not a character actor, you idiot. I'm a star."

"You ain't no star. Try another agent."

Martin was turned down a few times but got an agent soon enough. There weren't any lead roles, though, not in movies.

"This is a terrific opportunity," said his new agent.

"I'm not doing TV. If I crawl in that wretched little box, I'll never get out."

"You're kidding, Martin. Look at Burt Reynolds and Michael Douglas. Those guys did well on TV before getting established in movies."

"Another goddamn detective."

"People like detectives. You gotta make people relate to this guy."

Detective Frank Sparks was assigned to clean up and revitalize the corrupt and dispirited group of lawmen in Chicago's homicide division. Martin understood this could take a long time, so he decided to divorce his wife, a former Playboy bunny striving herself to become a serious star, sell his modest house south of Sunset Boulevard, and purchase a beautiful condominium near Lake Michigan.

He should have tried a hotel. Ratings were low from the start, off-screen scandal didn't help, and after but a season Detective Frank Sparks disappeared.

"Martin, I gotta ask you," said his agent. "Do you think you might've done this unconsciously? You know, to be like Flynn."

"Hell no. She told me she was nineteen."

And she had. There were witnesses. No one at the restaurant that night thought she was only fifteen. Even if they'd been sober they wouldn't have suspected that. The district attorney had started all this. He wanted to be governor and figured he could become a star protecting the innocent girls of Chicago from lecherous Hollywood actors. The guy preached pretty well but decided not to file charges. Unlike Flynn, Martin was spared a humiliating trial.

It was time to regroup, reassess, revise. It was time to return to Hollywood. Within a week, as he'd long done with unsettling frequency, Martin made his pilgrimage: he drove up onto Mulholland Drive to the house where Flynn had lived. Hollywood insiders had shown him where the place was, and it was always a letdown because the blockheads who'd moved in after Flynn changed everything. Martin could not imagine such unmitigated stupidity. Didn't any of them realize they were living in a historical monument, a place not merely of the most sublime and highly publicized debauchery, but a home where a van Gogh had once hung?

Martin considered lecturing the current occupant but decided he needed excitement. Lacking Flynn's yacht to whisk him onto the high seas, he settled for a franchise Mexican restaurant and started drinking beer with tequila chasers. After several quick rounds and not being approached by any of the lunchtime diners, he stood and announced: "Which one of you ladies wants to fuck Martin Stevens?"

No one responded, and this devastated him. Errol Flynn wouldn't have even had to ask, would he?

"Are you all so mundane, are you all so insipid, that you'd rather bury your faces in enchiladas than have a transcendent experience with me?"

"Sir, I'm sorry, but you're going to have to leave now," said the manager, a clean-cut fellow barely in his twenties.

Martin sat down and said, "Son, bring me three beers and three shots, and please do so before I dismantle you and this prefabricated house of shit."

Soon the police were there, telling Martin to stand up.

"On the contrary, boys, you sit down and join me."

This became Martin's seventh arrest, but only two of those had been DUIs, the second almost three years ago.

"Mr. Stevens, what do you do?" said the judge.

"I'm Martin Stevens, your honor."

"Yes, Mr. Stevens, what's your job?"

"I'm an actor."

"A working actor?"

"Of course."

"Why weren't you working the other day?"

"I'm taking some time off."

"Every man needs a job, Mr. Stevens."

"I've got a job."

"Who's your employer?"

"I'm self-employed."

"Do you make your own films?"

"No."

"Then you're unemployed," said the judge. "You need to keep busy, and I'm going to help you. Five days a week for the next six months, you're to attend an AA meeting."

"I'm not an alcoholic. I've read extensively about these matters."

"Then you failed to comprehend what you read. Also, Mr. Stevens, you're to find work immediately."

"I'm recharging my creative batteries."

"Fine, while doing so, you can work in another field. Do you have any other experience?"

"Of course not. I'm an actor for life."

"I'm assigning a probation officer to this case. Report to him in one week about the efforts you're making to find a job. If you don't have something, at least a promising lead, in a month, you're coming right back to this court."

Martin placed many calls and rushed around trying to get an agent. Everyone was too busy, booked with dynamic clients they had to commit all their time to. Screw 'em, Martin thought. How many have starred in two movies and one television series? Damn few, no doubt.

Marching in cold Martin knocked on doors of people who produced and directed plays in theaters where people could actually see him and none of his action would be snipped away. A number of the theater people knew about Martin, but that proved a disadvantage. They hadn't liked his minor stage work a few years earlier, and certainly hadn't been impressed by his work before the cameras. Martin moved from large theaters to medium-size and finally to those seating less than a hundred. They all had lots of talented and experienced actors vying to appear in their productions. Did he have a business card? Okay. Maybe someday they'd give him a call.

Despite the humiliation Martin strutted into a dingy theater of thirty seats on Pico Boulevard.

"We're casting a play now," said the young director. "It's about Jack Warner and his brothers. Not many know what Jack looked like, but we've got a dead ringer. We've also got a lady who looks just like Bette Davis and a guy who could be Bogey's twin. Naturally, we'd love to have a guy like Flynn, too."

"Here I am."

"Absolutely. You got it."

"When do rehearsals start?"

"Next week."

"Great. I'll be here."

"Next week's just for the main characters, the Warner brothers."

"Flynn was very important in the history of Warner Brothers movies."

"I know, but the story's primarily about the brothers themselves. Poor Jewish immigrants who achieved astounding things. We'll be focusing on what a compelling but reprehensible bastard Jack Warner was. He screwed the other brothers, you know."

"Yeah, I know all about the Warner brothers. I could help with the script."

"The script's already tight. My brother's worked on it several years. That includes at least ten rewrites."

"I assume everyone gets Actors Equity Association wages."

"All the stars, yes. The extras get twenty bucks a show. But, more importantly, you get experience and exposure."

Martin shook the young man's hand. Fine. This was what it took.

In two weeks he returned and met the Bette and Bogey actors, and all three periodically twinkled in the background as the Warner brothers talked about using them to build an empire. Each movie star briefly spoke in a few scenes, and Martin's best was based on an account from Flynn's ghostwritten autobiography My Wicked, Wicked Ways. Bad Jack has insulted the Baron, as he calls him, and Flynn, via studio telephone, announces he's coming up to the inner sanctum to kick Jack's ass. The movie mogul, more competent in matters of brain than brawn, skedaddles out a secret exit before Flynn, charging in, is left on stage, looking around.

During two weeks of rehearsals Martin was able to get the young Bette Davis actress into bed, which is something Flynn had never done with the real one. Flynn claimed he'd never wanted to. Bette insisted he did and she declined. Martin Stevens was invigorated by his thoroughly charming, albeit dramatically limited, Bette Davis. And he was ready on opening night.

They were all primed. And The Warner Brothers play was a hit. The L.A. Times came down and immediately awarded it Critic's Choice status. That designation, one must emphasize, was primarily due to provocative performances by the actors who portrayed the Warner brothers. Many theatergoers said they got a great feel for how the studio system worked during Hollywood's Golden Age. The play, originally scheduled to run six weeks, was extended another six, and then six more. Martin, meanwhile, was earning twenty bucks six times a week. That, combined with the prestige, was plenty to satisfy the judge. But, now that his savings were gone, it wouldn't have been sufficient to shelter him had the new Bette Davis not agreed to evict her old high school chum, a ballerina and cocktail waitress, and move him into her one-bedroom Hollywood apartment that must have been there the day the original Warner brothers strode into town.

During the day Martin's girlfriend was a secretary who typed a hundred words a minute. With their modest incomes funneled into one household, they were doing all right, and Martin was delighted to have time to take care of his AA commitment and call on agents, directors, office assistants, anyone who'd talk to him, and invite them to The Warner Brothers. Martin could make sure they got in, provided they let him know when they were coming. A number of show business people attended, including several that Martin had contacted, and the play led to the hiring of all the Warner brothers by an independent company committed to making a good movie adapted from the play. The company, however, had recently promised the supporting roles to other actors.

On closing night Martin was late. He'd called his girlfriend early that afternoon and said to drive to the theater alone. He would come on his own. Five minutes before curtain time, Martin wobbled in.

"Where have you been?" said the director.

Martin placed both hands around the man's neck and pushed, and then opened the curtains and took the stage.

"Ladies and gentlemen, tonight, the final night of this stupendous play, is going to be special. Indeed, it's going to be better than that. How? How, you may ask, do you improve an overwhelming hit? In this case, it is entirely simple. You simply remove the usurious and entirely unhandsome Warner brothers, and let the real stars take over. Tonight, therefore, you shall see Errol Flynn copulate, on this very stage, with the esteemed Bette Davis."

The director, stage manager, and set designer — the latter two were women — tentatively ran on stage toward Martin Stevens, who popped the director with a decent left jab to the nose before grabbing one lady, a hand on each breast, and snap kicking the other in the abdomen.

Martin was fortunate to have his jail sentence suspended and replaced by a mandatory three-month stint in a tight treatment facility. It was there that Martin first experienced delirium tremens. He was twenty-nine years old, and predictions of imminent death began. Those people didn't understand how much medications were helping Martin. They brought him out of DTs and gave him a greater calm than he'd ever known.

Pills not only rescued Martin from the revolt of an addicted brain being wrenched clean, they'd enabled him to weigh twenty pounds less. When he left the treatment center, he was the slimmest he'd been since his late teens. Live right, get good breaks. Martin was sure about that when he got a call to guest star on a detective show as the father of a little girl who is missing and later found molested and dead in a park not far from her suburban home. Every day Martin was on time and knew his lines and cooperated with the director, and still photographed well, but no one was enthused about him and he wondered if he'd lost it or ever really had it. But of course he'd had it and everyone would see as soon as he got hold of it.

His next chance came a year later as an ex-husband of the hot star of a daytime soap opera.

"I don't see many lines for me," Martin told the director.

"This part doesn't require a lot of words, but the dialogue's tight and explosive. Each of you four ex-husbands is showing up at embarrassing times for her, and the audience loves how she carves you guys up."

Alas, the social dynamics were frequently too complicated, even for this time slot, so Martin had to be killed off screen in a car crash. The camera closed in on the star and revealed a wickedly sexy smile. She had it.

In several months Martin next worked as master of ceremonies at the Miss Teen Orange County pageant and afterward persuaded one of the contestants to obediently return home with her parents and then sneak out her bedroom window. As they reached Martin's car, the girl's father opened the front door and said, "Get back inside, young lady."

"Lighten up," Martin said.

"You want me to call the cops."

"Go ahead. She's eighteen."

"Wait here while I get my gun."

"You're a bunch of fascists down here," Martin said, and headed back to the stars.

The following morning he awakened in a park near USC. His car was still there but his medications and wallet were gone.

"Hey," Martin said, waving at a man who looked like a regular in the area.

"How 'bout helping me with some change."

"How 'bout helping me with some weed," Martin said.

"All right."

Martin sat down and took off his loafers.

"What're you doin'?"

"I'm givin' you two hundred bucks right here," Martin said.

"They ain't shit to me."

"You can damn well sell 'em for twenty. That's worth a few joints."

The man reached into his old army-style jacket and presented four thin cigarettes.

"Let me smell 'em," Martin said, and then received a book of matches in the deal and started smoking right away. Relief came with the first puff and increased after every hit. This was unequivocally the world's finest cure for a hangover. Most people would rather endure pain than continue revelry by other means. In a few minutes, despite burning his throat, Martin finished the joint and within a half-hour he'd smoked two more. He put the last joint in his pants pocket and got in his car.

He knew where to go. When he arrived he couldn't imagine why so few people were there. Forest Lawn Cemetery was manicured pretty and green in the hills, and in all directions Martin could feel the famous people who had worked and lived and done great things, and the magic of Hollywood was within him as he marched to the best place. About an easy wedge shot from an elegant mausoleum, almost under a tree, close to a statue of a naked woman, lay Errol Flynn.

An employee had long ago told Martin where Flynn was. You had to know because for twenty years there hadn't been a gravestone or even a marker. What the hell was wrong with Flynn's three wives and four children? How could they just plant the man who'd been Robin Hood and General Custer and Don Juan, the unrivalled king of charm, as if he'd been a pauper? It was barbaric. It had been until his kids finally installed a small bronze marker containing the basic information. That was still not enough. Martin, as customary, was prepared to do much more. With considerable solemnity he unzipped his pants and began urinating in thick green grass next to the marker. His colorless stream had a lot of booze in it, and that had to make Flynn happy. Martin would have been happy, too, if only Flynn had known that today was his thirty-third birthday.

* * *

"Martin? Martin Stevens?"

"I guess so."

"This is William Atkins, the agent. I've been trying to find you. Pretty damn difficult. I finally got hold of your mother. Thankfully, she's helped you out."

"You implyin' I need my mother?"

"I'm not implying anything, Martin. I'm stating facts. You've frequently been homeless, and now you're living in a rat hole, from what your mother says."

"Screw my mother."

"Listen, Fred Bannister wants you for his next project."

"Who's Fred Bannister?'

"He's won about every award for documentary filmmaking the last ten years. Now he's doing one on actors who've had hard times. Troy Donahue. The blond hunk from the early sixties. Remember him? He's been homeless in New York City. We're gonna line him up."

"Good man."

"And we've already interviewed several others. Lots of guys have struggled. We want the best stories. Fred's positive you're one. Interested?"

"How much?"

"Fred's work is very dramatic but it's historical, it's journalism. He really shouldn't pay anyone for that. But he understands. He can go a hundred bucks a day, and meals. He wants to talk to you, follow you around. It'd be some good work. Interested?"

Fred Bannister and his cameraman arrived early in the alley beside a transformed garage behind an old house near downtown L.A.

"Roll it," said Bannister, approaching the door, then knocking.

The door opened to frame a gray and wrinkled man wearing a black scarf, a Hawaiian shirt, black slacks, and brown loafers.

"Martin Stevens?"

"Damn right."

"Fred Bannister."

"That thing on? Fine. Come in."

In one small room there was a single bed, neatly made, two wooden chairs, a wooden table, a little TV on a cardboard box, and a kitchenette.

"Martin, this world is vastly different than Beverly Hills," said Bannister.

"Beverly Hills bored me."

"You ever miss it?"

"Never."

"So you're reasonably content, despite your troubles?"

"I've had more fun than trouble."

"Martin, you've been arrested thirty-two times and hospitalized on several occasions, at least. I hope you'll tell the truth."

"I've never told anything else."

"Did you ever imagine this could happen?"

"Today's stars are tomorrow's casualties."

"Do you think you were a star?"

"No. But now I'm ready for character roles no one else can handle."

"Do you go to the movies often?"

"Never."

"Do you watch them on TV?"

"It doesn't work."

"Who'd hire you?"

"After this, plenty'll call me," Martin said.

"What does your day generally consist of?"

"Oh, I get up late. I'm definitely a night person."

"Movies are made early."

"Not if they're about the night."

"What do you do after getting up? Do you drink?"

"Just coffee."

"Really, Martin?"

"That's right, buster."

"How long?"

"Since the agent called. Eight days."

"Are you under a doctor's care?"

"Maybe."

"What are you taking?"

"What I need."

"So, after coffee, what do you do?"

"I generally read the paper."

"Where is it?"

"I already gave it to the people up front."

"After reading, then what?"

"I walk to the park."

"Can we go there?"

"Let's talk here," Martin said.

"A movie's always better with movement and some outdoor scenes."

"Not today."

"It's a beautiful day for a comeback."

Martin seemed to hold his breath and count before saying: "All right."

Crunching gravel in the alley, the three men provoked a dozen wicked dogs, and the cameraman got a startling close-up of a pit bull howling and slobbering through his chain link fence. After three blocks in the alley they turned left onto a street constricted by cars parked bumper to bumper on both sides.

"Do you have a car?"

"No," Martin said. "I don't need one."

"What if you're cast in a movie?"

"The studio'll pick me up."

"Is that your park?"

"Yep. Not much there."

Martin turned around.

"Hold it, Martin. Please. Let's take a look."

"You're lookin'."

Bannister put his hand on Martin's elbow and coaxed him to turn back around.

"Let's walk in your park, Martin. Show me what you do there."

"I like to sit in the shade."

"Do you have a favorite tree?"

There were six scraggly ones.

"This one, nearest the road," he said, and sat heavily on a tired rear end. Bannister joined him on the grass.

"You used to look so much like Errol Flynn."

"Still do."

"Respectfully, Martin, you don't really think you still look like Flynn, do you?"

"Better — at the same age. Haven't you done your homework?"

"You're fifty."

"Same age as Flynn when he died. Ever see Cuban Rebel Girls?"

"No. Who's in it?"

"The wrecked Flynn and his fifteen-year-old blond Beverly. Worst movie ever made. He's lucky he died, like Elvis. Nowhere to go when you're like that."

A large man was pushing a shopping cart full of bottles and cans toward the park. His open black jacket bared his torso and a dirty white cap was perched on an uneven Afro.

"Martin," the man said.

"Shoot him," said Bannister. "A friend, Martin?"

"No."

"Where the hell you been?"

"What are you talking about?"

"You know goddamn well."

"I don't need any bottles."

"You already drunk? You musta killed some dude and stole his clothes."

"Sir, please, I'm working."

"You workin'. Yeah, and I'm Denzel Washington. Listen, Martin, you gotta pay me for the shit. And don't disappear on me again. You been in jail?"

"You're clearly incontinent, sir. You and I have no business."

The big fellow left his cart in the street and walked toward Martin, Bannister, and the cameraman.

"I can't decide who to take out first."

Bannister jumped and said, "Relax. How much does he owe you?"

"Thirty-five bucks."

"Here's forty. Keep the change."

"Don't pull that shit again, Martin," he said, frowning, and walked back to his cart and pushed it away, bottles and cans tinkling over squeaky wheels.

"So you're not really clean," said Bannister.

"I'm clean. But the goddamn bums are always trying to get something."

"Don't you think that's denial?"

"No, that's a fact of the streets your audience should see?"

"How long do you usually stay here?"

"A couple hours. I usually bring some novels."

"Which ones?"

"Read 'em so fast I can't remember. Then I get up and stretch and run ten or fifteen wind sprints. I'm a lot trimmer than most men my age."

"What about eating?"

"I don't overdo it. Especially now. Diet's an important part of this business."

"Have you worked since the beauty pageant in Orange County?"

"Certainly."

"Where?"

"At various theaters."

"Which theaters? Which plays?"

"The Warner Brothers, an L.A. Times Critic's Choice."

"That was a generation ago. Which plays since?"

"Plenty of 'em. You ask a lot pointless goddamn questions."

Like an older man Martin struggled to stand, and said, "This movie's in the can."

"Not yet, Martin."

"The hell it isn't."

"We'd like to do some follow-up work."

"You just get this out there where it'll rekindle my career."

"Martin," a woman hollered, walking fast, almost running from the other side of the park.

"Roger," said Martin.

"Fred – Roger's the Englishman who ran the first sub four-minute mile."

"Yeah, good idea about the follow-up, especially after I'm back in business."

"Hey, Martin."

"Shoot her," said Bannister.

"Are your ears as infected as everything else?" she said.

"Madam, I haven't any idea who you are. Please cease these libelous statements or I'll contact my attorneys."

Laughter exploded from a toothless mouth.

"Get the camera off her or, by god, I will find an attorney."

"What's the matter? Ashamed of your girlfriend?"

* * *

Five weeks later Fred Bannister returned to the converted garage of Martin Stevens. As there was no response when Bannister knocked, he walked around to a side window and saw Martin Stevens stiff on the floor.

"Shoot him," said Bannister. "I'll call the police."

In about a year, when Fred Bannister's documentary Fallen Stars debuted on a wave of enthusiasm and praise, Bannister closed his segment on Martin with uplifting news: "Other than a single prescribed medication, Martin Stevens was clean. He died of natural causes as he struggled to make a comeback."

HUMPHREY BOGART

The Battling Bogarts

"Give us two more."

"Sure, Bogey," I say.

"Make 'em triples," says Mayo Methot.

"I told you, go easy."

"You drink faster," she says.

I look at Bogey. He nods. I return and put the drinks on their table. They blow smoke at each other.

"Maybe you should go back to work," he says.

Mayo swigs half her drink before saying, "I quit because you made me."

"No one makes you do anything."

"Only roles I ever got were smartass dames nobody liked."

"Pretty good casting."

"Too bad people don't know you're a balding little man with a big mouth."

"Cut back on the booze, your face and body won't be so fat. People'd like you more."

"People liked me fine before I got tied down with you."

"I wanted to talk about that."

"Don't be a sap. Lauren Bacall's half your age. She'd use you and leave you."

Bogey sips his drink.

"I'm gonna smack that skinny bitch."

"Stay away from her or I'll smack you," he says.

"Don't trust a girl who'd sleep with a man like you."

Bogey takes another sip.

"She doesn't really enjoy being with you."

"I love being with her and away from this hole we've fallen into."

Across her body Mayo unloads a right cross to Bogey's nose and scrambles up to throw three or four left hooks at his head. Bogey covers up and I run over and grab Mayo from behind, pinning arms to her sides. He picks his cigarette from the ashtray and inhales. I've never seen a man inhale cigarettes like Bogey or a woman who drinks like Mayo. At least this time he doesn't counterpunch. Using a cocktail napkin to dab his bloody nose, he says, "That's all. I'm moving out." And that's what he does. He divorces Mayo and marries Bacall and a few years later Mayo dies alone in an Oregon hotel room.

Duel in Casablanca

Early every morning screenwriters run onto this damn set and hand us their latest work and say memorize quickly so boss Jack Warner and production chief Hal Wallis quit demanding a great story going where no one knows. I learn whatever lines they give me and show up motivated and on time. Between takes I enjoy pounding people in chess. Today in exotic *Casablanca*, on the Warner's lot in Burbank, I've got my white pieces attacking Austrian pretty boy Paul Henreid.

"Hope you don't mind working with me, Paul."

"On the contrary, Bogey. I'm delighted."

He concentrates on two pawns I've pushed toward the center of his defense.

"I heard you were unhappy not being the lead actor," I say.

"I'm one of the leads."

"But I'm the star and know that bothers you."

I pull on a hot cigarette.

"Why don't we let the audience determine who is the star," Paul says. "After all, Bogey, you're already in your early forties and have generally played unpleasant characters in supporting roles."

"That changed with *The Maltese Falcon*," I tell him.

"I think I should get Ingrid Bergman in *Casablanca*."

"She's your bride in the picture. That'll help with the bluenose censors."

I move my bishop deep into enemy territory.

"I sense you're jealous I'm playing Victor Laszlo, the dashing resistance leader, while you're just Rick, a brooding saloonkeeper abandoned by the beautiful lady who loves me."

"You may lose her in *Casablanca*," I say.

"I'll have to speak to the screenwriters about that."

"They wouldn't listen to you, Paul. Your character may be sophisticated but he seems like a prude. That's why in the club it's me a lady asks, 'Can I see you tonight?'

"And I say, 'I never make plans that far ahead.'"

"A great line that should've been mine," says Paul.

I exhale and continue my chess offensive before saying, "I'm also the one who tells Ingrid, 'Here's looking at you, kid.'"

"You must be bribing the writers, Bogey, but I hope you concede I arouse your customers when I lead singing of 'La Marseillaise' to counter Nazis blustering 'Die Wacht am Rhine.'"

"That's pretty good, especially since I nod to the band it's okay to play."

In a series of moves I guess I haven't seen coming, Paul maneuvers a rook, a knight, and his queen into striking positions and says, "Two more moves, Bogey, and it will be my pleasure to say, 'Checkmate.'"

I stand and shake his hand.

"At least we agree about the need to defeat the Nazis," he says. "I'm a refugee in America, too, just like so many people making this picture."

"Maybe we'll make another one together before the shooting stops."

"Next time, I'll get top billing."

I understand Paul wanting to be a star but in a few weeks, when I embrace Ingrid Bergman, and by implication make love to her, and later tell her, "We'll always have Paris" and some other unforgettable stuff, I think he and audiences discover what I can do. Frankly, I just figured it out, too.

Bogey Meets a Prince

"Mike, where's my invitation to meet the prince?"

"Sorry, Bogey, but only my most cultured clients will be there," says Beverly Hills restaurateur Mike Romanoff.

"I've never met a real European prince and damn well want to."

"You'd embarrass me."

"The prince would be impressed to meet a movie star," says Bogey

"There'll be a lot of stars here tomorrow night, and I trust all of them."

"I thought we were friends, Mike."

"We are."

"What if I promise to behave?"

"I wouldn't believe it," says Mike.

"Maybe I'll start having lunch elsewhere."

"You'd miss me too much."

"How about I leave you a thousand dollar deposit, Mike?"

"All right."

"I'll drop off the dough tomorrow afternoon."

Mike says, "I don't need a deposit. Just your word you'll behave. No more than a half dozen drinks."

"Doubles or triples?"

"Singles."

"You'll have a coat and tie ready for me, won't you, Mike?"

"I'm already reconsidering. Maybe it's best you skip this gala."

"Relax, I'll bring my own coat and tie."

"That would be a delightful first."

The tall and distinguished prince, forged by several great central European royal families, smiles often as he charms celebrities, and the party proceeds famously.

"Prince, may I join you here?" Bogey asks, stepping to the table and exhaling smoke.

"You certainly may. You're a wonderful actor."

"Thanks." He sits across from Mike Romanoff, who's next to the prince.

"You were marvelous in *Casablanca*," says the prince.

"I appreciate that. And I wanna tell you your English is perfect. How'd you learn to speak so damn well?"

"I was most fortunate to have a British governess."

"Oh, yeah," says Bogey, "did you fuck her?"

Where's Captain Queeg?

On my cold Ohio farm I never watch *The Caine Mutiny* and won't allow my wife to, either. The conspirators who made it libeled me then and now, and I get my gun when people come here looking for Captain Queeg. I don't want to talk.

In the war they ordered me to take over an aging minesweeper infested with lazy and deceitful men. Right away I spotted some with shirttails hanging out. I retrieved ball bearings from my side coat pocket and ground them in my right hand as I demanded everyone tuck shirts in and shave every day.

I had to be wary. When I lectured an incompetent young ensign, my officers on the bridge shouted, we're going in circles and just cut our tow line pulling a big floating target. Nothing like that happened so what the hell were they doing? I'll tell you. They were trying to get me and pleased headquarters ordered *The Caine* to sail to San Francisco. After meeting the brass, I reached for my ball bearings and squeezed while I assured the men we just needed a new radar installation. The navy did receive some complaints but quickly dismissed them.

In a week or two we were in a storm throwing the ship around like a toy boat. Pull back, we're only a thousand yards from the beach, I ordered. No, traitors said, we're at least fifteen hundred out. I was captain of the ship and insisted we only had a thousand yards and couldn't survive so close. Then I walked away. Before long, sources revealed the officers were calling me Old Yellow Stain.

I was usually right but that's not why I called this meeting. I rolled ball bearings in my hand and told the men we were like a family on this ship. We had to be. We needed each other. Did they agree? Did they say, yes sir, Captain Queeg? No, they didn't say a damn thing. They didn't want me in their family. That's why they tried to frame me for cowardice. I'd been on naval duty forty years including seven in the Atlantic the last three during war. These men should've understood why I got a lot of migraine headaches. But that doesn't mean my nerves were shot.

I'd just rather look down than into hateful eyes. They'll pay for this. I ordered no movies for thirty days and everyone got tense. Thankfully, another ship, no doubt blessed with better officers, gave *The Caine* and me a pound of frozen strawberries, a wonderful gift. It should've been. But the men again betrayed me, and I demanded they attend this urgent meeting.

Gentlemen, we've got at least one thief and I'm going to bring him to justice, I said. How many servings of strawberries did you eat? And you and you and you? Each officer said two except one man had three and I ate four. I'd ordered sand put in a large tin can on the table, and a kitchen aide scooped with a serving spoon and dumped sand into a pan. That's twenty-four servings. But look in the can. What do you see, gentlemen? At least a quarter pound of sand. What happened to those strawberries? There must be a duplicate key. I want every key on board brought to me. Strip search all men.

A guy could throw a key overboard, someone said.

Not after the trouble of making the key, I replied, wagging my finger.

These men were liars. I wasn't spooked, even in a typhoon. I was in command and ordered an insubordinate man taken into custody. Panicky officers didn't think I could operate the ship. Someone shouted to change our position or the ship would blow over. Quiet, or I'll have you arrested, I said. Young and arrogant Van Johnson, a traitor since I arrived, said captain, you're a sick man. I'm relieving you of command and will be giving all orders.

The navy prosecuted Van Johnson for mutiny. According to my sources his defense lawyer, Jose Ferrer, told him he reviewed the case and thought what they did stunk since it was the first munity in the history of our United States Navy. Organized and aggressive prosecutor E.G. Marshall had an easy time, especially when another conspirator, Fred McMurray, testified he wasn't really involved but Van Johnson was. Marshall asked some elementary questions about mental health that Johnson couldn't answer. And this incompetent had tricked a psychiatrist into testifying I was damaged due to long conflicts at sea and had a paranoid personality. At least the doctor added that wasn't a disabling condition. I saw Johnson going to hell and wanted to be the one to send him there.

I took the stand and testified the ship was in lousy shape when I arrived but I handled her well even in a typhoon.

The defense attorney asked, Captain Queeg, did you ever steam over a tow line?

Of course not. The men were turning against me.

Did you ever turn the ship upside down looking for a key related to a quart of strawberries?

I got them on the strawberries, I said, taking out my ball bearings and working them in my hand. I proved by geometric logic what had happened. I'm not paranoid or incompetent. Van Johnson and his gang are mentally ill criminals. Imagine the damage to our navy if he and they get away with seizing one of our ships. No captain will ever be safe. We've got to demand the ultimate punishment.

Maybe the officers of the court don't hear or understand my rational explanations. They send me to a mental institution while bad guys get away. I don't know how long I'm in there or how many times they electric shock me or how much strange medicine they use to confuse me. All I know I'm back in Ohio and looking at my wife face down on the bedroom floor and sure someone's driving me crazy.

Bogey in Brief

Dad's a great guy and doctor until investments plunge and morphine soars. Mother paints pretty children far from her nerves. One sister dies young the other's not right. I escape to Broadway where some call me the next Valentino. After plays I caress ladies, smoking and drinking till dawn.

First time in Hollywood executives ignore me and later I try again. At forty-two I start knocking them out. At home, after three divorces, I find a beautiful wife who doesn't throw vases.

"You're twenty-five years younger and Hollywood's thick with Casanovas, be careful, your honor's at stake," I say.

"Yours, too."

"Come on, Betty, Evita just styles my hair and takes dictation."

We have two wonderful kids when Ava Gardner dumps Frank Sinatra who nightly slides into our home.

"You don't think he comes to see me, do you," I say.

"Oh, Bogey."

After throat surgery for cancer I hope switching to filtered cigarettes helps me get back like my wife expects. Where is she? I know she can't always be here but sense she's with him. I'm all bones and can't do much but close my eyes.

CLARK GABLE

Mutiny

I'm a nice guy and want Captain Bligh to like me. I can't help it he fidgets and won't maintain eye contact when we discuss our scenes. People tell me my looks make him feel uncomfortable. I don't know why. He's got a big expressive face, not as fat as he probably thinks, and is a superb actor. No man looks as mean and authoritative as the captain.

I follow his orders on the *Bounty.* In fact he's sailed with me before and this time wants me on board as a lieutenant. I'm honored. Maybe this will help me someday command my own ship. I know it'll be difficult controlling forty-six men on a ship for two years sailing to Tahiti in the vast Pacific and preparing breadfruit saplings to take to the Caribbean as cheap food for slaves.

A few weeks after leaving England I notice Captain Bligh is yelling a lot more and threatening half the people on board and rebuking most others. A month or two later he starts ordering men to be flogged and has one man hung upside down and when he dies Bligh demands we flog the corpse. He ties a rope to another man and drags him back and forth under the ship until he also expires.

"Captain, please restrain yourself," I privately tell Bligh.

"I'll restrain myself by not flogging you and merely deny you shore leave in Tahiti."

If he tries to bar me from paradise, I may strike, and other unhappy men would help. Thankfully, Bligh doesn't try to detain me and despair becomes joy on beautiful beaches backed by lush trees and plants. Also, God bless us, we meet many lovely young native women who're often in the nude and very receptive. My favorite is Maimiti. In five months it seems as if we've always been together, and I never want to return to the bloody *Bounty* of Captain Bligh.

"What should we do?" several trusted men ask.

"Be ready to act," I say. But we still lack resolve on Tahiti.

Back onboard and already lovelorn many of us become more distraught when Bligh blisters us with insults and flogs another man to death and cuts our water rations so his breadfruit trees can flourish.

"That's it," I whisper individually to seventeen good men.

"Tomorrow morning, we take over."

At the propitious moment I signal to arm ourselves with muskets, swords, and clubs.

"Captain Bligh," I say, "you'll be given greater consideration than many of our comrades."

"Lieutenant Christian, this is mutiny, punishable by death."

"Continuing with you in command would anyway lead to our deaths. Men, those who believe that Captain Bligh is a tyrant who's forfeited his right to command this ship, step over here and join us. Otherwise, go stand with the departing captain."

Twenty-one men, brave I readily concede, surround their deposed and shaken leader.

"Into the lifeboat, Captain," I order. "You'll be given a little food and water and a few necessities of navigation."

"Christian, you'll hang for this, you and the rest of the filthy traitors."

In addition to his fine acting, I sense real animosity.

"Captain, I told you to enter the boat. Or die on this deck."

Bligh shakes his fist at me and says, "I'll die in my bed in England. All of you better remember. There's nowhere a better seaman than I."

The man's competence is indisputable and I want him opposing me neither on the high seas or a movie set. I order that the *Bounty* sail forthwith back to Tahiti where we pick up ten women, including Maimiti, and supplies and eight comrades and six male Tahitians and sail away to look for a home where the Royal Navy won't find us. A couple hundred miles to the south we land on gorgeous Tubuao, glowing green and every shade of blue, but within a fortnight the natives resist our superior customs and authority and we barely escape.

"Men," I announce, "we're sailing far to the east."

Some fourteen hundred miles away we see small Pitcarin Island and our on-land reconnaissance reveals it to be green and hospitable and currently uninhabited. I ask what would Captain Bligh do. We agree he'd crash the *Bounty* close to shore and float as many supplies as possible to our new but eternally isolated home and then he'd burn the *Bounty*.

That's where the original script ends but, during a final discussion between executives and leading actors, Captain Bligh says, "We need to go on for perhaps fifteen minutes. There's so much more, isn't there, Lieutenant Christian?"

"I like endings that make the audience happy."

"Come now, Christian, don't you want to show everyone how you try to enslave your celibate Tahitian comrades and they either shoot or stab or stone you and all your fellow criminals save one, and I as a master seaman do in fact travel nearly four thousand miles to Timor, and then England, and send the Royal Navy to Tahiti where the worst of the scoundrels you left behind are returned home to be hanged or imprisoned, and I do breathe my last in a warm London bed surrounded by my wife and seven children. I suspect your lady and three infants didn't bid you such a graceful farewell."

"I myself am quite alive, Captain Bligh, and ready to remind our crew that you'll face more mutinies including one in which several hundred soldiers arrest your hateful ass."

As Bligh leers at me I lean to director Frank Lloyd and say, "I'm never working with that bastard again."

Notes: Charles Laughton plays Captain Bligh opposite the Fletcher Christian of dynamic young Clark Gable in *Mutiny on the Bounty*.

In Love

I'm not going back to Cadiz, Ohio or Akron or Tulsa or any other lousy place where I farmed and worked in oilfields and lots of other unpleasant stuff. I like it here in the Northwest even though the only acting work's in the boonies for damn little dough. I appreciate Josephine Dillon telling me I have potential and taking time from managing a theater in Portland to teach me how to act, speak, and walk on stage. One evening after lots of practice, she brushes my hair with her hand and says, "We've got to send you to the right barber and a good dentist."

"I can't pay for all that."

"Don't worry," she says.

She hugs me and I kiss her cheek.

Anyone who says I'm marrying Josephine to use her, I'll punch him in the mouth. I'm marrying for love. I'm twenty-three and she's forty when we move to Hollywood and she manages my career and helps make me advance. I do all right in some minor silent film roles until Josephine says we better head to Broadway where everyone can feel what I offer. I admit I'm amazed when ladies go crazy for me and critics write that whatever I may lack dramatically I replace with raw masculinity.

"Clark, do you really consider this a marriage?" Josephine asks.

"Well, sure. Don't you?"

"Not with you screwing everyone but me."

She tries to embrace me but I step back and say, "I can't help it."

I don't have any hard feelings when we separate and divorce, and don't think Josephine does, either. I've fallen pretty hard for Ria Langham, a stylish socialite from Texas. I like most people but make it clear I don't want to hear jokes about Gable marrying another woman seventeen years older. What does age matter? I learn it matters a lot when we return to Hollywood and I get starring roles opposite Joan Crawford and Greta Garbo and Marion Davies and Loretta Young and lots of others on and off screen. Life gets even more exciting when I win the Oscar for *It Happened One Night* with Claudette Colbert.

"I want you home earlier at night," Ria says.

"I work late to pay your bills."

"There's going to be trouble next time you stay out all night."

"I'll give you a divorce any time you want. How about today?"

"I'll never grant you one."

"I'm moving out."

"It will cost you a fortune," she says.

"Delightful."

"Please don't leave, Clark."

Ria doesn't understand. Carole Lombard's waiting for me. I can't control my love for this gorgeous blond actress who cusses and jokes and treats everyone well even though she makes more money than anyone in town. She even goes hunting with me and enjoys sleeping outdoors or in dirty old cabins without electricity or plumbing. She calls me Pa and I call her Ma and we're the most admired couple in the country, except President Roosevelt and Eleanor. Once I make enough in *Gone with the Wind* to get a divorce, Ma and I buy a ranch in Encino in the valley not far from Hollywood, and we raise horses and chickens and decorate our home with guns and photos and plenty of leather so everyone knows vigorous outdoor people live here.

We're having Sunday breakfast at the ranch on December seventh when news arrives the Japanese have attacked Pearl Harbor. I'm plenty upset but Carole's a whole lot madder and says, "We're going to do everything possible to win this war."

A few days later she says, "Pa, you should join the army right away. I'll help by selling war bonds."

"I'm forty-one. I can't join the army."

"They can't draft you, but you could join."

"There are other ways I can contribute."

"I'll write President Roosevelt," she says.

I don't expect the president to have time but am happy he responds that Ma and I and our friends in the movie business should continue to do what we've been doing, entertaining people in these difficult times.

"President Roosevelt's right, honey," I say.

"You can't just go on being a movie hero. You're no better than the guys who'll be fighting for our country."

"I'm no better, but I'm a helluva lot older."

She marches to the rifle rack and reaches for a gun. I grab an arm and spin her around, and put a finger in her face. "Don't get smart with me. You don't know a damn thing about war."

"And I suppose you do."

"I'll do my part, and right now that's making a helluva movie for the public."

"And what would that be? *Somewhere I'll Find You* with Lana Turner…"

"We clicked before and this time will be even better."

"Don't click too well."

I know Ma's proud of me when I'm named chairman of the Screen Actors Division of the Hollywood Victory Committee. People seem excited I'm involved, and we're going to raise a lot of money.

One afternoon at the Ranch Ma runs up to me just as I've mounted my horse. "Did you hear? They changed the draft law. Now men between twenty and forty-four are eligible."

"That's swell," I say. "Some of the brass at MGM have been talking to me about a special assignment."

She tightens her brow and says, "There'll be no phony commissions for you, Pa."

"Giddyup," I tell my horse.

In early January I'm proud Carole's going to headline fundraisers for war bonds in Indianapolis, not far from where she was born. All of us on the set are worried there's a war in the Pacific and in Europe, too, and we're trying hard to make good movies.

"Wonder why you're working so many hours lately," Ma says.

"I'm not interested in Lana, if that's what you mean."

"Then maybe it's that other little floozy. What's her name?"

"I don't know."

"Can't remember them all, Pa?"

"You're talking nonsense."

Ma leaves the Los Angeles train station on January twelfth but I'm not there to send her off. I had to get away and feel bad as hell about it and want to call her and make sure we're all right but there's no way to do that. Thank goodness she calls me every stop on the way to Indiana and I'm trying to figure what the hell was I thinking? This is the most wonderful, dependable, sexy woman in the world.

"God, I love you, Ma," I tell her every time.

"Yeah, but not as much as I love you."

I'm lonely back at our ranch but thrilled when the nation learns Ma looked beautiful, spoke passionately, and charmed everyone as she raised two million bucks at her war bond rallies in Indianapolis. No one's approached that. I don't think anyone will.

"I can't take a slow train to see you, Pa," she calls. "I'm flying home today."

"That's wonderful, sweetheart."

I decorate the house and invite a few guests and on the night of the sixteenth am excited she'll soon arrive at the Burbank airport after several stops across the country.

"Can't talk now," I tell a guy from the studio who calls.

"King, it looks like her plane disappeared just after takeoff. We've got to go to Las Vegas right away. I'll drive you to the airport."

When we get to Vegas I see a terrible glow in the mountains but can't stop looking and wishing it was me up there. A few days later we bury Ma in Los Angeles, and all I've got is an empty house full of booze I drink more than ever as I turn on our projector and watch my wife playfully kick John Barrymore as she becomes a star and try to hire wealthy William Powell as her butler and tell Jack Benny he's a prima donna who'd want to be the mother if he ever had a kid. She's wonderful in every role and even better at home. I know I'll spend the rest of my life looking for the impossible. I go into the Army Air Forces and train with vigorous guys half my age and hope the commanders will let me be a gunner or at least photograph what happens in battles in the sky and maybe I won't have to miss Ma much longer.

The Final Scene

It must be one-ten in the shade out here in this blasted desert near Reno and the stars and crew are sweating when Arthur Miller, sitting in his wife's unairconditioned trailer, says, "Did you have to degrade me?"

"I was more interested in Yves Montand than you, Arthur, and everyone knew it. Besides, he's back with his wife, and *The Misfits* is a new movie. Pass the champagne."

"No more for you today or ever."

"I'll drink as much as I want," she says, opening her purse to get a bottle of prescription pills several of which she washes down with champagne from the bottle she reaches around Miller to grab.

"You're destroying our marriage, Marilyn."

"We don't have a marriage anymore, Arthur. I'm moving to another hotel after work."

"You're also ruining yourself. You care about that, don't you?"

"Not really," she says.

The writer dejectedly steps into the sun and director John Huston, tall and majestically gray, walks to Miller and says, "How is she?"

"Worse every day."

"Arthur, I try not judge, since my own domestic affairs have generally been scandalous, but I think you should prepare yourself, and probably are already doing so. Marilyn is doomed. She's always been fragile but now she's irretrievably broken. I'm sorry."

Miller looks out into the desert. Huston slaps his shoulder and says, "Why don't you come into Reno with me tonight? There'll be plenty of booze, broads, and gambling to help you forget."

After adjusting his glasses, Miller says, "No thank you, John."

Huston approaches the crew and says, "Let's do a scene that Marilyn's not in."

It's already hot by ten the next morning at another location and everyone's waiting in the meager shade of a few downtrodden trees. Clark Gable steps out of earshot and with a glance summons Huston.

"What's wrong with that girl? When I started out, they fired people who showed up late even once. Marilyn's late every day if she shows up at all."

"It's irritating, Clark, but we need her to finish the movie."

"For the few grand a week she's getting, Paula Strasberg should coach Marilyn about good manners."

Marilyn arrives about two that afternoon in a car driven by Arthur Miller. He walks to Huston and whispers and the men take a short walk. "I worked on the script most of the night. She didn't seem interested when I picked her up this morning."

Marilyn stumbles over most of her lines but Huston, Gable, and Montgomery Clift don't complain. At the end of the day, Huston tells the two actors, "I want you guys to watch some of last week's rushes with me. Marilyn's really good. Both of you are, too. Our suffering will be worth it."

That night Marilyn invites Clift to her new hotel room. He enters looking more haunted than his hostess.

"Monty, I understand you aren't attracted to people like me but I want you to know you're a brilliant actor and I wish you liked me."

"I like you, Marilyn, but not in a romantic way."

"Just like with Elizabeth Taylor."

Clift, still handsome but marred after serious facial injuries in an auto accident several years earlier, looks down and wistfully says, "That's right."

Marilyn steps up and hugs him. "Let's have a drink."

"You have any tranquilizers?"

"Of course."

In the morning both fail to report to the set on time and after a couple of hours Gable, his face bloated and lined by years of heavy drinking and smoking, motions to Huston to step aside. "This damn waiting around is gonna kill me."

"Relax, Clark, we shoot the final scene tomorrow, you and Marilyn riding off happily in the pickup truck you're driving."

"I hope I don't look too old to romance a young lady."

After completion of shooting Huston says, "Clark, come on over to my hotel room tonight."

Gable shows up on time and they watch a lot of footage.

"Isn't she marvelous?" Huston says.

"She sure is. I don't know how she looks so pretty and delivers enough moments of magic to complete a picture, but she does."

Smiling gap-toothed and confidently, Huston looks several seconds at Gable. "And you also did a wonderful job. I think this is the best work of your career."

"Really?"

"Absolutely," says the director.

"You may be right."

Two days later Huston receives a call from Kay, Gable's wife. She's at a hospital near their ranch in Encino.

"Clark's had a heart attack."

"I'm very sorry, Kay. How is he?"

"Stable for now, but I'm just so worried about him, and our baby's due in four months."

"I'm confident everything will work out all right. Let me know if I can help."

Notes: Ten days later another heart attack, this one massive, killed Clark Gable before he turned sixty. Marilyn survived a year and a half, until age thirty-six, and that may have been longer than she preferred. Montgomery Clift struggled with physical and mental ailments until dying when he was forty-five. Arthur Miller and John Huston lived long lives. The *Misfits*, ironically titled and in edgy black and white, is more highly regarded today than in its time.

Gable on the Links

On a sweltering afternoon in the early sixties I'm standing on the green of a Sacramento public golf course and preparing to line up my putt when I glance right of the green at the maintenance man carrying a long sprinkler head. He's sweating and looks tired and gray like Clark Gable did before dying a couple of years earlier. Every second I'm more amazed at the resemblance. This guy's got star power too.

"Hey, hurry up and putt," says Joe.

I ignore Joe and the other guys in our foursome and watch the man, in a soiled khaki uniform, push the sprinkler into the ground, and walk toward his little tractor and trailer.

"Are you gonna putt?" says Joe.

"Look at that guy," I say.

"What about him?"

"He's a dead ringer for Gable."

"You've got sunstroke."

"Sir," I shout. "Just a minute, please."

He ignores me and steps onto his tractor.

"Sir, Clark, Clark Gable, please hold on."

I drop my putter and run toward the man who starts his little tractor and slowly moves away. Running hard in the heat I soon catch up, moving right up to him, and say, "Damn, this is unbelievable."

Looking straight ahead, he says, "Get lost, kid."

"But I thought you passed away."

"You're crazy."

"Okay, let's call the newspaper. Let's call your wife and friends in Los Angeles."

He keeps driving his little tractor, headed for the next fairway.

THE DOUGLAS BOYS

The Third Kominsky Season

Did you see the first two seasons of *The Kominsky Method*? Hell of a Netflix miniseries like two or three long movies good as anything I've seen. And I'm not saying that because my son Michael Douglas stars in and executive produces the project. I give plenty of credit to the rest of the cast and screenwriting team led by Chuck Lorre.

I love the start when Michael steps unshaven before his class and says actors make believe and pretend but really what they're doing is playing God and not for fame or money but love of their characters. Naturally, and I tell you this based on my own many delectable experiences, there'll be ladies rewarding you if they like your work, and Michael starts dating pretty student Nancy Travis who's only about fifteen years younger and that's more age appropriate than plenty he's known.

I should've told Michael to be careful or the sharp wit of Alan Arkin could steal the show. Alan's got a living wife who's dying and then a dead wife who sometimes reappears and Lisa Edelstein, a drug-addicted, thieving daughter in her forties and a couple nice ladies after his affection but they're already rich and not interested in his loot only outraged by his razor tongue. Alan slices everyone up, telling Michael he sure is peeing a lot. His urologist diagnoses an enlarged prostate and the biopsy reveals a few cancer cells but nothing that requires surgery or radiation. Just take Flomax to sooth the prostate and don't worry about those retro-ejaculations that, rather than erupt, sink into the bladder.

Maintaining tension and humor the writers show poor Lisa Edelstein newly arrived at her eighth rehab facility and already chasing Michael and Alan as they drive away. A little later I just don't believe my son would, as shown, fail to call blond Nancy for a week after their first time in bed. He's not irresponsible.

Financially, he better be careful. He and his acting school are three hundred grand in debt to the IRS and he asks Alan for a loan and offers to pay a thousand a month. Alan isn't worried about the money. He doesn't want to destroy his relationship with best friend Michael. Okay, he'll do it if Michael accepts the money as a gift and moves on. At their next lunch Michael writes a check for a grand and Alan flips it over and endorses it to the delighted waiter.

There's a lot more to the first season but I've got to move to the second and Michael's warning that ninety percent of the Screen Actors Guild is unemployed and most of the eager students before him will also end up that way. Michael's daughter and business partner Sarah Baker wants him to meet her boyfriend Paul Reiser, who's older. That's good, a little older means a lot more mature, Michael observes. Actually, this guy's in his sixties and twice as old as Sarah but they're in love.

More good news arrives with Lisa returning from rehab clean and sober and she likes her dad's current old flame, Jane Seymour, but the sophisticated lady resents his bad manners and subsequently freezes him on the phone. Meanwhile, Michael has implausibly given Nancy the ultimatum of student or lover but not both, so she now tells him no sex. Happily, a generous serving of wine resolves that problem.

Good fortune ceases when Paul, after bloating from gaseous meat in a restaurant and being verbally carved by Alan, is felled by a heart attack and taken to the hospital where bypass surgery is performed. Michael, who's battled and beaten tongue cancer off screen, now has to undergo cinematic immune-therapy for a cancerous spot on his lungs. The doctors think they've found it early. Octogenarian Alan, at least, has some good fortune when lady Jane gives him a call.

Michael collapses at home and Sarah, who's checking on him, sees a bloody face when he opens the door. What the hell? He confesses he has lung cancer but refuses to live with her and Paul. He remains adamantly independent even after he collapses in Nancy's bedroom. She decides to sell her home and move away. Michael desperately proposes but she isn't convinced. Like a vulture Sarah strikes, telling her father he's erratic and she intends to bring in working actors to strengthen the curriculum. The first guest is arrogant Allison Janney who barks all Michael's done is plaster his name on a window while she's won an Oscar. Who would the students rather have? Michael learns they want her.

I don't know what Chuck Lorre and those other writers are doing. And where the hell's Michael? Okay, you guys relax and stay safe. Ole Kirk will write the third season. Allison Janney doesn't have time to teach but since she implies she does I put her in the classroom where, tall and geeky, she berates rather than instructs and soon faces an academic – and almost physical – insurrection. She says you'll all be failures before storming out. Michael tells Sarah, go ahead, you run the damn school, but she can't deliver many stars and none for more than one evening class.

I didn't mention that in part two Michael signed over the school to Sarah. Sounds crazy but we have to understand he's a septuagenarian with an achy prostate and cancerous lung. But he ain't dead. He demands Sarah tear up the contract he wrote under medical and psychological duress exacerbated by the aforementioned difficulties. She refuses. He calls Alan Arkin to find out who's the best lawyer for this kind of case. Alan gives him the name of an expensive operator Michael can't afford. Okay, he says, I'll give you half the proceeds from the litigation.

What proceeds, asks the attorney? There won't be any.

Sarah's attendance is in the tank and she'll soon have to shutter the school. Come on, Sarah, get real, Michael says. She agrees. School's more efficient and fun when he's there and Sarah needs a stable relationship with her father. Her boyfriend Paul, who's hefty, suffers a second heart attack and is dead before he hits the boards of the stage at the acting school, where he's been studying.

Alan Arkin's got to be eighty-six but he's thin and tough and I've already torn up his letter of resignation after the second season. He survives to get another call from Jane Seymour and that's enough to motivate most men. She moves into his Beverly Hills mansion and they frequently travel to her three homes and have a good time.

Jacked up on Viagra or Cialis or perhaps both, Michael makes love to Nancy and points to Alan and Jane as people who should be their role models. Nancy, continuing to be kind, stable, and sensual, agrees to reside with Michael but not marry him. As a precaution, she proceeds with the sale of her home and banks twice what she paid. She also starts getting jobs in the growing advertising market for striking middle-aged actresses. Michael's delighted. He coaches her. She listens. After each commercial, he critiques. She tells him he's her boyfriend not her director. She's got several of those. Michael agrees. His cancer treatments, though not as debilitating as chemotherapy, are nonetheless taxing and he downshifts. After all, even Alan has retired.

During a happy sojourn to one of Jane's estates, Alan receives a call from police. I know, I know, he says.

Did someone already call you, the officer asks?

It's my daughter, right.

The officer explains Lisa has relapsed on several drugs, sold most of the furnishings in his home, and left town with two drug dealers, one of whom perished with Lisa in a high speed chase on Highway 1 south of Santa Barbara.

Alan loves his daughter but also hates her so we must assume his decline is due to age and he simply doesn't respond one sunny morning when Jane says, Alan, wake up, please wake up.

There's nothing more in L.A. for Jane and she departs to places we know nothing about.

I guess it's up to me to decide who gets Alan's millions. I've got his will right here. It says Lisa will get half of everything if she's living a sober and responsible life. Otherwise, Michael gets a quarter and medical science receives the rest.

Michael keeps teaching and, encouraged by Sarah, once or twice a month hires a working actor to address the class and do whatever, if any, dramatic exercises are deemed helpful. Sarah continues to be an assistant and business partner rather than a rival to her father. I give her a couple of scenes bookkeeping and using phone and email to set appointments for guest lecturers.

Michael and Nancy make a charming couple and are still together as the curtain drops.

Spartacus

Kirk Douglas enters an office where Dalton Trumbo stands, points at him, and says, "I am Spartacus."

"You're a helluva writer, Dalton, but I'm Spartacus."

"You will be, when the cameras start rolling. Until then, I'm molding a better man."

"We already agreed on the script you delivered," says Douglas.

Trumbo sits and motions for Douglas to do likewise. "Kirk," he says, "we shouldn't be melodramatic here. We can make a statement."

Placing forearms on knees and leaning forward, Douglas aims his cleft chin between Trumbo's eyes. "We're not preachers, Dalton. We're moviemakers."

"We must change history and make Spartacus and his men less violent. Otherwise, we're no better than the Romans."

Douglas nods. "And after my men loot, I warn them, 'We're becoming drunken sailors.'"

"But we're letting them remain so."

"What do you suggest?"

Dalton Trumbo rises, walks to a large wall map, and hammers Rome. "Here's the last place we should go."

"It's the heart of Roman power."

"Precisely. We can't defeat the Roman Empire with a band of slaves."

"We're compelled to try."

"Why?" asks Trumbo.

"Dramatic destiny."

"How about some common sense? After our escape and victories, we could easily head north, over the Alps, and into Gaul. We could survive."

"The Romans would pursue us."

"Not in anything like the numbers we'll face en route to Rome," Trumbo says.

Douglas gets up and moves to the map, stabbing Rome with his index finger. "We're attacking the tyrants."

"Your real goal is to rob, rape, and kill."

"That's not even in the script, Dalton."

"Only because the Romans will crush you first."

"Listen, since you're interested in being so realistic, you pay to make a movie about a bunch of roughnecks who run from the Romans and slaughter thousands of vulnerable people in Gaul."

"I can make it much more uplifting than that."

Gripping two fists in front of his muscular chest, Douglas says, "I am Spartacus, the producer, and ready to lose a vast battle to the Romans and be captured and crucified where my beautiful lady, our baby in her arms, will come and beg me to die. That's the brilliant way you wrote it, Dalton, and why Joseph McCarthy and his red-chasing phonies were so afraid. You know how to move people."

Avoiding Fatal Attraction

In my righteous hand I hold the script of the satanic movie *Fatal Attraction* and today emphasize the horrific events were only hammered onto paper as an exercise in cinematic fantasy and not meant to traumatize real people. I'm certain our nightmares will linger until I, the remorseful director, reshape reality by compelling Michael Douglas to make more prudent decisions which original screenwriter James Dearden, who's recording this conversation in an adjoining room, will fashion in a way that spares our sensibilities.

"Michael," I say, "couldn't you see that Glenn Close was edgy and likely unhinged from the start."

"Look, I was a horny guy whose wife was out of town. Going home with her seemed low risk."

"I certainly wouldn't have done that."

"Are you sure?" Douglas asks.

"I am, indeed."

"You get many hot offers like that?"

"That's not the point. At any rate, you certainly should've been alarmed about her wild sexual behavior, kissing you so frenetically in her elevator and then stopping it between floors so she could fellate you."

"Based on what I knew and felt at that moment, I can't see any changes there."

I adjust my thick glasses. "You should've bailed out when she called you at home and said she didn't like it when she woke up and you were gone."

"I agree with you there," says Douglas. "But what happens to the movie if I don't meet her in the park and bang her again in her apartment?"

"We're worried about lessening pain, not maximizing drama. Maybe we could instead focus on your law practice."

"That's not very exciting."

"It's better than what happens," I say. "She's outraged to learn you're married."

"I told her she's terrific, but I've got a family."

"She doesn't like that or the way 'you run away every time' you make love."

"What does she expect?" Douglas asks.

"After she starts crying and clinging to you, I'd have expected you to call it off."

"Okay, but she slashed her wrists. I had to help."

"If you'd walked out the door she would've died and that would've been the end," I say.

"But with more than half the movie to go."

I place my chin in one hand and think. "Though I disagree with the sin of adultery, we've got to find you another girlfriend."

"I guess we could've done that, but where's the tension? What's going to keep the audience hooked?"

"You don't need a series of obsessive and psychotic girlfriends to keep people interested."

In professorial style, Douglas says, "When the name of the picture is *Fatal Attraction,* I need at least one."

"All right, we must change the name of the film."

"We're too far in for that," says Douglas.

"I'm simply trying to make things less difficult for you. There she sat in your office, waiting for you to return from house hunting in the country. It's sad when this woman apologizes for upsetting you and invites you to a play."

"I told her it wasn't a good idea. That's as well as I could've handled it."

"I've got it. You can tell her she's obsessive and needs help. They've got some wonderful psychotropic medications."

Nodding, Douglas says, "Put that in. Maybe she won't call me at work and force me to tell her I can't talk to her anymore and I'm sorry if I've inadvertently misled her."

"We really should have this woman committed."

"On what grounds? I couldn't have done that even after she called me late at night and demanded an immediate meeting to claim she was pregnant and warn me to 'play fair' with her."

"We've got to intervene, Michael. Get a restraining order."

"Because a woman calls to tell me I've got her pregnant? Plus, she'd tell my wife."

"The latter doesn't matter, under the circumstances," I say.

Pointing at me, Douglas says, "As an attorney, I'm telling you we can't legally touch her so far. I couldn't have done anything even after I came home and found her pretending to be an apartment hunter talking to my wife who tells her where we'll be moving outside the city."

"I cringed when she told your wife she's pregnant. But you aggravated her the way you stormed over to her apartment."

"No matter what, she would've accused me of treating her like a slut and threatened to tell my wife."

"But you threatened to kill her if she told."

"Maybe I should've killed her."

"You'd have gone to prison."

"That's all that saved her," he says.

"You should've called the police when she burned up your car engine."

"I couldn't prove she did it."

"Why didn't you show the police the tape she sent you?" I ask. "You could've proved she was dangerous, yelling, 'you're a cocksucking son of a bitch… I hate you… faggot.'"

"The police would've questioned her but there's still no proof she torched my car."

"Michael, a little candor on your part and the police would've had to lean on her."

Screenwriter James Dearden shoves open the adjacent office door, knocking it into the wall, and shouts, "You unmitigated morons. It's too damn late to make major changes. You'll only increase suffering. We're sticking to what I wrote. She sneaks in and boils your family's pet rabbit, forcing Michael to confess to his wife. I'm certainly not taking out my line when Michael calls Glenn and tells her he confessed to his wife who takes the phone, identifies herself, and says, 'If you ever come near my family again, I'll kill you.'"

"We need to stop her now," I insist. "Otherwise, she's going to basically kidnap your kid at school and take her to an amusement park and upset your wife so much she rear ends someone and has to be hospitalized."

"You're right," says Douglas, looking at me before he glances at James Dearden. "What the hell else can I do but break into her home, fight with her, and frankly almost get my ass kicked before I choke her. I should've continued. She damn near killed me with that knife. After disarming her I should've stabbed her. In fact, that's what I'm going to do."

"You're not going to destroy my classic final scene," Dearden states. "Just like I wrote it, the police aren't going to find her, and you, Michael, are finally going to notice water from the upstairs bathroom come through the ceiling into the living room and you're going to sprint up there to stop Glenn from stabbing your wife and you're going to drown her in the bathtub and think she's dead but she's not and she's going to jump up and attack you and your wife's going to shoot her."

"This whole thing is crazy and dangerous," I say.

"How crazy is making three hundred million bucks," says Douglas.

"Maybe it'll be worth it," I say.

LAURENCE OLIVIER

General Patton Lectures Olivier

I could've delivered this rebuke in my underwear but of course donned my bemedalled uniform and a pearl-handled pistol on each hip before I shouted, "Attention, Olivier. Other than a coward in battle the last outrage on earth I'll tolerate is a ham on a movie set."

"You must forgive me, General Patton, for reminding you that I'm immeasurably more experienced in matters of stagecraft and moviemaking."

"I'm not impugning your talent or experience, I'm decrying your woeful performance, as well as that of Gregory Peck, in *The Boys from Brazil.* Moviegoers thought they were paying to see a mortal showdown between Dr. Josef Mengele, sadistic dissector of children at Auschwitz, and a character based on that intrepid hunter of Nazis, Simon Wiesenthal.

"Instead, what do we get? You and Peck squawk at each other in the most ridiculous Germanic English yet spoken. What the hell were you two fools thinking? You should've known, at least after the rushes, that when you wanted to be serious you were funny. Maybe that's it. Mengele and Wiesenthal were creating a comedy."

Still upright and stiff, Laurence Olivier says, "I perhaps should've spoken to the director, General Patton, but my health has been quite bad for a decade and I spend all emotional resources on my roles and young wife and our three children."

I point my riding whip at the aging actor. "You wouldn't have had to storm the beaches of Normandy, for God's sake. All you had to do was remind director Franklin J. Schaffner he'd had the honor to direct me as General Patton. I delivered everything in good tough American English."

"But you were an American actor portraying an American general."

"That's my point, Olivier. Be who you really are. You're an English speaker. Speak English and let your acting determine character. I would've court-martialed the lot of you and locked up Schaffner without a trial. And James Mason, too. Can you tell me why that formerly fine actor evidently forgot that a quarter century earlier he'd spoken English in his native British accent when portraying General

Rommel in *The Desert Fox?* Now he's as idiotic as you and Gregory Peck.

"Didn't you understand that after two hours of absurd speaking the climactic scene would be burlesque. It should've been a classic: Simon Wiesenthal battling Dr. Josef Mengele, eternal good versus unmitigated evil. Instead, I laughed as four Doberman Pinchers mauled Peck while you wrestled on the living room floor and shot each other and bled all over and continued to speak like Teutonic buffoons. And who's present for this high drama? The genetic Adolf Hitler as an Anglicized child. What a farce."

Olivier raises a slender hand from which he unsteadily wags a bony finger. "Enough, General Patton. You who had overwhelming advantages in men and material against an exhausted and surrounded German nation, you who slapped a mentally torn soldier, you who unlike George C. Scott had a high effeminate voice are not qualified to speak to me in that matter.

"Are you suffering from dementia or did you carefully neglect to mention that just two years earlier, in *Marathon Man*, I portrayed a Mengele-like Auschwitz dentist seeking to retrieve diamonds I'd purchased with gold I stole from the teeth of my Holocaust victims. And I played the role in subdued but otherwise straight English."

"I commend you for that, Olivier, and assume the director and screenwriter also merit praise for letting you explain you had certain linguistic characteristics enabling you to speak without a Germanic accent. I accepted the explanation, which really wasn't needed. When I played the Duce in *Mussolini: The Untold Story*, I spoke like a gruff Benito C. Scott. Or, when caressing my mistress and soothing my wife and children, I did so in dignified English that implied Italian intimacy."

The Right Cuts

I really shouldn't be upset. No one forces me to watch the current version of *Marathon Man.* I rather expect, more than forty years since starring in the movie and thirty after my demise, that filmmakers and the industry will be less barbaric than during my twilight period. Instead, they – the anonymous censors – snip away some delightful scenes of my drilling raw nerves in the teeth of Dustin Hoffman as he sits bound in my diabolical dental chair.

No actor wants to see his fine work swept up and tossed under the lid of an antiseptic metal wastebasket. And I must tell you, I cherish even pretending to send electrical agony through the mouth and brain of my fellow thespian who for three days has arrived on the set unbathed, hollow-eyed, and manic.

"Whatever is the matter with you, dear boy?" I ask.

"I've been starving myself and staying up all night to get ready for these scenes."

"Why don't you simply try acting?"

That's where most accounts stop. In fact, Dustin continues, "I make my scenes realistic, not like your dated and bombastic bullshit."

"You're a sniveling little boy far too much like the characters he plays."

"In fifty years I'll still be celebrated," he says. "You'll be irrelevant."

"Get in the highchair, method actor, and let history determine whom it prefers."

I want to throttle the little bastard or at least storm off the set. Other than my former wife, Vivien Leigh, no one but Marilyn Monroe has publicly spoken to me so disrespectfully. Alas, my electric drill isn't plugged in – the motorized sound being elsewhere generated – but I clang Dustin's upper incisors and say, "Oops, I'm so very sorry."

He never does answer sensitive questions about diamonds I'd long ago stolen from Holocaust victims, but I'm able to nervously reclaim them from a safety deposit box. I cannot blame subsequent dramatic imperfections on Dustin. It's director Franklin Schaffner who gets swept away by emotion when I enter a Manhattan jewelry store to learn the approximate value of my gems. It seems destined when a store employee, one of my Auschwitz victims, notices me at the jewelry case. The old man, unsure at first, figures out who I am and follows outside as I hastily walk away. Credibility weakens when yet a second victim, an elderly woman, spies me and begins stalking and denouncing me from the other side of the street until she tries to cross and a car hits her. The old man soon catches me but I slash his throat with the long knife lurking in my coat sleeve. One confrontation would've been poignant. Two almost prompted a chuckle.

In the ultimate scene Dustin, his teeth no doubt throbbing, enjoys pointing a gun and throwing my briefcase of diamonds at me, sending many into water below our subterranean service bridge. He insists I also eat the diamonds. I resist but finally swallow one before moving toward Dustin who clumsily drops his gun. I would've stabbed him but he throws the diamonds into water and in a panic I fall down winding steel steps and immolate myself.

When viewing this climax I'm not quite as moved as expected because the lingering slash of the old man's throat should be reduced, and the old woman and her sudden demise need to be altogether excised, leaving the old man to confront me. How shall I overcome him and thus proceed to my showdown with Dustin Hoffman? Very well, with only one death camp victim, I suppose it will be all right to let me rip the dear boy.

JOHN WAYNE

Searching for John Wayne

Hell, I should've written this more than sixty years ago when it was okay to say I like good whiskey and Latin women and they're part Indian so don't call me a racist killer, as some film historians have, because in *The Searchers* I do what any rugged pioneer would.

I know what you're going to say: I'm bigoted as hell from the start since I fought for the Confederacy before heading out West. Plenty of people died for the South and their way of life. Yeah, a lot of that was based on slavery but that was how they did things, and you weren't there so don't be too sure what you would've done. You don't know, Pilgrim.

Out in Texas the Comanches attack and kill my brother and sister-in-law and nephew and kidnap my two nieces. Damn right I go after them and get even madder when I find the oldest niece dead and no doubt raped in a canyon. Debbie, the younger niece, isn't even a woman yet, but when she is, if not before, I know what they'll do to her. While searching we find another family that was kidnapped and they're still alive but their minds are gone and I tell my men, "They ain't white anymore."

We know who's murdered my family. It's the Comanche chief Scar and his warriors. A few years later we find Scar and I tell him, "You speak pretty good American, for a Comanch. Someone teach-yuh?'" and he says, "You speak pretty good Comanch. Someone teach you?"

We enter his teepee, where his four wives huddle, and he tells us white men killed his two sons and he took many scalps for each one and orders one wife, my niece Debbie, to rise and display a lance with some of those scalps. She's now a beautiful woman dressed as an Indian. I can't do anything now so make a camp nearby.

In a little while Debbie comes running down a sandy hill, pretending to understand only Comanche before switching to English and telling her stepbrother, "These are my people." She can't go home with us. I draw my pistol and say, "Stand aside." I'd rather see her dead. Her stepbrother jumps between us but before I figure out how to handle this an Indian shoots me with an arrow from behind and the stepbrother and I escape on horseback, killing lots of Comanches with six-guns that never run out of bullets.

Debbie was my only living kin but she's gone and I try to bequeath my property to her stepbrother but he says keep it because I'm a rotten man who tried to kill her. He doesn't understand I was right because she'd "been living with a buck." Later on, when we get word that Scar and his killers are nearby, we make plans with the regional captain. Debbie's stepbrother warns not to charge or they'll kill her.

"That's what I'm countin' on," I tell him. "Living with Comanches ain't being alive.... One of those scalps on that lance was your mother's."

He insists on going in alone and quiet and finds Debbie sleeping in a teepee. She screams before understanding who he is. Scar must've heard and approaches the teepee from the rear where the stepbrother kills him with a straight shot. The cavalry and I attack and I find Scar's corpse, grab his hair, and take out my knife. Back on my horse, carrying the bloody scalp, I see Debbie who thinks I'm still trying to kill her and she runs till she falls and I ride in, dismount, and lift her over my head and then carry her like a baby as I warmly say, "Let's go home, Debbie."

Some think *The Searchers* is based on the kidnapping of Cynthia Ann Parker whose life mirrored Debbie's except Cynthia didn't want to return. I guess people who believe that would've liked to see Debbie resist, grab my knife, and kill me. I guarantee that wouldn't have been a happy ending for most of the nation but I reckon for some it would've brought war cries.

Notes: The screenplay for this nuanced John Wayne western was written by Frank S. Nugent and directed by John Ford, Wayne's frequent collaborator.

The Man Who Shot Him

"Listen, there's nothing wrong with Tom Doniphon."

"Sure, Duke, I know," says Jimmy Stewart. "He's a great guy."

"I don't mind you getting the girl, Jimmy. But I don't like the way people are saying Tom was disturbed. He couldn't have been. I played him like I've played a hundred characters."

Jimmy smiles. "That's right. You played Tom Doniphon tough as all the others."

"So what're they saying, Jimmy?"

"Well, Duke, people were wondering why this big heroic guy was still single in his mid-fifties."

He points at the world and says, "Are they saying I played a queer?"

"No, not that."

"Well, what's the problem?"

"I don't think it's a problem, Duke. It's just a little unusual. We don't know if Tom had girlfriends before Hallie. All that's unsaid."

"Well, they sure know Hallie was my girl till you came to town. And that I was adding a room to my ranch house so she'd be comfortable after we got married."

Jimmy pats Duke on the shoulder and waits a few seconds before he says, "I was wondering why Tom hadn't asked her a lot sooner."

"I kinda wondered that, too. If not for the script, I'd have sealed things long before you came to town."

"No offense, Duke, but she liked you as a friend, not as a husband. She wanted me for that."

"I guess you can thank the loudmouth director, John Ford, for that."

"I didn't have anything to do with how things turned out, you know that," Jimmy says. "You should've been recognized as *The Man Who Shot Liberty Valance.*"

"I probably should've told everyone."

"Something in Tom wanted me to get credit. Then Hallie tended to my wounds and you returned to your ranch and got drunk and burned down her new room."

Duke looks out the window. "People keep asking me, 'What did you do all those years after Jimmy and Hallie left town together?'"

"I think people assume you spent the rest of your life living alone and drinking too much."

"Jimmy, in that situation I might've been drunk but I wouldn't have been alone. I've been bringing in beauties all my life."

"Of course you have, Duke. But not Tom Doniphon, at least not as portrayed."

"I'll take a role like this once in a while but not so often people forget who John Wayne really is."

Notes: On this movie set director John Ford, after robust drinking, sometimes baited the actor about not having fought in World War II.

John Reviews Brokeback Mountain

I haven't had any offers in a long time, and director Ang Lee comes to me and asks if I want to be in a western with lots of action. Damn right, I say. Don't bother showing me the script. Let's just start rehearsing. I tell them I don't care if I play Ennis Del Mar or Jack Twist in *Brokeback Mountain*, so long as I kick his ass more than he kicks mine. You never did and never will see a movie end with my face being used to mop the floor of a saloon. But I certainly can play a sensitive man and don't always have to get the girl.

Ang Lee thinks I'll be perfect for Ennis, who's tougher and more masculine than Jack. That's great. In the rambling order of a movie shoot, I practice beating up two bikers and getting my wife pregnant and want to kiss Jack's wife too but they say that's not in the script. Instead, I wrestle with Jack and fight him and shiver in a blanket outside in the middle of a blizzard. Then I accept his invitation to share his tent so I won't freeze to death. And the son of a bitch kisses me. A man kisses The Duke right on the lips then drops his drawers and moves to all fours and the director says to open my zipper and act like I'm using spit to lubricate you know what. I jump up and kick Jack's bare fanny and then deck the director and run outside into the clean blizzard and climb on a horse and shout I'd rather be dead and ride hell fast down Brokeback Mountain.

At least go see the movie, they holler, and let us know what you think. Listen, one time at a party I chewed out Kirk Douglas for playing a whiny weak and suicidal Vincent van Gogh in *Lust for Life*. I told him real men don't act like that. We as leading men have an obligation to be strong and stoic and tough as hell. I still can't believe Kirk took that role. Imagine what he'd say if I'd done those things on Brokeback Mountain.

Still, I agree to see the movie, otherwise they'll send me back where I was. Disguised by a cap and shades, I slide in the back of a darkened theater. Several people twist anyway and wide-eyed ask aren't you…? Sure, I'm Martha Washington, now turn around and watch the goddamn movie. The scenery in Wyoming is stunning, and I love those mountains so beautiful and harsh and the way the cowboys ride around herding the sheep and eating beans and talking like cowboys almost tough as mine. Then there's that scene in the tent that had set me off. It's less hellacious to watch than be in. I don't enjoy the sight, but I'm not going to lie. I like the tension. I like real emotions. I've made a couple hundred pictures, many of them still damn good, and I understand moviemaking.

Turn around, I tell another lady. I stare her husband back around. The homosexuals in the theater know not to gawk. They're too busy. So am I. The movie starts getting good when Ennis and Jack meet fine horny women. The first night Jack's girl jumps on him in a car and rips off her bra and demands sex right there. The guy responds. Maybe this is going to be a happy movie. Maybe these cowboys are all right after all. Maybe they're going to be cured. That's it. Screwing those girls will make them studs and they won't want that other stuff.

But out of the blue a few years later Jack arranges to visit Ennis, and his wife and two kids, and Ennis runs outside, thinking they're out of sight, and grabs Jack and they start kissing in a way that'll shock most people, especially Ennis' poor wife who sees this and says nothing and doesn't protest when Ennis says they're going drinking and will probably get to talking so don't expect them home that night. The cowboys start taking fishing trips once or twice a year and their wives know what's going on. They never bring back any fish just a bunch of bullshit.

Ennis' wife leaves him and he gets an even prettier girlfriend but that doesn't do any good either. Maybe he wishes he'd accepted Jack's old offer to go off the two of them and get a little ranch. Ennis said he can't do that, he's got kids and responsibilities. And they could get killed. Years before his father had taken the little boy to see the mutilated corpses of a couple of cowboy queers. Ennis knows that could be them. He prefers what he has, child support and loneliness. Jack's got an unhappy wife and asshole father-in-law employer, and a girlfriend and a boyfriend on the side, and all this is damned entertaining, and of course I'm not going to reveal the end but I'll tell you privately I liked Kirk as van Gogh.

HEATH LEDGER

Pain

Last November I say I'd feel good about dying now, at age twenty-eight, because I feel alive through my two-year-old daughter Matilda. I quickly explain that doesn't mean I want to die; I want to be around for the rest of her life, and call this an interesting kind of little set up. Those close to me understand I love my daughter and her mother Michelle Williams, my former girlfriend, as well as my parents and sister and friends and colleagues in movies, and appreciate viewers worldwide who admire my work, but few realize I might not be with them much longer.

Studying the facts and observations now, you can see why. Friends and sources both named and anonymous say I'm jittery and an edgy smoker who often abuses alcohol. In early January I put a ski mask over my face and hood on my head and gaze through slits while downing drinks at a bar in New York City. That doesn't help and when hangovers invade I have to blow them away with cocaine and heroin, and I go down further when Michelle leaves me and considers demanding I be drug tested before visiting my daughter. Comments about my abuse of prescription medications come from authorities who around my floor-bound mattress find six bottles – two opiate painkillers, three anti-anxiety drugs, and a bottle of sleeping pills. I've got to have strong medications or I can't take it.

I've always been depressed. Most people don't understand what that means. They tell you to snap out of it. Would you say that to a man with a malignant tumor? Then don't be so fatuous with a man who's depressed. Direct him to a psychiatrist. Not a doctor lacking psychopharmacological expertise and who for money and the thrill of association will fill as many bottles as a celebrity asks for. Don't send him to Elvis' doctor. Don't send him to my doctors in Europe and the United States. How many am I seeing? That'll come out. But right now I can say you better not have more than one. If he's legitimate, he won't give you so many medications they shut down your brain and kill you with respiratory depression. Talk to experts at your local mental health clinics. At medium-size places they lose several patients a year through overdoses. And articles now reveal more than twenty thousand a year are dying of overdoses in the United States. Only car wrecks cause more accidental deaths.

I can't dwell on these things. Since my late teens I've been on a rocket, making movies and becoming a star but not clinging to less-challenging roles of heroes in period costumes. I have nervous energy and want characters to scare me. In *Monster's Ball* I play the son of a sadistic prison guard who insults and assaults me because my sensitivity makes him sick. Ultimately, I threaten to shoot his rotten ass but instead turn the gun on myself. Regarding *Brokeback Mountain* I must first credit Annie Proulx, author of the short story, screenwriter Larry McMurtry, director Ang Lee, and my fellow actors who include Michelle Williams. Together we make an especially fine motion picture, and as Ennis Del Mar, the cowboy who can't acknowledge the fallacy of his heterosexual existence and create a life with his gay boyfriend, I'm one of the most tormented and memorable characters in film history.

I follow as Dan, in *Candy,* introducing my girlfriend to heroin and then sending her to the streets to screw for our next fix. As I play this desperate character, I think about myself. Many times I obsess all night because I can't sleep. I'm nervous manic miserable and get worse playing the psychopathic Joker in *The Dark Knight* and that's clear when director Christopher Nolan says Heath "is extremely original, extremely frightening, tremendously edgy. A very young character, a very anarchic presence that taps into a lot of our basic fears and panic." This summer the public will stampede to see me implode. And if there's enough of me to salvage *The Imaginarium of Dr. Parnassus,* that too will attract both aficionados and vultures anxious to watch a young man on screen days before returning from London to his twenty-sixty grand a month SoHo apartment where he can't relax so takes an opiate then another then an anti-anxiety medication and another then one more combined with a sleeping medication, mixing them up, which one now, doesn't matter, two more of these, a few of those, can't remember which one's next, don't care, just want to quit hurting.

Ledger to Woods

Dear Tiger,

I'm not going to preach, from a faraway place, but I'm damn well going to tell you about prescription drug abuse. You may know I've been gone more than nine years now, and you must understand that mixed drugs taken together dramatically increase each other's effects and stop many young, strong hearts. Choose any statistics you want; they're all alarming. I'd say in the United States about fifty thousand people a year die after taking too many prescription medications or too much of a single medication. In my case, as I lay in my luxurious SoHo bedroom, examiners found two opiate painkillers, Vicodin (which you also took) and Oxycontin, three anti-anxiety medications, Valium, Restoril, and Xanax, as well as some sleeping pills.

No single doctor gave me all those – I'd have needed a quack for that. But I did look around, doctor shopped, as they say, and got what I felt I needed to lessen chronic tension. I hear you've had four back and a few knee surgeries in recent years so I assume your primary problem is physical but you're probably also dealing with psychological problems. Let's take a look at your drugs – isn't prescription medication a tidy euphemism? As noted, you took Vicodin, an "addictive painkiller (that can cause) drowsiness and confusion." What many people are trying to figure out is how and why you're taking some of the others. Vioxx? It's an anti-inflammatory that causes a "high risk of heart attacks and strokes" and is no longer approved in the United States. Who prescribes your Vioxx? You also said you take Torix, an anti-inflammatory "used to treat joint pain." This drug is also not approved in the U.S. And then there's Soloxex, which is used to treat dogs suffering from hypothyroidism. Why does some dealer with a stethoscope think that's appropriate? Millions need answers to similar problems.

I commend you for not having alcohol in your system and being forthright about what's in your medicine cabinet, but we must consider the issue of driving under the influence, and concede there's a serious problem when a guy's found sleeping at three a.m. in his car parked on a public highway and the engine's running and two tires are flat. Since both flats were on the left side, it looks like you were almost unconscious and lost control, veered left, and destroyed both tires by hitting a curb that probably bordered a sidewalk. Fortunately, nobody was walking nearby. Since you told police you didn't know where you'd been or where you were going, you wouldn't have seen anyone.

What this really means is you need to do what I didn't. Make sure all your doctors know about all your medications, and understand the reactions when various medications are taken together at certain doses. You've spent so much of your life analyzing how wind and length of grass and contours of fairways and greens affect the behavior of a golf ball. Quit walking blindly and do some homework about what you put in your body.

Sincerely,

Heath

BURT LANCASTER

Rescue Attempt

Ernest dashes up flophouse stairs and after asking a frail old man where's Ole rumbles through the hall and hammers the door. He waits a few seconds without an answer then kicks the door and kicks it again, splintering some wood but not removing the barrier, so he steps back to the opposite wall and, grunting like an offensive lineman, drives his strong shoulder into a door knocked open.

Ole's in bed, looking detached and dejected.

"Get up," says Ernest. "Two killers are coming."

"Nothing I can do about it… I did something wrong once."

"I'm not letting them shoot you."

"Why do you care?"

Looking insulted, Ernest says, "You mean you don't know I wrote 'The Killers,' a short story this is based on."

"Yeah, I read it. You know what's going to happen."

"Well, I've decided it's not going to happen," says Ernest, drawing a pistol from a holster under his jacket. "Get up."

Ole, a former boxer still muscular, doesn't move.

"I said, 'Get up.'"

"You gonna kill me, Ernest?"

"Don't be smartass. But I may wound you if you don't go kneel over there."

Ernest aims his pistol at the corner left of the entrance.

"I'm tired of running, sick of hiding. It's not worth it."

"Want me to carry you?"

"You don't have to stick around," Ole says.

"From now on, I'm the director."

Like rising from the canvas just before the ten count, Ole struggles out of bed and to his assigned position. Ernest crouches in the opposite corner. They don't talk. They wait and sweat and in a few minutes sense intruders before they hear steps getting closer.

"What the hell's this, Max?" whispers Al, pointing to the demolished entrance.

Max shakes his head meaning be quiet and they dash inside and fire at the bed before Ernest shoots Al in the side. Max turns toward that darkened corner, giving Ernest a straight shot into his forehead.

He stands and looks proudly at Ole while Al, still moving, raises his pistol and Ole shouts, "Ernest," who reacts firing twice into the gangster's head.

"Let's get outta here," he says, holstering his gun.

Ole walks to Ernest, extending his right hand, and when Ernest holds out his hand Ole floors him with a left hook, grabs Ernest's pistol, and shoots himself in the temple.

Notes: Burt Lancaster emerged from World War II in his early thirties but without professional experience except as an acrobat. Friends told him to try acting since he had the looks, voice, and demeanor of a leading man. They were right, and in 1946 he debuted in *The Killers* and became a star. Ernest Hemingway praised Lancaster and the movie his short story spawned.

Suburban Swim

"Great story," says Burt Lancaster. "How'd you create something so original?"

"It's based on my experiences," John Cheever says.

Lancaster laughs. "Come on, John."

Cheever inhales a cigarette and swigs his drink. Lancaster has temporarily shelved those vices in order to stay early-fifties sleek for his many scenes in a bathing suit, which he's wearing now.

"With only slight alterations the scenes in my story 'The Swimmer,' as well as Eleanor Perry's screenplay, could be appropriately placed in my biography."

"Care to show me how a guy gets home by swimming through the pools of gentrified Connecticut?"

"Delighted," says Cheever.

"I'd loan you one of my pairs of trunks but they'd be a little too big."

Cheever drops his cigarette in the drink and sets them on the lawn.

"Don't worry," he says, and steps out of loafers before unzipping his pants and letting them drop to reveal trunks dark as Lancaster's. After unbuttoning his shirt he tosses it onto his pants. Tall Lancaster looks like a gold-medal decathlete. He even played one, Jim Thorpe. Cheever, slight and several inches shorter, is a tad less athletic.

"This way," Cheever says, and runs to dive in a pool surrounded by curious cast members. Lancaster splits the water, too, and both swim a vigorous lap.

"See you later," says the author. "I'm helping Burt with his method acting."

"What're you doing, Burt?" shouts director Frank Perry, much younger husband of screenwriter Eleanor. "We've got a scene in twenty minutes."

"Let's do it tomorrow," he says, and joins Cheever jogging toward the next estate.

Under trees and around bushes they maneuver to a lovely layout owned by a famous Broadway playwright and his wife.

"Thurston," says Cheever, knocking on the big back door.

His wife, Emily, answers. She's wearing a one-piece bathing suit.

"Thurston had to stay in New York. His latest play opened last night."

"Of course," says Cheever. "How were the reviews?"

"Marvelous. Now we can buy a larger house but don't really need one."

"Mind if I take a lap in your pool?" Burt asks. "I'm preparing for a movie."

"Please do."

He runs and dives and churns through water almost as well as a college swimmer.

"John, hurry up."

"I'm afraid I must've stepped on something and my foot's afire. Emily, do you have something in your medicine cabinet that may lessen my pain?"

"I have some ointments, John, and a variety of liquid medications."

"Make mine strong," he says. "Burt, just continue through any passable places in the foliage and you'll come upon many wonderful homes with swimming pools."

Mouth hard and eyes sharp, he says, "I thought you were going to help me better understand the part. Evidently, drinking's a higher priority for you."

"That's not fair, Burt. Even this one stop has given you a feel for what it's like to make impromptu visits in these heavenly suburbs. Simply keep in mind you're playing a man who's moving into a psychotic state and doesn't realize he's already lost his wife, his daughters, and his house. Many people are correspondingly irritated to see him. We're all frontrunners by nature."

"I get it, John. And I got it before your hijinks. I can portray any character because I'm a serious actor. Good day."

"I won't be able to do my cameo today, Burt."

"Small loss," says the actor, dashing into trees.

After four hours of vigorous swimming through the enchanted region, Lancaster returns to the set where Paul Newman, clad in dark swimming trunks, stands with a beautiful actress before the cameras.

"What the hell, Paul?"

"Burt, hi. Told you I'd visit you on the set."

"Looks like you're stealing my part."

"Sorry," says Paul, "but you were AWOL and we had no idea if you'd ever return."

Visiting the Birdman

I guess I'm honored. I've read Burt Lancaster's a fine actor and here he is, preparing to play me in *Birdman of Alcatraz.*

"Why the hell's Alcatraz in the title," I tell him.

"I suppose that sounds better than *Birdman of Leavenworth.*"

"I hope you're making a fair movie."

"We're doing our best, Mr. Stroud."

Pointing through the wall, I say, "I only killed that first man because he mauled my girlfriend. Is that so bad?"

"I'm not sure, Mr. Stroud."

"Call me Bob."

"All right, if you'll call me Burt."

"And the guard I killed, that was self-defense. He was a big fellow about to brain me with a club."

"Why'd you have a knife, Bob?"

Extending hands wide and palms up, I say, "For the reason I just told you."

"I'm sure you understand that no prison can tolerate inmates walking around with concealed weapons."

"You ever done any time, Burt?"

"No, Bob, I haven't."

"The guards are armed, the other inmates are armed. I was within my rights."

"They almost executed you, Bob. Most inmates don't have to kill to survive."

"At least it got me into solitary where I could study birds and their diseases and how to cure them and write books about all this."

Lancaster smiles. "It's amazing they let you bring in all those birds and equipment and even gave you another cell at Leavenworth."

"They took all that away in minutes without even warning me I was headed for Alcatraz."

"In fairness, Bob, you used some of the equipment to make alcohol."

"That going to be in the movie?"

"Only briefly."

Sternly, I ask, "What about the fact I'm a homosexual?"

"We're not going to deal with that at all."

"Maybe you should. I think that's why I'm still in prison after more than fifty years."

Lancaster laces his hands together and squeezes them on the table between us. "Bob, you not only killed two people, you often fought guards and other inmates, and you were very aggressive about your sexual desires."

"I never raped anybody. Besides, I'm seventy-three now, way too old to be a dangerous wolf. My health has continued to go down here at this pen in Missouri."

"If it were up to me, you'd get your parole."

"Too bad I couldn't have been a bird and just flown away."

Lunch for Two

"Hey, aren't you Burt Lancaster?" asks an old man standing on the Atlantic City Boardwalk.

The actor stops and smiles and says, "That's right. What's your name?"

"Lou Pascal. I never thought I'd get to meet a guy like you."

They shake hands.

"I'm just a man headed for lunch. You hungry?"

"Yes sir."

They enter a restaurant two blocks off the main drag and Burt says, "Let's sit in back. I don't like being noticed when I eat."

"Me neither."

After they read their menus and order, Burt asks, "So, Lou, what kind of work do you do?"

He glances down then to his left and says, "I work independently. How about you?"

"I'm in town to make a picture called *Atlantic City.* I think it's going be a good one."

"What's it about?"

"I play this guy who loves a beautiful young lady named Sally. They live in the same apartment complex but she's not interested in an old guy. I think she still loves Dave, her ex-husband who ran off with her sister and got her pregnant then showed up back here."

Lou says, "She should stay away from that guy Dave."

Grinning, Burt says, "She'll have to since Dave ripped off a lot of cocaine from guys who tracked him down and killed him."

"So the dealers got their coke back?"

"Actually, my character's got the coke and has been selling it. The director, Louis Malle, and screenwriter John Guare and I are trying to decide what should happen next. You got any ideas, Lou?"

"I recommend you carry a gun. That way you can blow away the bad guys if they ever attack you and Sally in the street."

"What would Sally be doing with a guy like me?"

"You've got status and some dough now that you're dealing," says Lou.

"Yeah," says Burt, "I won't have to run errands for old bag Grace and listen to her telling me I'm worthless and how wonderful her dead husband was. He wasn't so great. I worked for the bum.

"What kind of business did you say you're in?"

"Just independent stuff around town," says Lou.

"Atlantic City?"

"That's right."

"So you think I might really have a chance with Sally."

"Damn right," says Lou, "I expect you'll get her in bed sometime soon."

"I'd love that."

"But be careful. If you get too close to her and run away together she'll rip you off and sneak away."

"You're probably right about that."

"At least you'd be able to go back to Grace," says Lou.

"I'm through with her."

Lou leans toward Burt and says, "Now that you've killed some guys and made decent money, I think she'll treat you nicer. But you better quit the rough stuff."

Notes: Burt Lancaster received his fourth Oscar nomination for his portrayal of Lou Pascal. He'd won playing *Elmer Gantry* twenty years earlier. *Atlantic City* was Lancaster's final great movie. In his late sixties the once powerful acrobat and fitness devotee began to endure chronic health problems including arteriosclerosis, two heart attacks, coronary bypass surgery, a stroke that left him partially paralyzed and barely able to speak, and ultimately a fatal heart attack at age eighty.

FRANK SINATRA

She Came Running

This is a dream. Frank Sinatra's coming to our little ten-thousand town in Indiana to make a great movie and I'm going to get him. I've loved him since I was a little girl. He's so handsome and charming and the greatest singer ever. Lots of people are downtown today after hearing the stars are going to be shooting outside. I can't believe how excited I am. I'm thrilled but scared. I'm pretty but not like Ava Gardner and other stars who chase Frank. I don't care. I know he'll feel the same about me as I do about him. He's got to.

There he is.

"Frank," I say, standing on my tiptoes and waving. "Frank."

He must not hear me.

"Settle down," says Ed, my husband.

"Go back to work," I tell him.

"I better keep an eye on you."

I push his hand away from mine.

Before they shoot, Frank talks to that tart Shirley MacLaine. I bet he's already sleeping with her. He is, if he wants to. I'm not worried about her. I'm cuter but to make sure Frank notices I dash by security guards and shove Shirley, saying, "Get away from him," and embrace Frank, pushing my cheek next to his. "I'm so happy to meet you."

He looks irritated. I hope he understands I didn't want this to be a bear hug. He pushes my shoulders and looks at a guard and says, "Get her outta here."

"Frank, you don't understand."

He keeps pushing my shoulders and two guys pull me away and Frank turns his back. Ed runs up and says, "Gladys, you don't even know the man."

That evening a policeman I've known for years comes over to our house and tells me I can't come to shooting anymore.

"You can't stop me," I say.

"We can, Gladys," he says. "Please cooperate."

"Listen to him, will you, Gladys?" says Ed.

I'm so nervous I have to go to bed for a few days. When I return to my job as a secretary people kid me so bad I cry. Don't they care? Frank

Sinatra's in town, carrying on with Shirley and icy blond Martha Hyer and probably plenty of others and all I've got is Ed who's no Frank. I'm happy when they leave town. Go on. Get back to Hollywood. Frank and Dean Martin and guys like that don't want wholesome girls from the Midwest. They want loose women no matter where they come from.

Several months later *Some Came Running* arrives in town and I don't want to see it but can't wait because I still love Frank. I didn't have a chance and don't understand why he wants Shirley who's stupid and mousy and goes to Martha Hyer's classroom to tell her she isn't rich or smart like Martha and doesn't want to cause any problems if she loves Frank, which of course she does, but Martha's shocked Frank's been seeing such a loose woman and doesn't want to see him anymore. After lonely Frank marries Shirley her no count boyfriend comes in from Chicago and shoots him and gets ready to fire again when Shirley jumps between them and is shot and falls on Frank and dies bleeding in his arms. I'd like to comfort Frank but he's not here and no doubt already has someone else.

CARY GRANT

Beware

I'm delighted to be invited to an advance screening of *Suspicion* in a lovely Hollywood theater. Alfred Hitchcock, round and distinguished, walks onto stage before the curtains open and says, "Good evening. We have an intriguing little drama for you this evening and ultimately want you to decide whether it's a murder mystery or a love story."

As the movie starts we watch Cary Grant try to sneak into the first class section of a train and pretend he's surprised his ticket's only third class.

"Can't believe how that leech is already putting the arm on Joan Fontaine," says my husband Gerald, leaning over. "She should have him thrown out."

"I hardly recognize her in those schoolmarm glasses. I'm sure she's enchanted to meet him."

In the English countryside, which in most cases is a Hollywood soundstage, Cary soon sees Joan astride a horse. She's beautiful without glasses, and another day he convinces her to leave church to walk with him.

"The man's trying to throw her off a cliff," says Gerald.

"He is not. He's only trying to kiss her, and she certainly needs to be kissed."

"She better stay away from him. I don't like the way he fusses with her hair and calls her Monkey Face."

"He's charming her," I say.

"He's setting her up."

I doubt Cary Grant would ever behave that way. He sees the kind of refined woman Joan is and what more she can be and is delighted she kisses him and doubtless has a pressing reason for cancelling his date with her that afternoon.

"Her father's right," says Gerald. "Cary's a tough and a card cheat and a womanizer and more."

"He's simply a man who ladies want to be with."

Cary and Joan have a fast and wonderful courtship and for the "first time" she understands what she wants and needs, and they elope on a romantic Riviera honeymoon.

Into my ear Gerald says, "I'm embarrassed watching this man bring his bride back to England into a beautiful home he can't pay for. Joan's understandably shocked."

"Her very wealthy parents should give her a larger allowance."

"It's not their responsibility to support this luxury-seeking deadbeat. What's wrong with Joan, staying with a man like that?"

"They're just starting, and she does tell him she expected that he had some money of his own and she at any rate tells him to get a job and quit borrowing."

I'm relieved when Cary's cousin Leo G. Carroll offers him a good job in real estate but concerned when his good friend Nigel Bruce lets it slip that Cary was at the horse races last week. You were betting rather than working, Joan thinks, and so do I.

"What would you do if your parents gave you two expensive chairs and I pawned them and wasted the money?" Gerald asks in loud whisper.

"You wouldn't dare."

"No decent man would," he says.

"But at least Cary bought back the chairs."

"That's a superficial gesture. His withering look at Nigel Bruce tells us what's in his heart and so does the cold way he tells Joan, 'One of these days brandy will kill' his friend by inducing an allergic attack. Nigel should run from this guy as fast as Joan.

"And here he is, lucking out again when Leo G. Carroll's tells Joan he won't prosecute Cary as long as his cousin pays back the two thousand pounds an audit proves he stole. I hope you don't think Cary's bereaved when he gets the telegram revealing Joan's father just died. He only cares her allowance will remain modest."

It's encouraging that Cary's ambitious, at least with Nigel's money, and wants to start a real estate development, and heartening he later saves Nigel's life by jumping into his car to prevent him from backing over a cliff. Like a good friend, Cary also tells Nigel he now believes the land is a bad deal after all and Nigel should go to Paris to understand why.

"Surely, Gerald, you're starting to change your opinion about the character of Cary Grant."

"Not a whit, my dear."

I get that oh no feeling when news arrives that Nigel Bruce died drunk in the company of an Englishman in Paris. I know Joan's thinking where were you? You were in Paris. No, he says, he was north of London.

"Maybe he was and maybe he wasn't," says Gerald. "He's certainly been talking to that old female writer about undetectable poisons and borrowed her book on the subject. I bet he was in Paris and killed Nigel."

Joan's already told Cary she doesn't feel well and wants to sleep alone tonight. He's angry but dutifully delivers a glass of luminous milk. Who knows what's in it? Joan examines it warily and doesn't touch it and in the morning tells Cary she's going to visit her mother.

"She better not get in the car with that madman," says Gerald. "God, what a fool."

Cary drives like a maniac and Joan's door flies open and she's about to be rescued or pushed out…

We see two endings. Lights come on and Alfred Hitchcock walks onto stage and, with a long dramatic pause, examines the audience. "Which climax do you prefer?"

Gerald stands and says, "You spent the entire movie creating a murderer. He killed her. That's obvious."

"No, no," shouts a woman. "Cary Grant would never do this."

Another lady says, "I simply don't want to see Cary Grant kill his wife, ever."

At least eighty percent agree. I do too. We want Cary and Joan to go home happy. Let someone else be a murderer.

Cary by Northwest

Hunched on a chair wedged into a far corner, Cary Grant rubs his hand over tired eyes and makes a sound alarmingly like a moan. Alfred Hitchcock walks fast as he can to his star and says, "Good grief, Cary, what's the matter?"

"Hitch, I just can't figure out where I am."

Looking worried, the director says, "Why, Cary, we're at an estate on Long Island."

"I know that. I mean I don't know where I am in this damn film. We don't even know its title."

"Don't worry. We'll get you oriented. I myself am only starting to figure it out. Let's review. Tell me what you remember so far."

Cary Grant stands and turns to tentatively face Hitchcock.

"I remember starting as an advertising executive having drinks with friends in a New York hotel and when I briefly left our table two unpleasant men grabbed me, one showed his gun, and suddenly I was hemmed between them in the backseat of a car driven away because they believed I was some man named George Kaplan."

"You're quite correct, Cary."

"But why was I kidnapped?"

"You don't need to know that so soon. Even I don't know everything. Let the tension build."

Speaking sternly to the shorter man, Grant says, "Why did I have to drink a bottle or more of bourbon?"

"That's a clever way for them to kill you, get you drunk and let you drive off the cliff."

"I mean why the hell did you allow them to force me to drink real bourbon? I can play a drunk. It's called acting."

Hitchcock extends a hand and pats Grant's shoulder.

"I swear I thought they were forcing you to drink tea."

"I was so smashed I couldn't remember whether I was being interrogated by Philip Vandman or Lester Thornhill."

"Names, especially surnames, can be rather confusing. Just remember the man in charge is James Mason."

"Why is everyone so intent on believing I'm this George Kaplan?"

"Precisely what we want the audience to ask," says Hitchcock. "Shall we return to the others?"

Shaking his head, Grant says, "You seemed quite content to run me off the cliff in that car, one wheel spinning over the edge."

"It's a compelling image, Cary, but not one I planned to come so close to disaster. I had offered you a stunt driver."

"I do appreciate your solicitude on that point but wish you, and the eminent screenwriter Ernest Lehman, had been more concerned at the United Nations where the real Lester Townsend was killed by a knife thrown into his back and I, the Good Samaritan, instinctively grabbed the knife and thereby framed myself for murder, an act immortalized by the newspaper photographer standing nearby."

In avuncular style Hitchcock says, "You should thank me for forcing you to go on the run. Otherwise, you wouldn't have met dazzling blond Eva Marie Saint on the train."

"Thank you so much, Alfred. That delicate lady made love to me all night and then sent me to meet Kaplan, or was it Vandman, on a rural Midwest road."

"You shouldn't complain about being in the Midwest, Cary, since this was filmed amid farmland north of Bakersfield."

"Couldn't you have warned me to beware after the local man waiting for a bus said it was strange that crop duster's dusting where there are no crops?"

"I could've, Cary, but that would've been tantamount to premature ejaculation. Despite an ostensibly dreary scene, the rich blue sky and luminous light brown fields are quite beautiful, and so are you. I thus offered our audience the sensuality of nature before the plane dove at you once, twice, firing bullets, then a third time, forcing you into a field where on still another dive the pilot bombarded you with pesticides."

Pounding his chest with a fist, Grant says, "I'm still coughing and have discussed this with my attorneys. One would expect after all that you'd get me safely out of there."

"What, and miss perhaps the most iconic moments in motion picture history? Most actors would be thrilled to have me film their horrified faces as a massive gas truck roars in and, just before crushing you, brakes hard, and forces you onto your back on the road and pulls over you before stopping and providing a dreadful dead end for that frightful crop duster. So I did save you, Cary."

"You left me in the dark but at least I got the chance to rebuke Eva for wanting my head on the road rather than my shoulders. And I got to tell insufferable James Mason about his lover's devious sexual behavior. In that regard, if you want to place Mason at an art auction, fine. But why put me there when I don't belong?"

"I wanted to release your creative instincts. It worked marvelously the way you improvised and disrupted the auction by shouting bids insultingly low and preposterously high."

"Glad you enjoyed it, Hitch, but your fantasies and those of your muse, Ernest Lehman, got me arrested again."

Hitchcock says, "I saved you again. Mason's men would've killed you had I not made many calls to arrange for The Agency and its leader, The Professor, to take you into protective custody."

"Rather belatedly I learned all those people pursuing George Kaplan were in fact trying to kill a man who didn't exist."

"Before continuing with this line of impertinence, you should allow me to tell you that I also believed Kaplan was real."

"You've been no more trustworthy than secret agent James Mason. I'm leaving."

Hitchcock tightens his mouth and says, "You're being paid five thousand a day, in addition to your contractual salary. You have some final scenes."

"I hope you don't think you're going to get me up on Mt. Rushmore."

"Let's at least go have a look."

In the national park beneath four stunning presidents, Hitchcock puts his arm around Grant and guides him into a beautiful glass-walled building.

"Don't worry, Cary, in this very room Eva will shoot you in a nonlethal way."

"She's not going to shoot me with bullets, blanks, or anything else."

Hitchcock reaches under his coat and from his belt draws a small pistol.

"Here is the very implement she'll be using. It's quite harmless."

Several inches from his temple he aims and fires twice.

"See?"

"Charming," says Grant.

"I hope you're not going to let personal feelings for Eva undermine your professional obligations."

"I despise the woman. I'm concerned about my own life."

"We mustn't let James Mason, a particularly dangerous spy, fly sensitive microfilm out of here tonight and into the hands of our enemies."

Suspiciously, Grant asks, "What's it going to take to stop him?"

"Just running away from Mason and his evil lieutenant and crawling around the granitic features of great presidents."

"It's awfully high up there."

"We won't take any chances. I've devised the greatest cut in history."

"What is it?"

"You'll pull Eva from the peril of a fatal fall right into your marital bed on a train speeding into a hot tunnel."

Notes: *North by Northwest,* one of the finest films ever made, was nominated for three Oscars and Ernest Lehman won for best original screenplay.

A Star and his Brides

Smiling as she approaches, an alluring lady says, "Cary, so nice to see you."

"Forgive me, Virginia, but I'm not sure I can say the same."

"I could be unpleasant, too."

"Because you left me just before I became a star and probably always regretted it."

"In fact, I always regretted your being so possessive and following me around."

"I apologize for not being as appealing off screen," he says.

"I accept. Look who's coming."

"What's this, a convention?"

Virginia Cherrill waves a soft goodbye, and to a slender woman with beautiful sad eyes he says, "Barbara, don't ask me to dine with you this evening or any other."

"I'd hardly do that," she says.

"I know your society friends would be there."

"The ones you so often avoided at my dinner parties, pouting in the bedroom upstairs."

Cary says, "They were boring, like you, nothing to do but play tennis and shop all day and dine and gossip at night."

"Your behavior insulted them."

"After getting up before dawn and spending hours on the damn movie set I needed rest, not chit chat."

"That's why we divorced," Barbara Hutton says.

"Better for both of us."

She walks away, typically grim, and a slim tomboyish lady approaches.

"I hope no one's filming this," he says. "It would be in such poor taste."

"I doubt anyone is, but one can't be sure," says Betsy.

"I suppose I should thank you for being my first wife who believed I didn't also like men."

"We screwed too much for me to feel otherwise" says Betsy Drake. "But you didn't love me."

"I wish I had."

"You didn't care I left."

Cary says, "I suppose not, but I always appreciated that your doctor introduced me to LSD."

"Those kaleidoscopic trips were necessary to rebuild my ego after you loved Sophia Loren on location. And when she rejected you, you needed emotional transformation, too."

"LSD should've helped Dyan, but she wouldn't let it," he says.

"She was too young for you."

"Only by thirty-three years. You're almost twenty my junior."

"You tried to mold her into your perfect little plaything," says Betsy.

"It's insulting you presume to know such things."

"I've read her book about you."

"Everyone's got a book or interview that's primarily fiction."

Betsy says, "You're saying you didn't pressure Dyan Cannon to take LSD and continue doing so even when she complained how nervous and unhappy the drug made her?"

"It would've enhanced her spiritual growth."

"She needed to determine her own way to mature, and certainly didn't need you telling her how to wear makeup and fix her hair. She was a beautiful girl."

"Wonder what she's like now. And my daughter, Jennifer, who gave me twenty years of joy. And Barbara Harris, my final and most loving wife."

"I bet they're doing well."

"I hope they remember me."
"Come on. You're Cary Grant."
"Not really," he says.
"Closest I've seen."

MARLON BRANDO

Brando's Title Fights

I thought they were only going to lean on Joey Doyle or I wouldn't have taken him up on the roof. I was shocked they threw him off. Now Johnny Friendly and other tough guys who get a cut of everything that comes and goes on the waterfront want me to keep my mouth shut. My brother Charley is one of them and says if I do nothing they'll pay me a few hundred a week. If I don't accept their offer, they'll kill me. He hands me a gun I don't want. For such a smart guy, Charley doesn't get a lot of things.

He thinks I started losing as a boxer because my manager brought me along too fast. In the back seat of his big car with a driver, I tell him, "That's not it, Charley. It was you. You came into my dressing room one night in the Garden and said, 'Kid, this ain't your night….' I could've destroyed that guy… You were my brother and should've looked out for me instead of trying to win big bets… I don't care you gave me some of your dirty money. 'I could've had class. I could've been a contender. I could've been someone.' Now I'm just a bum."

"Okay, Terry," he says, and tells the driver to take us to some address.

"Where the hell're we going?"

"To Budd Schulberg's."

"What for?"

"You don't like how life has turned out, talk to him."

Budd's happy to see us until I say, "Charley and I think I should be a champion or a least get some title shots."

"No way I'm going to cut the greatest scene I've ever written," he says. "You guys been drinking?"

"No," I say.

"Okay, then you better have a few. Honey, bring these guys a beer."

His wife Agnes puts two cold ones on a coffee table in front of the sofa where Budd motions to sit. He paces back and forth in front of us.

"What the hell's this all about, Charley?"

"I think the kid's got some good points. Maybe I should've made sure all his fights were square."

"Listen, Charley, it wouldn't have been your decision. If you'd crossed the bosses, they'd have put you on the same meat hook you'll soon be on anyway."

I down my beer and say, "Budd, you don't understand. I know I can win the middleweight title."

He walks to a bookcase and grabs some boxing reference books. "Let's see how that would work out. You were born in 1924, right? Okay, that means in your early twenties you'd have had to beat a real slugger, Tony Zale. Nope."

"Maybe I'd have needed a little more seasoning."

"Yeah, that would've given you Rocky Graziano and then Zale again. I saw some of your real fights and you were pretty good but not like those guys. Your next chance, if the mob had let it happen, would've been against Marcel Cerdan, who destroyed Zale. And Cerdan was mauled by Jake LaMotta."

"Cerdan was injured," says Charley.

"LaMotta fought the guy who showed up and looked terrific. And that brings us to the current champ, Sugar Ray Robinson, who's the best pound for pound fighter I've ever seen. You're not beating Ray Robinson, Terry. Sorry."

"I just want a chance. You aren't gonna beat Shakespeare but you've got a chance to write and make a living."

"Shakespeare isn't going to beat my brains into mush. You're lucky you got out of some fights early by taking dives. That spared you a lot of damage. Being a contender could've put you in with all those guys, some more than once, and you'd be worse off than in 'Balookaville.' You'd be stumbling down the street. Be thankful you've got your health."

"We did a pretty damn good scene, Terry," says Charley.

"Yeah, I guess we did."

"Agnes, please bring these gentleman two cold ones apiece, and get one for yourself. Let's celebrate."

Notes: *On the Waterfront* was nominated for eleven Oscars, winning eight. Among the principals in this story, Marlon Brando took best actor, Budd Schulberg won best screenplay, and Rod Steiger was nominated for best supporting actor.

PAUL NEWMAN

Questions for Luke

Paul Newman's latest film, *Cool Hand Luke*, has recently debuted and the star waits at a microphone on stage in a packed high school auditorium as students and teachers stand, cheering and clapping.

"I don't have a speech prepared but don't think I need one. Just ask me whatever you'd like to know."

He points to a boy in the front row.

"Why'd you keep getting up after that big guy Dragline kept knocking you down? And how bad were you hurt?"

"I had to keep getting up because that was in the script and the director as well as George Kennedy and I and the camera crew spent three days putting together the few minutes you see on screen. Thank goodness Dragline had good aim and didn't hit me square in the face. Our bodies were pretty sore after bouncing on the ground all that time."

A uniformed cheerleader waves and asks, "Mr. Newman, can I please come up there and get a close look at those pretty blue eyes?"

"No you may not, young lady. I have daughters older than you."

A tall female student rises to ask, "How in the world did you eat fifty eggs in one hour."

"Actually, and I hope this doesn't disillusion you, I didn't swallow a single egg. That's the beauty of editing. If I tried to eat fifty eggs in an hour I'd be dead rather than lucky Luke only passed out on the table."

An adult lady stands and says, "I'm Mrs. Evans, the drama teacher here, and I'd like to know if, after eating the eggs, you became a symbol of Christ."

Newman smiles as she continues, "You wore only a white cloth around your middle, like Jesus, and your arms were spread wide as if they'd been nailed to the crucifix."

"I usually avoid talking about symbols, but there was a brief and I hope subtle allusion to Christ at the end of that scene. And let me emphasize, we're not suggesting Luke is Christ-like. The symbolic opportunity just presented itself and is cinematically pleasing."

"Hi Mr. Newman, I'm Johnny, a freshman here. I'd like to know how long they made you stay in the box all those times they punished you."

"I spent one or two days there each time," the actor says.

Girls gasp and boys groan.

"I kid you, of course. I stayed in the box about as long as it took to open and close the door. I think my entering and exiting that stinkhole was realistic. I tried to be more decrepit and whiskery on the way out. That's where good writing, directing, cinematography, and acting come in. We're creating a world that isn't really there, at least not on our movie sets. Thank goodness."

"What about the leg-irons?" a boy asks.

"We made sure they were a loose fit and I never had to wear them more than ten minutes or so."

Standing, a big boy, maybe a football player, asks, "Were you scared when you escaped the first time and the dogs were chasing you."

"I had some jitters associated with acting but wasn't afraid of being torn up by enraged dogs since they were kept at a distance. I enjoyed walking in the stream to confuse them and running on railroad tracks and crawling upside down from a wire across a gully. I'm still young enough to do a number of my own stunts."

"How old are you?" asks the big guy.

"Forty-two."

Silence coalesces with disappointment in the auditorium.

"Listen, young ladies and gentlemen, I didn't mean to shock you with such a big number – big for kids between fourteen and eighteen – but remember this: forty-two ain't old, even if some of your parents are my age or younger. I try to remind myself of that once in a while. May you all have eighty years or more."

A girl raises her hand and Newman nods to her.

"Did you feel bad when that dog ran itself to death chasing you?"

"I would've felt bad if the dog had really died but our trainer just gave him a little sleeping injection."

"Really?"

"I swear," he says, raising his right hand.

Another girl asks, "Did you hate the Man With No Eyes, who never took off his sunglasses and never said a word but always made it clear he hated you and wanted to shoot you."

"I tried to hate him on camera, except when I was pretending to be broken by him and other guards after my second escape attempt.

But no, I liked him personally. In fact, the wicked Captain, who hit me in the mouth with a whip and said, 'What we have is failure to communicate,' is Strother Martin, a good buddy. On most movie sets, though not all, there's a feeling of camaraderie and common purpose."

A boy raises his hand and says, "My dad owns a construction company and I've had to dig some holes for him in the summer. It's really hard. How much of those holes did you really dig?"

"Dug 'em myself," he says, winking. "That way I was dirty and sweaty."

"Then," says the boy, "they made you fill them in and dig them out again and fill them in again."

"I make sure I never play the star on set, but I didn't do a heckuva lot of digging, just a little starting and a little finishing. We had a backhoe and a couple of landscapers to get what we wanted.

"Mr. Newman," says a girl, "was it difficult to cry like that and pretend to be defeated."

"Yes, it's very difficult to cry on cue. Imagine if all of you had to cry in five minutes when the director says, 'Action.'"

"Are actresses better at crying than actors?" a girl asks.

"They are indeed."

The big boy has another question.

"If you'd really been in a chain gang and faced all those problems, do you think you'd have stolen a truck and escaped the third time?"

"I hope I'd never be in prison in the first place and know damn well I wouldn't try to get away three times. Ladies and gentlemen, thank you very much."

Paul Newman waves to the audience and shakes hands with the drama teacher and principal, and a female student runs up to hug him, kissing his cheek.

MEL GIBSON

Making Peace in the Middle East

I'm an alcoholic. I've been an alcoholic all my adult life, and my disease has been a battle. I've struggled to stay sober and when intoxicated I've vowed to get drunker. I'm the same as any other drunk. It doesn't matter I'm rich and famous and handsome and a renowned authority on religious and moral matters. Every drunk says things he shouldn't. I really didn't mean that Jews start all wars. In fact, I don't remember saying so. Still, I'll trust the police officer, who also reported I asked him if he was a Jew. And indeed he was. But that's not important. We are all God's children.

And as a man of God, I have already begun to make amends. The day after my arrest – and I would remind those hammering me in the media, I am being punished by the law as well as my Creator – I go to a special clothing store in West Los Angeles and buy one of those fine black suits with a matching yarmulke, and – as I've always yearned to do – I put them on and begin walking the streets of Hancock Park. Imagine what Orthodox Jews think when they see me. They might attack if I'm not dressed just like them.

"Mel Gibson, what the hell?" they say.

"Let us walk to the synagogue," I say.

En masse we proceed, and during the service I'm acknowledged as a distinguished guest and allowed, as I request, to speak to the congregation.

"Please do not judge me by my recent and utterly deplorable drunken outburst," I state. "And I urge you not to associate me with the views of my father, who has addressed a conference of Holocaust deniers. I certainly do not deny the Holocaust, and unlike my father I've never claimed it is 'mostly fiction.' The Holocaust is fact. In fact, I was going to make a miniseries about it. But, as you probably heard, executives at a famous motion picture company just cancelled the deal, stating that in two years I hadn't provided so much as a preliminary script. They are factually correct and morally right and they are Jews.

"Trust me; I do not believe that most wars are started by Jews but we all certainly know – and you are inevitably proud – that almost all motion pictures in the United States are begun by Jews. Look at the history of Hollywood – the Warner Brothers, Samuel Goldwyn, Louis Mayer right to the present of Steven Spielberg and Harvey Weinstein. I revere these men. They are the fathers of the American motion picture colossus that has so rewarded my prodigious acting and directing talents and enabled me to 'own Malibu' and be confident enough to threaten police officers. Now, let me emphasize, I should not be confident in that regard. No one should. But it is the Jews who have given me this power. And I appreciate it. Thank you so much.

"I want you to know, most of all, that I am going to atone for my tequila-induced slurs. That wasn't Mel talking; that was Jose what's his name. I do accept responsibility, as well as critical praise and loads of money, for the content of my religious blockbuster: *Passion of the Christ.* I hope most of you have seen this thoroughly accurate historical tour de force. If so, you know that the allegation I portray the Jews unfairly is balderdash. The Jews are portrayed as evil but so are the Romans. They are all evil. They all conspire to kill Christ, who in my picture gets the worst whipping in motion picture history, and millions of people are very moved. They love Christ. So do I, and he was a Jew.

"I also love every one of you. That is why I am here. I am going to help you. I am going to delay entering rehab for alcoholism for two weeks and this very evening fly to the Middle East and broker a peace deal. Only I have the required credibility. I shall march into southern Lebanon and tell Hezbollah the truth. They are anti-Semitic warmongers and they must agree, first, that Israel has a right to exist. Then Hezbollah must withdraw, along with all its missiles, from southern Lebanon and allow itself to be replaced by an international peacekeeping force. If necessary, I will stay, undergoing on-the-job-detoxification, and lead the force myself. I am a heroic figure, particularly when attired as I am today and shall be forevermore. I shall smite the enemies of Israel. I shall create a buffer zone between Israeli Jews and their enemies to the north. I may not be able to take care of all other problems in the region this month, but I assure you my atonement shall continue to be most profound."

CHADWICK BOSEMAN

Boseman Meets Marshall

Thurgood Marshall stands tall and surprised in front of shorter and darker Chadwick Boseman. "Young man, you're playing me?"

"Yes, and I'm most honored to do so, sir."

"Who made this casting decision? I better have a talk with him."

Boseman's body language weakens.

"I'm kidding," says Marshall. "You'll no doubt well portray the NAACP's chief legal strategist."

"I'm determined to capture your essence, if not your physicality, and want to talk to you and do as much research as possible."

"Perfect timing. Let's go see Eleanor Strubing."

Confused, Boseman says, "Surely we don't have access to her."

"Let's drive up to her Connecticut mansion and see."

It's late Saturday night in the elegant suburbs. No lights are on downstairs but burn in an upstairs bedroom.

"That's the master suite," says Marshall, pointing. He parks down the street from her house and they walk to the front door which Marshall opens by turning the knob.

"Shouldn't we knock?" asks Boseman.

Marshall puts a finger to his lips and motions toward the stairs they quietly climb and ease down the hall. Around the corner Joseph Spell, the new butler, is knocking on a bedroom door. Eleanor Strubing, wearing a bathrobe, opens the door and says, "Hi, Joseph."

"Good evening, ma'am."

"Please, call me Ellie."

"I wonder if I could have a little advance on my salary."

"Come in," she says. "I guess you know, John's out of town on business. How's Virgis?"

"Asleep in the attic."

"I can help you with the advance."

"You're awfully pretty."

"Thank you, Joseph."

Talking ceases and Marshall and Boseman hear sounds of kissing.

She opens her robe and says, "Let's get in bed."

"I'd love to, but my wife might hear us. Can we go downstairs?"

She nods. The attorney and actor quickly tiptoe down the stairs seconds before Spell and Strubing do the same and the two men tiptoe into the living room.

"How about the sofa, Ellie?"

Marshall and Boseman look at each other, alarmed.

"Someone might see us from outside," she says.

"That big backseat of your limousine would work just fine, then."

She smiles and kisses him. "Hurry up."

After waiting a few minutes, Marshall and Boseman step into the garage where Spell and Strubing are already noisily entangled in the back seat. Several minutes later she says, "Not inside me." He quickly withdraws and pulls a handkerchief from his pants pocket on the car floor.

Spell and Strubing caress and talk softly before they dress and get in the front seat, as the intruders slide outside and to the side of the garage, and Spell backs out and they drive away.

"We know damn well he didn't rape her or bind her or gag her with a portion of her ripped dress," says Thurgood Marshall.

"But we don't know why in the hell these two are going for a drive," says Chadwick Boseman. "Let's follow them."

"Better not. They'd see our headlights."

"Shouldn't we intercede?"

"If we do, there'll be three Negroes in jail instead of one."

A few hours later Joseph Spell is arrested after drenched and distraught Eleanor Strubing waves down a truck driver who calls police. They interrogate and threaten the suspect sixteen hours and announce Spell confessed to rape, kidnapping, and writing a ransom note. Marshall hires local attorney Samuel Friedman who has local experience and the right complexion to strengthen Spell's defense.

Friedman and Marshall, accompanied by Boseman, their "new private investigator," question Spell in jail.

"Why the hell did you confess?" asks Marshall.

"I didn't confess to doing anything wrong, just having sex because she wanted to."

"I can't understand why you two left the house," says Marshall.

"She said she was worried about getting pregnant and her husband finding out and all her friends hating her. I wasn't comfortable driving around late at night, especially with a white woman, but she's my boss and she insisted. Sure enough, the police stopped me."

"Where was Eleanor Strubing?" asks Samuel Friedman.

"Hiding on the floor of the back seat," Spell says.

"You're sure she wasn't gagged," says Friedman.

"I'm positive. She could've hollered to the police."

"Did you at any time coerce the lady?" Marshall asks.

"No. I've never seen a lady more anxious for company."

"Why did you drive to the river?" Marshall asks.

"She asked to go there."

"Did you throw her off that bridge and throw rocks at her?" asks Friedman

"Hell no."

"Why do you suppose she went into the water?" asks Boseman, startling the attorneys. "Just a lay question, gentlemen."

"Fortunately, we don't have to answer that question, Chadwick, though we may speculate, if it's beneficial to do so," says Marshall.

"What we must do," says Friedman, "is overcome a racist prosecutor who'll portray Mr. Spell as a lustful African beast who stalks helpless white women. Our tasks regarding the evidence are rather less daunting. Watch this."

Friedman pulls a rag out of his coat pocket and pulls it tight into his mouth and ties it around his neck.

The three men are examining him when he screams, "Ahhhhhh."

"I'm using that in court," he continues. "I'm also going to ask where was the physical evidence inside a woman who claims she was raped as many as four times. I'm going to hammer every inconsistency, and then I'm going to soothe the jury by conceding Mrs. Strubing and Mr. Spell 'had an improper relationship through the night.' No offense, Joseph, but I'll then acknowledge that the 'formality of marriage and divorce means nothing to' you. On the other hand, 'Mrs. Strubing has strong moral fiber and dignity. She knows she has done wrong.' She threw herself 'into the water to kill herself' but the cold imminence of death 'changed her' and rekindled her desire to live."

"That's wonderful, Mr. Friedman," says Chadwick Boseman. "I

think you need a much bigger part in this film."

"That's quite impossible," says Thurgood Marshall.

"Why?" asks Samuel Friedman.

"Because you're not going to successfully argue and win many cases before the United States Supreme Court, including Brown v. Board of Education which integrated schools, and you're not going to be a key figure in civil rights and voting rights and then serve twenty-four years as the first black justice on the Supreme Court."

"Right," says Friedman, "I won't do that, but we're talking about this movie."

"Sorry, Samuel, but Chadwick's signed to play the lead in this movie and that can't be you."

Number 42 at the Plate

"Jackie, thanks for letting me come here as you prepare for this historic season."

"My pleasure, Chadwick. I figured Hollywood would make a movie or two about me. When's this one coming out?"

"We should have it ready by 2013."

Robinson looks at him doubtfully and says, "Try that on someone who didn't leave UCLA, for a job, just a few units shy of graduation."

"I'm serious. I thought you knew where I was coming from."

"No, Branch Rickey and Leo Durocher just asked me to help an actor get ready to portray me."

Chadwick Boseman wears a suit and tie when he watches games from a box seat behind the Brooklyn Dodgers' dugout where he hears opposing players and managers curse Robinson, and every game quite a few fans bombard him, and thus the actor, with the same words and hostility. In the locker room some teammates are unfriendly and after games don't mind Robinson often has trouble dining with them or staying at the same hotel.

"Why don't you leave all this?" says Boseman. "You're nervous as hell."

"Wouldn't you be?"

"I am, and I'm not even you."

"This is a historical mission."

"You've still got to sleep and relax."

Robinson sighs and places a hand on his forehead.

"I'm not supposed to reveal the future, but I'm going to," says Boseman. "This unrelenting pressure's going to destroy your heart and induce diabetes and send you to a grave in your early fifties."

"I can't leave Rachel and the kids."

"I've arranged for them to come."

"Are you God Almighty?" asks Robinson.

"No, but I'm in with the group that can move people, same way I got here."

"That still doesn't address what I'm doing for our people. You don't expect me to abandon them, do you?"

Placing a hand on Robinson's foreman, Boseman says, "Here's what I suggest. Leave after three seasons. You're going to win the MVP award in 1949 and at that moment be the best baseball player in the world. You're going to score a hundred twenty-two runs and drive in a hundred-twenty four and steal thirty-seven bases and bat three-forty-two."

"Why would I leave then?"

"Because you've made your point. A Negro can play as well as or better than all the white stars in the major leagues."

"So I just disappear and forget about my people."

"Jackie, you were the sole Negro for only fifty days before Larry Doby joined the Cleveland Indians."

"I guarantee my being the first brought intense pressure."

"Agreed. But there are already four other Negroes in the majors. And soon there'll be Roy Campanella and Satchel Paige and Monte Irvin."

"You aren't being realistic. If I disappear, the racists will say, 'See, you can't depend on blacks.'"

"I want you to be cheered and appreciated everywhere you go. I want to see a relaxed superstar who's paid thirty million dollars a year."

Robinson laughs. "Now I know you're putting me on."

"Really, Jackie, after your third season, you'll only be thirty and that's a very realistic salary in the next century."

Joining his hands on the table, Robinson closes his eyes and breathes deeply as he concentrates. "This isn't an issue of money."

"I just mentioned the money and adulation and, above all, respect, as motivations. What I'm most concerned about is extending your life."

"I'm certainly under a lot of stress, but my body's strong and fast and my reflexes are fine-tuned and I'm starring on a great team and I do have plenty of adulation around the country, and not just from Negroes. Many white fans appreciate a great player, and I feel I'm going to win rookie of the year. I can't give up all that because some actor appears and says he's from decades in the future and I should return to his fantasy world?"

"I had to try, Jackie."

"Maybe you're acting to trick me."

"I'm here to learn."

"All right, slugger. Pay attention to 1947 and the history that's happening right now."

Notes: Jackie Robinson and Chadwick Boseman are box office and their film, *42,* has generated good reviews and more than a hundred million dollars in ticket sales and rentals. Boseman died from colon cancer when he was only forty-three, ten years younger than Robinson at the time of his passing.

JAMES GARNER

Garner Mellows Out

I know people think I'm confident and easygoing and maybe I am, now, as an adult but as a kid in Norman, Oklahoma I was scared a lot especially after my mother died and my dad married a horrible woman who beat hell out of my two brothers and me and sometimes made me wear a dress outside. She evidently didn't understand I was getting bigger and when I was about thirteen she punched me, and I punched back, knocking her down. She said I'll kill you little wretch and meant it so I choked her enough she stopped talking and started packing.

I really didn't like Norman. Later, as an actor, I enjoyed going home and meeting people excited to see me walking the sidelines at University of Oklahoma football games. Things weren't that way when I was sixteen. I wanted out and joined the Merchant Marine and enjoyed the work and travel and being with the guys but was seasick all the time and had to quit.

The following year, as World War II ended, I moved to Los Angeles, where Dad was working, and attended Hollywood High. Really, I was amazed how much the girls, and the guys, too, liked me, and voted me most popular. I even got a job paying me twenty-five an hour, a fortune in those days, to model bathing suits but felt a fool doing that and returned to Norman where I continued to do poorly in school and didn't graduate. I joined the National Guard and later the army and fought in the Korean War. I gave up dreams of becoming a general when one of our jets shot me in the ass. A while later I got hit by more friendly fire but earned a second Purple Heart since I was shooting at the enemy. I hope those guys were the enemy.

After this I decided Hollywood had been better than I realized and returned to try acting. I'd give it five years to see if I could make a living. That's all I wanted. I didn't care about being famous. I wanted that girl Lois I met at a rally for Adlai Stevenson in 1956. We went out every night for two weeks and then got married, and the following year I became a TV star on *Maverick* and a movie star in the sixties, playing in *The Great Escape*, *Grand Prix,* and others, and was back on TV in the seventies in *The Rockford Files* and doing pretty well but knew those executives had a congenital need to lie about revenue and shortchange the talent and I had to battle them years to get what I earned.

For the most part I stayed pretty calm thanks to pot. Can't imagine what I would've done without it. Alcohol made me feel angry and bad as hell. I also hated cocaine John Belushi gave me a few times. Ever hear of anyone getting violent or overdosing on pot? Trust my fifty years of experience. Pot should be legal and alcohol and coke should not.

GEORGE REEVES

Superman

It probably surprises you to learn I appear in the opening scene of *Gone with the Wind.* I wish they'd put me on screen with Clark Gable and Vivien Leigh. Doesn't anyone realize my potential? I continue getting mostly minor roles, often uncredited, and the few times I star I perform competently but moviegoers consider me bland if they notice at all. At least kids like my work in the *Adventures of Superman*, one of the major TV hits of the fifties.

In that role I often feel like an object of infantile curiosity and adult derision. And some of the latter, I assure you, comes from envy. Personally, I'm not angry about the screenplay of popular new movie *Hollywoodland* but think it's ironic I'm George Reeves, the guy the story's about, yet they invent a forlorn detective and tell you about his divorce and ongoing difficulties with his ex-wife and son, and how his girlfriend is screwing a fellow acting student, and show him getting beat up and thrown around and ignore he's trying to find out what really happens to me.

I understand Ben Affleck is graciously taking a big pay cut, all the way down to three million bucks, in order to be me. Poor fellow. Even adjusted for inflation that's more than I make in a career. At my Superman peak, I receive twenty-five hundred an episode. And for most of the hundred four they shoot, I get a lot less. My Daily Planet newspaper colleagues, Lois Lane and Jimmy Olsen, and editor Perry White, who frequently barks at this mild-mannered reporter, are also poorly compensated and contractually prevented from taking good roles that require more than a month of work.

Despite this, I'm doing fairly well. I have a nice but not large house in Benedict Canyon and always drive fine cars. This is possible since my girlfriend, Toni Mannix, helps out with things. In fact, she buys them. That's why they're in her name. I don't mind. She adores me not her husband Eddie who's become a crude and wealthy executive at MGM. Eddie Mannix doesn't care about his wife. He has a mistress.

Toni and I have fun. I've always enjoyed myself. I can out-drink most men and not appear drunk and show up on time in the morning and deliver dialogue memorized in a single reading. Some old friends feel I've fallen in with a bad crowd in forties New York as well as before and after that in Los Angeles. What is bad? According to many, it's anyone who drinks and goes to bed late. I go to bed early enough, usually before making anyone mad. I like people and they feel the same about me. They'll tell you I'm a helluva guy. And I'm just being honest when I say women want me. I accommodate as many as I can. That angered the lady I met when we were part of the Pasadena Playhouse repertory and married in 1940, and divorced a few years later, and it often hurts Toni. I don't want that. I'm simply getting what I need. Toni's eight years older and fifty-two when the final Superman episode runs in 1958.

During a business trip to New York I meet a beauty named Lenore Lemmon. She's nine years younger and we fall in love. Some friends say be careful, she's a heavy drinker already twice divorced and has wrung out other guys. That won't happen to me, I promise. Lenore is special. I tell Toni right away. She should understand but instead becomes hysterical. I try to comfort her but can't, and she begins calling my house – all right, my residence and her house – a dozen times or more a day, screaming or pleading or hanging up, often all three. Toni will have to accept I'm marrying Lenore in four days.

Around this time I have a wreck and bang my head. The doctor says I have a concussion and gives me strong medication. In *Hollywoodland* they say someone empties the brake fluid from my car. Some articles claim I hit an oil slick. I don't know about brakes or oil but can tell you there's a bruise on my forehead and another on my brain because I was driving drunk again. The kids don't know Superman smokes and drinks. I think I'll give up cigarettes but don't want to live without booze. My head hurts like hell. The pills really knock me down but don't do anything about the pain. I need plenty of alcohol on the evening of June fifteenth. Lenore's already drunk and getting aggressive. She once demanded I stop a workout with my judo instructor or she'd break her expensive antique lamp. I ignored her, and she flung the lamp on the floor.

Tonight she says, "You're getting old and heavy. And your hair's thinning."

"Maybe I shouldn't marry you after all."

I don't need her. I'm in demand. They're soon going to film more Superman episodes and broadcast them in 1960. I dread putting on another cape and muscle-padded costume but know I have to. When I look at glistening photos of myself from the forties or my early Superman days, I cringe at a sagging hero who may soon be unemployable. I down another drink and more tranquilizers. Lenore and I have one invited guest, and two others come without notice after midnight on June sixteenth. I scold them for rudeness then drink another strong one before telling Lenore, "Quit griping." I need to sleep. My face feels big as a ham and my head's splitting.

In my bedroom I reach for the drawer as Lenore rushes in. She later says she's been downstairs with the guests, who evidently agree, but reveals that earlier in the day she accidentally fired bullet holes in the floor while playing around. That seems strange, and so does an out-of-place rug thrown over the holes. Get out, I tell her, and open the drawer. I don't remember anything else. When your blood alcohol content is .27 – about like guys on skid row – and you're twice that low because of pills, you don't care some people soon and forever insist there are no powder burns on my hand and the shot is fired more than a foot from my head. I'm not sure I believe that, but the immediate investigation should be more thorough. That's why all you get are allegations about Lenore, and Toni and Eddie Mannix, and others. My mother hires private detectives. They can't prove anything in three years before I'm cremated, and even today people don't understand. I felt bad enough to do it.

CHARACTERS

ROBERT DENIRO

LaMotta

In a steamy Manhattan gym Jake LaMotta, pushing sixty, attacks a younger man, staying close to pound his body and head, and lands a left jab to his nose after the bell.

"That's how it is, Bobby," he says. "You gotta kill the other guy."

"I'm getting better, aren't I, Jake?" says De Niro, puffing.

"You're improving but I'da killed you. Still could."

De Niro takes out his mouthpiece and says, "I don't box like you, Jake, but I can be as big an asshole."

"You and Martin Scorsese better not go too far."

"Our writers and Martin and I are creating a great script."

"I don't want any problems with my ex-wives."

Patting LaMotta's left shoulder with his right glove, De Niro says, "No worries, Jake, we're only dealing with the first two. In fact, I talked to Irma a few days ago."

"What'd she say?"

"She says after your first loss you yelled at her and upended the kitchen table because she was slow cooking your meat. And your neighbors shouted you were an animal. Maybe that's fair since you told Irma to settle down or you'd kill her."

"I guess I coulda been a better guy."

De Niro smiles at the former champ, who's at least fifty pounds over his fighting weight, and says, "I recently talked to Vickie, too."

He wistfully says, "What a beautiful woman. I was in love the moment I saw that face and blond hair. My brother Joey took her out before I met her, but he swears he didn't touch her. I couldn't wait. Irma knew something was up and screamed, 'You're married,' when I got dressed up to go out."

Pointing to a pigeonhole office near the ring, De Niro says, "Let's go sit down and make sure we've got the right details or at least the dramatic essence."

After a trainer removes their gloves and cuts their tape, they sit across a gnarled desk from each other, filling the room.

"Joey introduced me to Vickie at a dance. She trusted me. In a few days I took her for a drive in my convertible and we went someplace private and I almost died when she sat on my lap and I did die when we went into the bedroom. She knew she was with the guy who'd just beaten Sugar Ray Robinson. Knocked him down, too."

Looking concerned, De Niro says, "It bothers me how the managers, promoters, gangsters, all those bums, made you guys fight so often."

"Right, three weeks later I was back in the ring with Robinson. That's crazy, huh. I didn't question it then, though. I even told Vickie I couldn't let her kiss my body because I had to save myself for Robinson. I couldn't have held back unless I'd poured ice water in my underwear. That killed me. It was tough on Vickie, too."

The actor opens a folder on the desk and says, "Here's my list of all your fights, Jake. I've got notes, too. You knocked Sugar Ray down in the seventh round."

"That was our third fight, and I knocked him down each time. Ray's a great fighter but don't believe that shit about nobody ever decking him. I give him credit. He probably outboxed me our first fight. I won the second. And I think I won the third, too. Maybe the judges favored him because he was going into the army the next day. This was in early '43 when the war was a big deal."

Tapping his folder, De Niro says, "I've also got plenty of your personal highlights."

"You want to call 'em highlights, okay with me."

"You married Vickie and had some kids."

"That was wonderful for a while, but I couldn't trust the woman. There I was, around 1947, getting ready for a tough guy named Tony Janiro, and Vickie's talking about how good looking he is. I tell Joey to keep his eye on Vickie. What for, he says. Because she's sweet on this guy Janiro who a lot of broads like. When I took her and Joey and his girlfriend to the Copacabana, she made a big deal of getting up and going over to the table of some bad guys from the neighborhood and letting them kiss her cheek. One of them asked me what he should do about the Janiro fight. I told him bet everything he's got on me. I could've knocked Janiro out but made sure he lasted ten rounds so I could keep punching his bloody face. Vickie never said anything about him after that. But she talked to too many men. And some were dumb enough to act interested, even after I warned them. I slapped one bum who kissed her on the lips. Have some respect."

De Niro picks up a pen and aims it at blank paper.

"It pisses me off the way they made you guys throw fights," he says.

"They flat told me I'd never get a title shot, which I should've had years earlier, unless I took a dive against one of their stiffs."

The actor writes Billy Fox and says, "Must've hurt to pretend to be stopped, standing against the ropes in the fourth round."

"The guy's punches sure didn't hurt but being booed did. People knew that bum couldn't have beaten me square, so I got called a fixer and a gangster and was suspended."

"At least you got your title shot against Marcel Cerdan."

"Yeah, but I had to wait another year and a half, until 1949."

"Cerdan was a helluva fighter," says De Niro.

"He couldn't do much against me."

"Because he had a dislocated shoulder."

"That happened when I decked him in the first round. He'd have been tougher in the rematch. It was sad the way he died in that plane crash, flying to see his girlfriend, that French singer Edith Piaf. I kept busy with other guys but my toughest battles were against Vickie."

Pen poised, De Niro asks, "What happened?"

"I'd ask, where were you? And she'd ignore me. So I asked Joey, did that guy fuck Vickie? No, he said. I'm going to kill somebody, I warned him and Vickie. Did you fuck my wife, Joey? Joey said he wasn't going to answer that because I was sick and he was leaving. So I turned to Vickie and asked if she fucked my brother. I needed some answers. Why'd you fuck Joey? Then she got smartass and said, yeah, I fucked him, and I sucked his cock because it's a lot bigger than yours. I punched her out and hurried over to Joey's and beat hell out of him and when I got home Vickie was packing and I begged her not to go."

"All that stress must've hurt you in the ring."

"Probably… In 1951 I fought Sugar Ray Robinson for the sixth time. The record book says I was one and four against him before I gave him a shot at my title. I'd say it was more like three to two my favor. The last time, though, he beat hell out of me. He was so quick and had long arms and was getting stronger all the time. He stopped me in the thirteenth but, through my blood and bruises, I told him he couldn't knock me down. He knew who'd gone down in our fights.

"I wasn't even twenty-nine but felt about ninety. I'd had almost a hundred fights, most of them wars. I went up to light heavyweight and did okay until a strong guy named Danny Nardico nailed me with a right cross and I went down for the first time in my life. I got up but my corner stopped it when the round ended. No one ever put the knock on me. I quit for more than a year and only fought three more times and was done before I turned thirty-two. That's why I'm still so pretty and articulate. By the way, since I'm so much bigger than I was and you are now, how're you going to play the older me?"

Patting his stomach with both hands, De Niro extends them about a foot and says, "I'm going to our ancestral homeland and eat pasta till I'm bigger than you ever were."

"And how will you prepare for my comedy routines?"

"It's gonna be tough delivering jokes like yours, Jake."

Notes: Robert De Niro won the best actor Oscar for portraying Jake LaMotta, *The Raging Bull* in film as in life. He married seven times and lived to be ninety-five.

King of Comedy

After the show at a New York comedy club, I order another orange juice, scan a few dozen tables in a room where the lights just came on, and notice two old men in the furthest corner. One's about ninety and the other in his seventies. My eyes must be haywire. Is that really them? They look like Jerry Langford and Rupert Pupkin who in 1982 starred in *The King of Comedy,* a movie that upon release made more people uncomfortable than it entertained but has become, to sophisticated viewers, a celebrated study of obsession, mental illness, and comedy. I have to talk to those guys. I stand and walk tentatively to their table.

"Hi, good evening," I say. "I want you to know I think *The King of Comedy* is one of the greatest films ever made."

The older man, Jerry, looks at me like I'm on a Most Wanted poster and says, "We're busy. Goodbye."

As I turn, Rupert says, "Hold on. You really think so?"

"I do. Every scene's just right, every line of dialogue perfect."

"Sit down and join us," says Rupert.

I take a seat and shake his hand. Jerry keeps his right hand on a nonalcoholic drink.

"I watch *The King of Comedy* every year," I say. "I've been trying to break in as a stand-up for a long time."

"You must be the Rupert Pupkin of this generation," Jerry says.

"Would you guys like to hear some of my material?"

"Definitely not," says Jerry.

"You could email me a file," says Rupert, handing me his card.

"Thanks so much. I really didn't come over here to talk about myself, though."

"What're you here for," Jerry says.

"To talk about *The King of Comedy.*"

"Is that Rupert or me?"

"Both. I loved how Rupert spent years waiting outside the studio where you hosted your talk show, which I still feel was better than Johnny Carson's, and sort of forced his way into the backseat of your limousine."

"If I'd had a gun, I'd have shot him. Don't try anything like that."

I nod and say, "I don't have Rupert's conviction."

Jerry looks at Rupert and says, "I was dumb enough to give him my business card, and he barged into my goddamn office and security had to throw him out."

"Thankfully, all that's on film," I say, feeling like I'm at the movies. "Rupert, I still can't believe you and your lady friend, another aspiring comic, had the guts to kidnap Jerry."

"You must be a moron to think kidnapping's brave," Jerry says.

"I mean, despite the risks, Rupert believed so deeply in his comedic ability that he forced you, or at least those who worked for you, to put him on air."

Jerry takes his right hand off the glass and aims a wobbly index finger at my forehead. "He only got on air because he threatened to kill me if my people didn't put him on at the start of the show. That's sick, and Rupert soon realized it."

Shaking his head, Rupert says, "I don't think I figured it out right away, Jerry. I had to be a star for myself and that beautiful black bartender who I wasn't good enough for until I became somebody. I couldn't stand assistants and other flunkies always rejecting me without the great ones, like Jerry Langford, seeing what I could do.

"Once we had Jerry tied up, gagged, and stashed away in New York, I felt far more energy and confidence than ever. I knew I'd written the best monologue of my life. I couldn't have unless I'd been creating it for *The Jerry Langford Show*, and the wonderful lady I planned to marry."

"You're not that crazy anymore, Rupert," says Jerry.

"Since my monologue on that show attracted more than eighty million people, and I got a lot of publicity in prison, and my success has continued, I think I can cling to some sanity."

I look empathetically at Rupert Pupkin and ask, "What happened to the pretty bartender?"

"She filed a restraining order against me, and her boyfriend threatened to take me out. I'm happy to report she's had two divorces and gained fifty pounds. Look at the broads I have today."

"Does it ever bother you that some women like you because you're rich and famous?"

"Not at all. Does it ever both you, Jerry?"

"Only thing that bugs me is I can't get it up anymore."

"Thank you both for talking to me," I say, standing.

"Don't forget," says Jerry Langford, "you ever pull a Rupert and force your way into my limo, I'll shoot your ass."

Laughing, I ask, "What about you?"

"I gotta say yeah, cuz most guys who'd do that are violent," says Rupert Pupkin.

DUSTIN HOFFMAN

The Graduate at Fifty

People still love *The Graduate* and ask the same questions. What happened to Mrs. Robinson? How's her daughter Elaine doing? Is she still with Benjamin Braddock? No one ever asks how I am. I'm only Mr. Robinson, the trusting husband whose wife incessantly screws Benjamin, the son of my law partner. I should kill the little bastard, especially after he starts dating Elaine and compels my wife to accuse Benjamin of getting her drunk and raping her. I check that out and learn the truth. Mrs. Robinson is a nymphomaniac. At least I force my daughter to quit college and agree to marry a nice young man. Their union might help Mrs. Robinson and me rebuild our relationship. Instead, that obsessive runt breaks into the wedding chapel and disturbed Elaine flees with him. That's what you know. Happy ending, right? No sir.

I call the police and report a kidnapping. They quickly locate Elaine and Benjamin in a nearby motel room. The little punk accuses me of ruining their first night as man and wife. I try to explain what just happened but the police smirk and drive away. They should file a report because unstable guys like Benjamin never just miraculously become normal.

Right away Elaine gets pregnant and has another child a year after the first. Benjamin starts commenting she's getting chubby and my beautiful daughter, instead of saying shut up or leaving him, runs into the bedroom and cries. Benjamin works a lot of late hours for a guy who's often out of the office when Elaine calls. I know damn well what he's doing. I see it in his weird expressions.

One night two detectives come to their home to talk about complaints he's stalking a woman. Another woman accuses him of slapping her. Look at what you married, I tell my daughter. She's stuck at home caring for two babies and not ready to make a move. Meanwhile, Mrs. Robinson and I have had separate bedrooms since her betrayal. Every time I look at her I see Benjamin between her legs. She's disgusting. If they betray you once they'll do it again, and I'm pretty sure she screwing around with a friend of one of my clients. I confront her. She ignores me. I say I can do this too. She says she doubts it but go ahead and try.

I'm out of practice and don't have much luck so start hiring hookers to meet me in hotel rooms where, after twenty or so encounters, there's a knock and I'm arrested. Mrs. Robinson calls me pathetic. I tell her she's a whore. She says I ought to know. Elaine says, Daddy, how could you. The real question is why I don't kill Benjamin. He's not worth it. Neither is Mrs. Robinson. I don't even punch her. On occasion I just give her a couple of slaps. Once she calls the police. They don't see any damage. My destruction is inside.

Mrs. Robinson sues me for half our property and she can have it and whoever's unlucky to get her next. At least we both agree to help Elaine find a part-time job and go back to college and study business so she can build skills and regain confidence and leave that bastard as soon as possible.

Tootsie

When classmates ignore him, he shoves books off the desk and then prays they quit staring because he knows what they're thinking since they're saying it – Dustin Hoffman's got the biggest nose I've ever seen. No way he's going to give an oral report about a biography of Jimmy Durante. Either do so or get an F, says the teacher. The whole time his face burns explaining how sensitive Durante was about his own huge nose and their giggles make Hoffman cry and run from the room all the way home. He keeps his guard up, especially when he decides he's an actor. He just hasn't had any roles yet and works lots of terrible jobs. As a sales clerk he sometimes loudly accuses customers of stealing merchandise, and if they demand to see the manager he warns they're being filmed by Candid Camera. As a waiter he insults rude customers. Don't these idiots understand?

He's going to be a star. If directors don't like the way he's playing his small roles, he tells them they're dumb and sometimes quits before they fire him. Conflict intensifies his vision of how roles should be played. For years friends or maybe enemies tell him he's made himself unemployable. His current character, Michael Dorsey, can't find work so he secretly auditions as actress Dorothy Michaels and curses and jerks people around and says lines not in the script. Dorothy gets the role and makes the soap opera a hit and off camera the testosterone-fueled thespian chases an unwilling woman while an unknowing man pursues the dress-wearing actor, and the set of *Tootsie* sounds like a series of rush-hour wrecks as Hoffman argues with directors and other actors and harangues makeup artists – who bear the Herculean task of making him look like a passable woman – and in general behaves like an actor with rare talent and the ability to generate a hundred eighty million bucks at the box office.

CLAUDE RAINS

The Notorious Claude Rains

Slipping through a rear window of Alfred Hitchcock's mansion and down a hall into the study, Claude Rains finds Cary Grant and the host hunched over a script he knows is *Notorious.*

"Put down your sharp pens," he orders.

"Claude, you've been drinking," says Hitchcock.

"I've need for sedation rather than suffer your insults."

"What are you talking about?" asks Hitchcock.

Stretching tall as his short frame will permit, Rains says, "You very well know."

"This is most inappropriate," says Grant.

"I know what you're planning," Rains says, pulling his coat back to reveal a holstered revolver.

Hitchcock labors to stand. "Claude, I may have to replace you."

"No, Alfred, I have a rather more charming alternative. And do please sit down."

Rains sits at the opposite end of the table.

"What do you want?" asks the rotund director.

"That I shall explain."

Grim in an unpleasant way rarely seen on screen, Grant says, "Hurry up. This meeting is between the director and the star."

"I rather expected you, the eternally romantic hero, to be insensitive about this matter. A few devastating examples will suffice. In *The Adventures of Robin Hood* I was billed third among actors despite my dramatic abilities being immeasurably superior to those of Errol Flynn."

"You know the rules of cinema, Claude," says Hitchcock. "People who look like Errol and Cary generally play the leads and receive onscreen love as well as adulation from the masses."

"I'm sure that's rather painful for you, too, Alfred."

Hitchcock somberly says, "Yes, indeed it is. That's why I'm a fat and bald but brilliant director. And you're an attractive and superb character actor but you aren't beautiful. This man is."

"All right," says Rains, "what about my entertaining but subordinate role in *Casablanca* when I have to say if I were a woman I'd adore Rick, the rather worn-looking Humphrey Bogart."

"May I add something?" Grant asks.

"You may not."

"People like you and me, Claude…" says Hitchcock.

"Don't compare your physical presence to mine, Alfred. That's absurd."

"This evening the venomous mouth appears to be yours," says Hitchcock. "You're surely aware that Bogart in his early forties still maintained some of the Valentino looks that had prompted Broadway scouts to send him to Hollywood. Furthermore, the man's charisma dominates the screen."

"No more than mine," says Grant.

"I wasn't implying it did."

"I feel I could have played Robin Hood as well as Flynn and Rick better than Bogart," says Rains.

"No one could've matched Bogart in that role," says Hitchcock. "That's why Ingrid Bergman loves him."

"I'm also appalled by what they do to me in *Phantom of the Opera.* I spend myself into financial want while paying for the voice lessons of a young lady I love and then, trying to recover, I write a piano concerto that a devious publisher steals. He deserves to be strangled. If Cary committed this righteous act, he'd suffer no lasting consequences. But what happens to me? His assistant hurls acid in my face and I'm forever disfigured and doomed to live in the catacombs below the opera where I'll perish."

"You murdered at least two more people, didn't you?" Grant asks.

"I didn't write that script, Cary, but I'm going to rewrite this one. Both of you take notes about the following improvements."

Neither moves. Rains pats his coat. They pick up their pens.

"This is really quite simple, gentlemen, just a few nuanced changes. Instead of being a Nazi concealing uranium in Brazil after World War II, I'm a decorated veteran of the Royal Air Force who Cary offers millions of dollars to help the fascists develop an atomic bomb. I pretend to be interested but, instead, assign two investigators to monitor him. Meanwhile, gorgeous Ingrid Bergman visits Brazil and, by coincidence, rides past me on horseback one afternoon and we resume our romance from a few years earlier.

"Cary has dated her in the United States and is in love and tries to keep us under surveillance, using binoculars and hidden microphones and other devious means, but he gets that horrid feeling, one I've had in numerous roles and several real divorces, when he learns the woman he adores is in love with another man.

"We can retain the part when I marry Ingrid right away, but my troublesome mother, who's 'always jealous of any woman' I'm interested in, must this time sadly die. Let's have the horse she's riding bolt and buck her headfirst into a tree. Ingrid consoles me and, at the same time, urges that we continue to keep Cary under surveillance. This enables our agents to observe Cary meeting Nazis who've smuggled uranium into Brazil. They follow him to an eerie house where he hides the radioactive material."

Hitchcock and Grant listen noncommittally.

Since Ingrid is faithful and passionate I have no need to poison her. No, the enemy of justice must be punished. That would be you, Cary, not me. We may shoot you. We may stab you. Your car might explode. These particulars can be worked out by your talented but starstruck screenwriter Ben Hecht."

"What a coincidental reference," says Hitchcock, smirking as he peers behind Rains, who turns to look into a gun barrel.

"Touch my masterpiece and I'll kill you," says Hecht.

EDWARD G. ROBINSON

In My Gallery

People call my art gallery, and indeed much of my Beverly Hills mansion, The Museum because twice a week I invite the public to enjoy works by van Gogh, Gauguin, Picasso, Monet, Pissarro, Modigliani, and a few dozen more. Even my cook, maid, and butler are required, or rather honored, to if necessary serve as docents and speak knowledgably about these wonderful paintings. My celebrity pals can stop by any time. I'm forever delighted to stimulate lovers of beauty. That's also an important part of what makes an actor.

I've earned a rather lucrative living portraying wiseguy gangsters in movies like *Little Caesar* and *Key Largo* or shrewd investigators who trap criminals in *The Stranger* and *Double Indemnity,* yet I'm always broke or nearly so, and imagine you've already surmised why. The moment I'm paid for a movie I scurry to New York or London or Paris or anywhere I might find enchanting art. This isn't simply for the delectation of my eyes; it's for the nurturing of my soul. I feel the beauty I see and empathize with the dedication, skill, and pain of those who create great paintings.

Discovering little known artists is a particular joy. Some years ago my wife Gladys and I visited Mexico City and the suburban studio, built high into trees, of celebrated muralist Diego Rivera, who paints just as movingly on canvas. I bought a few fine pieces, including a penetrating portrait of an indigenous woman, and in Spanish, which I understood a little better than he did English, he said, "I'm sure you're familiar with Frida's work."

"Frida?"

"My lovely and talented wife, Frida Kahlo."

"I haven't had the pleasure, Diego, but would be delighted to meet her."

From Rivera's elevated space we walked across a bridge to Frida's adjoining studio.

"Frida thinks this place is a little cramped so she usually paints in our Casa Azul near here, but she's here today, in your honor, and has some of her quite unique works ready to view."

We entered Frida's studio and I was at once taken by her beauty and charm.

"You should be in movies," I told her.

"In starring or supporting roles?"

"Starring, of course. I'd only get second billing behind you."

Her laugh soothed me.

"I know you're a distinguished collector, Señor Robinson, and am anxious to learn what you think of my work."

"First, call me Eddie."

"If you call me Frida."

"Frida, your paintings are as alluring as you are, and in many cases I see you are your work. This self-portrait is superb. What's it called?"

"*Self Portrait with Necklace.*"

"I'll take it. And that painting and that one and that one as well. How much are they?"

Frida looked at Diego grinning above his massive frame.

"I hope you find two hundred dollars each congenial."

"Está muy bien," I said, and reached for a wallet laden with pesos and dollars. "You're going to be famous someday, Frida."

"I hope when I'm still alive," she said.

"Don't worry. You're young and healthy."

She glanced at Diego who stopped smiling.

I have many stimulating experiences seeking art treasures around the world and don't always burden myself with Gladys, who's growing as tired of me as I am of her. I meet Jane, a very bright lady who loves art and is a quarter century my junior. Let me concede this is a congenial combination. The three of us eventually admit to ourselves and each other how this is going to work out and Gladys and I hire attorneys to proceed with our divorce.

"Too bad about the art collection, Eddie," she says.

"What's too bad?"

"Half of it's mine, you know?"

Feeling like a gorilla's grabbed my stomach with both hands, I can't respond.

"You know the community property laws in California, Eddie. We must have an equitable division."

While I'm in New York starring in the hit play *Middle of the Night,* and squiring Jane to the finest clubs after shows, Gladys thrusts her dagger, inviting numerous stars including Elizabeth Taylor and John Huston to a farewell party for my art collection. She tells the guests and two invited newspaper reporters, "A van Gogh for Eddie and one for me, a Matisse for him and one for me…"

I'm so upset I forget a line that night and have to briefly leave the stage. In a few days I settle down and realize I'll still have half a great collection and the opportunity to keep collecting. When I return to Los Angeles, I meet with Gladys in my gallery as our lawyers watch.

"I've decided, Eddie, that I don't need art as much as I need money. We demand that you liquidate our collection forthwith."

I wonder what I would do if we were alone. I probably wouldn't do anything physical but can't guarantee what I'd say.

"Give me some time."

"How much and for what purpose?" says Gladys.

"I need a year to sell part of the collection and earn money from acting to pay you off."

"In addition to half our art collection and house, don't forget we're demanding a quarter of all your future earnings."

"Show yourselves out," I tell Gladys and her leering attorney.

Wealthy bargain hunters are much aware of my dilemma but I usually manage to stay calm when they offer unsuitably low prices. I simply exhale cigar smoke and say, "No thanks."

Following several months of this degrading process I get a call from Gladys' attorney who says, "It's time, Mr. Robinson. We need half the fair market value of the art collection soon. If you can't make an acceptable deal, we will."

"Come on over and we'll deal in person."

"Relax, Mr. Robinson. At least you'll no longer need a security guard in front of your house and another in back twenty-four hours a day. In fact, you won't even have a house, not the one where you currently reside. And please do get the home cleared out and cleaned up ready for sale."

Greek shipping magnate Starvos Niarchos, an acquaintance from the art world, agrees to meet me in New York. I sell him most of my collection for three and a quarter million dollars.

"I'd also like to request that we sign a friendly agreement allowing me, at your convenience, to buy back as many of these treasures as I in the future can."

"We don't need a written contract," says Niarchos, thrusting a hand I eagerly shake. "You have my word."

For a short, cigar-smoking pug from the Lower East Side via Rumania, I recover pretty well after being blackballed for alleged ties to communism, a preposterous notion, and resume getting jobs in movies, as a character actor now, and also in television, and earn enough money to help my only son, Manny, recover from alcoholism, mental illness, and legal problems. To relax I joke with great friends Groucho Marx and Jack Benny at the Hillcrest Country Club. And I continue to buy thrilling art even after a heart attack, a serious car wreck, and bladder cancer which doctors and I think we stopped but it returns and I have to tell everyone farewell.

Notes: One year after the death of Edward G. Robinson, his unstable son, Manny, suddenly died at age forty of what doctors ruled natural causes. He and Jane and the actor's granddaughter inherited his rebuilt art collection, which oil tycoon Armand Hammer purchased for more than five million dollars, about thirty million dollars today. Despite the informal oral commitment, Starvos Niarchos rarely sold Robinson any works from the actor's original collection.

KURT GERRON

Gerron's Academy Award

I'm planning to be a doctor but, after my wounds in the Great War, I need to laugh and bound onto cabaret stages of Berlin, telling funny stories and singing, and in a short time all my shows are sellouts. While Germany and much of the world plummet into an economic abyss I rejoice in every performance, live in an elegant apartment, and dine and travel first class.

I also yearn to be in movies and get many roles but directors won't let me star. You're quite charming, Kurt, even charismatic, but a hefty man smoking fat cigars can't be a romantic lead. I can play anyone else, though, and appear in *The Blue Angel* under Marlene Dietrich, and also direct. I'm always entertaining and believe many Nazis understand. They've surely heard me sing "Mack the Knife," but today storm troopers are singing the "Horst Wessel Song" as they march onto my movie set. Smiling, I stand to offer autographs and cabaret tickets.

"Get off the set, Jew, and don't stink it up again."

I walk away but know Germans will want me back. Meanwhile, I move to Paris. In this great city I don't need Hollywood like many German colleagues. When money becomes scarce I head to Amsterdam. No thanks, I still tell Hollywood and its offers. I'm doing a Dutch airline ad but it's soon cancelled. Okay, I write to director Fritz Lang, a fellow Germanic Jew. He doesn't answer but his agent does, warning an actor like me may not be popular in United States and he can't recommend I relocate on speculation.

Fine. The Dutch now pack theaters but I'm worried the Nazi propaganda film *The Eternal Jew* uses shots of me as a particularly repugnant sort, and soon I arrive at the theater to discover it's a transport center for Jews, and I'm on a train heading East. Don't worry, Nazis say, you'll be comfortable. I pray that's true.

At Theresienstadt guards take my clothes, watch, and remaining cash but people there are delighted to see Kurt Gerron ready to perform in plays. We have many actors, musicians, painters, and creative people here. At times it's almost like home, in a spiritual sense. Physically, we deal with more people, less food, more disease, and recurring whispers we could any moment be transported to a terrible place in Poland.

That won't happen. I'm on stage and people are cheering. There's hope. Nazis are fixing up part of the camp for Red Cross representatives who tour neat apartments inhabited by well-dressed people eating big healthy meals prior to going outside to stroll among flowers, and Red Cross folks say Theresienstadt's wonderful.

Following our successful live performance, the camp commandant tells me to direct a documentary film, and then I'll be free. I first ask our council of elders who say, don't feel guilty, survive. What thrilling experiences I have, orchestrating actors and elements of major production. Kids smile and eat bread and look happy and healthy like soccer players in a courtyard game hundreds watch from a pretty building around the field. After the game people go home to fine dinners and later gather in the auditorium and listen to our great orchestra. I'm creating a special place and ignore a guard who calls me a stinking Jew. I'll soon be rid of him. My film's going to win an award I'll receive when production ends in September 1944. Next month my wife and I are put on train that stops where a sign arcs over the entrance: Arbeit Macht Frei.

GEORGE SANDERS

Starring George Sanders

I believe I'm a leading man. I'm tall and have a well-shaped nose and patrician face and a deep distinctive voice and can plausibly win the girl or, if compelled, send her where she'll no longer displease me. I should star in the finest movies. Perhaps someday I shall.

For the moment, a decade or so into my career, I do concede, unless one wants to dominate B movie backlots, that it's necessary to tacitly accept that a handful of actors are simply prettier or more charismatic or dramatically gifted. Laurence Olivier, the gentleman starring in *Rebecca,* is a sublime example of such genetic good fortune. I often overwhelm lesser players but when I sign for this supporting role I in essence concede the other man is king.

I nevertheless sense a way to at least temporarily take the throne. I'm a cad in life and becoming typecast as one on screen so am rather comfortable telling Alfred Hitchcock I'd appreciate a brief but critical, and confidential, script change late in the movie.

"Our audience wouldn't like that," he says.

"Nor would they find this congenial," I counter, presenting a personal letter written in his hand that would distress Mrs. Hitchcock, his professional as well as personal partner.

Burdened by fifty kilos of fat, much of it in his face, Hitchcock generally bears an ominous expression and this one darkens. As he begins to turn away I snatch the letter and say, "I may add screenwriting to my resume."

For the present we proceed as planned and reveal Olivier's beautiful wife Rebecca died mysteriously at sea and he replaced the charming lady with a new and dear wife. Authorities are unalarmed until they discover the corpse of Rebecca offshore in Olivier's boat whose bottom was punctured with holes to facilitate sinking. That would be a strange not to mention physically impossible way for a distressed lady to commit suicide.

At this moment it is my profound duty to produce a letter, handwritten by Rebecca and dated the day of her death, in which she expresses love for me and her joy in living. This is not, I state at the inquest, the note of one planning to end her life that night. I could've suppressed this missive if Olivier had been of a more generous nature, but a star must always be dignified and victorious. Conversely, humble actors like George Sanders usually fail in ignominious ways.

Not this time. I disclose the name of Rebecca's doctor in London and lead a variety of relevant people to his office. She used a pseudonym but the doctor checks dates and medical records and remembers her great beauty and delight in being pregnant. What a wonderful experience she and I and our child could've enjoyed. The sheriff apologizes to wealthy Olivier for placing him under arrest.

Eyes widening like those of a provincial ham, Olivier says, "Alfred, what the devil is this? We agreed that Rebecca bore terminal cancer rather than a child and despondency overwhelmed her."

"Recent creative impulses have compelled me to improve the ending," says the director.

DAVID CARRADINE

Bangkok

When friends and I gathered in the mid-seventies for pot-fueled TV watching, we usually tuned to football, basketball, and boxing. The most significant exception was *Kung Fu,* a legendary series in which Kwai Chang Caine, played by David Carradine, embraced the wise and soothing philosophies of Asian martial artists before he righteously, and in mesmerizing slow motion, counterattacked and thrashed bigots in the Old West. At the time Carradine had little training in such matters but inexperience was no impediment to an actor born. The distinguished and haunting John Carradine had fathered him as well as three half-brothers who would also create characters on screen.

For some three decades I largely lost track of David Carradine, and that's primarily my fault, though Hollywood and its money-over-story mentality must also be blamed for the relative pigeonholing of a unique actor. I should have figured Carradine was doing something good but his films usually didn't play long, even at art house theaters, and many appeared before VCRs extended viewing opportunities. Online research now reveals Carradine in 1976 played folksinger Woody Guthrie in *Bound for Glory,* earning a nomination for the Golden Globe Award. The following year he was summoned by Ingmar Bergmann, master of angst and disturbed relationships, to play a Jewish trapeze artist in *The Serpent's Egg.* Not long before the Nazis begin to strangle Europe, Carradine and his prostitute cum cabaret girlfriend, Liv Ullmann, start working for a doctor who, they later discover, is conducting "cannibalistic human experiments that foreshadow the horrors of concentration camps." In 1980 the Carradine brothers joined the brothers Keach, Quaid, and Guest to make *The Long Riders*, "director Walter Hill's gritty retelling of the story of the James-Younger gang."

During this period Carradine directed and starred in *Americana,* a film about a Vietnam veteran coming home to rural Kansas and trying to regain a normal "life by rebuilding an old carousel. The townspeople are initially distrustful of the man, but eventually give him support. A labor of love for" Carradine. Critics shredded the actor – he vomited in a New York City hotel bathroom after reading the reviews – and moviegoers rejected him.

He didn't reemerge until *Kill Bill: Vol. 1* in 2003 and *Kill Bill: Vol. 2* the following year when Quentin Tarantino's film noirs inspired edgy and dynamic scenes, my final images of Carradine until the report of his death in Bangkok where he was making a film. The initial release from Bangkok police stated the actor had hanged himself with a curtain cord tied to a support bar in the closet of his luxury hotel suite. Was that plausible?

It seemed so. In a 2004 interview with the *Telegraph Newspaper*, Carradine stated, "Look, there was a period in my life when I had a single action Colt .45 loaded in my desk drawer. And every night I'd take it out and think about blowing my head off, and then decide not to and go on with my life. Put it back in the drawer and open up the laptop and continue writing my autobiography or whatever. But it was just to see." In other interviews the actor said he'd also had periods of intense drinking and taking many psychotropic drugs generally used to treat depression and anxiety. With so many disturbances, he perhaps did want out. But then Bangkok police released more information: Carradine not only had a curtain cord around his neck but another around his genitals. And his hands were bound to the support bar above his head. Police called it kinky sex. Psychiatrists diagnose it as autoerotic asphyxiation, a way to intensify sexual gratification by intentionally cutting off oxygen to the brain. Astonishingly, some men pop erections while being hanged and maintain them in death.

There are also troubling accusations by two of Carradine's former wives. (At the time of his death, the actor was said by family members to be happily married to his fifth wife.) Gail Jensen, number three, who divorced Carradine in 1997, said, "David was pretty strange. He would like to get tied up. He would tie himself up and I would walk in and see him and say, 'Oh my God, David, you got to be kidding me' - and I would (turn around and) walk out. I would leave him to his own devices... He spent days planning a different feature. He would go to a hardware store and buy the stuff." In a 2003 divorce document filed by Carradine's fourth wife, Marina Anderson asserted he was prone to "deviant sexual behavior which was potentially deadly." Indeed, every year in the United States several hundred people, virtually all men, die from autoerotic asphyxiation, seeking a thrill most can't fathom.

JESSE EISENBERG

The Eisenberg Network

There are lots of people in the ballroom tonight and scenes like this usually worsen my anxiety and depression. What will I say? I hope I'll be funny. I often am. But sometimes I'm impatient, especially if people say dumb things or remark I'm shorter than expected. I'm tall enough, same as Mark Zuckerberg, and think oh no here he comes.

"Mark, nice to meet you. I'm Jesse Eisenberg," I say.

"That's why I'm here," says the founder of Facebook.

"I hope you enjoyed *The Social Network*."

He doesn't frown but says, "I didn't like the film at all. You and the screenwriters got me wrong, not because you're incompetent but because of malice. Instead of admitting I had a pretty boring life, writing computer codes and working twenty-four/seven to start an online business, you invented a bunch of insulting things that still bug me."

I smile at Mark. I hope I'm smiling.

"This isn't a documentary," I explain. "Some of the dialogue has to be invented. We tried to present you in a cinematically accurate way."

"Nonsense. You guys show me being hypercritical on a date and the young lady saying my problem isn't that I'm a nerd, it's that I'm an asshole. Shortly after that you have me starting a website so I can find girls. For your edification, I was already dating my girlfriend, Priscilla, and she thought I was nice enough to stay with and marry."

"I'm happy for you, Mark."

Extending a hand toward an imaginary silver screen, he says, "You've also got me insulting the huge Winkelvoss twins and stealing their concepts so I could launch Facebook."

"Well, they did contact you about their ideas for starting the social site ConnectU, but instead of doing their programming, as you agreed, you ignored them and about six weeks later Facebook debuted."

As if talking to a child, Mark says, "Do you think the Winklevi could've made Facebook happen. No sane person believes that."

"They did win a judgment of sixty-five million dollars against Facebook," I remind him.

"By then that was pocket change to get rid of them."

I offer my hand to Mark Zuckerberg. He takes it, and I ask, "Have you seen *Café Society*?"

"No."

"I think you'd like it. I portray a charming character like I really am."

Silently, he walks away.

Notes: Aaron Sorkin wrote the screenplay for *The Social Network.* At press time, there are no public reports of fisticuffs between Sorkin and Mark Zuckerberg.

ERNEST BORGNINE

Marty

In 1955 they release a movie about me called *Marty*. I'm embarrassed by the public opening of my private life but no more uncomfortable, really, than I am every day when people bombard me in the butcher shop where I work. Marty, you've got a younger brother and three younger sisters who're all married, they say. When are you going to get married? What's the matter with you? You should be ashamed. They're the ones who should be, talking to me like that. But they're right. I'm worse than ashamed. I'm thirty-four years old and don't get out much. Really, I don't get out at all.

My best friend often asks: what do you feel like doing tonight? I don't know, Ang, what do you feel like doing? I want to do something romantic but worry about the consequences. I try calling a woman I met a month earlier. She can't remember me until I explain a lot. Then I ask her out for tonight. Yes, I understand that's not much notice. Okay. How about next Saturday night? Well, I say, eyes tightly closed, how about the Saturday after that? Maybe I sound nervous. I wouldn't have been with a little more time. They're always so impatient.

My traditional mother doesn't understand. I live with her and she's always pestering me. Tonight she's trying to force me to go to the Stardust Ballroom and doesn't let up until I snap that girls make me feel like a bug and give me nothing but heartache. I'm just an ugly fat little man. I don't like the Stardust Ballroom. But Ang and I head there anyway, and he starts dancing right away. I stiffly walk up to a woman and ask her to dance. She says no. Here I am again, standing around.

A guy comes up to me and offers five bucks to stand in for him with his blind date because she's a dog, he says. I tell him he can't do that so he finds a jerk. That guy dumps her too so I go over and we start talking. Right away I can tell she's special, and I assure her that dogs like us ain't such dogs as we think we are. We're just fine. We take a walk, and I've never talked so much. I'm having the best time of my life. When we have coffee we laugh together. Being with her is so natural. I tell her how frustrated I was after World War II, walking the lonely streets until I considered jumping under the train.

All that's over now. I take her to my home. Everything is very proper. I know my mother will be home soon. I've still got to kiss this girl. I've never wanted to do anything this much. I lean over but she pulls away, like all the other girls. I erupt in self-pity she eases by telling me she wants very much to see me again. This is still my happiest moment. Ang and my mother must be jealous. They start telling me the girl's a dog and looks too old for me even though she's only twenty-nine. I'm so shocked I don't call her when I say I will. She's home with her parents, getting more upset as she waits, and starts to cry. I feel the same way, and announce I'm going to call her and if necessary someday get on my knees when I ask her to be with me forever. The movie ends there and I win the Oscar.

The movie should have gone on. She's happy to hear from me and we soon get married and are very happy. I certainly am and will be forever. But after a while she starts getting cranky. She probably thinks I'm boring. And for sure she's upset when I lose the money I borrowed to buy the butcher shop I work in and even unhappier when I lose the shop itself. I get another job right away. I promise I won't take any more business risks. I'm a good butcher. That's enough, isn't it? It should be. Why does she start complaining I put too much oil in my hair and it looks bad. Okay, I use less oil but that doesn't help. She stays thin as I get fatter, and she finds a handsome guy who makes a good living. Those guys always seem to have money.

I move back in with my mother until she dies then I decide on a big change and move into the next century, which is a lot better time. Now I've got the gym. Everybody can go to the gym. I'm taking an aerobics class. The ladies still ignore me but that's all right because I pretend not to notice them either. I'm just there for the exercise. I've already lost twelve pounds and washed that oily stuff out of my hair and gotten it styled real nice. I look pretty good in the pictures I post on the internet dating site. I've met quite a few ladies already though nothing so far has lasted more than one date. I know I'm not the only one struggling. Things are still pretty awkward sometimes but I'm learning not to try for the real flashy women. They'll never be interested in me and I shouldn't be interested in them.

I really don't think I have to have a woman when I go to the big cineplexes. They're terrific. And I also join an online film club that lets me rent movies from all over the world. I can have a great time home alone. Church is pretty good too. They have dances and pot luck dinners and a singles club. No woman really likes me yet but I'm going to keep exercising and sending my profile to ladies all over New York City and going places and pretty soon something'll happen.

CHRISTIAN VALE

Vice

I expected cheap shots and lies from liberals and they unload bundles in *Vice,* their movie about me. Right away they gleefully recall I have a couple of drunk driving arrests as a young man and drop out of Yale to repair power lines and almost get dumped by my fiancée, Lynne. At least they're right I promise her I'll shape up and do, and you'd think the moviemakers would appreciate that from distant Wyoming I soon work my way into the halls of Washington, D.C. power, aiding Donald Rumsfeld, then a congressman.

I assure you I don't have horns or a tail and neither does Rumsfeld or Henry Kissinger or President Nixon or his media consultant Roger Ailes. They're already men of great accomplishment and I'm thankful to observe and emulate. I make myself indispensable and therefore ready when Nixon resigns and Rumsfeld becomes President Ford's chief of staff, and I gain more influence, and then Rumsfeld takes over the Department of Defense and I become the youngest presidential chief of staff.

The movie's already suffering because the lefties can't decide whether they're making a drama, a satire, a comedy, or delivering a sermon. Actually, they're doing all those things, shuffling the deck and undercutting any narrative momentum. I should stop the video when they essentially accuse Lynne's father of drowning her mother. That's despicable.

They present their next holy theme as the unitary executive theory whereby the president must have absolute power especially in times of war. I suppose the cinematic wizards forget that Lyndon Johnson manufactured the conditions he needed to escalate the war in Vietnam. Nixon did the same. Don't fear presidential authority, especially in times of war. Be thankful decisive leaders like Franklin Roosevelt yearned for and got wars in Europe and Asia.

On screen we move to 1978 as I become the lone congressman from Wyoming and have my first heart attack, an event hardly portrayed with empathy. I serve in Congress ten years and during this period the Koch brothers fund conservative think tanks. Damn right. You think the other side isn't financing theirs. Not long after Ronald Reagan is elected, I have another humorous heart attack, and later, after George Bush becomes president, we meet his drunken son, W, as he stumbles into a gathering. Soon the movie gloats that my daughter, Mary, is gay, and groans that the great oil company Halliburton hires me to run it. I'm proud I do a hell of a job and make millions.

As George W. Bush prepares to run for president he invites me to his Texas ranch and asks me to be his vice president. I can't accept, I say, it's a lousy job, but I'll help you search for the ideal candidate. Look at my resume. I'm clearly the only man to help W win and, according to the moviemakers, all I need is a different understanding that enables me to oversee the military, energy, and foreign policy. Do you think any presidential nominee would accept that? Don't worry about things getting too serious or political. I have another entertaining heart attack. And on December twelfth, 2000 the Supreme Court stops the recount in Florida and I become Vice President-elect Dick Cheney.

Remember, I've run the Department of Defense during Operation Desert Storm and organized a massive military campaign and also learned it's disastrous the elder President Bush let Saddam Hussein keep power in Iraq. Young President Bush agrees about that all along and so do oil company CEOs, as the movie tremulously notes. After 9/11 we rapidly crush the Taliban and waterboard any terrorist we want and put others in boxes and choke-chain others before letting our dogs chew. We have this great momentum and now aim it at the most wicked man in the world, Saddam, who has to be removed since somehow he's schemed with his enemy Osama bin Laden and the Taliban in Afghanistan to incinerate three thousand Americans.

We get Great Britain's Tony Blair on the war train and, look at that, even young Mike Pence and liberal Hillary Clinton who's as patriotic as anyone. She knows she has to be a hawk to win in this country. Colin Powell, the too-celebrated general from Desert Storm and now my secretary of state, reluctantly explains matters at the United Nations, and we go back into Iraq and start kicking asses. No, as I'm sure you'll note, I didn't serve in Vietnam. I got deferments. I had other priorities. But I guarantee I know a lot about war and feel empowered sending young soldiers into battle and killing several hundred thousand Iraqis. That's what we have to do and I don't care what you or anyone else thinks.

I'm damn happy to get a heart transplant when my original ceases pumping enough oxygen to keep vital organs alive and think it's crude moviemakers show my big old heart on a table and the dead donor disrespecting me.

Notes: The preceding opinions are those of Dick Cheney, and his doppelganger Christian Vale, and in no way reflect the views of this publication.

JACK PALANCE

Palance Estate Auction

At age seventy-two, celebrating his Oscar for best supporting actor in *City Slickers*, Jack Palance launched himself onto the academy awards stage and cranked out several one-arm pushups. I'd been proud to do those in my twenties. Afterward, the two-armed variety was challenging enough, and before age forty I altogether abandoned the exercise as a concession to popping elbows. I assumed Palance, through genetic good fortune, admirable discipline, and the magic of celebrity must have discovered a way to if not defeat the aging process then at least batter it back. Accordingly, I was surprised to read last year that he'd died of natural causes at one of his homes, in Montecito. He was only eighty-seven and should've lasted another century. On screen he'll endure for portrayals of tough guys from urban killer to hired cowboy gunman to soldier, boxer, film producer, Jack the Ripper, Fidel Castro, and cattle trail boss. Whether despicable, frightening, stoic or crusty, he was always entertaining.

Before World War II he'd charged out of the Pennsylvania coal country – his Ukrainian immigrant father would die of black lung disease – to become a heavyweight boxer standing six-four and weighing a taut two-ten. Records from that era are often undependable or non-existent, so one can choose from press accounts that say Palance either won fifteen in a row, twelve by knockout, until losing a brawl to a contender or – more likely – usually took as many blows as he delivered. Either way, he emerged with a battered nose that precluded leading-man roles but ensured an ominous presence. During the war Palance trained as a B-24 pilot in Arizona and had to jump from a burning plane. His face was disfigured and, despite plastic surgery, "retained a distinctive, somewhat gaunt look" that first arrested theatrical audiences at Stanford University, where he graduated in 1947. He bounded to Broadway and was soon Marlon Brando's understudy in *A Streetcar Named Desire* and ultimately assumed the lead. Hollywood then called, and in 1952 he received his first of three best supporting actor nominations for his portrayal of a man plotting to kill his wife, Joan Crawford, in *Sudden Fear.* His second came as the thug gunning for homesteaders in *Shane.*

In his personal life Jack Palance was as robust as on film. He married, fathered two daughters and a son, traveled widely and bought a few thousand pieces of art and antiques and several classic sedans, sometimes drank too much, quarreled with his wife, acquired a ranch in Pennsylvania and another in the mountains outside Tehachapi, California, named the spread Holly Brooke Ranch after his two daughters, divorced, married another woman, painted landscapes and wrote poetry, lost his son to cancer, continued acting, and left memories and many collectibles recently sold at the Jack Palance California Estate Auction.

Why hadn't I gone up there several years ago when Palance put on a sale of his work and from his collection? I would've enjoyed talking to him, I think. Depends who you ask. A lady at the auction said, "I saw him around Tehachapi several times, and he was a gentleman. There was a gentleness about him, despite his image." Several months earlier another local lady had told me that he scolded her over the phone for sending an improper part from the hardware store where she was filling in. Before that another Tehachapi resident told me that Palance had simultaneously kicked the asses of three, four, or even five drunken yokels who trifled with him.

Let's assume he was a man both rough and sensitive, and be clear that for stretches every year he lived on his California ranch entered through a gate yielding to a dirt road that runs between some stunning boulders and back toward oak-covered brown hills that face a one-story stone ranch house, a couple of other dwellings, a big three-section barn, fenced areas no longer occupied by horses and cows, a huge statue of a chicken and an even larger chrome-plated steel rendering of a winged Pegasus horse weighing more than a ton and valued at thirty-five grand.

The live horses must've been removed just before the auction since their paddies still decorated dusty fields serving as parking lots. In a scene from a country fair, scores of people browsed the premises, eating hot dogs and chicken, rubbing Palance's fine antique furniture displayed under canopies, and picking up his old rock and classical record albums. Those planning to participate in the auction lined up at a cash register in the barn's first room to fill out forms, get their driver's licenses scanned, and receive numbered cards to signal bids. On the way out they stopped at tables covered by informal photos of Palance with celebrities, many of whom – like Joan Crawford and Jimmy Carter – are gazing at the big actor. Before bidders sat in plastic folding chairs under a large canopy, they strolled through the second and third sections of the barn, examining an array of paintings and antiques. The setting was prepared by fourteen employees of Keystone State Auctioneers who'd flown out from East Williamsport, Pennsylvania. Last year they handled four days of bidding on Palance's holdings at his ranch in Butler Township. His artifacts at the California ranch were similar but more extensive.

A trio of machine-gun talking auctioneers spearheaded the effort to sell more than fourteen hundred items in three days, a frenetic pace requiring fifty transactions an hour. Many of the least expensive items, for those wanting a Palance keepsake, went on the block Friday at ten a.m. Gruff trail boss Curly in *City Slickers* undoubtedly used cast iron frying pans, metal cook pots, an iron ladle, a leather two-gun holster, a lantern, and an old metal cow bell. Curly threatened to kill Billy Crystal's character for playing a harmonica and would have been glad to see it sold along with some belts adorned with noisy brass bells. On Saturday cowboy tools like branding irons, horse shoes, and a lasso rope continued to sell along with antique rifles, pistols, swords, an axe and a dagger, but emphasis on art increased. Fred Duran's pastel portraits of Billy the Kid, Jesse James, Doc Holiday, Wyatt Earp, Calamity Jane, and General Custer brought a few hundred dollars each, and so did statuettes of cowboys, Indians, horses and a stage coach.

Energetic auctioneers kept the money flowing in, and every hour they yielded to a fresh speaker who would immediately announce – What a beauty, a thousand dollars for this one - okay, five hundred, do I hear five hundred? – It would look great in your office – two hundred? Okay, get me started now with a hundred-dollar bill. One hundred right there – one-twenty-five – one hundred – one-twenty-five right there – one-fifty – one-fifty – one-seventy-five – one-fifty in front – one-seventy-five – one-seventy-five – one-fifty – one-seventy-five over there – Come on, where you gonna get another one? – two hundred right there – two-twenty-five – two-twenty-five – two hundred – two-twenty-five. It's only money. You'll get another check next week – two-twenty-five, two-twenty-five – You bought it for two hundred.

What's your number? Let me see your card. And our next item – what a beauty…

After four hours of this increasingly addictive activity, I didn't want to leave but had an appointment in Bakersfield, an hour down the mountain in the smoggy Central Valley. Sunday morning, I returned to the ranch. That's when the best art would be auctioned. Bidders warmed up buying a hundred-dollar beaded purse, a brass calendar for one-sixty, a silver pitcher for two-thirty, a hundred-buck brass barometer, a nineteenth century Viennese urn for seven hundred, and a silvered bronze statuette of a sheep shearing from France for thirty-five hundred; everything was selling, six hundred for this, three hundred for that, five hundred for a pair of Italian carved marble angles, a hundred forty for a magnifying glass, three hundred for a French cast iron Ram's head, and the deluge continued.

I wanted to get involved but restrained myself during bidding for Gen Paul's contemporary portrait of an emotional "Guitar Player." Four collectors from around the world were on the phone, battling local bidders, one, two, three, four, five all the way to eighteen grand offered by someone in Germany. Maybe I could play a little when Number three-zero-nine-four came up, indicating the ninety-fourth item on the third day. I'd been waiting for this beautiful African painting of village life almost three feet high and five long framed with thick wood. The artist's name is Dusso. My hopes dissolved when they opened too high. But they kept coming down – one hundred, one hundred, let's get started with a hundred-dollar bill. I raised my card – one hundred right here – one-twenty-five – one-twenty-five – one hundred – one-twenty-five over there – one-fifty – one-twenty-five – one-fifty right here. Again I raised my card. One-seventy-five – one-seventy-five – one-fifty – one-seventy-five – you bought it for a hundred-fifty dollars, the auctioneer said, looking at me.

I started bidding on paintings I couldn't afford without using a credit card, and even by that means should've bought at least one of the five sports paintings by former professional football player and internationally-collected artist Ernie Barnes. I'd seen his work in L.A. galleries and knew it was usually worth five grand and up, but I timidly avoided risk and thus the chance to acquire creative pieces that this day sold for five hundred to seventeen hundred, about ten cents on the dollar. Let's go, I told my friend. I retrieved my very heavy African work, shoved the seats all the way forward in my Honda Civic hatchback, barely got the big frame inside, and driving scrunched up didn't say much on the way home. At least as I was leaving the appraiser for the auctioneers had patted my shoulder and said, "You got a steal. For years Jack had that painting over his mantle in the main ranch house."

Some Noteworthy Films

Panic in the Streets (1950) – Palance debuts with verve, murdering a man infected with a potentially catastrophic plague. Unaware of the medical problem, the now-stricken Palance concludes the massive manhunt is fueled by something of major value he hasn't had a chance to learn about and steal. Seeking the prize, he strong arms a dying man in bed and then throws him off the stairs. When health official Richard Widmark arrives, Palance conks him. And while hand climbing the dock rope to a ship, in a hopeless escape attempt, he exhibits intensity and fanaticism that will distinguish other roles.

Shane (1953) – Wearing a black hat, a black vest, and black boots, Palance is a nasty gunslinger hired by cattlemen to kill some farmers and scare the rest away. Unlike in other roles, Palance doesn't have much to say, but his silence is ominous and builds tension for the showdown with Shane, played by little Alan Ladd.

I've heard about you.

What have you heard, Shane?

I've heard that you're a lowdown Yankee liar.

Prove it.

Blond-haired leading men don't lose many gunfights with sinister character actors. *Shane* remains a classic primarily because of Ladd's laconic and dignified performance and George Stevens' precise directing.

Attack (1956) – It's World War II, Americans are fighting Germans, and cowardly captain Eddie Albert trembles when he should be giving competent orders. Palance, only a lieutenant, tells his captain that if any more lives are wasted he'll come back and shove a grenade down his throat. Young Lee Marvin outranks both men but is a close childhood friend of Albert and covers for him. When the drunken captain again shrinks while his troops are under fire, Palance storms back. Even after a panzer runs over one of his arms, he keeps coming, and when he can't walk he crawls.

Contempt (1963) – How do you combine a young and often naked Bridgette Bardot, a legendary director, Fritz Lang, playing a director, and Palance as a callous producer, and let celebrated director Jean-Luc Godard guide them, and still make a wretched film? Ignore its cult status in France. Bardot is boring. Lang is feeble. And Palance is robotic. He and Bardot either didn't want to kiss each other, or Godard instructed them to act like their lips were made of cardboard. This isn't film noir. It's pretension. And its utter badness is of mild historical interest. Celluloid adventurers should simply watch the first half hour and avoid the final hour of agony.

City Slickers (1991) – Palance arrives late, roping the neck of a boor who's harassing a blonde, and leaves early propped up by a boulder after his fatal heart attack, but while present he captures the screen. Never more dynamic and intimidating, and at the same time philosophical, Palance had to be axed so Billy Crystal and his two New York pals wouldn't be overwhelmed on their dude ranch holiday. Palance's Oscar reception prompted his most memorable role, that of the septuagenarian stud popping out those one-arm pushups.

SACHA BARON COHEN

President Ahmadinejad Praises Borat

In a letter to President Bush last spring I demonstrated profound understanding of United States foreign policy, and outlined many diplomatic steps that unrighteous nation must take to correct its barbaric behavior. Nevertheless, I did not, as I should have, offer substantive commentary on American society and psychology. I simply didn't know much about them. That's a dangerous shortcoming for the new president of Iran, and I resolved to overcome it, daily devouring the Koran as well as mounds of written matter most Iranians would be arrested for possessing. I also prayed many times a day and stared at the stars and shouted at the heavens. Insight was still denied, and perplexed I remained until the seminal moment a servant guaranteed I'd experience everything essential if I watched the recently-released movie *Borat.*

What painful revelations are in this movie, which I know I can trust since at the beginning it proudly presents our brothers in half-Muslim Kazakhstan during the annual Running of the Jew pogrom. Once the offensive Hebrew is surrounded, she lays her egg, and children pounce on it before it can hatch more problems into our region. Borat, that nation's finest television journalist, is there. And he's going to America to find out more.

Right away, in New York, heart of the imperial beast, Borat is berated on the subway by uncouth Americans who do not understand his friendly desire to kiss their cheeks and exchange names. I am being too generous. New Yorkers not only rebuff Borat, they curse and threaten him. They should have embraced him. He could have saved them. He knows Jews were behind the 9/11 attacks and that he better avoid airplanes and instead drive across the terrifying American heartland.

Borat's route is soon bisected by a Gay Parade whose perverse marchers fondle him between the legs. On the opposite American ideological precipice, the organizer of a rodeo tells him to shave his mustache so he doesn't look like a Muslim terrorist. Borat tests the redneck crowd by stating he supports the war in Iraq and wants the boys to kill every terrorist and for Bush to drink the blood of everyone in Iraq. Their cheers betray lust for the destruction of Islam. I confess, however, that I can't fault the rodeo organizer for advocating hanging homosexuals since in my Iran we can hang anyone, especially unmarried women who spread their legs.

Borat is a very brave man: he and his obese producer stay in the house of Hebrews, who pretend to offer them sustenance. Borat knows better and spits out the food, which doubtless contains poison. Later that night, at three a.m., the Jews transmogrify into bugs, crawl under the visitors' bedroom door, and prepare to attack. Borat and his friend, praise Allah, are awake and aware, and throw dollars at the insects before dashing down the stairs.

Oh, how racist are the Americans. In a Southern mansion his hosts evict him because he invites a black prostitute to the dinner party. In an antique store there are many images of Confederate flags, which symbolize and celebrate slavery. Those flags should be outlawed. There indisputably was slavery. But the existence of the Holocaust is still in doubt, according to yours truly, the eminent World War Two historian.

Not even Borat can remain righteous in decadent America. He's obsessed by the sexual allure of a silicone-busted, bleached-blond TV-star. There must be laws to protect men from women like her as well as insulate other women from such influence. That's why in Iran we would probably hang Pamela Anderson. Woman like her always cause great distress. In their hotel room, Borat catches his once-trustworthy friend masturbating while he ogles magazine pictures of wicked Pamela. The two temporarily-deranged men engage in a horrific wrestling match during which Borat has the fat fellow's gargantuan ass planted squarely across his face. All this because of an immoral woman.

America may be three thousand parched miles from sea to sea, but the horrors never fundamentally change, as desperate Borat learns when his former friend absconds with his money, passport, and their bodyguard bear. Hitchhiking, Borat is picked up by drunken college students in a camper. They brag about screwing bitches then disrespecting them for not being decent females. They encourage Borat to drink like them. In that uncivilized environment, he's unable to resist. He drinks and listens to them declare there should still be slaves. At least the drunken louts denounce Jews. That still doesn't compensate for their showing lovelorn Borat a video of Pamela Anderson engaging in unbridled sex.

Borat is now so bereaved he asks to be let out into darkness along the perilous American highway. He sleeps outside that night, and the next morning, dirty and unshaven, he desperately enters a Pentecostal church. What a nation of religious fanatics are the Americans. They're talking in tongues and convincing Borat that Jesus, praise be upon him, can help him. Under the influence of these zealots, Borat rants and writhes and nearly faints during a disgusting process that does not work. He still decides to pursue Pamela, aided by Jesus, praise be upon him.

Degradation is inevitable everywhere in America, particularly California where temptations overwhelm: Borat learns Pamela Anderson will be appearing at an obscene publicity event in a strange place called Orange. When Pamela walks into the store, many libidinous men leer like Borat. I do not fault any of them personally. The fault is that of a vile nation permitting women to be free. Men cannot deal with that and neither can women. That is why in a Muslim nation Borat would never propose in public – and be humiliated by the rebuff – before putting a cloth sack over the head of the tramp who, quite unjustifiably, is rescued by security guards.

Finally, Borat can bear no more and returns to Kazakhstan. On the way home he stops and picks up the black prostitute to be his wife. That is tragic. In my kingdom, we also have this problem. More and more women are forsaking Islam and becoming whores. This is primarily the work of Americans and Jews. We're trying to fix things and think nuclear power is the answer.

General Aladeen Assails The Dictator

Obscene, self-righteous, and unfunny Sacha Baron Cohen has earned a few hundred million dollars, as *Borat* and *Bruno*, by insulting rubes in Kazakhstan and the United States, and then either deflecting or burying their lawsuits. Now you can be assured that I, General Aladeen, supreme leader of Wadiya, will by all necessary means forever seal the malicious mouth of a Hebrew who in unforgivable ways blasphemes me in *The Dictator*.

Dishonest from inception, Cohen, grandson of gangster Mickey

Cohen, asserts I was born with a beard and pubic hair, and implies that trauma caused my mother's immediate death. In fact, I entered the world anatomically normal and my mother not merely survives but flourishes, albeit in prison after trying to seize my office. Cohen portrays me, an impossibility given his dorky ways, as an ungainly and malicious Olympic competitor who, during competition, shot my closest competitors and various officials. I'm indeed a fine athlete, though not of gold-medal stature, and am most comfortable telling you so.

Cohen's assertion that I'm enriching weapons-grade uranium, and need but two months before producing nuclear warheads, is preposterous like his claim that all my friends have nukes, even President Mahmoud Ahmadinejad of Iran. In fact, Mahmoud is my only friend nearing that soothing state of armed readiness, and I don't need to spend money or risk preemptive strikes to develop something that will soon be given me just prior to our dual launches.

Predictably, Cohen alludes to hapless Saddam Hussein, foremost employer of doubles, by showing one of mine getting killed in an assassination attempt. I have lost some lookalikes, yes, but this is not a humorous matter. They were brave men. And contrary to Cohen's slur, through the malodorous mouth of my nonexistent uncle and most powerful aide, the unconvincing Ben Kingsley, my doubles do not have their penises shortened to resemble mine, but in fact undergo major augmentation. And, straightforwardly I tell you, I have no use for the hookers Cohen burdens me with. Ladies flock to my desert boudoir.

Cohen lies that my seminal diplomatic trip to New York, for a speech at the United Nations, cost me much money and time on earth. I was not kidnapped. I addressed the General Assembly. I wasn't a halfwit who swigged his urine from a jar before offering some to the Israeli delegation. My speech, about the obsessive and paranoid nature of American interventions in the Middle East, and civilian casualties thereafter incurred, evoked a howling ovation from eighty percent of diplomats in the U.N. chamber.

The episode about my working in a feminist vegan store, and punching a customer, throwing a garbage can at a vehicle, and kicking a child, are of course apocryphal. I did visit the store, for cultural enrichment, and was smitten by the charming young lady who managed it. She indeed accompanied me back to Wadiya, and we did marry whereupon I learned she's Jewish. I certainly did not give my feared double left-hand slices across the throat. I accepted her, and she was thrilled that even after I ordered my country to become fully democratic I won almost ninety-nine percent of the vote.

PHILLIP SEYMOUR HOFFMAN

Capote in Kansas

I spent months portraying Truman Capote and that's not easy despite my character being relatively young, healthy, and sober, and I'm anxious to learn what he thinks.

"You were wonderful, Philip," says Capote, sitting next to me on a sofa. "I love your high, distinctive voice. I thought I was listening to myself. Let me hear it."

"Sorry, but I don't talk like that anymore."

"Just a line or two.

"I can't do it because it puts me in your character and isolates me from my own. That's unhealthy."

"I apologize for traumatizing you."

"I didn't mean it negatively. I'm simply saying that I have to be myself."

Capote places a hand under an elbow and uses the other hand to prop up his chin as he examines me.

"At times in the movie I felt you didn't approve of me."

"You call *In Cold Blood* a nonfiction novel," I say. "That's a contradiction. A book is either fiction or it isn't. If novelistic techniques are used, like realistic dialogue and fact-based conjecture about what characters are thinking, then it's literary nonfiction."

"I invented those genres."

"Let's call you one of the pioneers. At any rate, I'm not questioning the essential accuracy of most of the book. What disturbs me are the truths that emerged after studying what it took for you to write the book."

Capote keeps his hand under his chin and looks at me in a way at once amused and impudent.

"As I say in the movie and quite a few times to others, 'When I think how good my book can be, I can hardly breathe.' Certainly, I sacrificed. I was writing for history and history has appreciated this work, don't you think?"

"That's why I took the part. I wanted to show the world not the debauched Truman Capote of later years but the dynamic man who rushed to rural Kansas to investigate the murders of the Clutter family, four people slaughtered in their own home, and became progressively more involved in the lives of the two suspects, ex-cons Perry Smith and Dick Hickock."

"I know I'm quoting myself again, Philip, but 'I couldn't bear the thought of losing (Perry) so soon.' I had to make him stop fasting and ensure that he had a competent lawyer during the appeals process. I didn't want those boys to die."

"You didn't want them to die too soon or live too long."

"I resent that."

"Then let me note that your editor, excited after reading some of your manuscript in progress, asked when you were going to finish. And what did you tell him, Truman?"

Removing his hand from his chin, he shakes his head and smiles resignedly. "I told him 'I have to talk to Perry about how he killed the Clutters.'"

"Right, and the editor tells you to do it soon because, after losing their appeal, Perry and Dick will be dead in months. You went to Spain for some intense writing and then gave a public reading in New York, yet you told Perry that you'd 'hardly written anything.'"

"What did I really owe two convicted murderers sentenced to die?"

"You didn't owe Perry the romantic love you'd been feeling for him," I say. "But, having offered friendship and trust, you owed him more than the cold insult that learning the specifics of the murder were the only reason you'd ever stood in his prison cell. You must've been uncomfortable lying that you didn't know the book's title is *In Cold Blood.*"

Capote rises to a full five-foot-three and says, "I couldn't have been sure about the title since I didn't know what really happened. I still told Perry he didn't have to tell me anything he didn't want to."

"He had to tell you everything or you'd have abandoned him."

"I was writing a book, not serving as his attorney or a relative, none of whom gave a damn about him."

I stand, several inches taller than Truman, and say, "You must've felt less affection for Perry when he told you he looked into the eyes of 'very nice gentleman' Mr. Clutter and then slashed his throat before he shotgun blasted his head and that of his son before running upstairs and doing the same to Mrs. Clutter and her daughter."

"Perry says he prevented Dick from raping the girl."

"There's no way to confirm that, and it doesn't mitigate his crimes."

"Why don't we sit back down," Capote says, placing a soft hand on his temple. "I think the stress of researching and writing this book and dealing with all the difficulties caused many of my subsequent problems. I had four years invested in the book and was getting tenser and drinking more and using medications to sleep."

Joining the author back on his sofa, I say, "It looked bad when you got upset by the stay of execution and said, 'All I want to do is write the ending and there's no ending in sight.'"

"I couldn't have saved Perry and Dick even if I'd felt well. I had to save myself. I was having a 'nervous breakdown.'"

"Were you relieved when the Supreme Court rejected their appeal?" I ask.

Ignoring my question, Capote says, "I didn't want to go to the execution but couldn't stop myself. I needed to say goodbye to Perry. I thought it was touching he told me he needed to 'have a friend there.'"

"You said you'd never get over it. I suppose you didn't."

"Philip, you know who you remind me of?"

"Who?"

"Myself."

"I'm portraying you in this movie, Truman."

"The movie's over. I've read you began using and liking alcohol and every other drug out there when you were a student at NYU. Too bad we hadn't met. I'd have joined you."

"I was only an undergrad, not a candidate for your elite social circle."

"Did you really have twenty-three years of sobriety?"

"Yes," I say.

"I rarely had twenty-three days. I suffered more breakdowns and was in and out of rehab too many times to recall. I suffered hallucinations and seizures, and they x-rayed my brain and said it had shrunk and that my liver was shot. Everything was wrong."

"I'm surprised things turned out that way since I've seen an uplifting interview you gave F. Lee Bailey in 1968."

Capote laughs and slaps each thigh just above the knee.

"God, wasn't I a fount of discipline and insight? I denounced drug use, which is the 'worst thing that can happen to any writer,' and said, 'I have no particular affinity for drugs.' I also proclaimed, 'Alcohol is the worst' and that Aldous Huxley was wrong when he said 'drugs aid creativity… Being a classic artist requires the most disciplined action… The mind must be surgically balanced.'"

"Couldn't you control yourself, given your artistic ambition and discipline?"

"Of course I couldn't or I would've. As bad as alcohol and prescription drugs were, they weren't nearly as hellish as dealing with my unsedated brain. When I was hospitalized and battling for my sanity people were calling me a drunk and an addict and a queer and a gossip and, evidently, praying I'd die and suffer like hell before departure. I was glad I never woke up in the guest bedroom at Joanne Carson's, one of Johnny's exes. My body was saturated by vital but destructive medications. Which leads to this question, Philip. What the hell happened to you?"

"I don't know how I stayed sober so long. My inherent anxiety never disappeared. Like you, I made enough money so I could deal with my pain my way which forced my girlfriend to kick me out, to protect our three children. In an apartment nearby I continued taking heroin and tranquilizers and cocaine and amphetamines and a friend found me with a syringe in my arm."

"I understand why you won an Oscar for portraying *Capote.*"

"So when are you going to write a book about me?"

ROBERT BLAKE

In Cold Blake

Three guards lead me into death row at the Kansas State Penitentiary and stop in front of the cell of a guy I at once recognize.

"Perry Smith, pleasure to meet you. I'm Robert Blake."

He looks like me, having thick black hair and muscular arms and is even shorter, and I'm only five-four.

"Thanks for coming."

"Looks like you're a weightlifter, too," I say.

"Used to be but haven't gotten back all my muscle since I almost died while fasting."

"Yeah, heard about that."

I turn to the guards and say, "Gentlemen, the warden says I can talk to him in his cell. Right?"

"If Truman Capote can, why not you?" says one.

"There are a lot of short guys hanging around this cell," I say, laughing.

Somber faces don't respond. The cell door slides open and I enter and shake Perry's firm little hand.

"We'll be right down the hall," says another guard.

Perry sits on his Spartan bed and I stand since there's nowhere for me to sit and I'd rather stand anyway. Makes me feel taller.

"I've done a little reading about you but most is pretty superficial stuff," I say. "I already know the most important thing. You had to have been abused as a kid."

"That's very insightful, Robert. My father was a drunk and beat hell out of me and my brother and both sisters. My brother killed himself and so did one of my sisters and the other hates me as bad as I hate her."

"What about your mother?"

"Worst woman I ever met. Every time my father left town, she'd be out drinking and screwing around or bringing guys home and carrying on so loud we couldn't sleep. She was once a beautiful Indian lady but drank herself into a mess and an early grave."

I pause respectfully before saying, "My dad was a bastard. He hit me, touched me in the wrong places, and my mother wasn't much better."

"At least you had a commendable acting career. You were one of

The Little Rascals, weren't you?"

"Yeah, that was exciting but didn't last because I grew up, or at least I got older, and had to join the army. After getting out I struggled for years before I could support myself as an actor. What did you do after high school?"

"I never made it past the third grade. I fought in Korea, mostly against guys in bars and the barracks, and just did shit work until I almost died in a motorcycle accident. My legs are useless except for giving me incessant pain. It's unsurprising I got into crime and went to prison and fell in with bastards like Dick Hickock.

"Watch your mouth," Dick shouts from the adjacent cell. "Who killed all four Clutters. You did."

"Which imbecile said Mr. Clutter had a safe with at least ten grand in it," Perry says. "Which psychopath preached every day that we couldn't leave any witnesses. Lamentably, I did leave one witness, didn't I?"

"Screw yourself, Perry," says Dick.

I walk to the bars, take one in each hand, and try to shake them. "You've been here about six years, haven't you, Perry?"

"That's correct."

"Guys on death row can't work in this prison. I hear you only get to leave the cell once a week for a shower. What do you do?"

"I read and look up the definitions of words and have developed an articulate speaking style. Words make me feel better than people ever have. I presume you know Dick and I have run out of appeals and will soon be dead. Are you going to the uncivilized ceremony they call an execution?"

"No, Perry, I don't think I'll be there for that."

"I feel good knowing you'll be portraying me."

"Thanks, Perry, and God bless you," I say as I embrace him.

Forty years later I know what you're saying or at least thinking: how ironic Robert Blake played a killer and then became one. Listen, I swear I didn't murder my second wife, Bonnie. I couldn't have. I'd returned to the restaurant to get the pistol I'd forgotten there and when I got back to the car she was dying from a head wound. My pistol wasn't the one some animal shot her with. The police found the murder weapon in a dumpster nearby. They must've known I couldn't have put it there. There was no gunshot residue on my hands or clothes. Why was I being framed? Because a couple of unhinged and drug-addicted stuntmen say I tried to hire them to kill Bonnie.

I loved my wife. I didn't care I was her tenth husband and she'd tried to shake down most of the others as well as some boyfriends. I didn't care when I married her because I was lonely in my late sixties and had no life. I guess I cared about that stuff later. Nobody likes being used. Fine. All I had to do was divorce her. I wasn't going to kill the mother of our little girl who, surprisingly, turned out to be mine. What a thrill that was. An even greater thrill came when the jury said not guilty of first degree murder with special circumstances which, if I'd been convicted, would've put me in the company of guys like Perry Smith and Dick Hickock. Life is wonderful but I'm miserable as hell.

Notes: Robert Blake starred as a detective in *Baretta,* a popular TV series lasting four seasons in the seventies. During that period into the eighties Blake appeared scores of times on *The Tonight* Show with Johnny Carson. Arms pumped in short sleeves, charismatic Blake entertained audiences with earthy stories and sometimes pulled out a piece of paper, holding it with one hand and pointing to it with the other, and saying he'd had a lot of problems and knew a lot of you did too and if you needed help here was the place to go to get it. I wonder if Robert Blake later lost contact with mental health officials he'd once urged people to visit.

BEHIND THE CAMERA

WOODY ALLEN

Woody Reviews Everything

Why do you want to know? It's been almost half a century but I've already explained *Everything You've Always Wanted to Know About Sex.* Sure, I was joking. That's what I do. I write funny things and make people laugh. At least that usually happens. Thank goodness the gags worked in this movie because I was still a young and not very handsome filmmaker but determined to control my movies and the only way I could was to make money and this one brought in about nine times the budget and I'm still independent.

Okay, I'll deal with the seven key questions addressed in this movie. Go ahead.

1. Do aphrodisiacs work?

First, let me emphasize I disapprove of a court jester or anyone else giving love potions to unknowing young women like the queen. This is especially so when the queen is wearing an impenetrable chastity belt and the king catches the frustrated rascal and cuts off his head. Today, the aggrieved husband would shoot you and so would the victimized woman. I think chemistry, intangible but overwhelming, is the best aphrodisiac. I've never drunk much but don't mind providing a large glass of wine to women who ask. You pose an intriguing question. Can women light up men with aphrodisiacs? I've seen women loosen men up with alcohol but they better not get the guys too loose. I never needed unnatural boosters in my youth or middle age or even early old age but am eighty-five now and recently told my wife I was a bit too tired but after dinner I spontaneously became a tiger and afterward praised myself before she said, "Veggies and Viagra…"

2. What is sodomy?

Gene Wilder is a great actor and convincingly falls in love with a sheep. I never dwell on this issue but have actually talked to two men, separately, who said they'd had sex with a sheep. I don't know why they told me but wish they hadn't except their insights enhanced this film. Like Wilder, both men were caught in flagrante delicto by their wives. I have no objection to sodomy, or pederasty, as long as two or more consenting humans are involved.

3. Why Do Some Women Have Trouble Reaching an Organism?

I hope you won't think me a braggart but very few ladies have had any trouble heating up when they're with me. I've been proficient since my teens. But this segment is about my wife falling asleep or watching TV as I try to arouse her. I'm inconsolable until, mercifully, she starts getting naked in public and mauling me all over Rome. This worries friends who think we'll be arrested for indecent exposure but in Italy that kind of stuff is more or less okay, I think. Ironically, this lusty lady is played by my second wife, Louise Lasser, who had spontaneous orgasms every time men touched her.

4. Are Transvestites Homosexuals?

Not all or even most of them are gay but a much higher percentage than among men who don't dress as women. Sadly, the consequences of being a transvestite can be quite severe. I wrote this segment of the movie based on an unassailable source, the man himself. Just like Lou Jacobi, he and his wife went to an afternoon party and the man excused himself to go upstairs to the bathroom. He instead scampered into a bedroom, took off his clothes, and put on a short red dress, high heels, and a big red hat and pranced and posed and felt quite feminine until he heard someone climbing the steps and approach the bedroom. Hurriedly he opened the window and jumped out and tried to blend in with neighbors on the sidewalk but two ladies tried to chat and asked why he was holding his hand over his mouth and screamed when they saw he was concealing a moustache. He dashed behind the hosts' house and tried to secretly enter a window but was spotted and his wife became hysterical and they separated and divorced after a brief attempt at therapy. In the movie, I imply Lou's wife is going to try to stick with him.

5. What are sex perverts?

Don't you love *What's My Line?* I watched it on TV in my teens and sometimes still get on YouTube and enjoy the celebrity mystery guests. *What's My Perversion?* is just about a regular guy. I can't risk someone famous suing because he thought he was being portrayed. Our distinguished panel of four should ask the guests more penetrating questions. They never figure out he simply likes to expose himself on subways. I hear about people doing a lot worse on subways, believe me. They're aroused by a captive audience. I'd like to thank the rabbi for writing us and flying in from Indiana and letting our audience watch what most excites him: a statuesque blonde ties him in a chair and whips him while his aged wife sits on the floor and eats pork. I should tell you I don't know this rabbi and am not religious.

6. Are the Findings of Doctors and Clinics Who Do Sexual Research and Experiments Accurate?

It depends. If eerie John Carradine owns the clinic, call the police before he confiscates your cell phones, which he doubtless would have if they'd existed fifty years ago. A young female journalist and I see a hippo being treated for premature ejaculations, and plenty of other weird stuff is happening, and these images evoke what forty years later befall Carradine's son, the noted actor David, who perished during an autoerotic experiment. Not all of father John's experiments are sinister. After escaping his laboratory, I enjoy fleeing a monstrous tit that undulates over the countryside, firing streams of milk at all who dare stand in her path. We eventually trap the tit in a giant bra and send her to prison.

7. What Happens During Ejaculation?

As Tony Randall, Burt Reynolds, and a large cast on duty inside an industrial penis so ably demonstrate, it's what happens beforehand that makes ejaculations possible. A man and a woman have to talk sweetly to each other and the woman's got to want him and he must achieve and maintain an erection or there's no ball game. His chances for sustained arousal improve when the lady is sexy like Erin Fleming when I film her in Sidney's car. We know she's promiscuous since she studies at NYU and pants about Norman Mailer and eagerly asks struggling Sidney, "What's the matter?" We never see him but know Erin invites him in and moans the music of love ending in mutual orgasms and as we leave they're preparing an encore. I think I might use Erin in a future role and assume other directors will, too, but she seems to forsake acting to become Groucho Marx's secretary and manager and companion and archivist and alleged abuser. Groucho's son sues her and she has to repay almost half a million to the comedian's estate. In time she's diagnosed as suffering from paranoid schizophrenia and spends much time in institutions or on the streets and kills herself when she's about sixty and the only way I don't feel bad thinking of her is when I recall the young lady who still delights viewers of this film.

Notes: In around 1974 I was looking for menial work in Los Angeles so I'd have plenty of energy to write. After a couple weeks of rejection I said hell with it, I'm going back home to Sacramento but before doing so I'm not going to drive on any more streets with warehouses, I'm cruising down Sunset Boulevard in Beverly Hills. About a mile east of the Beverly Hills Hotel I saw a short slender old man in a black beret. He carried a long thin black cane as he walked west on the south sidewalk of Sunset with a tall lady I recognized as Erin Fleming, not from her performance described above but from television appearances with Groucho. During one of them, he said, "She makes my life worth living."

Woody Testifies

There are some misconceptions about me that I have to correct in my memoir. Before I get to the biggest one, let me tell you I may be short, skinny, and bespectacled but as a kid and young man I was a hell of an athlete especially in baseball. I could run and catch and throw and hit, though not with the power of Babe Ruth, and didn't think it was unrealistic to dream of someday playing in the major leagues. Okay, I wasn't that good but I could play and all my classmates knew it.

Many people think they know me because they've seen *Play It Again, Sam* and are convinced my role as Allan Felix is autobiographical and I really am a shy, inept guy who rarely gets a date and blows it when he does. Listen, that's called screenwriting and fantasy and filmmaking. I'm not like that. I was popular in high school and lots of girls considered me cute and I socialized plenty and had a pretty girlfriend named Harlene who I married when I was twenty and our problems didn't result because she considered me a schlemiel. I was a successful comedy writer producing jokes for big names when I was still in high school and had a wonderful future in the business but felt confined so started performing live comedy. I wasn't worried people would consider me dorky. I was terrified they might not laugh at my jokes. Most comedians have the same fear. But I usually got some laughs and in a few years began appearing on all the shows and not only performed on the Tonight Show but sometimes guest hosted when Johnny Carson was on vacation.

Harlene didn't drop me. We just didn't get along and split but pretty soon I met Louise Lasser, and let me tell you she was beautiful and charming and always determined to jump into the nearest bed. On film I've referred to myself as a sexual athlete and that's accurate. Unfortunately, Louise was very unstable and intemperate and every time I left Manhattan for work I'd get calls from people telling me she was pounding the sheets with other guys. Okay, I counterpunched by doing the same with a variety of beautiful actresses, playmates, and other hotties.

I admit Louise's behavior hurt but when we divorced I moved right into romance with delectable Diane Keaton. Even after we broke up, I starred her in several fine films culminating in *Annie Hall* for which she won an Oscar for best actress. I couldn't have been more delighted.

I know I'm a lucky guy meeting all these lovely and talented actresses. And I was both flattered and surprised Mia Farrow started pursuing me. I may be pretty confident but this lady had been married to Old Blue Eyes, Frank Sinatra, and then she stole brilliant conductor Andre Previn from his wife and married him and began bearing children, three by Previn, and adopting others, and by the time Mia and I became involved she had eight kids. In those days she was beautiful and sexy and fun to be with.

I realized I couldn't live in a house with eight kids since I hadn't really been able to handle cohabitation with Harlene or Louise or Diane. I needed a quiet place to write. I'm getting ahead a little here but need to mention I've been nominated for sixteen best original screenplay Oscars and four times for best director and I've won three for writing and one for directing and couldn't have written, directed, and often starred in a movie a year for decades unless I focused. For a while Mia was okay with our arrangement. I visited her and the kids whenever I wanted and had a key to her apartment on the other side of Central Park, and she came over to my place, too.

I suppose taking care of so many children and making thirteen straight movies together caused a lot of stress and she stopped being intimate so I was stunned when she told me she wanted to bear my child. She'd already adopted another, giving her nine, a complete baseball team, and I was thrilled when Satchel was born. You probably know him by the name he uses now – Ronan Farrow. Despite a full apartment Mia kept adopting and had thirteen kids by the time she told me Soon-Yi was tense and needed to get out and why didn't I take her to a Knicks game. She had selected Soon-Yi from a Korean orphanage at age eight. Now she was a wonderful young woman of twenty, thirty-five years my junior but in many ways more mature, and began to reveal to me the physical and psychological abuse Mia had inflicted on her and the other kids, especially the adopted ones.

I enjoyed talking to Soon-Yi very much. We went to more ball games and took walks and ate in restaurants and visited art museums and went back to my apartment many times. I hadn't been so aroused in eons but kept thinking, no, she doesn't want me. She thinks I'm too old. She'll be mad if I try something. Still, I couldn't wait any longer, and nervously leaned over and kissed her, and she smiled and said she'd been waiting, and we both made moves we didn't know we had and with technology today I'd probably have filmed us but thirty years ago polaroid camera shots were a pretty big deal and I accidentally on purpose left out a few beautiful images of Soon-Yi in the nude and

Mia found them and you may have heard what followed.

Let's be logical. Mia had been breathing fire and denouncing me to all her children and everyone else, and I understood that but still can't comprehend why I accepted the invitation to her country home in Connecticut. I hate the country and all those mosquitos and crickets far from theaters, restaurants, and the place I play clarinet in Manhattan. And I don't like being around people who hate and distrust me. This was the first time in my life for that, by the way. I can't imagine anyone believes what Mia and our adopted daughter Dylan say happened. Mia went on an errand and I may have put my head in Dylan's lap, and I may not have, and if I did, so what, while a group of us watched TV, and some days later I discovered I was being investigated for sexually abusing seven-year-old Dylan, not while watching TV but a little later supposedly taking her up to a crawl space and doing things no one before or since has accused me of and that I, as a loving father, would never have done to Dylan or anyone else.

That's the allegation. According to Mia, I ventured into enemy territory where everyone had been told to keep me under surveillance, yet I suddenly decided to molest Dylan. It's preposterous. Why did I choose such an absurd time and space? No logical person would, and I didn't. The police investigated. So did doctors, psychologists, and social workers. And the Yale-New Haven Hospital's experts in child abuse declared no physical abuse had taken place. They further explained that a vengeful mother coerced her increasingly disturbed daughter to try to destroy me. I'm thankful they couldn't.

Mia would rather continue to damage Dylan than accept I fell in love with Soon-Yi and we're still married and happy almost thirty years later. And the Me Too movement, which insists you must always believe every accusation made by women, has forced distributors in the United States to bury my latest movie, *A Rainy Day in New York.* Fine. It's doing quite well in Europe. A number of actors and actresses, who were delighted to work with me, have been me-too-ed into proclaiming they regret having done so and certainly will never work with me again. That hurts, but I'll find other actors. If I don't, no sweat. I've already made more than forty films and am almost eighty-five. And Mia, Ronan, and Me Too – nice job defending the First Amendment. You forced

Hachette to back out of publishing *Apropos of Nothing.* Okay. Arcade stepped in and the book's selling well and getting good reviews. I'm a lucky schlemiel. Plenty of people still believe in due process.

Spike Hosts Woody

"Woody, listen to this," Soon-Yi says, yanking his hand to stop on a Manhattan sidewalk and reading news on her cellphone. "Spike Lee says, 'Woody Allen is a great, great filmmaker and this cancel thing is not just Woody. When we look back on it we are going to see that – short of killing somebody – I don't know you just erase someone like they never existed.'"

He smiles and pulls her other hand and tries to keep walking.

"Let's turn around," she says. "Spike only lives a few blocks from here. Let's go see him."

"We can't just drop in. We barely know him."

Soon-Yi shakes her head and says, "Check this out. 'Woody is a friend of mine, a fellow short and bespectacled Knick fan, and I know he's going through it right now.' Come on, Woody."

He waves a hand of surrender, and they change directions, guided by Soon-Yi. In a short while they arrive at the mansion of Spike Lee and introduce themselves to a security guard who says, "Mr. Lee isn't home right now. May I take a message?"

"Here's Woody's number," says Soon-Yi. "Please text Spike."

The guard complies and Spike Lee soon calls and says, "Woody, perfect timing. Tonight's the premiere of my latest, *Da 5 Bloods.* I'd be pleased if you and your wife can join us there."

"I'm not sure if we can make it tonight, Spike."

Soon-Yi, learning toward the speaker, takes the phone from surprised hands and says, "Spike, we'd love to attend."

"Great, we'll save two seats next to my wife and me."

That evening Woody puts on a black tux and bowtie and Soon-Yi dons an elegant black dress baring her shoulders. Their driver deposits them in front of the auditorium adorned by spotlights and fans, and they introduce themselves to the doorman. He checks his list and says, "Sorry, but your names aren't here."

"We just talked to Spike this afternoon," Soon-Yi says. "Maybe he didn't get the information to you in time."

"I've got to go by what's here, ma'am."

Turning to Woody, Soon-Yi orders, "Give me your cellphone."

He hands it over and she dials Spike Lee. An automated voice directs her to voicemail. "Spike, Woody and I are out front. What's going on? Please pick up."

"No problem," Woody says, "Let's go home."

Soon-Yi examines Woody's text messages and sees one from Spike that says, "Sorry, Woody, but got pressured from all over this afternoon and had to tweet, 'I Deeply Apologize. My Words Were WRONG. I Do Not And Will Not Tolerate Sexual Harassment, Assault Or Violence. Such Treatment Causes Real Damage That Can't Be Minimized. – Truly, Spike Lee.'"

Tapping reply, she types, "Sorry to hear you've forgotten due process, Spike. – Best, Soon-Yi."

SPIKE LEE

Wall of Fame

Two long black limousines roll into Brooklyn and stop on Stuyvesant Ave. in front of Sal's Pizzeria. A couple of serious men in tailored suits exit the first vehicle and join two comparable men stepping out of the second and one opens the rear passenger door for the man in charge who steps onto the sidewalk and asks, "This the place?"

"This is it, Frank."

"Hotter than hell today. Let's get inside."

"We bringing the chauffeurs in, too?"

"Better let them keep an eye on the cars," says Frank

Through a door held open he walks into the pizza parlor and heads to the counter where a stocky man's mouth opens as his eyes liven.

"Frank, I can't believe it. I'm honored to meet you. Thank you so much for coming."

They shake hands, Sal using both his for a vigorous pump.

"What can I get for you and your friends, Frank? We've got great pizza and pasta, you name it. On the house."

After they order, Sal seats them at two tables he pushes together and his son Pino hands him a red and white tablecloth he spreads and says, "This is just for you guys."

"Have a seat, Sal," says Frank. "Tell me about your problem."

Sal looks at Pino and points behind the counter.

"I don't know what to do, Frank. It's about the Wall of Fame. My photos of you and Dean Martin and Robert DeNiro and Joe DiMaggio and Rocky Marciano and lots of our other heroes should hang here forever."

"They're a beautiful tribute," says Frank.

"The problem started a few days ago when a guy named Buggin' Out complained there were no blacks in the Wall of Fame even though most of my customers are black. I told him it's been my place for twenty-five years and only I decide what goes on the wall."

"Buggin' Out?"

"That's what everyone calls him. Who the hell knows what his real name is," Sal says, squeezing beefy fists on the table. "It's not only him. Radio Rahim came in with his radio booming and I told him to turn the damn thing down. Then he and Buggin' Out came back and demanded I start putting blacks on the wall. I told them to go to hell. After that they started going around trying to organize a boycott of my place. Can you believe that, Frank?"

"It's something I hate to believe."

Pino steps around the counter and walks over. "Dad, we should sell the place and move to a different area. I'm sick of all the blacks around here. They should stay in their neighborhoods and we should stay in ours."

"I'm not moving my place, Pino."

"Your dad's right, Pino," says Frank.

Pointing at a slender young black man, Sal says, "Mookie, come on over here. He's been delivering pizzas for years and is like a son to me. Mookie, you've got to help me deal with this."

"Sure, put some pictures of blacks on your walls," he says, rubbing a hand over his Brooklyn Dodgers jersey Number 42. "Start with Jackie Robinson and Willie Mays and Martin Luther King and Malcolm X and Michael Jackson and Louis Armstrong and Aretha Franklin…"

"All right, Mookie, I know your heroes, but you've got to work your ass off like I did so you can get your own place to hang those pictures."

"Okay, Sal, but there's going to be trouble."

"Are you threatening my friend?" Frank says.

"No," says Mookie, pulling rolled up papers from his rear pants pocket. "I'm giving you a fair warning. Either put some of our people in the Wall of Fame or deal with the consequences."

"What consequences?" says Sal.

Mookie glances at the papers.

"What the hell's that?" Frank says.

"It's a screenplay about all this."

"I've done lots of movies. Let me have a look."

Mookie opens the script to a key part and hands it to Frank. Everyone watches him read several minutes.

"Who the hell wrote this, Mookie?" Frank says.

"I did."

"You oughta be in your high school class."

"I'm a college graduate."

Frank says, "Then why the hell're you working in a pizza joint?"

"Hold it, Frank. Mookie's got a good job here, two-fifty a week."

"I'm directing the film," Mookie says.

"What's the name of it?"

"Do the Right Thing. Don't you know who I am?"

"Some skinny kid with a big mouth."

"You used to be a skinny kid with a big mouth until you became a pudgy old man with a bigger mouth."

Frank looks at the front page of the script and says, "So your real name's Spike."

"Right."

"Someone hand me a pen so I can fix this damn story."

"You're not touching my work," Spike says.

Frank looks at him, shakes his head, and says, "This is a problem that doesn't need to happen."

"This shit happens every day."

"You're exaggerating," says Frank. "No way Sal would take a bat to Radio Rahim's radio."

"He might."

"Why don't you pay more attention to what blacks do to each other in the inner cities," says Frank.

"I deal with that stuff, too, but at this stage in my movie Sal's going to freak out and say the magic word and Radio Rahim's going beat his ass and people are going to tear this place apart until the police come and choke Radio Rahim to death."

"Maybe that's the only way to stop him," says Frank.

"He was subdued," says Mookie.

Eric Garner and George Floyd enter Sal's Pizzeria and announce, "Radio Rahim was subdued and so were we."

"Who the hell are those guys?" says Frank, looking at Spike.

"Brothers, have we met?"

Spike Fever

On a Bensonhurst residential street lined by brick homes mortared together, a swarthy man says, "Hey Spike, come here a second."

"Sorry, but I'm busy making a movie."

"Yeah, I know," he says, stepping toward the diminutive director. "That's why I need to talk to you."

Spike stops in the posture of a walk briefly paused. "Who are you?"

"Jimmy."

"Jimmy who?"

"Jimmy Tucci, Angie's brother."

"Nice young lady," Spike says, and takes a step before Jimmy grabs his arm.

"Take you hand off me, Jimmy."

"Sure, Spike. I'm just making sure you don't try anything with Angie."

Spike adjusts his glasses and says, "Try what."

"I know how you guys operate."

"How's that."

"You can't get enough of the white stuff."

"Doesn't a hotshot like you read Playboy, Jimmy? I said in that interview and others as well as in everyday life, I'm not attracted to white women. You got that? I'm not saying they aren't pretty. But it's black women who move me."

"Okay, but behave yourself."

"I'm behaving quite well, but you aren't," he says, walking away.

Two weeks later Jimmy eludes two large but immobile security guards and rushes up to Spike Lee. "I told you to take care of my sister."

"You told me to lay off and I did, because I wanted to. You didn't say anything about Flipper Purify."

"That's one of the blackest guys I've ever seen," Jimmy says.

"Look, they fell for each other. Nothing I could've done about it."

"You're the director…"

"And the screenwriter, but righteous words flew onto the page and I captured the passion."

"Our dad beat hell out of Angie and called her a disgrace. You like that?"

"I don't like it. I don't like a lot of things that're wrong. Your family's not the only one affected. Flipper's wife threw his ass out of the house and cursed him as she fired his clothes at him from the second floor window. Imagine their little girl having to watch all that."

Jimmy says, "That's my point, Spike. The races don't mix after a point."

"That's not for you to decide."

"I decide if it's my sister."

"No, Jimmy, she decides what's right for her."

"Her boyfriend Paulie's devastated by this."

"You don't give a damn about Paulie. That's why you threatened him about having sex with Angie."

Spike points at the exit and the security guards standing on either side of Jimmy take an arm each and almost carry him from the room.

"You gonna throw me out, too, Spike," says Drew, Flipper's wife.

The director spreads his arms in exasperation.

"I agree with Jimmy," she says. "We're losing our men to thousands of white bitches who throw themselves at black men. Once they've made it professionally, they want the lightest women they can get. I'm half white and that's not good enough for Flipper anymore."

"Those are some of the key points I'm making, Drew."

"At the expense of my family? Go to hell."

She leaves and passes Reverend Purify, Flipper's father. Walking slowly, he stops a few feet from the director and says, "Spike, I told my son and his unholy girlfriend that Southern whites put their wives on a pedestal never to be approached by black men, and the whole time they were going to their slaves' quarters and screwing all our lovely young women. Now the big black bucks are getting what they were denied."

"Hey, Reverend, I know all that. I wrote it, right. I appreciate your passion but want you to focus on the camera."

Head down as he walks toward Spike, Paulie slowly lifts his eyes and says, "The way you took my girlfriend made everyone degrade me, and then when I get a date with a pretty black woman you send the neighborhood punks after me and I have to show up bloody at Orin's house. That's not how things really are, Spike. The guys in the neighborhood might razz me for going out with a black lady, but they're not going to assault me."

"Guys in neighborhoods like yours have killed black guys for even being there."

"That's tragic but rare," Paulie says. "Besides, I'm talking about my life."

"Move on," Gator tells Paulie. "Look, Spike, we've got to adjust a few things here. I don't mind being a crack addict in the movie. As you know I've been a crack addict in life. But I didn't steal TVs and money from my parents for another blast. You're making me look bad."

"I'm giving you the opportunity to do some great acting."

"And I do appreciate that, Spike, but does my father have to shoot me in the balls to get rid of me. An immaculate shot to the gut would be just as effective."

"I'll shoot it both ways, okay? Then I'll choose the best one when I'm finished."

"How about loaning me a hundred, just this once?"

"Get your ass outta here," says the director.

Drew Purify waves at Spike and motions come here. He walks over and she hugs him and says, "Thank you so much."

"What for?"

"For putting my husband back in my bed for at least one night. We're going to reconcile, aren't we?"

Spike lifts his shoulders. "I dunno."

"I do," she says.

Directing David Duke

Based on an online preview, I'm very concerned how Spike Lee's portraying me in his new movie *BlacKkKlansman* and, as a lifelong activist, I'm going to speak out. For the New York premiere I put on a tux and long, curly wig, so anti-whites won't recognize me and bar the door, and ease into the theater and wait in the lobby until lights dim.

"Where's Spike sitting?" I ask an usher, who gives me an unpleasant look as he points.

"Thanks, brother," I say.

I ease to the seat of honor Spike always has at movie premiers, basketball games, and restaurants. I think the woman on one side is his wife and will be hard to dislodge. The other lady must be an actress.

"Excuse me, ma'am. I have very important business to discuss with Spike. May I have this seat?"

"You may not," she says.

"Fine," I say, looking at Spike and removing my rock-star crown before turning to the audience, which has damn few whites. "Listen, everybody, don't believe how Spike Lee is representing me in this film. It's a distorted image that keeps you from dealing with the facts."

"Get your ass outta here or my guys'll throw you out," Spike says.

"Listen, Spike, I respect some of your work but this one's way out of line."

"Which of my movies do you like? I better go back and edit."

"You're portraying us as caricatures," I say.

A mountainous security guard asks, "Should we toss him, Spike?"

"You take my seat," Spike stands and tells the guard. "Duke, I've always wanted to straighten you out. Come with me into the lobby."

We walk up the aisle and I hear lots of buzzing and a few obscene threats.

"Would you like some popcorn, Spike?"

"No, Duke. What the hell's your problem?"

"I don't like coming off as an ignorant and hateful cracker."

"Let's see, you used to be Grand Wizard of the Ku Klux Klan. You want me to make you Gandhi?"

"That was more than forty years ago. I've changed. Now I spend a lot more time worrying about Jews than blacks. Look how the Jews control our media and our foreign policy."

"About ten years ago I saw you on TV with President Ahmadinejad at that conference of Holocaust deniers in Iran."

"The Jews are trying to get us to start a war with Iran."

Lee says, "Donald Trump and his group are the ones doing that. Do you really believe the Holocaust didn't happen?"

"There were atrocities, no doubt, but not as bad as the media claim. I'm more concerned about present and future bloodshed. The white race in the United States is in genocidal danger. We need white civil rights and segregation and we've got to reduce welfare and busing."

"There are about two hundred million whites in the United States and they still control most of the money and political levers, but you've always considered yourself oppressed. You need a shrink, man. That's not an insult. That's good advice."

"Listen, Spike, I'm trying to help all people. I was conservative but moderate when elected to the Louisiana House in 1989, and even more reasonable when I ran for the U.S. Senate and for governor."

"You got blown away both times."

"The media, and that means the Jews, tricked people into opposing me. I've studied this stuff quite thoroughly, Spike. I hope you've read my doctoral thesis 'Zionism as a Form of Ethic Supremacism.'"

"Who'd give you a PhD?"

"The Interregional Academy of Personnel Management in Ukraine."

Spike pulls a cell phone from his pants pocket, pokes the screen several times, reads a little, and says, "That place isn't even accredited in Ukraine. Quit calling yourself Dr. Duke."

"I'm a scholar as well as an activist and am dedicated to stopping the Jews from destroying the white race."

Shaking his phone, Spike says, "I don't need this to tell me you're more jailbird than academic. About fifteen years ago you pleaded guilty to mail fraud and tax violations. You, the savior of the white race, told poor white followers you were in 'dire straits' and needed cash right away. They responded. After all, in those days you looked pretty good with all that plastic surgery. And what'd you do with the money? You spent it on your gambling addiction. How'd you like prison?"

"I only pleaded guilty because the media made sure I couldn't have gotten a fair trial."

"That's weak."

"Why don't you admit Trump's doing a great job and lowering unemployment for blacks."

"He's unworthy of comment except to say he's Agent Orange."

"You've been self-righteous so long, Spike, I bet I spend more time than you worrying about victims of black on black violence."

"How much?"

JOHN HUSTON

Huston Directs Bogart

During vacations from boarding school I watched my father Walter, one of the preeminent actors of stage and screen, perform on Broadway and elsewhere, and I appreciated the talents of Aunt Margaret Carrington, the finest voice coach of her generation who helped transform her brother from a popular vaudevillian into a consummate actor and developed the lyrical voice of John Barrymore as he prepared to play Hamlet and also helped me add warm honey to a voice I'm told is deep and alluring.

You may not know that as a young man I aspired to be an artist and sketched and painted for hours and eventually years and felt I was rather good but belatedly discovered I was broke and not long afterward spent several months almost starving on the streets of London. At the not terribly young age of twenty-four, I resolved to develop my other creative talent, and began to write dialogue for movies in Hollywood and was soon writing or rather co-writing screenplays and my skills were rather highly regarded on the lot of Warner Brothers and particularly so after my contribution to the script of *Jezebel*, for which Bette Davis won an Oscar for best actress.

As my directorial debut at last approached, I was delighted at age thirty-six to have a great dramatic source, *The Maltese Falcon* by Dashiell Hammett. Two other movies had been improperly made of this work. I vowed to outperform my predecessors who frankly lacked talent and insight. I mined the novel for its most affecting passages, and wove a seamless screenplay enhanced by my sketches of every scene in the movie. I thus ensured we would shoot this film rapidly and in order but worried who would be in front of the cameras. I certainly did not want George Raft, a limited actor, to star as Sam Spade but executive producer Hal Roach had offered him the part and, despite my bold tendencies, I understood rookie directors do not win many confrontations.

I occasionally saw Raft on the lot and ignored him as he did me and in a few days I celebrated when Hal Wallis said, "Nothing personal, John, but George is worried you've never directed and has signed for another film."

"May I suggest Humphrey Bogart," I said. "He's quite good and too often passed over for good roles."

"I'll ask him."

Bogey immediately agreed to play Sam Spade, and we brought in Mary Astor, beautiful and talented but a heavy drinker, and British stage veteran Sydney Greenstreet, a gentleman of sixty-one who had never acted in a film and weighed more than three hundred pounds, and eerie but intriguing Peter Lorre.

One night early in production Mary Astor called where I was staying and said, "John, I've got to see you. I'm so nervous about this role."

"Have you been drinking, Mary?"

"Just a few, so far. Please come over right away."

"I'm a married man, Mary."

Her laughter rang my right ear. In my capacity as a dedicated director and devout hedonist, I met Mary in a private place and comforted her for a couple of hours and we periodically resumed this practice as needed.

Everyone faced a variety of rapidly developing events. Bogey's partner is murdered on a dark street. A mysterious man named Thursby is also killed, on a ship docked in San Francisco. The widow of Bogey's dead partner thinks he killed her husband so he could have her. The cops believe Bogey killed Thursby. Peter Lorre offers Bogey five grand for the Maltese Falcon and then pulls a gun Bogey snatches after a short right to Lorre's jaw. He suspects Bogey has the valuable statuette or knows where it is. Now the cops warn Bogey they know he is involved in his partner's murder.

Despite my determination to finish this picture on time and under budget, I several times invited actors and others in the production to a restaurant so we could talk and laugh about matters unrelated to *The Maltese Falcon*. I much enjoyed mixing liquid spirits with those of the soul while my charm enthralled the group.

Back on the set I maintained momentum scene after scene. In the lobby of Lorre's hotel Bogey tells a gunman named Wilmer, who's following him, that "the cheaper the crook, the gaudier the patter." After more action Wilmer points his gun and takes Bogey to Sydney

Greenstreet who tells him the black bird is quite valuable and offers twenty-five grand now and more later. Bogey can't consider this long as he passes out from a spiked drink the Fat Man gave him. Peter Lorre and Wilmer come in and Wilmer kicks unconscious Bogey in the face. A wounded man called Jacobi, captain of the ship where Thursday was killed, staggers into Bogey's office and hands him a package before he dies. In a little while Astor, Lorre, Greenstreet, and seething Wilmer await Bogey at his apartment. I shall not tell you more except everything is exciting and at the end one character tells another, "You're taking the fall," and we've got a hit and Bogey, at age forty-two, finally becomes a star, and so do I, and Lorre and Greenstreet enhance their careers while Astor regains some influence.

Sierra Madre

"Why didn't you ask me?"

"I did," says John Huston.

"When?"

"Back in Los Angeles, Dad, when I offered you the best part of your career."

Running a hand through his scraggly beard, Walter says, "I grew this to look old and crusty."

"You promised – no dentures when we film *The Treasure of the Sierra Madre*. You look great in the dailies."

"I look terrible."

"Precisely what I mean. Besides, I'm both director and screenwriter."

"Okay, but I'm using my damn dentures when I eat," says Walter.

"Long as that's off camera."

It's very hot and dry down here in the heart of Mexico and lots of people are struggling, some like Humphrey Bogart who doesn't have a dime. Three times he asks cocky John, playing a cameo, if he's got some change. That's the last handout, John says, and Bogey and fellow bum Tim Holt go to work for a fellow who rips them off and almost kicks their asses when they try to collect in a bar but they eventually pound him and get enough money to join Walter in the Sierra Madre to look for gold.

Bogey and Tim can't work hard or smart as veteran gold miner Walter and want to run home but they'd die alone and Walter's not leaving because they're too dumb to understand he's dancing where they stand and saying there's a fortune in the mountains right there. Like Walter promised, the gold's up there and they about die mining in the heat but start bringing in treasure and packing it in sacks, each guy with his third of the stake hidden, but Bogey's getting more paranoid, saying if he goes to town for supplies Tim and Walter will take his gold and run, or if he takes his share with him bandits will get it, and he accuses Tim of stealing his gold and hiding it under a rock that Tim says in fact conceals a deadly gila monster and if Bogey doesn't believe him go ahead and stick his hand in there. Tim's right but Bogey doesn't apologize he just rants, "I've got to finish this damn picture and get back to L.A. for my annual yacht races."

The Sierra Madre is a tough place to make a movie, especially with John being a perfectionist bastard and Bogey's character's getting crazier and the real Bogey going the same way. Worried John Huston rides a horse several hours to the nearest town and calls Jack Warner.

"When the hell are you guys going to finish the movie," Jack says.

"That's why I'm calling," says John.

"I'm losing a fortune."

"Bogey's slowing things down."

"Go ahead and use some of your boxing skills on him," says Jack.

"I slapped him around last night but he just got worse. Come on down and threaten to fire his ass."

"You're the director. Fire him."

"You could overrule me."

"I won't. Go ahead."

"We've been here weeks and would have to start again if we replaced Bogey," says John.

"Then kill the bastard."

"I'm not willing to go quite that far, Jack."

"I mean in the script, smartass."

"We'll deal with that remark upon my return, Jack."

On horseback coming back John makes key changes in his head and passes out the actors' lines day by day. Walter saves a little boy and grateful villagers demand he return with them to be properly honored.

"That's damn stupid, John. They wouldn't thank a guy by virtually kidnapping him."

"Bogey, I advise you to keep your mouth shut except when delivering your lines."

Walter, the steadiest man on site, leaves with the villagers, and Bogey and Tim become ever more suspicious of each other and manic Bogey tries to kill him and after Tim subdues him Bogey warns they'll have a contest to see who can stay awake longest. John Huston's revised script mandates that Bogey stay awake and whenever he falls asleep John gives him a few small white pills that wake him right up.

"These things are about killing me. Why don't you let me go to sleep and finish me off?"

"Be patient and accept my judgment about dramatic propriety," says John.

When Bogey stops cooperating, crew members hold him down and John grabs his face, thumb on one side of his mouth and fingers on the other, and forces him to open up and swallow more pills washed down by tequila. At last, Tim's asleep and Bogey shoots him and packs heavy gold sacks on several mules. When he returns to bury Tim the body's gone and that makes Bogey even edgier as he talks to himself and laughs maniacally while he and the mules suffer from thirst and despair until, mercifully, Bogey is attacked by bandits who, in this code-restricted era, hit his head with sticks that are supposed to be axes.

"You two Hustons have a great time," says Bogey, bearded and filthy but heading north.

The culminating particulars of John's script needn't be elaborated here but we can report a final confrontation. After Walter and merely-wounded Tim are reunited they learn the bandits believed the sacks were laden with sand weighing down furs underneath and foolishly scattered *The Treasure of the Sierra Madre* to the winds. By now Mexican authorities have begun monitoring the dailies and reporting "insulting portrayals of Mexicans" to newspapers and politicians.

President Miguel Alemán Valdés speaks for millions in this terse message: "Our people have skillfully mined the Sierra Madre for centuries and know its treasures better than anyone. Your yanqui arrogance is laughable. All United States citizens on your film crew must leave Mexico within forty-eight hours."

President Harry S. Truman sends a military plane for the task and urges Mexican authorities to be patient since John Huston, Walter Huston, Tim Holt, and others are being held at a secret prison. Thankfully, the moviemakers are located within a week and, without ceremony, flown back to Los Angeles where Humphrey Bogart does not meet them at the military airfield.

African Queen

As the *Queen Luise*, a large German boat, floats on this beautiful blue African lake during the Great War, Humphrey Bogart and girlfriend Katherine Hepburn stand on deck. Enemy officers sentence them to death for spying and place nooses around their necks.

"Go ahead and hang us. That's dramatic justice."

"That isn't in the script, Bogey," says director John Huston. "And remember, I'm also the screenwriter."

"One of at least four, and I don't care which one of you is responsible. I'm not going to let you throw away the best performance of my career so you can send everyone home happy with some sappy ending."

"I think Bogey's right," says Kate.

"I admire both of you personally as well as actors and know you respect my authority."

Shaking his head, Bogey says, "Look at the great work that precedes this. People will always remember my stomach growling as I drink tea with Kate and say, 'You'd think I had a hyena inside me… Ain't a thing I can do about it.'"

"A superb line, indeed, Bogey, and one I crafted just for you."

Katherine, elegant even in a noose, says, "John, we must maintain the poignancy established when my dear brother Robert Morley loses his mind and dies after the Germans burn down our church and the village of the natives."

John walks close and looks down on each before he says, "If reality is your paramount concern, why didn't you complain about the notion that a religious spinster and drunken old boatman could team up in a creaky boat and navigate an increasingly treacherous river whose rapids become a veritable waterfall? We had to shoot those scenes with a small model boat. "

"That's an exciting adventure, dangerous but possible," says Bogey.

"Do you really think you and Kate could make two torpedoes and detonators out of blasting gelatin? In everyday life would you conclude you'd make it all the way to the lake and blow up the hundred-ton *Queen Luise*?"

"I'd believe we should try," says Kate.

"I'm not saying everything has to be literal, John. I'd never let Kate or any dame force me out of the boat's only canvas-covered area and into tropical rain. And I'd never let her me call me a coward for getting drunk and telling her the whole thing is crazy. And if she dumped my gin in the river, I'd dump her."

She turns to Bogey. "If I sensed that level of violence, I'd probably bash your head with a bottle and push you overboard into the mouths of crocodiles."

"Come on, Kate. The best part of the movie's when we finally start to touch and kiss."

"Those moments are quite tender," says John, "and would be more so had I not been a gentleman and stopped shooting."

Looking sternly at John, she says, "You have no idea what transpired behind our canvas retreat."

One doesn't know but is nevertheless thankful that Lauren Bacall, Bogey's beautiful young bride, has gone sightseeing with guides.

"After your unlikely survival of the rapids, could Bogey, without equipment, weld and repair the seriously damaged propeller and rudder? How about you, Kate?"

"You're shredding your own movie," she says.

"Not at all. I'm building dramatic momentum, scene by scene, and prosecuting my case that modest suspension of belief is part of making and watching movies. Our viewers will forever recall the *African Queen* gets stuck in a swamp, surrounded by suffocating plants, and Bogey climbs into the water and pulls the boat, and has to jump out because he's covered with leeches Kate helps him remove, and Kate eventually joins him in the swamp and with a machete hacks a trail until the muddy morass compels him to say, 'We're finished... I'm not one bit sorry we came... It was worth it...'

"Should I stop the movie there? Should I show your agonizing descent into death? Is it necessary to see bugs and reptiles devour your rotting flesh?"

"Stop it, John," says Kate.

"John, I love the way you let rain lift the *African Queen* out of the swamp and onto the great lake where we see the *Queen Luise* which may see us until we turn back into the reeds and hide while activating our detonators and torpedoes."

"All that's wonderful," says Kate, "and I really don't object to a storm overwhelming us and sinking our little boat. It's also logical that Bogey thinks I drown, and, though you don't show it, I naturally conclude he perishes. But it's illogical for Bogey, captured by the Germans, to plead guilty to spying, a capital crime during war."

"Your death devastates him," says John.

"Even losing me," says Kate, "I think tough old Bogey would offer the Germans believable reasons for being on the lake. He needs supplies. He wouldn't place that noose around his neck. Then, when they bring me on board, I wouldn't confess either. The Germans still have no physical evidence against us."

"She's right, John. The best ending, and it ain't too late, would be to either hang us or keep us prisoners a little while before letting us go. What we can't have is the *African Queen,* underwater but just beneath the surface, miraculously be where the big boat runs into it and gets blown up and Kate and I end up happy and by ourselves in the water. People are going to ask where the hell are all those Germans? Don't they have lifeboats or preservers? Can't they swim? We've got an extraordinary movie here, John. But at this stage you shouldn't have a fairytale ending."

John Huston steps back, looks at the captain of the *Queen Luise,* and orders, "Hang them."

Let There Be Light

I've made four documentaries about World War II, and while in the midst of filming *The Battle of San Pietro* I see many soldiers shot and maimed but only later learn that some who survive, even without physical damage, suffer from severe wounds of the spirit. I begin to consider the psychological consequences of war and conclude that men who clubbed each other in and around caves assuredly suffered from the stress of combat as did Alexander the Great's warriors wielding swords and spears and Civil War soldiers firing rifles and cannons. Put people in hell, we're learning, and twenty in a hundred will emerge with the devil in their heads.

The war ends in Europe and will soon be over in the Pacific and back in the United States my crew and I are at Mason General Hospital on Long Island. All soldiers under treatment are in uniform. Listen to them describe their feelings and watch doctors try to help and note narration by my father Walter Huston. Individually and in groups there are men who tremble and can't sleep or remember things and suffer from "unceasing fear and apprehension" in a world of "impending disaster… hopelessness and isolation." Their problems aren't physical in origin but as if they're "paralyzed by their minds."

This man always looks down when people talk to him. Over there, a young black soldier, in a documentary I insist be integrated, cries as he talks of homesickness intensified by a picture of his sweetheart, "the one person who gives me a sense of importance and cooperation."

Here's a man who hopes "something would happen" because he's "tired of living." The next man is asked if he's aware he's changed. "Yes," he says, "I'm more jumpy. I used to go places and have fun. I don't like to do that anymore." Another man has also changed, noting "I was never nervous before the war."

"I can only stand so much of seeing my buddies killed," says the next soldier. A man nearby suffers from crying spells he thinks are related to his mother's illness. All these ailments require treatment, for, as narrator Walter Huston reminds us, "modern psychiatry makes no distinction between body and mind."

I'm never on camera or listed in the credits but am becoming fascinated by hypnosis and how it's used for therapy. The doctor presents a young man who doesn't know his name after a shell burst near him in Okinawa. After putting him under hypnosis, the doctor asks, "What do you see in Okinawa?"

"Shells are thrown at us," he says. "We're told to get cover. One guy's hurt. They're carrying me across the field to a stretcher. I want to forget all this."

"Okay," says the doctor, "but you remember who you are. What's your name? And your last name?

The soldier gives correct answers we must keep confidential.

"Good," says the doctor. "This is past and no longer threatening your safety."

Soldiers relax making art and playing baseball and share feelings in group psychotherapy designed to get them "out of isolation" and help them understand they're "like other men." Getting relief from anxiety is essential. When they rejoin society they'll inevitably face pressure competing for jobs.

"Many wonder what the public will think," says a doctor. "Some employers might not understand psychoneurotic. We're conducting educational programs. You can work in groups as trained, and this will be of much value to you. You're no longer shut up in the inner recesses of yourselves. You're coming out. You're enjoying ice cream and sports and you're getting over nervousness and you're being accepted. We have a guy who couldn't walk. Now he's hitting home runs. One man who couldn't talk is today behaving normally."

I shoot seventy hours of film, cut it to fifty-six tight minutes, and am anxious to share what I believe is an important work. The United States Army, no doubt encouraged by various unnamed government officials, also considers the film vital but for other reasons. My print and others are seized "in order to protect the confidentiality of the soldiers." I suppose appearing in *Let There Be Light* wouldn't help a guy at a job interview. And I damn well know the armed forces want the public and future recruits to believe all fighting men come home happy and healthy.

Notes: *Let There Be Light* was finally released in 1981.

ALFRED HITCHCOCK

Hitchcock Visits Perkins

I watch Alfred Hitchcock struggle out the back seat of his chauffeured limousine and slowly walk into the office of my Perkins Motel.

"What a marvelous place you have here," he says.

My motel is clean and quiet and safe but no sincere person would describe it as marvelous.

"For my next movie I'm searching for a quaint roadside motel with a sinister mansion high on the hill behind it."

"We can't shut our hotel or we'd lose our regular customers," I say.

Rather a ham than an actor, Hitchcock rotates to survey my empty parking lot.

"Must be your off season. Let me use this establishment for three weeks, four at most, and I'll pay your gross receipts for the preceding twelve months. The publicity would help as much as the money."

I double the real total, surmising he won't ask to see the books.

"Deal," he says, shaking my hand. "Whose name shall I write on the contract?"

"Anthony Perkins."

"Is there a Mrs. Perkins in that ornate home behind us?"

"No, just my mother," I say. "Taking care of her and this motel is all I can handle."

"I'd be delighted to talk to her."

"She'll no doubt be pleased."

Hitchcock and I walk up shaky wooden steps and he's huffing before we reach the porch. We enter and I shout up the stairs, "Mom, guess who's here?"

"I have no idea, Anthony. Who is it?"

"Alfred Hitchcock."

"Don't be silly," she says.

"Are you decent? We're coming up."

"Wonderful."

I worry Hitchcock won't survive more stair-climbing but he does and, upon entering my mother's large bedroom overlooking the motel, says, "Madam, it's a pleasure to meet you."

"I'm thrilled, Mr. Hitchcock," she says from her wheelchair.

"You're the greatest director in history. Before my fall I used to go to all your movies."

"I hope you watch *Alfred Hitchcock Presents* on television."

"Every week," she says. "And sometimes your old movies, too."

"Where is Mr. Perkins?"

"He died many years ago," she says.

"He must've been quite young. May I ask the cause of his demise?"

I frown at Hitchcock before Mom says, "He died of a heart attack, just like Anthony's grandfather."

"Was there an autopsy?"

"Oh, yes. But we all knew he was dead before he hit the kitchen floor."

Hitchcock surveys the bedroom and says, "So you've been alone a long time."

"Well, I wish I had been, except for Anthony. About ten years after his father died I married a no good man who wanted my money. And he tried to get it by pushing me down the stairs. I'm lucky I survived but I could never walk again. He probably would've finished me off but Anthony heard the ruckus, rushed out of his bedroom, and shot him."

"Fascinating," says Hitchcock.

"You could make a movie about our adventure," says Mom.

"We certainly could, but I already have an even more horrific tale in mind."

Many of you know what that is. The director portrays me as a matricidal maniac and sends me into psychotic outer space. Maybe I am haywire or I'd never have let Alfred Hitchcock into my family history. At least my attorney tells me he'll soon be paying plenty to get out.

Janet Leigh Debates Hitchcock

"I've decided I can't do that scene," I say, crossing my arms.

"My dear, it's all make believe and will make you a star."

"I'm already a star, and I plan to survive," I say, but stop there instead of accusing Alfred Hitchcock of complicity in on-the-set deaths of actresses in two early British films and the recent severe injury of an actress here in Hollywood.

After looking at me disgustedly, he turns and waddles out of my motel cabin on the set. The following day, at home, an attorney knocks and hands me a document warning I'll be fined and fired if I don't uphold my contractual commitment. The document closes with an assurance that several crew members will be present to protect me. I call Hitchcock's assistant and say, "All right. When do we do it?"

Two days later I'm naked in the *Psycho* shower, water pounding my chest, when Anthony Perkins rips down the plastic curtains with one hand and raises his knife with the other. I aim the derringer in my right hand and shoot Perkins between the eyes. He tumbles onto my bloody feet where I grab his knife and bound out of the tub and stab the right shoulder of an astonished Hitchcock who screams, "Good god, what's this?"

"Keep shooting," I order.

Hedren v. Hitchcock

I don't like birds but am quite young and want to become a director and one of Alfred Hitchcock's assistants hires me to work on the set of *The Birds* and care for his snake-eyed creatures.

"As we shall begin filming the climactic scene tomorrow, make sure you don't give nourishment of any kind to the birds," Hitchcock says, the first time he's ever spoken to me.

"Nothing?"

"That's what I said. But do rattle their cages periodically."

I don't need to harass the crows and other extraterrestrials; they snap and claw the cages and flap their wings and squeal and squawk like their feathers are being pulled. In the morning Hitchcock tells me, "Carry the cages into the attic of the house and don't utter a word to Miss Hedren."

"Yes sir." That really lets me down as for months I've been yearning for a reason to talk to beautiful Tippi Hedren, a sophisticated blonde in the Grace Kelly style. Hefty Hitchcock has ordered everyone to stay away from Tippi and seems the only person authorized talk to his star, a model making her first film. He coaches her before scenes, he invites her to his private office for drinks, he gazes at her frequently and seems to be in love, and Mrs. Hitchcock has undoubtedly noticed.

When Tippi arrives I smile and say, "Good morning," and am thrilled she does and says the same.

Hitchcock greets her at the front door. "Go inside a moment, dear, and in a few minutes we shall walk upstairs and into the attic where some harmless mechanical birds await you."

Several men protected by thick leather gloves and jackets and heavy plastic goggles, all of which I now don, already stand in the attic, its only window darkened by a tarp, and when Tippi enters I rush in behind her and, after Hitchcock slips in, I close the door. The director orders, "Action," and the men begin throwing birds at Tippi's face, at her shoulders, at her legs, but mostly in her face, and I do, too, and she says, "Stop this," ducking and holding her arms up.

"Don't hide your face, dear," Hitchcock says.

As she opens her hands a big bird bites her left cheek and blood emerges.

"Didn't get you in the eye, did it? Continue shooting."

Tippi turns and staggers into a corner, pushing her face into the intersection of walls and covering each side of her head with her arms, and screams, "Get these birds off me."

One of the commando squad, a braver man than I, snaps off a bird's head, throws it and the body on the floor, jerks the tarp down and opens the window, shouting, "Any bird that doesn't fly dies right here."

"Keep shooting," Hitchcock orders.

I, at least, open the door to the stairs, and in a minute or so most of the birds have either flown out the window or the door, and Tippi, who weighs about a hundred pounds, wheels and attacks Hitchcock, kicking him in the belly and, as he bends and grimaces, gouges his eyes with both hands and crumples him with a kick to the groin. The original hero escorts her out of the house.

Hitchcock groans on the floor several minutes until he says, "Mercifully, that's the final shot."

Ladies in Neckties

Sitting heavily on the plush sofa in a London hotel suite, Alfred Hitchcock says, "Excuse me for not rising but at age seventy-two I'm not quite as agile as I once was."

"That's all right," says Barry Foster. "It's an honor to meet you."

"Please be seated."

Foster pops into a soft chair near the director and leans forward.

"I'm considering you for the vital role of Bob Rusk in *Frenzy*, which I assure you will be a splendid film. Have you read Anthony Shaffer's script?"

"Yes, it's wonderful."

"I should like to determine your fitness for the part."

Foster nods go ahead.

"Were you abused as a child?"

"No, not at all."

"Are you sure? You seem rather anxious to deny the possibility."

"I'm as confident about that as any man can be," says Barry.

Hitchcock examines the actor's face.

"Do you hate women?"

"Of course not. I love the birds and, frankly, they think I'm pretty jolly, too."

"Have you ever desired to see women behave in a sexually masochistic way?"

Red-haired Foster reddens in the face and says, "No. What the hell line of questioning is this?"

"Consider it an aesthetic cross-examination. If I hadn't made films I'd have been a first-rate barrister. You don't have to answer any questions that could incriminate you."

Heatedly, Foster says, "I beg your pardon."

"Relax, Barry. If you do have any pathological urges to rape and kill – and I assume they'd be unrealized – then I want you to draw on them while playing Bob Rusk."

"I'm no longer sure I want to play him."

"It would be the best role of your career. Michael Caine turned it down, you know."

"I wonder if Michael declined the part or didn't want to work with you," says Foster.

Hitchcock exhales frustration. "He thought Bob Rusk was disgusting. Evidently, Michael Caine doesn't think he can convincingly play the part. I respect his diffidence. Only a rare actor can play a serial killer in a movie that will also have moments of comedy."

Barry Foster mellows as he says, "That's a challenge but one I'm prepared for."

"Perhaps I did probe a bit too deeply, but I have to be sure. A serial killer is loose in London Town, leaving his ties taut around the necks of naked ladies who are fished from the Thames. Can you be a good fellow, offering money to your friend Dick after he's fired, and then darkly enter the lonely hearts office of his former wife, who in exasperation says she can't help you because you want women who submit to your 'peculiar' needs?"

"I can do all that," Foster says. "And I've been practicing the great line, 'You're my type of woman' before I attack and rip off her dress and rape her and tell her she's 'lovely, lovely' and call her a bitch like all women and remove my tie pin before taking off my tie and strangling her. Look how I grimace as I finish her off and make her hands slowly fall from her neck around which I leave my lethal tie."

"It doesn't bother you that Dick's onscreen a lot more than you?"

"Not at all, Mr. Hitchcock. Every moment I have I'm either ominous or violent."

"His character's far more appealing."

"To an audience, yes, but not to a serious actor."

Hitchcock points at the script on the coffee table and says, "I believe the audience will enjoy the sequence during which you invite Dick's girlfriend Babs up to your apartment, 'no strings attached,' and in a scene we don't see we hear you say, 'You're my type of woman,' and then you wheel her out in a sack on a dolly and toss her into the back of a potato truck, and back home you realize your distinctive tie pin is missing, and you rush back to the truck but can't dig through the sack and potatoes so you crawl into the back just before the driver pulls away and you're in a jam now and can't find her and then you can't find her hand and when you do her rigor mortis hand won't yield your tie pin and you have to break her individual fingers to retrieve your pin while many dusty potatoes are rolling out the rear of the truck. At least you can exit when the driver pulls into the parking lot of a roadside café but after dining the fellow drives away unaware the departed lady's foot is hanging out the back and then she falls out, shocking the police in pursuit."

"I read this passage for some friends and they reacted as if I were Peter Sellers," Foster says.

"It's sad when other friends boot poor fugitive Dick but fortuitous you, his good friend Bob Rusk, let him stay at your apartment into which the police soon charge and arrest Dick and, portentously, open his bag in front of him, revealing the clothes of his departed lover Babs. You and Dick know who the murderer is but the police and the judge think he's the culprit. We shouldn't, even among ourselves, reveal all the surprises, but I must say I liked the prison guard being given an overdose of sleeping pills that enable Dick to escape, rush to your apartment, and beat you to death with a steel rod. Alas, his covers-concealed target isn't you, Bob Rusk, but a nude and necktied lady who appears ready to laugh when the chief inspector rushes in. Wait, there's a sound clomping down the hall and getting closer. What could that be?"

BILLY WILDER

Wilder Hires a Writer

Maybe making a movie from the novel *Double Indemnity* isn't such a swell idea. The book's author, James M. Cain, is busy somewhere else in this crazy town and my usual partner is fleeing like a schoolgirl because he thinks the material's immoral and degrading. Doesn't he understand that's why I'm excited about the script? Except we really don't have a script yet. I've read some fine detective stories by Raymond Chandler. Get him for me. He sounds like an exciting guy who knows lots of criminals.

The following week Chandler walks into my office and I say, "So, you're the detective."

He takes a smelly pipe out of his grim mouth and exhales. "I'm a writer and before that I was an oil executive and prior to that I was a failed journalist."

"Ever done any movie writing?"

"I don't know that I'd call it writing, but no, I haven't scribbled anything for films."

"This will show you the format and maybe give you some ideas," I say, handing him one of my screenplays.

Chandler acts as if he's holding a dead possum. "Okay, I'll take a look. And I'll have a finished script for you in one week."

"It usually takes several months to write a good movie script," I say.

"Pleasure to have met you, Mr. Wilder."

On time in his fantasies Raymond Chandler shoves a stack of typewritten pages at me. I read them that night and the next morning tell the muse, "This is a hundred pages of horseshit. I'm not hiring you for camera instructions. I'm interested in your dialogues. From now on we'll work together, right here in this office. You want a drink?"

"Certainly not. I'm committed to Alcoholics Anonymous because I'm powerless over the poison that so many times has almost killed me and certainly will if I ever relapse. I pray that God will 'grant me the serenity to change the things I can and the wisdom to know the difference.'"

I pour myself a drink. "Let's get to work."

I sit on a sofa. He sits at a desk and writes on a large notepad.

After a few hours of arguing, Chandler says, "You have a rather thick accent, Mr. Wilder."

"Because I'm from what's now Poland. Where are you from?"

"Chicago."

"You ever a member of the Capone gang?"

He puts his pen down and raises the pipe, lighting it and inhaling like a vacuum cleaner. I get up and pace around the room and find this helps as do frequent trips to the men's room or anywhere I can get a break from this stiff.

We've been collaborating a few weeks and I'm getting more concerned by how much of James M. Cain's original dialogue he's cutting and replacing with his own.

"*Double Indemnity* is a damn good book," I tell Chandler.

"Did you read it in Polish or English?"

"German was my best language but at this point I read and write English pretty well," I say.

"Better than you speak it, I hope."

"Plenty good to know Cain's dialogue's a helluva lot better than what you're shoveling in."

"What I'm writing is much better for a movie," he says.

"You don't know which end of a camera shoots the actors."

"All right, Billy, if I may presume to use your delightful first name, let's bring in a couple of actors to read some of Cain's dialogue and some of mine from the same scene."

"You got it," I say, pouring a drink and toasting Chandler's pipe.

Son of a bitch. His dialogue overpowers Cain's.

"Okay, Shakespeare," I say. "You're great at dialogue but need me to shape the script."

In a couple of weeks Raymond Chandler resumes drinking and I've never seen a worse drunk. He's slurs, he staggers, he belches, he tells me to get off my sofa so he can lie down. But sometimes he's sober and we finish the script and both know it's damn good.

Now I'm ready to film but don't even have my three stars. Nobody wants to play a guy who has an affair with a married woman and schemes with her about murdering her husband to collect his insurance money. Gregory Peck and Spencer Tracy and plenty of others have turned me down. Even grouchy George Raft said no but that's a good sign because he often ignores roles that become classics. Jolly Fred MacMurray certainly doesn't want the part, either, but decides to take it. He must be as soused as Raymond Chandler. Or at least as tipsy as I am. Barbara Stanwyck would be great as the treacherous female even though she usually plays a heroine.

"I'm sorry, Billy, but a role like this could alienate my fans and ruin me at the box office."

"Are you a mouse, Barbara?"

"I beg your pardon."

"I'm not looking for a mouse. I need a fine dramatic actress. Is that you?"

"I certainly think so."

"Then get ready to become a promiscuous murderer."

All right. Who's going to play the smart and relentless claims adjuster who knows something ain't right. It's got to be Edward G. Robinson.

"I love the script, Billy, but I've been a star for years and wouldn't be comfortable with third billing."

I put a hand on my head and extend it several inches over Robinson's noggin.

"Look, Eddie, you're a tiny guy in his fifties and not likely to be taking roles from the pretty boys. Prepare for life as a character actor."

"I expect to be compensated at a level commensurate with my dramatic achievements."

"What the hell's commensurate? If you're talking money, we'll pay you the same as Barbara and Fred and for less work."

"I love to work, Billy."

"You'll have a ton after this picture."

I guess Raymond Chandler will have plenty of work, too. But not with me. I don't even want to talk to the guy after he writes a magazine article complaining how he wasn't included in our cast party. I'd have invited him but was worried he'd either be too drunk to attend or would stagger in and embarrass everyone.

CLINT EASTWOOD

Fistful of Fame

Clint's getting small parts in movies like *Revenge of the Creature* but producers at Universal conclude he'll always be a wooden actor and terminate his contract. He doesn't want to resume packing groceries or golf bags so elsewhere accepts roles he usually doesn't like but that get him attention until he's hired to play upright cowboy Rowdy Yates on *Rawhide*. He makes a little dough while improving his craft and after a few years on the popular TV show he starts asking to direct an episode but bosses always say no. Fine. It's time for his three-month vacation.

He learns co-star Eric Fleming just turned town an Italian director named Sergio Leone to star in *A Fistful of Dollars* in an obscure part of Spain resembling the U.S.-Mexican border, and when Leone offers Clint the part, for fifteen grand he doesn't need anymore, the actor almost says no thanks until realizing he could escape always playing the same guy inside a small tube. Okay, he'll try, concluding this little movie will either do well or do nothing, probably the latter.

He takes three sets of hats, ponchos, pants, and boots to Spain because Leone tells him he can't provide more than one outfit, and the tall actor knows his scenes can't be duplicated if any of his clothes are damaged or lost. The script is based on a movie by Akira Kurosawa but this version's a primitive combination of Italianized English with a little Spanish and there's really no flow to the story just a bunch of episodes. Clint asks an interpreter to tell that to Leone.

"You don't like the picture, fine, I'll get James Coburn," Sergio says.

"He already said no because you couldn't pay him twenty-five grand. Everyone's turning you down."

"Sí," he says. "That's why I hired you. Follow the script."

Clint decides to improvise a little. Leone and his crew won't detect the difference. Early in the movie they agree it's pretty cool the man with no name tells a local carpenter, "Get three coffins ready." He singlehandedly approaches some bad guys and says, you boys apologize to my mule for shooting at his feet and laughing at him. Instead, they try to shoot him but he fans his pistol hammer, killing them, and turns to tell the carpenter, "My mistake. Four coffins."

He doesn't like a lot of flowery dialogue anyway. This movie's about stopping Ramón and his desperados from terrorizing Sheriff Baxter and citizens of this parched little town. Nearby, aiming a hot Gatlin gun in a wagon, Ramón cuts down gold-laden soldiers who've been grimacing on their horses rather than trying to kill the guy who's shooting them. Viewers may forget why this scene happens but don't need to know. What matters is Clint soon blows away a roomful of men before throwing a machete into a man's chest.

His enemies strike back, punching and kicking until he's bloody and swollen on the floor where, as an unseen man laughs maniacally, someone grinds the heel of his cowboy boot into Clint's left hand. Don't the fools realize he's right-handed and has amazing powers of recuperation and luck? The warehouse where he's locked up offers a wooden ramp down which he rolls a huge barrel to crush two captors. Their friends chase Clint but he sets the place afire, stumbles away and, moments before being detected, crawls under an elevated wooden boardwalk along the main street. As he escapes in a wooden coffin pulled by a wagon guided by a friendly man, Clint periodically lifts the lid to watch as Sheriff Baxter and his clan, including his wife, are burned out of a building and shot by Ramón and his gang. Evidently the bad guys don't wonder why a coffin's being wheeled out of town at night.

Clint has time to recover and resume target practice. At first he's only good but soon fires multiple rounds into a single bullet hole and knows he's ready to retake the town. In a street menaced by five armed men, he tells Ramón to shoot for his heart, and the bandit complies one, two, three, four, five, six, seven times, knocking Clint down twice but only briefly as he rises and approaches the men and lifts his poncho to reveal a steel breastplate. Thank goodness Ramón didn't shoot for the head. Now he's out of bullets. So is Clint.

We won't divulge the particulars but you may guess the outcome. The biggest revelation is the birth of a movie star. Put most actors into this sequence of silliness, some of which is here omitted, and they'd be guffawed at by moviegoers. But for Clint Eastwood, they cheer. When a man's that handsome and charismatic, he plays by different rules.

Evelyn Draper on Misty

Are you watching the TV interview with Clint Eastwood a few years after making his directorial debut in *Play Misty for Me.* It disgusts me he says a woman has the best part in the picture. He's right but doesn't explain the consequences when I call his radio station to request he play *Misty* and pick him up in a bar and sleep with him and then care so much I surprise him showing up at his house with groceries to make him dinner and blow my horn at a neighbor who tells us to be quiet and I sit in his car as he leaves a bar and grab his keys to slow him down and that night wait at his house and greet him in a fur coat I open to show I'm nude and call at work to rebuke him for not calling me and he says we've got to talk so I give him a beautiful pair of shoes he rejects and says he never told me he loved me and I tell him he's not going to dump me, he's not even good in bed, he's just a poor pathetic bastard, and I know his blond girlfriend's back in Carmel because I watch them kiss in a meadow and think I'm dying and storm over to his house that night and accuse of him screwing around but he's alone and I tell him I love him and cry on his bed and he offers to take me home and I agree to go after I wash my face in his bathroom where I slash my wrist and he can't go to his girlfriend now, he's got to hold me all night, and in the morning as he sleeps I borrow his car and make a duplicate key to his house and know I'm earning his love and am very upset he says he has a business lunch at the wharf when I get there I see he's romancing a disgusting old woman and I tell him he's a dirty old bastard and resist as he drags me out of the restaurant and up stairs to the street where he shoves me into a taxi and pays the guy to just get out of there and I know where to go and at Dave's I tear the place apart and when his housekeeper comes I slash her and she almost dies and the police come and arrest me and I'm sent to a mental institution and Dave thinks he and his little blonde have everything but I call him at the station and say play *Misty* for me and not to worry since I'm cured and released and heading to Hawaii for a job he evidently believes and late that night I use the key I'd hidden above his door to enter his bedroom and have the knife almost to his throat when he wakens and rolls, and I escape to the home of my new roommate, Dave's girlfriend, who spots my slashed wrist and I have to grab big scissors and tie her up and gag her so I can talk as I cut her hair and when the phone rings I say we're waiting for you David and I'm ready when a detective shines his flashlight out front where I plant my scissors in his chest and when Dave arrives I stab him in the shoulder and leg and am trying to punish him for what he did to me when he punches me in the mouth, knocking me through the glass door and across the deck through the rail and over the cliff into the ocean.

Clint's right. I had the best part and received a Golden Globe nomination for best actress. Combine that with an earlier Golden Globe nomination for best new star of the year and you'd think my career would skyrocket. I certainly expected it to. I'd dominated a major picture that made ten times what it cost. What did I get for my performance? I got the back of the hairy male hand of moviemaking and didn't appear in another movie for five years. That's an eternity for actresses. We're always viewed as either getting old or already too old. I got some work in TV but nothing commensurate with what I deserved. I ask you, why the hell didn't Clint Eastwood play the deranged lover and I the smooth and steady disc jockey. I'd have accepted that role. You think Clint would've played the head case. I've called him many times, saying, "Don't you have any more roles for me? I'm not box office poison. I'm box office gold. How do you men justify treating me like this? I'm tired of you and others telling me you'll keep me in mind when something good comes up. I'm thirty-five now. You'll soon want me to play the grandmother. That's not going to happen. Threatening you? No, Clint, I'm not but I should. I certainly could. I've still got your door key. I don't care you changed the locks. I'll find some other way in."

Notes: Actress Jessica Walter swears she portrayed a fictional character. As a precaution, however, call 911 immediately if any women who look like either Jessica or Elizabeth approach Eastwood or screenwriters Jo Heims and Dean Riesner.

Actors on Iwo Jima

Five hundred feet above land and sea Mt. Suribachi's smoking and quaking from naval and air bombardments prior to an American invasion twenty thousand Japanese troops have been preparing for. Outnumbered four to one on the ground and hundreds to nothing in air and on water, they've been digging tunnels and bunkers and laying mines and adjusting their guns to riddle every inch of Iwo Jima, a hot and humid hellhole dominated by mosquitos. The commanders know their men are going to die. Most soldiers understand. It's their sacred duty to fight and delay an overwhelming and bestial enemy so for a little longer the Empire of Japan can delude itself the war may not be lost.

"What the hell're we doing here, Clint?" asks John Wayne, ducking against the wall of a dark tunnel.

"Welcome to my Iwo Jima," he says.

"These animals will kill us."

"Everyone's an animal in war," says Clint. "We'll be okay. You're watching my second movie about this battle, *Letters from Iwo Jima*."

"You shot it here on Iwo Jima?"

"Not really. Our tunnel scenes were filmed near Barstow. We did other stuff in Bakersfield and L.A."

"We made *Sands of Iwo Jima* in nice places like Catalina Island, Thousand Oaks, and Universal Studios," says John.

"I hate shooting in movie studios because they look like it on screen."

John Wayne stands tall at six-foot-four, same as Clint, and pokes his finger into the younger man's chest. "You could've asked if I wanted to come here."

"It's an educational opportunity for both of us. You missed World War II making movies. I spent the Korean War giving swimming lessons in California."

"I would've fought," says John. "I didn't make a big deal about being in my mid-thirties and a married guy with kids."

Clint looks at Japanese troops as he ponders. "I guess I'd have fought too."

"Aren't there any white guys in your film?"

"Not many and only as extras. All these actors are Japanese and fluent speakers. I want our Japanese audience to feel this is real."

"You're gonna dub it in English back home, aren't you?"

"Most Americans can read, John, even if they're lazy about it at movies. We'll use subtitles."

John Wayne shakes his head. Clint motions to an opening where they look at American soldiers rushing from their landing crafts and coming ashore uncontested. They think their ceaseless bombing has rendered the Japanese helpless but, as General Tadamichi Kuribayashi had planned, most defenders were uninjured, protected in tunnels from which they emerge to fire machineguns and artillery at stunned invaders who start falling, some headless before they hit the ground. But there are so many and they keep landing and bringing equipment as their ships and planes hammer Iwo Jima and the island becomes a meat grinder for both sides.

"As you know, John, this battle lasted about five weeks but well before the end, rather than surrender, Japanese soldiers started killing themselves with grenades, pulling pins and holding them to their chests. Look at those young guys. Everything to live for."

"What a waste," says John. "Screw that guy from headquarters who's sending the message, 'We earnestly hope you will fight and die for your country.' Why doesn't that brave commander get out here?"

Clint says, "I imagine he'll be shooting himself in Tokyo before long. We'll never know, but here on Iwo Jima I bet two or three thousand Japanese committed suicide."

An American soldier falls through a weak point at the top of a tunnel, and Wayne says, "I'm saving him."

"You can't but would be dead if you tried."

They watch Japanese soldiers bayonet the screaming young man before Colonel Takeichi Nishi intercedes and says, "Treat that wounded soldier."

"But, sir, we're short of morphine."

"I said, 'Treat him.'"

The colonel kneels by the wounded soldier and asks if he knows Douglas Fairbanks and Mary Pickford, stars from the silent film era. The soldier says everyone knows them but not personally. Aristocratic Nishi says he met them during the 1932 Olympics in Los Angeles where he was the equestrian champion. He speaks English softly and well to a young man hearing his final words.

The Japanese run out of food and water and even some fanatical defenders attempt to dessert but are shot by officers or, in some cases, American soldiers rapidly dehumanized by hellish conditions. General Kuribayashi leads his men not on a masochistic bonsai charge but an adroit early-morning attack that strikes attackers in their sleep but ends in the general's death and the disappearance of his body, as he'd hoped. Almost all the defenders never leave the island alive and many still molder in graves on a tiny piece of land that didn't have to be fought for.

"Years later archeologists found thousands of letters buried here," says Clint. "They've been translated. Want to read some of them?"

"Sure do," says John.

Eastwood Battles Snipers

I don't spend much time arguing with critics of my movies. Today I'll just refute those who accuse me of glorifying war or, at minimum, celebrating a man they scream online was a "psychopathic killer." Listen, I'm not trying to transform Chris Kyle, the *American Sniper* who killed more than a hundred sixty enemies during the war in Iraq, into a perfect man. Watch the movie. I portray Kyle as a soldier who from the first shot was disturbed pumping bullets into people and who shot by shot during four tours grew more tormented. So did his wife, Tara. They had a baby, and Chris kept reenlisting even after their second child. He said he had to eliminate enemies of the United States and those who were trying to kill his comrades in Iraq and Tara warned that others could now do his job and he had to come home soon or she and the kids wouldn't be there.

Some say I should write a prologue about why the United States shouldn't have invaded Iraq in 2003 since either the George W. Bush administration lied about a link to Al Qaeda and weapons of mass destruction or, at minimum, made a tragic decision based on faulty intelligence. I let viewers interpret the story. They already know how they feel about the second invasion of Iraq, and they're going to bring those feelings to the movie even if the director preaches.

I don't glamorize the war. There aren't any immaculate corpses in *American Sniper.* They're bloody and maimed. That's why Chris and many others suffered from post-traumatic stress disorder. They couldn't leave it behind. Like I've said, "When a man has that many kills he's got to have some baggage." Wouldn't you? But you haven't been there. And the loudest critics of Chris Kyle have never been in combat, either, and might hide if the draft returned. If you believe there's no such thing as bad guys, you must've been sleeping in history class and today read fairytale news accounts. Okay, you think Americans are sometimes the bad guys, like in Vietnam and Iraq in 2003 and beyond. That's your opinion. I'm not trying to change it. Let politicians and pundits do that. I make movies. This one's about Chris Kyle hiding on rooftops and shooting our enemies. We've always needed guys like that and, trust me, we're going to need more. We also need guys like Chris who tried to help fellow vets also suffering from PTSD. One of them shot him in the back. I doubt the guy wanted Chris face to face.

MARCO BELLOCHIO

Mussolini Reviews Vincere

They wouldn't have made *Vincere* in Italy when I was the Duce. If they tried, you know what I'd have done to director Marco Bellocchio and his traitors. The Duce did not permit unflattering articles, photos, speeches, or thoughts, and no one save a deranged and masochistic individual would have contemplated thrashing me in a feature film. Ironically, in what I'm sure is unintentional honesty, much of the cinematic story is about a criminally disturbed woman, Ida Delser, who harassed me in intolerable ways.

I will give you some history. Before and during the early stages of the First World War, I did have an affair with Ida Delser. Like so many women, she was overwhelmed by my charisma and political destiny, though I was then merely the editor of a socialist newspaper. We made love often. We made love passionately. I embraced so hard she sighed. In bed I pounded till she screamed. The Duce knew sex was war with women I had to win. And I did. Ida Delser loved me. She sold her belongings to help me start my own newspaper, *Il Popolo d'Italia*, and in 1915 she bore a son she called Benito Mussolini. The movie claims I acknowledged the child. I don't recall doing so. Prove I did.

I'm equally certain I did not marry Ida Delser, as she fervently claimed. Show me the marriage certificate. You can't. Don't tell me my agents found and destroyed it. I had no agents then, anyway. I didn't need any. I married my hometown girlfriend, Rachele, with whom I already had a daughter age five. Then I went to war and loved the sounds of machinegun fire and exploding bombs and artillery shells. Violence and death ennobled me. I enjoyed being wounded by metal shards and hospitalized. I reveled in my blood as everyone could see what my commanders at the front already knew and officially reported: Benito Mussolini is a brave and resolute warrior.

Italy craved me after the war, and I rose fast. In 1922, at the youthful age of thirty-nine, I led the glorious March on Rome, a coup d'état that installed me as prime minister with the sacred atheistic duty – God didn't exist or he would've killed me, as I often dared Him to do – to establish myself as the supreme leader, the Duce, of a fascist nation ready to recapture the glory of the Roman Empire. Imagine how irritating it was, and potentially threatening to the health of Italy, when Ida Delser persisted with claims that I was her husband and her son my child.

I ignored them. I tried to. But she shouted in public and wrote letters that I, while Italy was still neutral, accepted French bribes to influence my country to join the First World War. She also ran up to various fascist officials, insisting I was hers and that a court in Milan had ordered me to make support payments for her and the child and referred to them as my wife and son. The Duce was correct in protecting himself and the nation from this delusional woman. For her protection, as well, she was placed in a mental hospital. She nevertheless continued to proclaim I loved her and was just testing her loyalty and would come for her if she didn't crack.

She had already cracked and clearly could not take care of her son. He was adopted by a fascist former police chief who assured him his mother was dead. Her mind was dead but dangerous and had to be medicated regularly. That finally reduced her outbursts, though not enough to release her from the asylum where she crumbled and died of a cerebral hemorrhage at age fifty-seven and was buried in a common grave. Her son was equally deranged and obsessive, and even during his protective hospitalization he declared he was my son, and sometimes imitated my speeches in an unflattering manner, as the movie shows. Decency compelled his doctors to administer a series of coma-inducing drugs that settled the young man down and allowed him to die peacefully in his mid-twenties and be buried in a common grave. Three years later, my own end was less dignified.

JEWISH FILM FESTIVAL

Eichmann Appears

This afternoon at the San Francisco Jewish Film Festival, before a capacity audience in a large theater, Adolf Eichmann – looking typically banal, bespectacled, and grim – is wheeled in a glass cage onto a stage after completion of *Eichmann's End: Love, Betrayal, Death*, and he demands: "Let me out at once."

"As the most dedicated and efficient bureaucrat implementing the Final Solution during World War II, you better stay in your bulletproof public home, compliments of the Jewish people," says the moderator.

"I only followed the orders of Adolf Hitler and other superiors, as I stated after being kidnapped and drugged in Argentina as well as at my trial in Jerusalem in 1961."

"You not merely followed inhumane orders but many times went far beyond their scope with a fanaticism that earns you a place in an oven before your ashes are dumped into the Mediterranean," says the moderator. "I therefore direct you to share a few professional anecdotes and comment briefly on this cinematic fusion of drama and history."

"I'm angry Klaus, one of my four sons, romanced a Jewish girl in Buenos Aires and bragged about my importance in the annihilation of six million European Jews. He knew secrecy was essential but I too must accept blame since at home I sometimes raged about Germany's enemies and that we obviously had too many since we lost the war. Our demise was decidedly not my fault. About this I must insist.

"I served the Reich well. Following my dreary academic imprisonment, during which I failed to complete the equivalent of high school, and some menial jobs, I found a cause – National Socialism – that rescued me from boredom and potential indigence and allowed me to become a proud and successful man. I became an expert on the Jewish problem. I read books and learned a little Hebrew and Yiddish and traveled to Palestine where I tried – quite briefly, before being thrown out by the Arabs and British – to arrange for the Jews to emigrate and establish a homeland. That might have solved the problem. Or if we could've made a similar deal with Madagascar. Or if the United States and other supposedly sympathetic countries had opened their doors to our problem. They did not, and Germany ordered me to act.

"Once the war in the East had begun, and roving SS Einsatz Groups began killing thousands of Jews and other enemies of the Reich, I knew what was going to happen before being explicitly told and was ready to help and in 1941 went to Poland but reported I wasn't going to look through those peepholes in vans any more. Too many people dead or alive bore horrific expressions and had defecated on themselves and each other. This was frightful and inefficient and too hard on German officers. I said only Jews should unload these vans until we developed something better.

"In January 1942 Reinhard Heydrich, after Himmler the most powerful man in the SS, presided over a conference in a villa in Wannsee, near Berlin, and pronounced, 'Our measures to date, though promising, have not been sufficient. We must shift our efforts from the casual to precise. There are still eleven millions Jews in Europe. They are all going to end up here in the East, the asshole of the world… Eichmann, please report on the steps we're taking in the Reich. Be brief.'

"Thrilled by this opportunity, I rose and pronounced, 'The Jews must be detected. Second, they are to be registered and segregated. Third, they will be arrested. Fourth, they will hand over their house keys and sign over their possessions to the Reich. Next, the Jews will be allowed to take one suitcase and fifty marks each to a remote railroad junction. Then they will be placed in freight cars for transit to ghettos, work camps or direct operations.'

"In a few months I went to Auschwitz to confer with the commandant, Rudolf Hoess, and told him about my ghastly experience with vans and also stressed that shooting wouldn't be adequate for a project this size. We drove around the camp and spotted an old red farmhouse we designated Bunker I and ordered that it be remodeled and made airtight. I told Hoess to find the right gas, and he found some handy canisters of Zyklon B, which had been used to kill rodents and insects, and when Bunker I was completed we found everything worked damn well."

"You're more forthright in the hereafter, and for that we reservedly thank you," says the moderator.

My So-Called Enemy

You're invited. Tune in to *My So-Called Enemy* in the summer of 2002 at a retreat in gentrified New Jersey where for ten days teenage girls from Israel and Palestine are gathered to discuss their lives, seek common ground, and learn conflict resolution skills. The latter two goals are challenging. It's the second year of the Second Intifada and fifty-five hundred Palestinians and a thousand Israelis have died, each side blaming the other.

Listen to Gal, an Israeli Jew whose parents were harassed and forced to flee their native Iran. She was born in Israel, considers herself very liberal, and questions the religious beliefs of her devout family. Rezan, a Palestinian, resents always having to wait in checkpoint lines one or two hours depending on the mood of guards who view her as a person without a country. Hanin, a Palestinian, is also angry about issues of sovereignty, telling Gal that no, she doesn't understand, even after the Holocaust, the Jewish need for a homeland in Israel. Why should Jews from Europe torture us, kill our people, and take our land, Hanin wants to know? There are lots of empty places you could go, she tells Gal, who covers her mouth and almost cries. Gal counters she cannot return to a country, Iran, where she has never been and where her family would again be persecuted. She avoids the communal lunch and says she doesn't want to build bridges with someone who wants her out of her native country.

Inas, a Palestinian, later laments that Jews took her people's land and killed them. Adi, an Israeli, doesn't want to hope for too much progress with Palestinians, just something realistic. She says when Israelis see Arab children throw stones they think even the kids are violent, like their parents. Inas defends the children, noting they have nothing to do since Israelis have closed many of their schools.

Hanin suggests that a bridge could be built from the ass of Yasser Arafat to the ass of Ariel Sharon. More good fellowship develops one night when keffiyehs, Arab scarves many Jews see as war symbols and masks, are passed around as the girls frolic and dance and Gal wraps one around her head.

Tranquility quickly vanishes: Hebrew University is bombed after

Israelis kill a Palestinian leader and, in the process, thirteen others. The girls argue about what to discuss. Facilitators urge them to honor each other by listening. Inas concludes they can't have good relationships.

Still, they're getting to know each other. Gal says she has so much feeling for every girl in this circle. Inas reveals she once wanted to be a bomber but now she's changed and thinks too many people in villages are closed minded. Some Palestinian girls express sympathy for those who died in the attacks of September eleventh, 2001, but stress the nineteen suicide bombers yearned to prove something that day. The girls, however, want to be good Muslims. Goodwill abounds. Back home, Gal and Rezan become best friends.

A year later, there is a reunion, and Gal cries because she will soon be in the army – all women serve two years and men three – and obligated to take care of security, not peace. A year after that Gal, a sergeant in the Israel Defense Force, says she was once radical left but now is different and committed to maintaining security. In Hebrew she delivers a sharp series of orders to attentive female soldiers. Gal knows her relationship with Rezan has changed because she now wears the same uniform Rezan sees every day at checkpoints.

Gal and Rezan reunite in Jerusalem at the Separation Barrier that divides Jews and Arabs. Rezan touches the massive wall, smiles resignedly, and says you can come here but I can't go there. In December 2008 Palestinians fire eighteen hundred rockets into southern Israel and the Israelis respond by killing eleven hundred Palestinians and choking off the area. Gal and Rezan communicate by email. Both are saddened by the carnage, but Rezan notes Gal can still move around while she can't.

Gal and Rezan are still friends but not best friends.

Notes: Director Lisa Gossels and Rawan, one of the Palestinian women in the film, appeared after the showing of *My So-Called Enemy* at the film festival.

Budrus 2109

I'm tired of my parents telling me how lucky I am to live in a country with the highest per capita income in the world. I'm bored with reminders that life is infinitely easier for me than it was a century ago for my great grandparents. Too often I must endure the same stories about how they risked their lives to save our town and secure my future. I appreciate all that, in a detached theoretical sense, but prefer to enjoy my freedom and privileges without being reminded of unpleasantness. Only to silence my parents do I agree to watch the ancient documentary film *Budrus,* released in 2009 when dinosaurs roamed the region.

I don't recognize Budrus in the first decade of the twenty-first century. It's not really a town, and certainly not the high-tech suburban marvel of today, but a hardscrabble village of fifteen hundred people who for generations had lived here, about twenty miles northwest of Ramallah in the northern region of the Occupied West Bank, a name that strikes my ear about like East Germany and North Korea. We still have some olive trees and a few plaques I've barely noticed, but in this film olive trees symbolize the soul and economic survival of the people. Bulldoze the trees and build a wall around a dying city to ensure it becomes a cemetery; that's what the Israelis were trying to do in Budrus. The Israelis weren't unjustified feeling rage and fear. Hundreds had been killed by suicide bombers the first two years last century. They decided to build a wall, a Separation Barrier.

It's unfortunate, said an Israeli officer, but less unfortunate than the death of an Israeli civilian.

The people of Budrus agreed that violence was unwise and had long been a peaceful group from which not a single bomber emerged. So why build a wall around us, they asked? Build your wall on Israeli land. Ayed, the politically adroit and oft-imprisoned village leader, protested that the Israeli plan would confiscate three hundred acres and demolish three thousand olive trees and damage the psyches of children leered at by a wall forty meters from their school. The men of Budrus demonstrated and stopped the bulldozer the first day. A female Israeli soldier, who looked like a leading lady, stressed her side didn't want to damage things important to Palestinians, simply to protect Israeli lives. Nevertheless, eight olive trees were soon uprooted.

The day before, Ayed said, people sat under those trees.

The women of the village stepped forward. Demonstrations and political activities became the focus of life in Budrus, and this commitment attracted international supporters. Israeli soldiers countered with "crowd dispersal methods" like firing tear gas canisters and striking with sticks. Citizens of Budrus responded, in the nonviolent tradition of Gandhi and Martin Luther King, with larger and more frequent and effective demonstrations. Palestinian unity grew. Ayed, long a critic of Hamas, embraced it as a legitimate part of society. For all Palestinians the wall was a symbol of occupation.

It must not encircle Budrus. Demonstrators strode into the fields. Ayed's daughter said Israelis were very bad when she visited him in jail but she now realized not all Israelis hate Palestinians. Nevertheless, Israeli soldiers announced those who failed to leave in twenty minutes would be arrested. Some who demonstrated were Israeli Jews. Others came from South Africa where, one notes, there were but two choices: either the whites left or everyone stayed. In Israel, in Palestine, in Budrus, the same principle applied.

Israeli soldiers were ordered to push back the demonstrators.

One shouted, this is a peaceful demonstration.

Three minutes to leave, came the response.

Soldiers waded in, swinging sticks, and Budrus was declared a closed military zone and a curfew established.

Ayed said, my people have staged forty-three peaceful demonstrations but the Israelis are becoming violent.

Palestinian children threw rocks. More demonstrations followed. Israeli soldiers fired live ammunition high over indignant heads. At night protests continued and a wire fence, part of the barrier, was torn down. The fence was repaired. Demonstrations proceeded.

On a portentous day, Israel announced it was changing the route of the barrier, which would avoid ninety-five percent of the olive trees and stand out of sight of children at the school and miss the town cemetery. Peaceful action averted a punitive land grab. My parents stood and cheered and so did my brother and sister and so did I.

And then all over the old West Bank and Gaza and everywhere else people started doing the same thing, I conclude.

No, my father responds, for years Budrus was the only such success.

Palestinians sometimes blew up Israelis and Israelis killed Palestinians and walled off the survivors, and who did what first no one ever agreed until they concluded it was irrelevant. Generations passed before people in Israel and the occupied territories understood there could not be separate states, only one nation of many religions and ethnicities, a united state we now proudly call Israel, an economic and cultural powerhouse for all who reside here.

Notes: *Budrus* was shown to a large and enthusiastic audience at the film festival. Julia Bacha directed *Budrus* and Ronit Avni served as executive producer.

Avni, who appeared at the festival, is a United States citizen as well as an Israeli peace activist. In a Washington Post column from June 2009 she noted that Israel's policy of expanding settlements is contrary to international law, as established at the Fourth Geneva Convention, and that much funding for this inflammatory policy, which is not in Israel's interest, comes from "evangelical Christians" and "wealthy businessmen" in the United States. She also writes that the "settler organization Amana held 'housing fairs' in New York and New Jersey to encourage American Jews to buy property in the West Bank."

LEE HIRSCH

Bullies at School

Thirteen million kids will be tormented at school this year. Several of them are studied in Lee Hirsch's documentary film *Bully.* Let's focus on two.

Bespectacled Alex is skinny, awkward, and nervous. He says he likes learning but has trouble making friends. When he tentatively tries to be congenial on the school bus, a much bigger boy next to him says, we're not friends, I'll shove a broomstick up your ass.

Alex's father lectures him that nobody respects a punching bag and urges him to be tougher. That's going to be difficult. His sister tells Alex she's embarrassed they're related because that might make kids reject her. Alex doubts that. She tells him, other kids don't like you and think you're creepy. His mother says, Alex tries to fit in but just can't because he comes across as weird. For that, he gets pushed and slapped around a lot. Viewers assume Alex is still trying to be accepted.

Tyler, born after only twenty-six weeks gestation, remains weaker than most kids. His dad says he knows Tyler is vulnerable and laments that kids shove him against lockers and curse him. When he's in the school shower, some punks take his clothes. One time, standing at the urinal, Tyler is pushed into it. His pants are soiled. In the classroom his books are thrown on the floor and he's told, pick them up, bitch.

Tyler's father goes to the school many times but administrators always tell him they can't stop people doing bad things. They may be correct. The day after Tyler hangs himself in his bedroom closet, some kids come to school with ropes around their necks.

Maybe those ropes should be tightened, just a little, before the heathens are lectured.

HARVEY WEINSTEIN

Inside Harvey

I love these parties celebrating my movies that have generated more than three hundred Oscar nominations. I'm the guy everyone wants to talk to. I confess it wasn't like that in high school or college or when I started in show business as a concert promoter. I saw those looks a million times: hey, you're fat and ugly, women might as well have said as they turned to better looking guys. I don't know how I survived. I deserved the best. I was smarter and more creative than all those women and their pretty pickups who didn't notice as I stood by walls and watched.

Now it's different in Rome and London and Paris and Cannes and New York and Beverly Hills where people look at me and smile. They're enchanted by my intelligence, charm, and power. And I sense some of these beautiful young actresses think I'm sexy, too. Frankly, I know a lot of them do. Tonight I'm in… It doesn't matter. I only go to wonderful places where the hottest women hover. Here's one standing sleek next to me. I know she's afraid to speak. She's thinking, there's the great Harvey Weinstein.

"Hello," I say. "I've seen your screen test."

"Really?"

"I sure have, and it's wonderful. I'd like to discuss your career as soon as possible."

"Thank you so much. I'll ask my agent to call you tomorrow."

"Why wait? Come on up to my office."

"You have an office in this hotel?"

"Yes."

"Right now?"

"Absolutely."

I nod for a female aide to follow us. Upstairs, I sit at my desk and motion for the lovely actress to relax on my sofa. I always make sure I have an official desk in my suite. "Let's drink some champagne."

My aide walks into the kitchenette.

"No thanks," says the actress."

"Oh, just one."

"I don't drink at all."

"Okay, then only a sip."

I sense discomfort.

"Let's talk about your career."

She brightens.

"You have so much potential, and I have many great stories I'll produce all over the world."

"I love your serious movies and the way you develop characters," she says.

"Thanks," I say to her, and smile at my aide as she hands me a glass of bubbly. She then gives the actress her glass.

I raise mine and say, "Cheers."

She puts the glass to her lips but doesn't drink any.

"Here," I say, rising and moving to the sofa. I sit next to her, my right leg touching her left. "Let's drink to your getting a good supporting part very soon."

She reluctantly clicks my glass.

"What experience did you have before the screen test?"

"I was in lots of high school and college plays. After that I did some commercials and got small parts in a couple of movies."

"Speaking parts?"

"Not yet."

"We'll change that."

I drain my glass and put it on the coffee table. She holds her glass between us like a shield

"When do you think I could get a good part?" she asks.

"I'll look into that tomorrow. How about a massage?"

"Pardon me?"

"Just let me rub your shoulders a little."

"Where'd the lady go?" she asks.

"She's got to entertain the guests downstairs."

"We better join them." She puts her glass on the table and braces to stand.

I place a strong hand on her arm. "Come on, just a little massage."

"I have a boyfriend."

"He wouldn't mind what I'm talking about."

"Yes he would."

"He doesn't have to know."

"I'm really uncomfortable."

"Okay, I respect that. We'll go downstairs in just a minute. First, excuse me while I dash to the men's room."

She's going to leave, I know it. She'll be gone before I get back. She doesn't want to be with me, but I need her, and underdress rapidly and put on a big robe and, smiling, enter the living room. She looks alarmed and jumps to her feet. I walk fast between her and the door.

"Please relax," I say. "I just want us to take a little shower together."

"Mr. Weinstein, I'm not going to do that. I came up here for business."

"Okay, I get it. I only ask, then, that you watch me take a shower."

"I don't do things like that."

"Just a little while. You wouldn't have to touch me."

"I'd like to go now."

"Okay."

"You're blocking the door."

I open my robe and place a strong hand around myself and pump hard and in only a minute or so exclaim, "Oh," and she rushes past me out the door.

QUENTIN TARANTINO

Hollywood Ending

Two famous guys are seated in the living room of a cool Hollywood Hills mansion. I turn on my camera.

"How the hell is it I'm living out at hot and dusty Spahn Movie Ranch and you're here with all this luxury," Charlie says.

"All this comes from my talent writing and directing movies," says Quentin. "I've been obsessed, that means dedicated, all my life."

"If producers and other musicians weren't screwing me, I'd be a great songwriter and performer."

"Charlie, I don't think you can honestly claim you've committed yourself to music."

"How could I, being in jail half my life till I was thirty-two?

Quentin says, "Yeah, that's a big consideration when building a career, staying out of jail."

An elbow planted in each thigh, Charlie leans forward, "It's also big having a mom and stepdad who take you to movies and encourage you. I love my mom but she was a drunk and a thief who went to prison. I don't remember seeing my father or much of Mom and her boyfriends when she got out."

"You had disadvantages but still should work harder to develop your talent."

"Prison was home. I'm not sure I even wanted out."

"Come on, Charlie. Lots of young women do whatever you tell them."

"They have to show loyalty. And they're happy to. They love listening to me sing. So does Dennis Wilson of the Beach Boys. He said I was a genius after I played him my song 'Cease to Exist.' I didn't hear from him but several months later found out he stole my melody, changed the lyrics, and recorded my song as 'Never Learn Not to Love.'"

"Dennis Wilson's scared of you," says Quentin.

"He should be."

"The guy just spent a hundred grand housing, feeding, and drugging you and lots of members of your family."

"He did that so he could use my women and talent," Charlie says. "Tex, girls, get in here."

A good looking man and two pretty ladies dash into the living room where Quentin says, "Brad..."

He doesn't appear, and Charlie's followers engulf Quentin and wrestle him to the floor.

"Brad, you're on, get out here," orders the director.

"You've got maybe three minutes to live," says Charlie

The front door breaks open and in charges Brad Pitt chased by Bruce Lee, the martial artist smacking Brad around the room until he falls near Charlie's feet which kick Brad in the ribs.

"Bruce, delighted to see you're in such wonderful form," says Quentin.

"I'm surprised you approve, given your plan to portray me as an arrogant buffoon and incompetent fighter."

"That would've been dark comedy, Bruce, nothing more."

"Who's side you on, you little Chinaman?" asks Charlie.

Bruce snap kicks him in the face and rolls onto the floor, under Tex's pistol fire, and springs up with a simultaneous eye gouge and groin grab maintained until howling Tex collapses. Each woman, armed with a knife, eases toward Bruce.

"This would be rather easy for me, Quentin, but in light of your historical distortions I think you should resolve matters. I've read you sometimes 'bitch slap' your business adversaries."

"That's just Hollywood hype, Bruce. Don't you want to be the hero, vanquishing these hippies and saving Sharon Tate and her friends next door?"

"No thanks."

Quentin pops up and dashes to a nearby closet, retrieves a flame-thrower, aims, and ignites two shrieking ladies.

Bruce walks to Quentin, takes the weapon, and fries Charlie and Tex on the floor.

"Well done," says the director.

"I've still got to deal with you and Brad."

Quentin twists toward me and shouts, "Cut..."

"The camera won't stop," I say.

Sources

Allen, Woody – *Blue Jasmine; Everything You've Always Wanted to Know About Sex; Café Society; Wonder Wheel; Apropos of Nothing* by Woody Allen.

Bellocchio, Marco – *Vincere.*

Berry, Halle – *Monster's Ball; Bulworth.*

Blake, Robert – *In Cold Blood.*

Blanchette, Cate – *Blue Jasmine; Carol.*

Bogart, Humphrey – *The Maltese Falcon; Casablanca; The African Queen; The Caine Mutiny; Lauren Bacall By Myself and Then Some* by Lauren Bacall*; Bogie: The Definitive Biography of Humphrey Bogart* by Joe Hyams*; Bogie and Me* by Verita Thompson.

Booth, Shirley – *Come Back, Little Sheba*; *Hazel.*

Borgnine, Ernest – *Marty.*

Boseman, Chadwick – *Marshall; 42*; "Saving the Race," LegalAffairs.org April 2005.

Brooks, Louise – *Pandora's Box; Diary of a Lost Girl*; *LuLu in Hollywood* by Louise Brooks

Carradine, David – Netflix; Wikipedia; TMZ.com; TheSmokingGun.com; StarPulse.com.

Clark, George Thomas – "Fallen Star" originally appeared in the short story collection *The Bold Investor. Hitler Here,* a biographical novel by George Thomas Clark; "Jack Palance Estate Auction" debuted in *Paint it Blue.*

Cohen, Sacha Baron – *Borat; The Dictator.*

Crawford, Joan – *Letty Lynton; Mildred Pierce; Humoresque; Possessed; Sudden Fear; What Ever Happened to Baby Jane; Hush… Hush Sweet Charlotte*; *Mommie Dearest* by Christina Crawford

Davis, Bette – *The Letter*; *Now, Voyager; Dead Ringer; All About Eve; Of Human Bondage; In This Our Life.*

De Havilland, Olivia – *The Adventures of Robin Hood; Captain Blood; They Died with Their Boots On; To Each His Own, The Snake Pit; Hush…Hush, Sweet Charlotte.*

De Niro, Robert – *Raging Bull; The King of Comedy;*

Dietrich, Marlene – *Shanghai Express*; *Desire*; *Destry Rides Again; Witness for the Prosecution; Stage Fright.*

Douglas, Kirk – *Spartacus.*

Douglas, Michael – *The Kominsky Method; Fatal Attraction.*

Eagels, Jeanne – *The Letter* (1929);

Eastwood, Clint – *A Fistful of Dollars, Play Misty for Me, Letters from Iwo Jima, American Sniper.*

Eichmann, Adolf – *Eichmann's End: Love, Betrayal, Death*, a movie; *Hitler Here,* a biographical novel by George Thomas Clark; *The Capture and Trial of Adolf Eichmann* by Moshe Pearleman; Wikipedia – Adolf Eichmann.

Eisenberg, Jesse – *The Social Network; Café Society.*

Flynn, Arnella – Article by Kevin Smith in Splash News, October 1998.

Flynn, Errol – *Captain Blood; The Adventures of Robin Hood; They Died with Their Boots on; The Santa Fe Trail; My Wicked, Wicked Ways* by Errol Flynn and Earl Conrad; *Errol Flynn: A Memoir* by Earl Conrad; *The Films of Errol Flynn* by Tony Thomas, Rudy Behlmer, and Clifford McCarthy; *Errol & Olivia* by Robert Matzen; *Errol, Olivia, and the Merry Men of Sherwood* by Rupert Alistar.

Gable, Clark – *It Happened One Night; Mutiny on the Bounty; The Misfits; Gable & Lombard* by Warren G. Harris;

Garner, James – *Grand Prix; The Great Escape.*

Gerron, Kurt – *The Blue Angel.*

Gibson, Mel – *Apocalypto; Bravehart; The Passion of the Christ.*

Grant, Cary – Suspicion; Notorious; North by Northwest;

Hirsch, Lee – *Bullies.*

Hitchcock, Alfred – *Rebecca; North by Northwest*; *Psycho; Vertigo*

Hoffman, Dustin – *The Graduate; Tootsie; Marathon Man; Kramer v. Kramer.*

Huston, John – *The Maltese Falcon; The Treasure of the Sierra Madre; The African Queen; Let There Be Light; The Hustons: The Life and Times of a Hollywood Dynasty* by Lawrence Grobel.

Jentsch, Julia – *Sophie Scholl: The Final Days*; The White Rose and Sophie Scholl from The White Rose website; Excerpts from

Leaflets of The White Rose, Hans Scholl, Alexander Schmorell, Christoph Probst, Willi Graf, Kurt Huber, & Roland Freisler from Spartacus.schoolnet.co.uk; Sophie Scholl: The Final Days from Movienet.com; Marc Rothemund on Sophie Scholl from Emanuellevy.com.

Jewish Film Festival – *A Film Unfinished; My So-Called Enemy; Budrus; Eichmann's End Love, Betrayal, Death*

Lancaster, Burt – *The Killers; The Birdman of Alcatraz; The Swimmer; Atlantic City; Burt Lancaster: An American Life* by Kate Buford.

Ledger, Heath – *Brokeback Mountain; The Dark Knight.*

Lee, Spike – *Jungle Fever*; *BlackkKlanxman; Do the Right Thing.*

Leigh, Vivien – *Gone with the Wind*; *A Streetcar Named Desire.*

Lohan, Lindsay – *Mean Girls; Georgia Rule.*

Mayer, Louis B. – *Hollywood Rajah: The Life and Times of Louis B. Mayer* by Bosley Crowther.

Mitchum, Robert – *Robert Mitchum: Baby I Don't Care* by Lee Server.

Monroe, Marilyn – *Niagara; Some Like it Hot; The Misfits; Don't Bother to Knock.*

Novak, Kim – *Vertigo; Jeanne Eagels.*

Olivier, Laurence – *Marathon Man; The Boys from Brazil; Rebecca.*

Palance, Jack – *City Slickers; Sudden Fear; Shane; Contempt.*

Rains, Claude – *Adventures of Robin Hood; Phantom of the Opera; Now, Voyager; Notorious; Casablanca.*

Reeves, George – *Hollywoodland*; *Adventures of Superman.*

Robinson, Edward G. – *Double Indemnity*; *Key Largo*; *Little Caesar; Little Casesar: A Biography of Edward G. Robinson* by Allen J. Gansberg.

San Francisco Jewish Film Festival – *My So-Called Enemy; Budrus; A Film Unfinished; Eichmann's End: Love, Betrayal, Death.*

Sanders, George – *Rebecca; All About Eve.*

Sinatra, Frank – *Some Came Running.*

Streep, Meryl – *Kramer v. Kramer; The Iron Lady; Sophie's Choice; Julia & Julia.*

Swanson, Gloria – *Sunset Boulevard.*

Tarrentino, Quentin – *A Hollywood Ending; Kill Bill: Vol. 1; Kill Bill: Vol. 2.*

Turner, Lana – *The Postman Always Rings Twice; Peyton Place; Another Time, Another Place; Imitation of Life.*

Vale, Christian – *Vice.*

Velez, Lupe – *The Mexican Spitfire*; *The Life and Career of Hollywood's Mexican Spitfire* by Michelle Vogel.

Wayne, John – *The Searchers; The Man Who Shot Liberty Valance; Brokeback Mountain.*

Weinstein, Harvey – Miramax Films.

Wong, Anna May – *The Toll of the Sea; Picadilly; Shanghai Express; A Lady from Chungking.*

About the Author

George Thomas Clark has written numerous books including *Hitler Here*, an acclaimed biographical novel, *They Make Movies*, a collection of creative stories about actors and actresses, *Paint it Blue*, stories about painters, *The Bold Investor*, a short story collection, *In Other Hands: Revised Edition*, portraits of people mired in prostitution, human trafficking, and poverty, *Basketball and Football*, and four books of political satire.

If you enjoyed any of the author's titles, please leave a review.

Visit the George Thomas Clark page on Amazon.com or on Barnes & Noble, Apple Books, Kobo Books, and other easily-accessed digital stores and websites that focus on books.

www.ingramcontent.com/pod-product-compliance
Lightning Source LLC
LaVergne TN
LVHW010223110826
845148LV00022B/1346

* 9 7 8 1 7 3 3 2 9 8 1 4 8 *